THOUGHTLESS

PAT LUTHER

ISBN 978-1-7367515–3-4

Cover by Chantel Saban

For Thomas Marsh

For three decades of friendship and conversations, without which this would be a very different book, if it even could have been written at all.

CONTENTS

ONE
ATMOSPHERE AND VOID

Del was two million kilometers out from Ceres when she heard the distress call. She spun her bike around and hit the thrusters hard. Her seat conformed around her as two G of acceleration pressed her into it. She pulled up the information about her destination on her helmet's faceplate. It was a minor asteroid registered to Rimedo, one of the largest mining corporations in the Belt. Jackpot. The corp bonus from this could set her up for months. She pushed the thrusters to three G.

Her bike's computer would have already transmitted her acceptance of the call, but she broadcast a message anyway. It would give Kenny something to edit into the video when he sold this footage for her later.

"BeltSec Enforcer Delokita SC9-370-176 en route in response to a distress signal from asteroid 1327-27," she read the designation from the display. She did not mention who it belonged to. "Currently under attack from an unknown party. ETA thirty-seven minutes."

Nineteen minutes later, her small craft turned itself around and began slowing down to match the speed of her destination.

She had heard no further signals in all that time, and her calls to the asteroid went unanswered.

When Del was close enough for her bike's sensors to pick up a visual, she brought the feed up on her suit's faceplate. A jagged cut marred the side of the rock. There must have been a contained atmosphere inside. Contained no longer, debris was floating away from the damaged area. She glanced over her shoulder in the direction she was heading, but was still too far away to see anything with the naked eye. She zoomed in on the display and saw bodies amongst the debris. Exactly what she'd feared.

"*Egido! Protektu viajn infanojn*," she said out loud, a quick prayer to a goddess she didn't believe in. If there were any survivors, footage of a rescue could end up being worth more than the bonus. She only felt a little guilty for thinking it.

She was close enough to see the small asteroid directly when the platform ship slid out from behind it, its powerful mining laser aimed straight at her. She spun her bike to the side as it fired.

With nothing to scatter the light, the laser itself was invisible. It could only be seen if it hit something. She didn't intend to be the something it hit. The platform ship was slow to maneuver. They were built to be highly precise and stable, not fast.

She closed on it in an erratic spiral, switching vectors every two to three seconds to keep it from locking on. She'd done the maneuver a hundred times in simulation. Whoever was operating this thing, though, wasn't following the same procedures the programmers of those simulations had.

The platform tilted and spun and twice she had to perform a high-G dodge to avoid being directly in front of the laser. The operator knew what they were doing. Given the bulk of the mining platform her bike's little missiles would be worthless against it. She would have to get inside to stop it.

When she drew close, the gray metal side of the mining platform dominated the sky. A long tether ending in a claw, two meters across, shot out toward her. She changed course again, dodging out of its way, and the platform tilted in an unexpected direction. She hit the thrusters again, turning the bike sharply, but half a second later the acceleration stopped, leaving her floating free. A mental command to her suit brought up a linked display, where she checked the bike's status.

There was no response from either engine. She was headed straight toward the platform. She glanced over her shoulder again and saw two large chunks of metal floating away from her. Both engines had been sliced cleanly in half. Another half a degree of arc and the laser would have hit Del herself.

Without the engines, she couldn't dodge the laser again. She leapt off her small ship and into the void of space. As her crippled craft tumbled away from her, she oriented herself toward the platform and used suit thrusters to launch toward it.

In her suit alone, she hoped she was too small and maneuvering too erratically for the laser to target. That didn't seem to stop them.

The operator ignored the bike and for another long minute of harrowing twisting flight, the platform tilted back and forth and grew ever larger. Without her bike's sensors, she couldn't tell if it fired again or not.

At last, she slammed hard into the platform and caught a hand-hold set in its side. Hugging the hull, where the laser couldn't target her, she pulled herself along the row of handholds, using them as much as her suit's thrusters to propel herself forward. She assumed they would lead to an entrance of some sort.

A slight shudder ran through the platform just as she

reached a hatch and she looked wildly about to see what had happened. A tiny spacecraft, not much bigger than her bike, had just launched. The operator must have realized they couldn't stop her.

KILL HIM!

It wasn't a voice so much as a sudden insight. A packet of instructions delivered straight to her brain. She knew exactly what she had to do.

Her own bike was still drifting, close to the platform whose laser had destroyed both her engines. There was no way she was going to be able to repair them here, but it wasn't the engines she needed right now. She pushed off the mining platform and, keeping the fleeing scooter in view, she used her suit's propulsion system to reach her damaged vessel.

When she got there, she caught the maneuvering yoke to stop herself and tried to pull the whole bike around to face her fleeing adversary. Its own propulsion useless, she used her suit thrusters to turn it the direction she wanted it to face. She brought up the linked controls to her two missiles while her bike slowly turned. The fleeing scooter was too far away to be seen by the naked eye now, but her suit knew where it was. She fed the targeting information into the starboard missile, armed it, and let it go.

A soft double-beep told her it had acquired the target. She zoomed in close with her suit's sensors until she could see the fleeing scooter.

The pilot had turned sideways, trying to dodge. He failed. The missile streaked into view, then there was a sudden bright flash and only the darkness of open space. Whatever pieces were left were too small to be seen even by her bike's sensors.

NOW THE BASE! DESTROY IT!

The words pierced her skull, and again she knew what action she had to take. The bike was already slowly turning, and she gave it another quick boost from her suit's thrusters and waited for it to come around, facing the asteroid the mining laser had already carved.

Before it got all the way back around, though, she realized what was happening. Acting quickly, fearing that this moment of lucidity would be fleeting, she disarmed the missile and hit the release, letting it float gently away from her tiny craft. She swung herself around and, holding on to the bike, planted both feet on the missile and unwound, kicking it away as hard as she could before pulling herself back into the seat.

She tried to think and was relieved she still could. *What had happened?* She hadn't had an episode like this since Mars. She had hoped with the steady supply of the medicine she'd secured from Kenny that they'd be behind her forever.

She had her suit's medical module do a quick blood test. The advanced option was an expensive modification, but worth every credit. The report scrolled across her faceplate.

Everything was within normal levels. The only thing out of optimal range was the compound meant to fight bone loss in low gravity, but that shouldn't be an issue. With her current living situation, she wouldn't even take it except that BeltSec required it and provided it for free.

She double-checked the antipsychotics. The computer had been giving her her standard dose, and the supply was exactly at the level it should be.

Something was wrong, though, or she wouldn't be hearing the voices. Could Kenny have given her a bad batch of the drugs? The blood test should have shown that. Could she be developing a resistance? That wasn't supposed to happen.

She remembered those early days, after leaving her last foster family. Living in the tunnels, hiding from the Martian Authority, unable to trust her own mind. She couldn't go back to that. She didn't dare go to a physician. There was too much chance that BeltSec would find out, and then where would she be? Unemployed and still unable to get the medication she needed. Out here where, as Jie kept reminding her, the slightest mistake could be fatal, she wouldn't last long.

To the void with that thought. The future could take care of itself. She was here now. She reached back into childhood memory as she stood and pushed gently away from her broken spacecraft. Floating alone amongst the vastness of the stars, she reached over her head. With no other frame of reference, "up," like fate, was whatever she decided.

She imagined a mass of energy floating above her. She reached into it and pulled a thick strand down into herself as she began the ritual her foster parents taught her all those years ago.

It didn't matter that the angels she invoked as guardians didn't exist, or that there were no demons for them to guard against. The wards would work because she decided they would. She shaped the energy around her into a pentagram and extended it above her and down below her feet, creating a three dimensional cage of force, surrounding and protecting her.

Performing the ritual had the other practical benefit of distracting her from her own thoughts, breaking the cycle of fear feeding upon itself.

Her imaginary lines of force were fading in her mind, though she could still feel their presence. She found herself drifting peacefully, surrounded by the rubble of her recent adventure. The asteroid, the mining platform, her dead bike.

No, the bike wasn't quite dead. It still had power from the batteries, just no propulsion. She used its transmitter to inform BeltSec Headquarters of the situation and ask for help.

While she waited for a response, she investigated the asteroid. It had the standard airlock, and the standard tunnels created by Hanzhong borers. Offices, living quarters, all identical sizes, and a large chamber at one end used as a cafeteria and rec center. That was the area that the mining laser had breached.

As she feared, there were no survivors. Under normal circumstances, the dozen or so former inhabitants wouldn't have needed vacsuits inside. If Rimedo had provided them, or fitted all the rooms with pressure doors, some of these people might still be alive. Even her own small apartment had a pressure door on the bathroom and a main airlock where she could go if something happened to the main chamber. In the Belt, such safety measures were considered a necessity. Del smiled as she thought what Jie's reaction would be to her saying it.

Apparently Rimedo didn't want to bother with the expense of redundant pressure doors to all the rooms. This was probably some satellite office handling whatever local business they had in this area of the Belt, built as cheaply as possible decades ago and never updated. As cavalier as BeltSec was with the lives of their Enforcers, Rimedo seemed even worse with their employees. There were always more where they came from, she supposed. She knew what Jie's reaction would be to that.

She went back to her bike and sent her report to BeltSec. She left out her opinions about Rimedo's design that let this happen. It was unlikely there'd be any corporate bonus for this, but it wouldn't help to annoy the people who'd be making that decision.

Nothing to do now but wait. She floated near her bike, surrounded by stars and the long expanse of the Milky Way. Normally she slept well in zero G. Now, however, she kept waking up from bad dreams, and each time had a moment of panic as she tried to remember where she was and frantically searched until she saw her bike.

Finally, she saw the approaching lights of an automated craft bearing two new engines. She spent another hour swapping them out. The damaged parts, she pushed off toward the asteroid. BeltSec could pick them up when the Salvage and Forensics crew got here. With full power restored, she connected her suit to the bike's systems and let the suit charge as the bike replaced her recirculated air and water with its own. She pulled a balloon cover from the back over the entire bike and let it pressurize.

When it had finished filling, Del opened her helmet and took a deep breath of the fresh air. Then she retrieved a pair of nutrition bars from a small compartment. It was the first solid food she'd had for nearly twenty hours.

When she was done, she put her helmet back up, stowed the balloon, and started back toward Ceres.

Fifteen minutes later, she turned off her transponder and changed course. Turning off the transponder was technically against protocol, but a common enough practice amongst BeltSec Enforcers that there was nothing inherently suspicious about the act. There were any number of legitimate reasons an Enforcer wouldn't want to announce their presence somewhere. In her case, the location of her next stop was a carefully-guarded secret. It was eight hours away at a nice comfortable one G.

She sat back and relaxed, watching the stars. Even as fast as she was moving it seemed like she was standing still. They were so far away, the closest wouldn't seem to move in her lifetime. She stood up and had the seat transform itself again, into its treadmill configuration. Another expensive modification that she'd added after her first corporate bonus. She'd never regretted it, as it allowed her to stay fit and alleviate boredom on long trips through the void.

As she ran, her helmet displayed one of her favorite courses: an open plain on Mars, strewn about with boulders she'd have to occasionally jump, vault, or climb over. Olympus Mons rose above the horizon in the distance. She had run across similar terrain, wearing a bulkier suit than she was now, in school competitions. Strange how she could get homesick for a place she'd dreamt her whole life of getting away from.

As she ran over the desolate plains of Mars, she thought more about what had just happened. Checking how much of what she experienced was real was a simple feat. Her suit's logs confirmed that she hadn't blown up the base. The distress call was real, someone had used the mining laser to attack the base, killing everyone inside before she'd arrived on the scene. The existence of a killer wasn't her memory playing tricks on her.

She didn't have to kill the attacker, though. She could have reported them. She could have recorded the transponder of their small craft and they would have been found next time they docked or even passed near any Zono Mastro client or affiliate anywhere in the Belt.

Launching the missile may have been excessive. It was still justifiable. Whoever they were, they'd just killed almost a dozen people. Who knew what they might do next?

Exhausted at last, she stopped the treadmill, but left it flat so she could lie down. Her helmet display cleared, and Mars disappeared to be replaced by the now familiar view of outer space. The Milky Way stretched above her, illuminating her tiny craft speeding between distant points. Lying comfortably on the soft surface, she pushed the acceleration up to its maximum three Gs.

When it came time to turn around to slow back down, she returned the seat to its usual configuration.

THE ASTEROID ahead was registered to a small corporation on Venus that seemed to have no other interests in the Belt.

According to the listing, it had no exploitable resources. There was an airlock set into one side, though, a standard Hanzhong Medium, two and a half meters square. The lights had been covered, so to find the airlock you had to know exactly where to look. Del knew where to look.

She sent the code to open the outer door. Unlike most Belters, Kenny kept his outer door locked. By convention, outer airlock doors were always left unlocked. In case of emergencies, someone could always get into a nearby airlock, though not all the way through without the owner's permission.

She parked her bike just outside, setting it to keep relative station. She had to wait for the airlock to depressurize, then wait again for it to fill back up with air while she floated freely inside. By now, the man she'd come to see would know she was there and was probably watching on some view screen somewhere.

He wouldn't speak to her yet. Communications would all have to go through the net, and net access was blocked from anywhere near this place. His assistants would be alert and ready in case she tried anything, and scanning the area to see if she'd led anyone here.

At last, the inner door opened. She pushed forward into the central chamber, a large workshop full of various gadgets, tools, and machines of all sorts, floating freely through the area. On a ship, this would be incredibly dangerous, as any course change could send everything flying at high speed. On the asteroid, though, there was no chance of that. Everything would stay wherever it was placed, drifting with whatever momentum it had when let go.

She wondered how he ever found anything, though. Half a dozen people flitted about, either working on various tasks, or waiting on others who were. There were a few she hadn't seen before, and they gave sidelong looks when they saw the

Enforcer uniform she wore over her vacsuit. At the center of all the chaos floated a bulky pale man with graying hair and beard. This was the person she'd come to see. He wore his usual overalls, with no vacsuit.

"Delokita!" his voice boomed across the workshop. "What brings you to my humble abode?"

Taking their cues from him, his assistants turned from her and went back to whatever tasks they were working on.

"Hello to you, too, Kenny," she replied. She used a brief jet from her suit thrusters to avoid his embrace. "I need you to check my suit," she told him. "Something's off with the med dispenser. I hope."

"You hope?" He frowned.

"The alternative is something wrong with me, and if that's the case I have no idea what to do about it." She tried to keep her fear out of her voice, but wasn't sure she succeeded.

Kenny looked concerned. "If that's the problem, we'll take care of that, too. Can't have you flying around broken. You're too valuable to me in working condition."

Del appreciated the sentiment. "I've also got the location of some good salvage for you. Send a crew who'll be respectful. There are bodies amongst the wreckage."

"Respectful grave robbers. Sure, 'Kita, I'll pass the word along."

She pulled up the coordinates on her suit's interface and gestured toward him.

He lifted a small console attached to his belt by a cord. Del's suit would analyze who was in front of her and transfer the data to his profile.

"They need to hurry, before BeltSec F&S gets there," she told him. "Also, there's an inactive missile there that I'd be interested in purchasing if I can raise the money by the time you get it, which will hopefully be before BeltSec notices it's missing."

"I'll let them know to look for it." He tapped a few more words into his console before dropping it, letting it drift freely, attached by a cord to his belt.

"I've got some vid you might like, too," Del said, and transferred her suit's record to him, starting with her acknowledgment of the distress call.

"Excellent. You know, you could make a lot more from these if you'd talk to your fans."

"Not interested." She knew the kind of people who paid for life vids, and she wanted nothing to do with them. "As far as I'm concerned, my part in all this is over once I get paid."

With a sigh, Kenny pushed off a corner of a workbench and floated over to what looked like half a manikin made of plastic and metal, rooted by its feet to a stone wall. "Let's get that suit off of you and onto my friend here and see what's up."

"In your dreams," she replied.

"I can't run diagnostics when it's on you."

"Where can I change?" She was feeling more confident again after having no more episodes and had no desire to be floating here naked in front of Kenny and his assistants, despite him being one of her closest friends in the Belt. Or maybe because of it.

"You Martians and your taboos," Kenny said. "You're a Belter now, 'Kita. It's time to move on past your childhood traumas."

The mention of childhood traumas hit too close to home. She didn't say anything, but he obviously sensed her mood.

He gestured to one of the many doors. "That door leads to my bedchamber. You can change there."

The room he pointed her to was as disorganized and cluttered as the rest of the place. Mostly softer materials floated around, largely pillows and clothes. She didn't know why he'd need pillows or blankets when there was never any gravity. She ignored the clothing around her as she stripped off her own. She had already been wearing her BeltSec uniform over the vacsuit, so she put it back on once she'd peeled off the nearly skintight suit under it. The vacsuit itself she carried back to Kenny draped over one arm.

He took the suit from her and placed it over the manikin, which then extended to fill it as a human would. When it had finished unfolding, he pulled his console back to him.

"The good news is there's nothing wrong with your med dispenser," he said after a moment. "Or maybe that's the bad news?"

"I don't even know anymore. What kind of medical equipment do you have here? Can you do a full blood work? How about a brain scan?"

"Your suit's fine. Your blood level's fine. That's a top of the line med module I put in there, you're not going to find a better scanner outside of a Ceres hospital. If you really want, I can get access to one. I can get access to anything." He paused and looked at her. "But in order for me to help you, I have to know how. Which means, you need to tell me what's going on."

Del took a deep breath. "Remember how I told you when I was younger, I'd get these...compulsions?"

"Your voices, yes. Have they come back?"

He said it so casually, as if it were just a question. As if it didn't mean the entire universe was crumbling around her. She couldn't even speak in reply, she just nodded quietly, not meeting his gaze.

"It's a problem then," he said, "So we'll fix it. That's what I do."

"How?" she asked. She realized that his cheerful optimism was meant to reassure her, but it had the opposite effect. It just made it seem like he didn't understand how serious the issue was. His next words didn't allay that impression, either.

"Don't know yet. Don't worry. Are you sure this is actually a problem?"

"The fact that I can't trust my own mind? Yes, I'd say it's a pretty major problem."

"I mean, how likely is this ever to happen again? You told me it's been years since the last time."

"Except for today—" she started.

"It might not recur," he said. "Sometimes drugs work differently in zero-G. After a long time at zero G, followed by a series of high-G maneuvers, while accompanied by increased heart rate and adrenaline? Who knows what could happen?"

"That doesn't make me feel better."

"One episode, during a highly stressful time, and you handled it without hurting yourself or anyone else, right?"

This was more reassuring, but not necessarily true.

"I can alter the limiter," he said. "Let you increase the dose when needed, but still prevent an overdose. I don't want to just remove it since you won't be in your right mind when using it, so I'm going to add a hard limit and only I will have the code to override it, okay?"

She nodded. "I still hate the idea of just waiting to see if it happens again. Are you sure there's nothing else you can do?"

"I'm not a physician, but I can do a bit of digging and see if there's other medicines we can try."

"I'm not sure I like the idea of experimenting with mind-altering drugs on myself."

"A lot of people do it just for fun," he replied with a smile.

He had a point, though. If it was carefully controlled, how dangerous could it be?

"I'm aware," she said. "That's half the reason I had to leave Mars, remember?" She said it as a joke, and he laughed appropriately. She had never told him the other half, and he had never asked.

"Give it a few more minutes to upload the protocols and you'll be good to go. I also went ahead and ran a clean and refresh routine while it's there."

"Thanks," she said, "What do I owe you?"

She knew what the answer would be, but the question had to be asked, out of politeness.

Kenny waved one hand in the air. "Bah. I didn't even use any resources on this. If you want help on that cash-flow problem, though..."

And there it was.

"Wouldn't mind a job, no," she replied.

"You still have contacts on Mars, yes? I need a package delivered to a certain public official, with no record to trace it back to me, and without passing through any inspections before it gets to him."

"No problem. How big of a package, and is it going to explode on the other end?"

"I like how you say yes before asking if it'll explode. But no, no boom today. The whole thing's less than a fifty centimeter cube."

"Then yes, I can arrange for it to be shipped on a Zono Mastro transport with a pre-approval label, and taken off at the other end, delivered to a secure carrier. Anyone who wants to trace it back will have to go through four different people to get to you, and none of them will be cooperative."

"That's why I like you, 'Kita. You always come through. Standard rates once I have confirmation of delivery."

It would have to do. Del didn't really think it was explosives. What reason could Kenny possibly have to assassinate any official back on Mars? Not that she cared much if he did. She didn't owe anyone there anything. If he was involved in

Martian politics to the degree that an assassination would be advantageous to him, he'd have his own contacts there and wouldn't need her. He might have his fingers in everything in the belt, but Del was fairly certain his influence didn't extend beyond it. Most likely this official just wanted a discreet shipment of cosmo or something.

This could be a recurring gig if she worked it right. The drug was currently popular amongst the idle rich. It produced mild hallucinations and a sense of euphoria. Mostly harmless, but banned on Mars. She'd worked on the other end smuggling it in from some other unknown manufacturer in the Belt back when she was there. Somewhere out there someone was manufacturing it, buried in some unknown asteroid. She wasn't surprised Kenny knew where.

She took the box with her when she left and put it into the small storage compartment behind the seat of her bike. It could sit there for a few days until she found a transport to put it on.

TWO
LIES AND MISPERCEPTIONS

Another long trip and the familiar lights of her asteroid home were visible. She could see her own home and the kilometers-long cable that attached it to another asteroid somewhere out there in the void. The two were tethered together and spun around a mutual center. The cable was being slowly lengthened while they accelerated the two asteroids to keep a constant linear speed. It was a complex system with the end result of slowly increasing perceived gravity. Half a dozen families had gotten together and set the system up so they could acclimate ahead of their planned trip to Earth. Del had no intention of heading to Earth, but after one couple had dropped out of the group, a room in one of the asteroids became available. It was luxury accommodations for a fraction of what they'd normally cost. She even had her own bathroom. Keeping accustomed to higher gravity was a bonus.

She parked her bike alongside an airlock that opened into her room. There was another one at the other end that someone could take an elevator from a central point to reach. If she'd been coming by transport and didn't have a vacsuit, she could have gone that way. She never did, though, and just used the inner airlock as a closet. Consequently, she almost never saw the family that lived in the other half of her little rock. She clamped the bike into place at the bottom of the short ladder and climbed up, sending the code to open the outer door as she did.

As she waited for the airlock to pressurize, she looked through the inner window at her apartment. The bright colors of the silks she'd hung around the dark stone walls and the blanket still draped on the couch where she'd left it days before made a welcome change in scenery from the endless dark space of the last few days. She unfortunately couldn't stay long. Her side trip to Kenny's had delayed her for several hours. People would be expecting her.

Once pressure was equalized, the inner door slid open. She took off her uniform and tossed it in a corner before releasing the seals and peeling off her vacsuit. She hung it on its dummy as she always did. This one was sleeker than Kenny's and made specifically for this suit. She let it run the refresh and cleaning routines, despite having been done only a few hours before.

When it complained about the new protocols installed, she assured it they were safe. She could only assume they were. What possible reason would Kenny have of wanting her harmed? She was almost always willing to help him when he needed it, and it's not like he could turn her in to the authorities. Any reward he'd get for such an act wouldn't come near to what he could make by keeping her as a contact. He was, by virtue of his dishonesty, the most trustworthy person she knew.

She took her time in the shower. One of the great luxuries of this place - a private shower with real falling water you could stand under. No waiting in line or scheduling in advance, this entire room was dedicated to her exclusive use.

The water itself had to be shared. Of course, it was recycled, but recycling took a while. When she had first moved in, the other family had complained about how much of the water she was using. She called in a favor and had a second, larger tank installed. Now she could take a real hot water shower as long as she wanted and there were no complaints.

When she was done, she retrieved her vacsuit, now cleaned and replenished, then picked up her BeltSec uniform again. There was a laundry on Ceres she could have used for it, but except for a brief time at Kenny's, it never touched her skin and constant exposure to the vacuum of space kept it cleaner than laundering would have.

Refreshed and rejuvenated, she headed back out. Time to head to Ceres.

SET into the rock at the end of the tunnel there was a standard pressure door with the word *Rokoj* written on it in large ornate lettering. There was no other indication of what this place was.

Game face on, Delokita, she told herself as she approached the door. It wouldn't do to show any weakness here. Kenny, she could confess her fears to. The worst he would do would be to exploit them for criminal gain. The people here, though, could ruin her life. Get her kicked out of BeltSec. Maybe worse.

She fixed a broad smile on her face as the door slid open and brought her the excited babble of conversation from the room beyond.

Men and women sat or stood around a dozen tables scattered around the room. At one end stood a counter behind which the bartender was already drawing a flask of beer. Over the last couple of standards she had been here often enough that he knew what she wanted.

"Thanks, Zak" she called, catching the cylindrical flask that he tossed to her before she even made it to the bar. The credits would already be deducted from her account. She gave him access the first day she was here. She could feel her mood lightening as she went. For better or worse, this was where she belonged.

She thumbed open the lid on her drink and took a sip while she turned to scan the room. She was happy to see Bilan and Jie sitting together at a table watching her. They'd both been in BeltSec longer than she had and had befriended her shortly after she'd joined.

Jie waved her over while Bilan watched with a strange smile.

Del nodded a friendly greeting to other patrons, many of whom she knew from BeltSec, as she went.

Before she could sit down, however, Bilan raised her own flask, stood up and loudly proclaimed, "Hail the hero of the day!"

People nearby applauded and cheered. Even Jie nodded politely as he raised his flask.

Del took a seat at the same table and asked, "What in the void was that about?" She kept an affable smile glued to her face as she said it.

By way of answer, Bilan gestured to the table their drinks were sitting on. The top lit up with the video she broadcast to it.

The image was from her bike's sensors, as Del was trying to swing it around. Her face, visible through her vacsuit's helmet, contorted with the effort.

"You won't get away with it, you bastard," she heard herself say, before the video cut to the outside and she saw the missile speed off toward the enemy craft.

"Did I really say that?" She couldn't remember. "Isn't this supposed to be restricted footage?"

"Afraid we're cutting into your market?" Jie said, a tone of disapproval in his voice.

"Hey, there's no rule against selling the vid from my suit, as long as I don't compromise operations," she said, keeping an easy smile. "What I meant, though, is how did you get it?"

"It was attached to your report," Jie said.

"That answers where it came from, but not how you got it."

"I got it from your report..." Bilan started, then stopped. "You haven't checked your messages, have you?"

Del sent the mental command to her suit to bring up the interface. From a small square in her front collar, her suit's menu projected onto her retina. With quick eye movements and a wave of her hand, she brought up her messages and scanned through the recent ones.

"We need to talk?" she asked Bilan, seeing the message waiting from her. She probably should have done this on the way over here.

"Check out this morning's briefing," Bilan replied.

She probably should have done that already, too. As a far patroller she wasn't expected to be there in person every day of course, but she should at least review the recordings.

Bilan brought it up on their tabletop for her, and Del picked up her own beer while it played so she could see it better. Bilan fast-forwarded to the relevant part, and she recognized the footage from her own bike.

She realized the footage had been shown to the whole corp. They seemed to be making a much bigger deal out of it than she had. It was a senseless attack that had left a dozen people dead. But people died out here. It was an accepted fact. Sometimes Del was appalled at just how accepted it was. People went crazy sometimes, too. Given the dangers of the Belt, and the ever-present hard vacuum so close to everything, people going crazy, or even getting a little careless, could mean death for them and everyone near them.

"I don't understand," Del said. "I didn't do anything. Everybody died and I got my bike slagged and had to sit there for fourteen hours waiting for a rescue. How does any of that translate into hero?"

"Are you kidding?" Said Jie. "Since when do you go in for false modesty?"

Del gave him a look. He seemed serious.

"What false modesty? I didn't do anything!" she repeated. She looked around.

Everybody was ignoring her now, doing whatever they were doing before Bilan called on them to cheer her as a hero.

"You killed the terrorist!" said Jie.

"Alleged terrorist," Bilan corrected him.

"Oh come on, he killed eleven people..."

"And we don't yet know why."

"Okay, I'm lost," Del said. "Why do we think he's a terrorist and why does it matter?"

"We think he's a terrorist because he left a manifesto about humans destroying the Belt."

"It wasn't a manifesto. It was an opinion piece posted to a public discussion forum before he even came here, about how humans shouldn't be exploiting the asteroid belt."

"Why shouldn't humans be exploiting the Belt?" Del asked. "It's not like anyone else was doing anything with it."

"And nothing indicates he still felt that way by the time he got out here."

"Wait, we know who this guy was?" Del asked.

"If it's who we think it is," Bilan said. "We're pretty sure it is."

"He's an Earther," Jie said.

"We're assuming," Bilan answered.

"Who else could it be?" Jie said. "You've seen the recordings."

"The ones that got out at least," Bilan said. "Wish I could have got ahold of the whole thing."

"Why couldn't you get the whole thing?" Del asked without thinking. Then she realized she knew the answer.

Bilan confirmed it. "Illegal salvagers got to the site before we did." She turned back to Jie. "I'm not saying you're wrong, but we need facts, with evidence, not supposition."

"Okay, let's look at the facts," Jie said, and held up one finger. "One. Bartran's ID was used to access the mining platform."

"Could have been stolen, or hacked," Bilan said.

"Ah ah. We're only looking at facts right now."

"Bartran?" asked Del, suspecting the answer.

"Jeremy Bartran, our assumed deceased alleged terrorist," Jie answered her.

"Assumed?"

"Did you verify that he was actually in that scooter?"

"I didn't even know that it was a 'he.'"

"Could he have stayed on the mining platform and sent the scoot out on its own?"

"No. I checked the mining platform."

"How thoroughly?" asked Bilan.

"Pretty darn. I was stuck there for fourteen hours with nothing much to do, and the place wasn't that big."

"Two," Jie raised another finger and continued as if he hadn't been interrupted. "How would you rate the skill of the person controlling the platform, Del?"

"High. He made it do things I've never even heard of before."

"So, fact two is that Jeremy Bartran was rated class E, the

most skilled level of operation, for that particular model of platform."

"Which still proves nothing," Bilan said, "There's probably a hundred or more Belters with the same rating."

"Facts only, remember?"

"That is a fact."

"Oh, right. Well, three: There was a transmission from someone in the cafeteria just before the laser pierced where they can be heard very clearly saying, and I quote, 'Jeremy, what are you doing?', 'Knock it off Jeremy,' and 'Stop it, Jeremy, you're going to kill us!'"

Del laughed out loud. "That's some pretty compelling evidence. It still doesn't answer the most important question."

"And what's that?"

"Why do we care? Whoever he was, whatever his reasons, he's dead. It's over. He's not going to attack anyone else."

Neither of them spoke for a second.

Finally, Jie looked at Bilan.

"What? What is it?"

"I mentioned he was from Earth, right?"

"Yeah?"

"He's got family there. Old money family."

"What does that mean to us?"

"They've called for an investigation into his death."

"And BeltSec agreed? How come they haven't talked to me?"

"No. BeltSec agreed with you. Guy goes crazy. Guy kills people. Hero Enforcer stops crazy guy. Case closed."

"Then why—?"

"The family is paying for an independent investigation."

"Damn, he must have been important."

"He is," Jie responded, "Or rather was, their son."

"I mean, they must have a lot of money to be spending it

like that. So, if they have that kind of money, what's he doing out here?"

"Maybe he wanted to accomplish something on his own, outside of his family's wealth."

"Idiot," Del said.

Jie shot her a look at the vehemence of her response.

"He reminds me of the people we used to fleece back when I was running in the tunnels on Mars. 'Oh, woe is me, I have everything but I'm unhappy. I know! I'll go live like a poor person for a while then when I get tired of it, I can go back to my normal life and brag to all my rich friends that I know what it's like to have to work for a living!'"

"Wow, Del, tell us how you really feel," Jie said.

"Slag him. He deserved to get blown up."

He looked like he was about to say something else, but Bilan interrupted. "I guess it's a good thing you did, then."

There was something about the way she said it that disturbed Del, but she couldn't quite put her finger on it. "This investigation..." she started.

"I picked it up, yes," Bilan said, looking at her.

"And BeltSec's okay with it?" Del asked.

"I cleared it with Lakshminarayanan. He approved it as long as I don't let it interfere with my official duties." It was the standard line for outside work.

"Since when do you care what BeltSec thinks anyway?" Jie asked.

"Always. As long as they're paying me, their happiness is near the top of my list of important things."

"I'm more worried about what you think of me investigating this."

"Is that why you didn't tell me at first? Didn't want to hurt my feelings?"

"Mostly I wanted to see what you'd say when talking freely."

"Low."

Bilan shrugged apologetically. She knew the score. They both did.

"Now that I do know, what do you want to ask me?"

"We're good? No hard feelings?"

"For tricking me into an interrogation, hoping I'd let something incriminating slip?"

"Not how I'd put it, but...yeah."

Del had a sudden image of herself walking into the bar, and Bilan silencing Jie with a look before plastering a smile on her face. She pushed it aside and brought her attention back to the conversation.

"Did I let anything incriminating slip?"

"No," Bilan said.

"Then we're good." She meant it. "I don't resent you for taking the job. I certainly don't begrudge you making a bit of extra coin on the side. You are buying the next round, though."

"Fair enough."

"You're just reporting the facts, right? Then my facts are your facts. If your client doesn't like them, they can come here and say so to my face."

"I'll need to get into your suit."

"It's gonna take more than one drink for that."

Bilan laughed and raised her hand toward the bar. "Zak! Another one for Del, on my tab. Come to think of it, another for me as well."

Jie raised a finger as well and the bartender nodded. A few seconds later, three blue cobalt cylinders flew toward the table. A trick that would only work in the low gravity of Ceres.

Del thumbed the top open on hers and took a drink before

setting it on the table. She tossed her empty in a high arc into the bin in the corner.

A light that only she could see flashed and she pulled up the suit's interface and saw the request for access from Bilan. She didn't know exactly what Bilan would need so she just gave her complete access. The recorders had been off during her entire trip to Kenny's of course, so she wasn't worried about a record of that.

Bilan looked at it for a minute then said, "Part of this has been erased."

"Has it?" Del responded innocently, trying to stall for time to think up a legitimate excuse for erasing the recording.

Bilan just gave her a look that indicated she wasn't fooled for a second.

"It wasn't relevant to your investigation."

"What was it?"

"I'd rather not say. But I promise it had nothing to do with the attack."

"Four hours' worth of deleted records right after you killed this guy? It's suspicious, Del, you gotta give me something."

"It's nothing. Call it a glitch. I was trying to make sure my storage wasn't too full and hit the wrong control."

"Okay, now that we know that Del didn't do it, what's our next step?" Jie asked.

Del was about to ask about that "our" when Bilan responded, "She did do it. That's the one thing we already know."

"So, what are we investigating?" Del asked.

"What's with all this 'we'? I thought you didn't care."

"That was before I knew there was free beer involved," Del said, indicating her newly empty cylinder.

"Screw it, I'll put it on my expense list," Bilan said and gestured toward Zak, who soon flung another her way.

"If you can do that," Del said, catching it before it could get to Bilan, "I want whiskey."

"Don't push it."

"All right. So..."

"Two things." Bilan changed the display on their table top again.

Del picked up her beer so it wouldn't obscure the image.

"First, our late friend Jeremy Bartran - was it really him? I know," Bilan said, forestalling Jie's objection, "we have lots of circumstantial evidence. I want to be sure. Was he on the mining platform, and was he on the scooter that Del blew up?"

"Yes, and yes," said Jie. "That was easy. Next."

"If you're not going to take this seriously, you're buying your own beer."

"I got it. Establish Bartran's presence on the platform, and make sure he got off the platform and onto the scooter in time to get blown up by Del."

"Can we maybe stop all this 'Del blew the guy up' talk? I'm starting to get nervous again."

"The second thing," Bilan continued, ignoring her, "and this is what's really important: Why? Was he a terrorist? If so, in what cause? Was there a group that trained him? What do they want? If he's not, did he just go crazy? Were there any signs of it beforehand? What other motive might he have had? Did someone owe him money?"

"What else do you have besides a name?" Del asked.

"Here's everything I found before I got here."

The table changed again to show the picture of a young man with short hair, bronze skin, and an easy smile.

"Asteroid miner. Maybe six months out from Earth. Well-liked by the rest of his crew. No gambling debts, no addictions, and they say that, while he enjoyed arguing politics over an occasional pint, he never showed any extremist views."

"That's what they were willing to tell you over an open feed anyway," Jie said.

"Exactly. I plan to follow up with in-person conversations in a bit. Are you bored already, Del?"

Del had pulled up her own suit's interface while she was talking and was looking into it. "Just thought he looked familiar," she replied. "There he is. It's Jay."

She pushed the image to the table where the other two could see it, next to Bilan's image of the same man.

In the new image his hair was longer and shaggier, though in an endearing rather than slovenly way, and he was wearing a miner's vacsuit.

"I met him about six months ago," Del said.

"You met him? Where?"

"Here."

"On Ceres?"

"No, I mean in here. Rokoj." She scanned through the video file and stopped at another image. This one showed more of the area around the man.

It was clearly Rokoj and he was just rising from a table close to where they were now.

She replaced the image on the tabletop with the new one. It started moving on its own and she gestured to stop it. When that didn't work, she looked up to see Bilan with her hand over her wrist console.

"Sorry, I wanted to see where this is going," Bilan said. She was controlling the playback from Del's suit.

Del let her continue.

They all watched as Del accompanied "Jay" out of the bar and down the hall to the open garage. The garage was never pressurized and was used only by those who had their own vacsuits. She smiled remembering this night. She had been pleasantly, though not excessively, drunk, and he had broad shoulders and the muscles of a man recently out from Earth.

Bilan skipped forward to see them flying through space on her bike, then again to them standing in the airlock as it cycled.

"Um..." Del started, once Jay and she had both removed their helmets. "I think we can all see where this is going."

"I wanna hear what's being said."

"Conversation wasn't really the point."

There was no sound playing from the table. She pulled it through the bone conduction from her suit. At Jie's querulous look she added him to the output as well. She didn't give him full access to the suit like she did for Bilan.

"Damn, that's where you live?" Bilan said as the inner door slid open to her apartment.

"Nice," Jie agreed.

"How come we always meet up here instead of your place?" Bilan asked.

It had never occurred to her to invite them to her little rock. It was only half an hour—just over a hundred thousand kilometers—away from Ceres, right at the edge of the exclusion zone. But the only reason to go there would be to see her. Del was aware that having friends over was a thing that people did, it just never occurred to her to do it. She realized she had no idea where they lived, either, and had never been to either of their places. Could they still be living in the Zono Mastro barracks? Or maybe in the lower apartments, which weren't much better.

On Mars, she'd had, for a little while at least, an apartment that was twice the size of her current one and it had been considered small. Out here, where there was infinitely more room, living space was much more severely limited.

On the video, Jeremy Bartran, "Jay", had taken off his vacsuit, an older, bulkier model than her top of the line one, and was beginning to peel off the garments he wore under it.

Del smiled at the memory of what was to come.

"Wait a second," Jie said. "He dropped it on the floor?"

"In a hurry I guess."

"No, I mean he *dropped* it. On the *floor*." He stressed the words. "Gravity?" he added when she looked confused.

"Oh, yeah. It's part of a pair of tethered rocks. The families I'm leasing from are slowly spinning it up so they can get used to Earth gravity. They're all planning on visiting or moving there at various times."

There were a lot - maybe as many as a hundred nearby - similarly spinning tethered pairs. Possibly thousands scattered throughout the Belt.

"You must work out there, then?" he said. "Explains the muscle tone." He had a funny sort of smile when he said it.

She had been looking up at him while explaining about the gravity. She followed his gaze now back to the table where it showed her, having stripped out of her own vacsuit, now walking away from it, toward the waiting man.

"Nice butt, too," Bilan said, trying not to laugh.

That was too much. She stopped the playback, then closed the connection to the table.

"Just when it was about to get good," Bilan said, still with her broad smile. "If I'd known this was the kind of content you had, I would've subscribed myself."

"Sorry," Del said, forcing herself to laugh as if merely embarrassed. "It isn't. I thought the sensors stopped recording when the suit was off."

"Should've. Maybe yours only stops recording when you specifically tell it to?"

"I'll have to remember that in the future."

THREE
THE MINDS OF ANGELS AND DEMONS

Surprisingly enough, Del did remember it late that night, or early the next morning, or whatever it was when she stumbled into her apartment. Her chronometer was set to Earth time. A convenient standard, but with no real meaning in the Belt.

Twice she tried and failed to take down her helmet before the airlock had finished cycling. If she had one of the older models, like Jie's, that were operated manually and actually removed from the suit instead of folding into the collar, she might have done it. She wondered how many so-called suicides by spacing had really just been drunken mistakes. That was likely a good part of the reason that cosmo, the drug that had caused her so much trouble back on Mars, had never been made illegal here. It didn't have to be. Anyone who got careless while on it would only do so once.

Once she had entered, she thought about the issue with the suit recorder. Just to make sure, she double-checked that it was off before she stripped off the suit and hung it on its manikin.

She picked up the remote console then from its place on the table and took it with her to her couch. She connected to the suit and searched the video log. Everything that happened since she turned off the camera was there. She watched herself walk across the room, put on her robe, and pick up the console. She checked the status, and the recorder was clearly off.

She got up and walked around the suit before sitting back down and checked the video again. It was there. She wasn't sure what to make of this. She would have to have Kenny look at it. *Or did Kenny already know? Did he do something to the recorders? To what end, though? Trying to spy on her? Sell footage when she thought it was off?* That seemed likely. Whoever he was selling the footage to was being discreet about it. If it had gotten out onto the public net, there'd be no end to the hard time her fellow Enforcers would give her. She wasn't sure if she should be angrier about Kenny selling vids of a type she specifically told him she wouldn't include, or that he wasn't cutting her in on any of the profits.

Slag it. She was too drunk to figure it out. She tossed the blanket from the couch over the suit and dropped her robe over that, then went to bed.

SHE WAS AWAKENED by the sound of rushing air. She bolted upright in her bed and looked around. Her vacsuit was in one direction, the bathroom and the closet, each with their own pressure doors, in two others. Could she make it to either one in time? How much time did she have? Even as all this rushed through her mind, she congratulated herself on starting to think like a Belter. Jie would be happy. On Mars, a sudden air leak was a problem, not an emergency. The worst that was likely to happen is that you'd have to move to another room, then call someone to come deal with it.

She got up, and almost fell back down again. It felt like

someone was driving a spike through her forehead and her stomach was trying to escape into her throat. Bathroom it was, then. She scanned for the source of the leak on her way there, and realized it was the sound of her airlock cycling.

She ran back to her suit where it still sat on her dummy, covered in blanket and robe. From across the room, she could tell the outer door had closed and the airlock was pressurizing again. There wasn't enough time to put on the vacsuit. She shrugged into the robe instead before crossing to the airlock and peering through the window.

With her head still pounding, she looked through the small window to see Bilan looking back at her. She'd been watching the whole time she was standing there, with a strange expression on her face. It wasn't the lecherous expression she'd worn during so much of the previous night, when she and Jie had joined in teasing her about the vid. That alone told her it was something serious. She thought about it for a moment, then hit the unlock button then moved to get dressed.

"We need to talk," Bilan said as soon as she entered.

Her mind raced. What did Bilan know? She had to make sure to react appropriately to whatever it was. Instead, she grimaced in pain and raised a hand to rub her temples. "Sorry. Long night. What about?"

Bilan shot her a strange sort of look, like she wasn't sure where to begin.

"Mind if I sit down?" she asked. "This is a bit more gravity than I'm used to."

Bilan would train at high G, of course, but that was still different than living in it the way Del did.

Del gestured to the couch then retrieved an analgesic from a cabinet. She poured herself a flask of water from the chef and offered a second to Bilan.

"Thanks. I..." Bilan started, then she hesitated again, then finally blurted out, "I know about the voices."

"What voices?" Del asked, almost instinctively.

"Don't. I understand, and I'm not reporting you, but I need to know the truth."

"I don't know what you're talking about," Del said and took a sip of her water while fighting down the rising panic.

"I had hoped to find something at the site of the Rimedo massacre."

"Is that what we're calling it now?"

"Don't change the subject. Forensics and Salvage went to investigate. You know what they found?"

"My head hurts way too much for guessing games right now." Del crossed to the bed and took a seat there, facing Bilan.

"What they found was a surprising lack of wreckage. No broken engine. No mining platform. No port missile. Nothing."

"Didn't you say illegal salvagers had already been there?"

"As if someone tipped them off. And there was only one living person who knew what had happened."

"The location was in the report I sent back to BeltSec..." Del started.

"Are you going to deny that you were the one who tipped the salvagers?"

Lie. Conceal. Don't let anyone know. Every instinct told her to keep quiet. Bilan was her friend. Her closest friend. Her only close friend unless you counted Kenny, who was almost certainly spying on her.

"No." She looked down. "I didn't know there was going to be any kind of investigation, or that you'd be in charge of it. I know a guy..."

"Kenny."

Del snapped her head back up.

"And thank you," Bilan said. "Like I said I'm not here to

toss you into the engine. Enforcers can't claim salvage. Even for BeltSec that would be too much conflict of interest. Doesn't mean we can't point someone else to it. We've all done it."

Del didn't know if she was being truthful or just trying to make her feel at ease so she'd confess. She obviously knew something, though. "How do you know about..."—she wanted to say *the voices* but didn't dare— "Kenny?" she said instead.

"After I found that the salvagers had already taken everything I wanted, and after I'd stopped screaming and crying about being betrayed by my best friend..."

Del tried to say something then, to apologize, or explain, but Bilan silenced her with a raised finger. "Like I said, over it now. But at the time..." she shrugged. "Since I already had access to your suit, I thought maybe it's worth a closer look."

"What?"

"Since we're being honest with each other, I'll admit last night I went back to watch the rest of your encounter with Jeremy Bartran."

"Oh deities." Del was mortified.

"I wanted to know if you said anything incriminating. You did not."

"That's good to know, I guess. Especially since I had no idea who he even was at the time!" She stood up and walked back over toward the chef.

"Then I skimmed through some of your other footage. You have a much more active social life than I realized."

"What I do on my own time is—"

Bilan raised her hand. "Not a criticism. Just jealous is all. Do they know you leave the recorder on?"

"Funny story about that."

Bilan raised an eyebrow.

"I'll tell you after you finish yours."

"All right," Bilan accepted her reticence and continued.

"I'd left your video alone since after a few minutes it started to feel like a violation—"

"Because it was." She was trying to keep herself from yelling.

Bilan seemed to notice. "Yes. Anyway, this morning after the full report from F&S came in, and after I finished cursing your name, I remembered that I still had access to your suit. You'd erased four hours of footage, but you were at 1327-27 for fourteen. It was where you went after that that I found interesting."

"My suit recorded that whole trip, didn't it?"

"Yep. You really should turn it off if you're going to do clandestine meetings."

"I did." She filled her in about her discoveries the previous night.

"So that's why it's under a blanket," Bilan said. "Of course, he can probably hear everything we're saying right now."

"Fine. You hear that, Kenny? You tried to spy on me, you only exposed yourself!"

"Hold on," Bilan stood and crossed to the suit where it sat on its stand. She pulled off the blanket and dropped it on the floor then carefully removed the suit. Crossing to the airlock she hit the button to open the inner doors, then tossed it inside.

"Hey!" When she realized what Bilan was doing, Del sprang to her feet. She wished she hadn't. She was still feeling woozy.

"Trust me," Bilan said, and cycled the airlock.

"That's my only vacsuit," Del told her.

Bilan just held up one finger as the air evacuated.

Del sat back down on the edge of her bed and watched in trepidation.

"That should be enough," Bilan said after a few more seconds. "It can't hear us now."

It. As if it was the suit itself that was listening.

"First, are you sure it's Kenny overriding the off switch and not somebody else?"

"He's the only one besides you who's ever had access."

"It's just from what I've seen of Kenny, this doesn't seem like his work."

"You can tell that from one recorded conversation?"

"Pretty much. I think if he was going to tamper with the recording system he'd hide the playback from you, too. I watched him write and install a new protocol in fifteen minutes, and code-lock you out of it at the same time. Which you never should have allowed, by the way. But he's someone who thinks of those details."

"I know you didn't do it. Could someone have hacked it remotely?"

"No. That's not possible. By design, you can't alter anything in these suits without a manikin. Nobody wants to take even the slightest risk of a remote hacker getting into them."

"Then it has to be Kenny."

"Or, and don't take this the wrong way, but you've had quite a few people over here. Could one of them have done something to it while you were sleeping?"

"Void. I hadn't even thought of that. If they did, it might have recorded video of it. Or at least I might be able to tell when it started recording when it's supposed to be off."

"They probably have the data sent to themselves as well. You should check the data transmit logs."

"The what?"

"You don't know how to read your suit's logs?"

Del just gave an embarrassed half-shrug in response.

"Ah, Delokita. This vacsuit is your life. You need to know everything about it." She sighed, picked up the remote console and joined Del sitting on the edge of the bed. She put the device in Del's hands and sat beside her.

The last thing Del wanted to do right now was to have anything to do with the suit. She'd spent so much time with it, depended on it so much she'd come to think of it as part of her. Now she found herself thinking of it as some alien creature. It didn't help that it was trapped in the airlock, blinded and deafened. She half expected it to force the door open and come slithering in on its own. She shook her head to clear the thought.

For an hour, though, she sat next to Bilan, as she showed her how to access the logs, run diagnostics, which she thought she knew but they went deeper than she expected, and how the custom connections fed into the system.

Bilan was impressed with the medical module. It could not only dispense meds and do immediate blood analysis, it could also analyze its own status.

"That makes sense. A lot of drugs can be altered or destroyed by exposure to vacuum or extreme temperatures," Bilan said when she discovered that.

Del looked at the analysis display. "Looks like my psych meds are all in good shape."

"That's good at least."

"Not really. If they were bad, I could just replace them. Good means there's something wrong with me, instead."

Bilan didn't have an answer to that. They both knew it was true, and to pretend otherwise would be more insult than reassurance.

When they got to the list of protocols, Del was surprised at how many there were.

"You really had no idea these were here?"

"It did everything I wanted it to do. When it didn't, I had Kenny upgrade it."

Bilan shook her head. "It's one thing to rely on experts, but you have to have some idea of what they're doing."

"It's worked so far."

"You're in the Belt now—" she started.

"I wish people would stop telling me that."

"Sorry. But it's true. You've got a top notch suit here, but it's not going to do you any good if something goes wrong when you're a million kilometers away from anyone else and you can't fix it."

"Okay, I got it." Del felt chastised, and knew it was her own fault. Less than an hour ago she'd been congratulating herself on learning to think like a Belter. Bilan was hammering home just how far she had to go.

"A lot of these are pretty standard across all suits," Bilan said, continuing down the list of protocols. "This is what's letting you talk to your bike." She pointed to a small icon of Del's bike on the console. She tapped it and the display went back to an image of her suit and the bike next to it, with lines running from the suit to the bike's engines and missile racks. She tapped again and it went back to the list.

"These regulate your pressure and air mix. This one came with your medical module - see how it can analyze your blood and control each dispenser?" She opened it up with another tap. "If you need to make any changes, this is where you do it."

"Umm..." This was too much. She couldn't understand most of what she saw.

Bilan, seeing her face, swiped it back closed. "You don't have to worry about that. If you need changes you don't want to do them yourself anyway until you're sure you know what you're doing. Ask Kenny, I guess. You don't want to let any of the BeltSec techs look in here. Maybe Jie. He's pretty good at this stuff and can be discreet as long as it's not too over the line."

Del nodded, feeling a little better. She realized Bilan was helping, but she felt like a child being tutored.

"For instance, he probably wouldn't be so understanding about that package hidden in the back of your bike."

"Void."

"Forgotten about it already?"

"No, I just...need to take care of it soon."

"Did you scan it?"

"No. Pretty sure it's just a delivery of cosmo."

Bilan shook her head. "I understand why you need the med module. But if I ever find out you've loaded cosmo or any other fek like that in there, I am going to pound you bloody, understood?"

"Not to worry. I tried it when I was younger. It doesn't affect me the same way as other people."

"I can imagine! No, actually I can't, but I don't want to." She brought her attention back to the console. "Here's what I really wanted to see. Looks like this is your friend Kenny's addition to your med module. Notice anything different?"

Del looked at it, then repeated Bilan's hand-opening gesture to open it up. It didn't open. She hit the information icon. Nothing. "It won't open."

"Exactly. He's got it locked down so only he can see in it. Now, the overdose protection, that makes sense. If you're not in your right mind when you use it, you don't want to rely on your memory for how much you've taken or what your limits are. No reason to lock down everything else, though."

"You think Kenny's up to no good?"

"He's a fixer. Of course he's up to no good. The question is, what nefarious schemes does he have planned for the Belt's favorite miniature Martian?"

Del scowled. At a hundred and fifty-one centimeters, she was not that much shorter than average, but popular entertainment from Earth or the Belt always portrayed Martians as gangling giants. That kind of mistake made sense for Earth, as Mars' lower gravity meant the people from there tended to be a bit taller on average. She supposed the Belt got its aesthetic from Earth, still by far the most prolific producers of popular entertainment.

"I mean, you think he's the one who altered the recorder?"

"I don't think so," Bilan answered. "I think I know where the recording is being reset. See if you can spot it."

Del looked at the display. Amongst all the icons listed there was one black square. She waved her hand near it and the label "DelPeepFun" appeared. She felt a wave of anger surge through her. She didn't know which was worse: "peep" or "fun." Someone had tampered with her suit and violated her privacy for fun?

She opened it the way Bilan had shown her and saw it was a very simple list of instructions with only two functions: one that just turned the recorder back on any time it was ordered off, and another that uploaded the data to the net every twenty-four hours.

"They're going to pay for this."

"Good. Who?"

Del had no idea, or how she'd find out. She just looked blankly at Bilan.

"Access logs?" Bilan prompted.

"Yes!" She pulled up that page, remembering and eager to show Bilan that she had been paying attention.

There was only one entry for "DelPeepFun." It was installed a couple of months ago. She noted the time then brought up the video for that moment. It started, to the second, when the protocol was installed.

On the video was a man sitting on the edge of her bed with her console in his hand. He hit a button, then waved at the suit, then looked back down at the console and smiled. He stood up and Del could see herself sleeping behind him, which made her even angrier.

"Who is he?" Bilan asked, after Del had stopped the video.

"Prospector, or so he said. I think his name was Dario or something like that." She gritted her teeth expecting a disapproving comment from Bilan and when it didn't come, she wasn't sure to feel grateful or even more worried. She was glad it wasn't Kenny who messed with her suit, though. "I met him at Rokoj. Seen him there a few times before; he might be back. I'll keep an eye out for him."

"Might want to send his picture to Zak," Bilan replied. "He can alert one of us if the guy comes back in."

She realized what Bilan had said. No words of judgment, no pointing out that this was her own fault for her carelessness, just help and an offer to help in the future.

"Thank you," she said. Impulsively, she reached over to hug her. "I mean it. For..." she floundered for the words and ended with, "everything."

Bilan smiled in return. "You're welcome."

"Now how do we get this fek off of there?"

"For that, we're going to need to put the suit back up on the manikin. Since the data only gets sent once per day, we should be safe."

Del pressurized the airlock and retrieved her vacsuit. She picked it up tentatively, still with mixed feelings, and arranged it back on its service dummy. She erased the offending protocol without issue.

After testing it to make sure it was working properly, Bilan said, "Good. It's gone. Of course, if it wasn't for your perverted friend there, I never would have known about you, and Kenny. Speaking of which..."

Del looked at her apprehensively.

"You ready to talk about it yet?"

"I met him through one of his agents, about six months after I got here..."

"You know that's not what I mean," Bilan said gently.

Was this, all of this—the training on the suit, removing the rogue protocol—just to get her to calm down after dropping that initial bombshell "I know about the voices"?

"The thing is..." She took a deep breath then continued, "I have to trust you if you know this."

"Do you not, by now?"

"I mean completely. Absolutely. Literally, I have to bet my life that you won't lie to me or use this to mess with me, even as a joke."

"You're...kinda starting to scare me, Del."

"Good. You should be scared. It terrifies me."

"If it makes you feel any better, I won't lie to you. I appreciate you being honest with me, and I'll do my best to do the same."

"Swear it." She held her hand out in a fist, little finger extended.

"Del..."

"I'm serious. This is a pact."

Apprehensively, Bilan extended her own hand, hooking the small finger across Del's own.

Del continued. "Swear that any time I ask you if something really happened, or is happening, you will always tell me the truth, no matter how embarrassing it is, or how you worry it'll make me or anyone else feel."

"All right. If you swear that any time I ask you something you'll be honest with me. I'll forgive you if you just lied, but when I ask, you have to tell me the truth afterward."

"I swear it."

"I feel ridiculous," Bilan said, still holding her little finger wrapped around Del's.

"Good. That means you're more likely to remember this moment. It'll stick in your mind that way." Del withdrew her hand.

Bilan gave her a dubious look.

"Hey, this is the deepest magic, stretching back to earliest childhood. It's not to be trifled with."

Bilan laughed, then immediately sobered up. "So, tell me."

"They're not really voices," Del began. "More like...information packets, or flashes of visions. It always seems like they're coming from outside my head, which is why some of my families thought they were demons."

"Wait...back up. Some of your families?"

"You knew I was an orphan, right? On Mars, we have the *Nobeleco Postuloj* system. Obligations of the rich."

"I've heard of it. Wealthy households reduce their taxes by contributing to art and science, right?"

"Sort of. It goes beyond that, but one of the things they can do is foster children. They take in the kids, contracted one year at a time. That's a Martian year, so about two standards. At the end of the contract, they pass them off to someone else."

"That sounds terrible!"

Del shrugged. "It wasn't that bad. Mostly they leave you alone. Some of them make you do chores. Cleaning, running errands, helping out. Nothing horrendous. At least, I was never asked to. Worst I ever had to do was dress up fancy and attend dinner parties so all the other rich people could coo at me and tell the fosters how wonderful and generous they were for taking in such an unfortunate little girl. Sometimes you hear horror stories, but I never knew if they're real or just something they tell you to frighten you into showing gratitude. At any rate, I was never beaten or starved or raped or anything, though they do make us all take classes on how to identify and report early signs of such things."

"Still. Just having a new family every year. I can't imagine."

"Why? How do they do it on Venus?"

"I…uh…I don't know. I assume their extended family would take them in."

Del shrugged again. "Didn't have any family. None that they could find anyway. Near as they could figure, I was born on a ship, maybe just a couple of people on it. The ship had been stolen fifty years earlier. Probably bought and sold and stolen again a dozen times over since then. They had no idea who'd been operating it when they found it orbiting Mars. All the pressure doors were open but one. Behind that one was baby me."

"What happened to your parents?"

"Apparently, they made it to Mars then accidentally spaced themselves. Somebody opened the cargo bay doors while it was in orbit, anyway, and by the time the Martian Authority got to it, I was the only one on board."

"Wait…so your parents were pirates?" Bilan said with a laugh.

"Guess so. Why?"

Bilan looked down at the floor before looking back up. "Nothing. Just, kinda badass."

"You've dealt with pirates. You know they're nothing like in the vids."

"I know, but still. Maybe I was just too fixated on them as a little girl. Doesn't matter. Go on. These voices…"

She took a deep breath, then looked out through the window at the distant stars. "They first manifested when I was five. That's about ten standards."

"You must have been terrified."

"Not at first. I didn't really think anything of it. I told one of my foster dads what happened - information that I learned that coincidentally turned out to be true - and he decided I was hearing the voices of angels sent by Ares."

"Ares, the god of war?"

"That's Earth's misrepresentation. On Mars, it's Ares, the goddess who created humanity then waited for them to grow up enough to reach her."

"I've never heard that one."

Del shrugged. "Apparently it's a pretty common belief. I've known a few other Ares worshipers, though none took it to quite the level my fosters did."

"And she has angels working for her? Sounds like they've got a few different religions mixed together in there..."

"Probably. That's generally how it works, isn't it?"

"I suppose. You should ask Jie about his some time. His parents believed that the Belt was the original heaven. Their God abandoned it when humans started arriving, and that's why it's such a mess now."

"That sounds...interesting."

"Gets more so. Since he was born here, that makes him an angel."

"Jie the angel. Huh, figures."

"Sorry, I'm getting us off track. You said your parents thought they were demons..." Bilan started.

"Foster parents, and that was later. They changed their minds a few months before the contract was due to expire."

"Why?"

Del looked out the window again. Somewhere out there was the tiny red dot where she grew up. "They...the way it works...sometimes it seems like information. Other times, more like a compulsion. An action I should take. I...I was playing with my foster brother; he was about a year younger than me, and we were on the balcony. I don't remember exactly what he said, but I knew—knew with no doubt at all—that I should push him over it."

"Depths below! Did you...?"

"Push him off the balcony? Yes. I realized what I'd done as he was falling, and ran down the stairs."

"Was he...?"

"He was breathing when I got to him. I was bawling. His parents ran in, and took him off to the hospital, and told me to wait there." She had never told this story to anyone. She took another moment to calm herself, and was grateful to Bilan for waiting, quietly, and allowing her to. "I don't know how long I sat there, right at the spot he'd fallen. Hours, maybe. But two people from the fostering system came and got me. The family had canceled the contract and they were going to place me somewhere else."

"What about the child?"

"I never found out. I tried to ask but was just told that it's over and not to try to contact the family again, but I did find out that that's when they claimed I was possessed by demons. They said so on the official forms."

"That's awful! What a horrible thing to do to a child. And to just leave you alone like that? They should have at least let you know..."

"I was told it wouldn't make any difference. They reminded me it was worse for my foster brother and that it wasn't about me."

"That's even worse," Bilan said. "That must have made it hard to place you again."

"Not...that hard, strangely. I was in the group home again for just over a month before they found a family, in another city, who'd heard and specifically requested me."

"And that didn't raise any issues?"

"They promised to get me help. They didn't, and I think

they lied on the reports. Turned out they were members of a kind of fringe religion. They believed in demons the same as the Ares worshipers did, but to them, they were tools to be manipulated, not worshiped or feared. They had rituals they used to summon or bind them, and one they taught me to banish them."

"You needed professional help!"

"Yeah, that's what the next set of fosters said. And I got it, eventually. But these...the ritual actually does help. Sort of. I think the biggest thing is, the episodes never last for more than a few minutes, and the ritual takes a few minutes to perform."

"So, by the time you finish it, the episode would have passed naturally anyway."

"Maybe, but also while I'm doing it, I can't do anything else and I'm not thinking about how my mind is being taken away or how maybe my original fosters were right and I'm really being possessed by demons."

"You don't...actually think there's such a thing as demons, do you?"

"Not usually." She laughed. "Do you not have demon-believing religions on Venus?"

"If there are, I'm not familiar with them. I was taught that demons were something only primitive Earthers believed in."

"I guess some of them made it off of Earth."

Bilan laughed, but not loudly.

"Anyway, during an episode my mind can warp in weird ways, and I don't know what's real or not. That's why I said you absolutely have to be honest with me, because I'm likely to believe anything you say. You could...if you even joked about something during such a time, you could destroy me."

Bilan looked her straight in the eyes then and said, "Then I won't. Ever. I promise."

Del felt tears welling up. It was such a simple statement,

yet nobody had ever said that kind of thing to her before. Again, she fought down the tears before proceeding. "That's the footage I erased. I was doing the ritual and didn't want to take the risk of anyone finding out."

"So this ritual they taught you actually worked."

"More or less."

"But you didn't stay with that family."

"No. I thought I was going to. I was so happy with them and thought maybe I'd be with them forever." She gave a snort of laughter at her own naivety. "But at the end of the year they didn't renew. I don't know why and haven't spoken to any of them since then."

"Depths, I'm sorry."

"Also, that's why I dropped the second missile from the bike. I was afraid I'd listen to the voices again and fire it into the office. I almost did the first time. If it hadn't taken so long to get the bike pointed the right way...I don't know what I would have done."

"You didn't, though. That's what's important."

"Is it? I mean, is it really? What happens next time?"

"You've proven you can ignore it."

"Maybe. The problem is, I don't always know. Is something a real memory, or is it something my fevered brain just conjured up?"

"I don't understand. How can you not know? You said it feels like it's coming from the outside, right? Can't you just ignore it in favor of your own perceptions?"

"It's...it's hard to explain. I've never actually tried to explain this to anyone before. In the past, if anyone found out, they'd have run away by this point."

"I'm sorry. And I promise, I won't."

"Thank you. I mean it. I...I don't know what to say."

"Then you don't have to say anything. It's okay."

She thought about it again for a moment. "Try this. And here's information you know is coming from the outside. Imagine that we met after a morning briefing two standards ago."

"We did meet after a morning briefing two standards ago. At Rokoj."

"You followed me there because you thought I was cute and wanted to bed me."

"Yeah, that's true," Bilan said with an embarrassed smile.

"You offered to buy me a drink and told me it was tradition to welcome a new team member. I accepted the drink, but we never bedded."

"Right. It turned out you're monosexual like me, but with the other sex."

"And now you believe that," Del finished.

"I believe it because that's what happened."

"No," Del said. "None of that happened. You believe it because I just put it into your mind."

"No. I...uh...wait..." Del could see her considering the possibilities. "Shining stars and the depths below!" Bilan said, finally. "Is that what it's like for you all the time? You could never trust your own mind!"

"Not all the time. But sometimes. And sometimes, it's information, but it's also compulsion. Like, *this* fact is true, and I must do *this* about it. But at the same time, I know this *other*, contradictory, thing is true."

"So, you have to choose which competing reality is true."

"And they both seem equally plausible, and I have to make that choice with my heart racing, my vision unsteady, and my hearing overwhelmed with static, and ten thousand other thoughts crashing through my mind."

"How often does this happen?"

"That's a trickier question than it seems. When it first

started, all the time. Sometimes it seems like it's going on, but it's just a background buzz. And the medicine helps control it. That's why I got the med module out here in the first place. I knew BeltSec wouldn't let me out on patrol, and would probably just fire me outright if they knew, so I kept it secret and made black market connections to get the medication I needed. The other day was the first episode I've had since I started taking it."

"You said you can't tell what's real? The hallucinations from real input?"

"Sometimes."

"What do you do? How do you choose what's actually going on and what's your brain making stuff up?"

"Sometimes, I can measure against objective reality. I can look at a gauge for instance and see there's really air in my vacsuit even when I think it's all leaked out. I can measure against past events. Like, if I start thinking you're planning to kill me, I can remember that you could have done so easily many times in the past and didn't, so my perception is probably wrong."

"It must be hard for you to be dealing with people like Kenny."

"Ironically, no. I know I can trust Kenny because he'll only sell me out if the profit from doing so outweighs the profit of dealing with me in the foreseeable future."

"What about me?"

"You're more difficult. The pact will help, I think. I know I can trust you, it's just a matter of remembering that when the time comes."

"I will do my absolute best to abide by the pact, then. And if I don't, and you ask me, I swear I'll remember to tell you the truth. No matter what."

"Thank you. I've..." Del fought back tears. This was ridiculous. She had just confided her deepest, most dangerous secrets to this woman. In the last hour, Bilan had seen video of her committing crimes, and of her having sex, and now she was afraid to let her see her cry?

Despite her best efforts, she could feel her eyes growing moist and there was the slightest quaver in her voice as she said, "I've never had a friend like that before. I've always thought it would be nice."

Bilan reached over to give her a hug, which she returned. "I almost hate to ask now," she said once she'd released her. "But I need something from you."

"Name it."

"I need you to talk to Kenny for me."

"What? Why?"

"His salvagers got the data core from the station. I want it."

"He's not going to just give it to me. Something like that could sell for a lot."

"I have an expense account."

"I don't know if he takes corporate credit transactions."

"There must be some way you can funnel it—"

"You want me to launder money for you?" Del said with a laugh.

"Is there another way?"

"Another problem is that I start a long range patrol tomorrow. They're sending me to the Hygiea sector. I'll be gone for almost two weeks."

"Can you call him before then?"

"You don't call Kenny. To talk to him, I'd have to go there."

"He's about six hours from here, right? Can you go before your patrol starts? I know it's asking a lot, but it's important."

"It's not a lot," Del decided. "Not for a friend. I'll leave now."

"Thank you. I'll toss you some of that expense account money for your help, too."

"I thought you said they specifically asked that I not be involved?"

"Then I won't give them your name."

FOUR

EXTORTION, PIRACY, MURDER, OR NOT

"Delokita!" Kenny greeted her as she again exited the airlock into his workshop. "What's wrong? I was not hoping to see you again so soon! Is my new protocol not working?"

On the way over, she had considered how she'd handle her misgivings about what he did with her med module. On the one hand, if he thought she was suspicious he might be eager to prove she could trust him. On the other hand, he might play the injured party and expect concessions from her for hurting his feelings with her doubts. She decided to take a page from Bilan's book and see what he let slip while having no idea what she knew.

"Haven't had a chance to try it yet," she said. "Hopefully never will."

"Then are you here about my little package?" he asked.

"No interest in your little package," she replied. "But the box you gave me is on its merry way to Mars as we speak." She'd received confirmation that the package had shipped without inspection just about an hour ago.

"If not the package and not the protocol, what does bring you out to my little rock? Could this be a social visit?"

"I'm here as a customer this time."

"Ah. I see. And what might I have that would be of interest to you?"

"There was a data core in the salvage I pointed you to," she said, intentionally including the not-so-subtle reminder of why he had it.

"Now, that's interesting," Kenny replied. "I think I charged far too little for that core."

"What do you mean?"

"You are the third person to ask for it."

"What? Who else?"

"You know I can't tell you that."

"I don't suppose you kept a copy."

"Sorry. The purchaser wanted exclusive access."

"I don't suppose they'd be willing to sell part of it? I don't care about the industrial data. I just want maybe an hour or so of the vid. I can pay well for it."

"How is this possible? Yesterday you were having difficulty meeting rent."

"I'm working as an agent for another in this."

"Who?"

"You first."

He nodded, conceding the point. "It doesn't matter. It's gone, and I guarantee whatever you want it for they're not interested, and whoever you're working for doesn't have enough money to make them interested."

"Void. There must be some way."

"Believe me when I say there isn't. You seem to be attaching a lot of importance to this. I've never seen you this worked up."

"It just..." She didn't want to tell him how much she didn't want to let Bilan down, not already. "It just is."

"Then I'm sorry. I can tell you I got the impression that getting the data themselves wasn't nearly as important as keeping anyone else from getting it."

"WE WON'T SEE you for another two weeks?" Bilan asked.

Del had met her at Rokoj for a last round of drinks before heading out on her long patrol. As usual, Jie had come with Bilan. Del had nothing against Jie, he was one of her favorite people at BeltSec. She'd just wished to get in a private conversation with Bilan.

"You're doing the whole patrol on your bike?" Jie asked.

"It's the only transport I've got," Del said.

"It's not really meant for that far of a distance. You can probably arrange—"

"I like my bike. I'm used to it. It'll be fine."

"Have you done the fuel calculations for such a distance?"

"It's fine," Del said again. "I can refuel on Hygiea itself, and there's bound to be a bunch of corporate spots I can ask at if I need to."

"We'll miss you," Bilan said, heading off the argument. "Stay in touch."

Del took a sip of her beer and set it down on the table. A lot had happened since the last time she'd been drinking here, just over twenty hours ago. "You, too," she replied. "I've put a search up on our perp, Dario. If he shows up anywhere, you'll both get notified as well as me."

"What should we do if we find him?" Bilan asked.

"Space him."

"What?" Jie exclaimed.

Bilan laughed.

"Too much?" Del joined her in laughing. "Maybe confiscate his local storage. Force him to delete any images he took from my suit. I wouldn't arrest him. I don't want BeltSec to know about it."

"Agreed," Bilan said.

"Yes," Jie said as well.

"Really?" Del asked him.

"You wish me to reconsider?"

"No!"

"But yes. BeltSec doesn't need to know you let your suit get compromised. At the very least, they'd insist on a full inspection."

Del wondered if he knew how bad that would actually be. She wanted to ask Bilan what she'd told him.

"It's only two weeks, she's not leaving us forever!" Jie chastised a tearful Bilan after several more rounds. Several more for Del, at least. She didn't think Jie had more than a couple. Void, that man could drink slowly. She didn't usually get this drunk twice in a row, but it had been a trying day and she wasn't likely to see any alcohol for another two weeks.

Which is why she was so miserable as she flew away from her home early the next morning, heading to a remote section of the belt.

BeltSec had to pay extra bonuses for these long patrols, or else nobody would volunteer. The extra money, combined with what she'd received from Kenny, meant she'd be able to pay rent for at least another month. During half of which her home would be sitting empty. If she could pick up any side work, or even a corp bonus along the way, even better.

She suspected this particular route would be a dud. The Enforcer it was originally scheduled for, someone named Johanka, had canceled at the last minute, leaving BeltSec scrambling for a new volunteer. Really, though, she enjoyed the deep patrols. She could go days without seeing another human being or any signs of life. She could feel like she was the only person in the universe.

Of course, after a couple of days of that, she'd be longing for the hustle of the Ceres marketplace or the chaos of Rokoj. She felt a twinge of nostalgia for the buzz of activity around the spaceport at Bradbury Point, which eclipsed that of Ceres even on the dwarf planet's busiest of days.

For nearly twenty-four hours she accelerated toward her first stop, eighty million kilometers away from Ceres. At seven percent of the distance around the Belt, it was faster to leave the Belt entirely, cutting sunward as she went. Not that she got close enough that the sun grew any larger than the tiny dot it always was.

She settled into her usual routine: cutting acceleration to deploy her balloon and engage in a zero-gravity meal, sleeping a few hours at a time, without regard to any set schedule. Watch an occasional old vid. Bilan and Jie shared a love for old pre-spaceflight vids and were constantly sending her recommendations, some of which she decided weren't entirely without merit.

At the turnaround point, she let her bike drift and kicked off slightly from it, allowing herself to float free. Killing all lights inside her helmet, she turned away from her bike and from the sun, looking out onto the stars and the ever-present Milky Way. She was millions of kilometers away from any other being or anything else. She could just stay here, set her bike on a one-way course sunward, and let it accelerate until it ran out of fuel. If she opened her helmet now, nobody would ever know what happened, and nobody would ever find her remains. She'd just drift out here alone amongst the stars until the sun itself went nova and killed them all.

Enough of that. She pushed the thought away with a burst of anger. She was overdue for a run. She used her suit thrusters to return to her bike then sent the command to flatten and extend the seat into a treadmill. She brought up the surface of Mars on her helmet display and spent the next hour or more running across her favorite course on Arcadia Planitia, vaulting boulders and jumping the narrow ravines.

Finally, she stopped the treadmill but left the seat flat as she napped then, held down by the acceleration of her tiny craft away from its destination. It would take it another twenty or more hours to slow down to where it matched the velocity of the rock at her first stop.

The next day, she repeated mostly the same routine.

Once she arrived at the tiny asteroid, Del checked in at the small mining office and spent just enough time to remind them that BeltSec still existed and to confirm that the base hadn't been taken over by pirates. If it had been, the pirates were wearing the uniform of the local corp and following standard bureaucratic procedures, which was close enough. Forty-six hours of flight to spend less than half an hour there.

It was after another two days of the same routine as the first two when she got two calls within an hour of each other. The first was from a smaller independent mining group. She hadn't heard of it before, but they were registered as Zono Mastro shareholders, which meant they were BeltSec clients. There seemed to be some kind of dispute over ownership of a particular asteroid, and they'd asked for an Enforcer. These calls were gold to BeltSec, and usually worth at least a small Corp bonus to the Enforcer who answered. They were just over a million kilometers away - practically next door by Belt standards. She set the new course and sent acknowledgment of the call and her ETA.

"It's a pretty clear case," she narrated for her later vid audience, after she'd looked over the details. "One party registered the rock, the other did not. The unregistered one is currently occupying it. Usually, my presence alone—or that of my uniform—is enough to resolve the issue. We'll see how this one goes."

Most likely, whoever was squatting there would be persuaded to move on to wherever people in the Belt moved to when their home was yanked out from under them. At such times she felt less like the long arm of the law and more like its middle finger.

Fifteen minutes after she'd sent confirmation, another call came in, from somebody who'd picked up her post looking for Dario. He'd been spotted in a bar, nearly twenty million kilometers away from her current location. If she set out right now, she could be there in twenty-four hours. She was tempted. It was off her assigned route, but Enforcers had a great deal of latitude when it came to such things. They had to, at the distances they traveled. But it would be the opposite direction of the client whose call she had already acknowledged.

She had to choose between profit and revenge.

Profit it was. She continued on course toward the disputed asteroid.

Her alarm woke her an hour out. She sat up, took hold of the manual control yoke, and turned to face her destination. She was close enough and the difference in her velocity was small enough that she could go the rest of the way on the forward engines.

Using the bike's sensors, she zoomed in on the rock, sending the image to her visor. She could clearly see the lights around a standard airlock, identical to the one around her own. That was unexpected. If the rock was only recently claimed, there shouldn't be a pressurized atmosphere inside.

She looked around. A small cargo ship stood outside the

rock. No base for it to be shipping cargo to, and no mining platform nearby. The whole thing looked like smugglers, but if that was so, why call an Enforcer?

She was close enough for realtime communication now. She hailed the freighter first, after pinging its transponder to get its name.

"*Zheng He*, this is BeltSec Enforcer Delokita, on approach to your position. What is your situation?"

"Enforcer Delokita, good to hear from you." A woman's face appeared in a window on her faceplate. "We've got some illegal squatters here and could use a bit of help persuading them to leave."

"This is a mine, then?" Del asked. "I don't see any equipment."

"The asteroid's full of volatiles, so we can't use lasers. We have to do it from the inside the old fashioned way. The squatters are willing to talk - they said they wanted to speak to Zono Mastro. Our captain's over there now if you'd like to join them. If it helps, we can even transport them as far as Newman. I think mostly what they need is reassurance they won't all be spaced. The presence of an Enforcer would go a long way toward that."

"All right. I'll head in. Let them know I'm coming."

She brought the bike in alongside the airlock. There were no external clamps, but it wasn't accelerating, so she just set it to keep station nearby.

She pushed off gently and floated toward the airlock with a couple of bursts from her suit thrusters. They had already opened the outer door for her. She flew inside, hit the button beside the door to close it behind her, and listened through her suit as it pressurized.

There was a curtain over the inner door's window, on rails on either side. That was common for residential spaces. She had the railing on her own, but had never bothered to put a curtain on them. It still increased her sense of unease of the situation, though. She willed herself to relax. It was just a routine eviction. She'd done it before many times.

Then she knew someone was waiting for her. Without a doubt, someone was waiting on the other side of that door to kill her.

She took a deep breath. *There's nobody there.* She pulled up the interface to Kenny's new protocol. Then pushed it away. What if she was right? Somebody was right there, on the other side of the wall, waiting for her to step through.

No, stop it. Nobody is trying to kill you.

Ready, she didn't quite hear someone say.

No! Not now!

She activated Kenny's protocol and pushed herself up to the ceiling. She could feel the soft pin prick as an additional dose of the medicine entered her bloodstream.

Stop. Check. What's real?

There was enough air now that a sound could conceivably carry. She didn't hear a voice, though. Her heart was racing, and black spots grew at the edges of her vision. She forced herself to take a deep breath and tried to calm down.

Three...Two...One...

Someone was counting. When they hit zero, the door slid open. On the other side was a long-time residential area, much like her own. These weren't squatters who just moved here and this wasn't an active mine, either. And there was nobody visible inside the room waiting for her. No squatters, no miners, no ship captain wanting to talk to her.

She thought back on Bilan's words. What would she do, on her own, a million kilometers from anyone else, when she couldn't trust her own perceptions? Her own mind could be the biggest danger to her. If she just went crazier and crazier until

BeltSec had to send somebody to stop her, then so be it. She had nothing else to rely on.

Three...Two...

Someone was counting again. She knew it. He was expecting her to come out and she didn't, so he was about to come in. She had an image of a man pressed up against the side of a door with a weapon in his hand and she knew what she had to do.

Just as he got to *one*, she activated suit thrusters on full power, launching herself into the room along the "top" of the airlock. She twisted around to face the opening as she went by.

Two men hovered inside, both of them holding weapons in their hands.

She raised her right arm and with the needler mounted there shot them both in rapid succession.

Now all she had to do was survive the next three seconds while the drug in the needles did its thing.

She slammed hard into the wall behind her, taking most of the impact on her upper back, then shot down along the floor as bullets hit the wall where she had just been. She twisted again, launching off the floor diagonally, desperately seeking cover, but could find none.

They each fired again as she shot around the room, bending, twisting, keeping her course as erratic as possible.

Finally, she launched herself low again and slammed into one of the men, pulling herself around so his mass was between her and his friend. While he was trying to recover his balance, the drug took effect and first one, then the other collapsed, hanging limply in the air.

She took two pairs of restraint cables from a pocket on her suit and applied them both, binding the men hand and foot, checking that they didn't have any other weapons. She tossed both pistols gently into the airlock.

She had an antidote to the needle guns poison, but she decided against giving it to them yet. Not out of kindness, though the side effects were unpleasant. There was still another threat to her. The ship outside, with an unknown number of people on it.

Stop, Del. Think.

Both of these men had guns. They had already drawn them and were prepared to fire before she entered. Slug throwers, not stunners or needlers. They were planning on killing her, not taking her prisoner. *To what end? Why lure an Enforcer out here to kill?* There were plenty of easier people to rob.

For whatever reason, though, they had tried to kill her. That was objective reality. She didn't imagine it. She looked over toward the airlock, where the two handguns were floating. They were still there. They were real. It wasn't just a fake memory her mind had conjured up to justify the violence. Which raised the question, how had she known? Some subconscious cues. Their movements causing vibrations through the rock and her broken mind had conjured up their thoughts? And their images?

She checked her suit recorder. It had been operational the whole time. She scanned quickly through it. One corner of her mind was calculating where to edit the footage for maximum effect. It would certainly be an exciting moment, even if it was only a few seconds long. She could splice in the part where she applied the restraint cables, and maybe an interrogation later.

It could be worth quite a bit. Especially if she pulled off the next part. The *Zheng He* had told her their captain was over here in peaceful negotiations. There had been nobody here except the two who'd tried to kill her. Which had to mean whoever she'd spoken to on the ship had been involved. That meant she'd have to take them out, too, before they could complete their friends' mission.

In the airlock, after the inner door closed, she picked up the two guns. She briefly considered taking them to Kenny; he'd no doubt be able to give her a decent price for them. But she had a feeling if she did that they'd just show up again, probably to be used against some other Enforcer.

When the outer door opened, she stepped out into space, unloaded the weapons, and hurled them, one after the other, toward the sun. Floating alone in the vastness of space, they'd never be found. Still, she threw the bullets in a different direction, scattering them. In maybe a thousand years they'd reach their destination and their molten or vaporized remains would be swallowed up by the great star at the center of the solar system.

The freighter was the immediate concern. She launched herself from the asteroid and headed straight toward it. Once there, Del cut her speed and grabbed a handhold set into the hull to stop herself. She pulled herself along it to a standard airlock in the ship's port side. There was no way they didn't see her coming, and would likely be ready for her. She opened the outer airlock door and was surprised to see it worked. The inner door had a large window, looking into an empty hallway. Once the small chamber was pressurized, she found it was locked, as she'd expected.

Del pounded on the inner door, knowing the sound would carry, hoping whoever was on this ship would surrender and open the airlock. They did not. She called them anyway. As expected, there was no answer over the com, either.

She took her vacuum torch from its belt pouch and set to work. Hopefully whoever was still here was trying to hide, hoping she'd go away, rather than setting up a plasma cannon in the corridor.

She considered that for a second. Someone had already tried to kill her. This was the type of operation that should really be undertaken by a team of Enforcers with breaching cord, explosives, and armored vacsuits, not one woman with a wrist-mounted needler and a hand-held vacuum torch. But she wanted answers. This would be a great time to have a mining platform handy. Or maybe a missile or two. She'd really have to get those replaced when she got back to Ceres.

The airlock fell open as she finished cutting off its latch. She hoped the inhabitants had a different way out. Or at least vacuum suits because when she left, she'd have to open that outer door and all the air in this hallway would rush out behind her.

She lowered her helmet and a rancid smell assaulted her nose. The scent of molten metal mingled with that of a ship that had been a long way out of port. She listened for movement and heard none. No heavy breathing or bump of heavy equipment along the narrow corridor. And most importantly, no ominous hum of a plasma cannon getting ready to fire.

She pushed up the hallway toward the cockpit. Either someone would be there, or she could control the ship from there. She still wasn't sure what she'd do once there, maybe announce her presence over the com and threaten to pull all the air if the crew didn't surrender. She assumed those were both things she'd be able to figure out how to do once she got there.

A pressure door at the end of the hallway was, surprisingly, unlocked, and opened to her touch. Past it, another pressure door to the bridge was closed and locked. Del looked in through the window and saw the woman who had answered her original call. She sat with her back to Del, frantically hitting some control that Del couldn't see.

Del banged the window with the butt of the torch and the woman started and glanced her way, a look of terror on her face. Not exactly a hardened criminal, then. She wasn't even wearing a vacsuit. Del pointed at the handle of the sealed pressure door, and then to the BeltSec seal on her chest, then to the door again, making it clear this was an official demand.

The woman again shook her head and looked frantically around the cabin.

Del pulled the cutting torch off her belt again and held it to the window. She looked meaningfully at the woman without a vacsuit on the other side of the window.

The woman once again looked around. There was nobody to help her. Resigned, she turned to the console and hit a button.

The door Del had come through slammed shut, and the door to the bridge slid open.

Del entered, helmet still down. She put her torch back in its pouch as she entered, but kept the needler pointed at the woman.

"How many more?" she asked as she entered.

Sensibly, the other woman had both hands raised, palms visible. "Are Ned and Felix dead?"

"I'm asking first." Del decided to let her worry a bit. "Who else is still on the ship?"

"Nobody. They left me here when they went to..." She stopped.

"To kill me, yes. Why?"

"Somebody had to watch the ship."

"I mean," Del said through gritted teeth, "why did they try to kill me? What did you hope to gain?"

"It wasn't about the money!" she yelled, and looked like she was about to leap at Del.

Del raised the needler and pointed it at her face. "So there is money?"

"We got paid. So what?"

"Who's paying you to kill me? And why? And if you're not doing it for the money, why are you doing it?"

"Because of what you did to Ashur!"

There was so much to unpack in that sentence. It was revenge, then? Revenge against her specifically? But how did they know she would even be in this area of space? And once they found out, they'd lured her here. Because of Ashur. That begged the next question, and she asked it: "Who in the void is Ashur?"

"You don't even remember his name?" She cried out.

Void, did she sleep with this woman's husband or something? The woman looked like she was going to attack Del again. That was enough of that.

"All right. Turn around," she said.

"What?" Her eyes grew wide. She had asked if her friends were dead. She probably thought Del was going to kill her. Afraid was good, but too much would be counter-productive. Hoping she hadn't read her wrong, Del lowered her arm, no longer pointing the weapon at her and reached into a pouch at her side and pulled out a restraint cord.

"You're under arrest," she said, letting the woman see it. "If you cooperate, you will be taken back to Ceres to stand trial."

"You're not going to kill me?"

"If I wanted to do that, I'd've just punched a hole in your ship and let you drift off into space."

The woman shuddered. Either she was new to all this, or she was a good actor. Considering how easily Del got here, she decided the former was the more likely possibility.

"I'm not going to hurt you. Give me your hand."

The woman held out her hand tentatively.

Del snapped one end of the cord around it then took her wrist and twisted. The move spun her around so her back was to Del and her arm trapped behind her. Del reached for the other arm and pulled it around. When she touched the other end of the cord to her wrist, it wrapped itself around it and pulled the two ends together. Her prisoner cried out in alarm.

"You're not hurt, right?"

She shook her head.

"Good. Behave yourself and you'll stay that way. What's your name anyway?" Del asked.

"Nurayda," she answered.

Del took her by the arm and kicked off from a nearby seat back toward the door. Outside the cockpit, she closed the door behind them. The door wouldn't lock from this side, but if somehow her prisoner got free it would slow her down for a couple of seconds as she opened it, which might give Del enough time to catch up to her before she could do any harm.

Outside, Del let go and pushed her gently down the hall.

Nurayda struggled to get her bearings as she tumbled in the lack of gravity, which only caused her to tumble more. Which, in turn, only reinforced Del's opinion of her.

"Let's try this again," Del said, letting her slowly tumble ahead. "Tell me who Ashur is."

"From Aluna," she replied, trying to look over her shoulder at Del.

"What's Aluna?" Del said with a sigh.

"Where you met Ashur!"

She'd had enough of that, too. She waited until the woman was almost but not quite facing straight at her, then used her suit thrusters to shoot forward, catching her by the collar and carrying her to the far wall, which she slammed into with a cry of surprise and pain.

"You think this is a joke, Nurayda?" Del yelled, her face centimeters from the other woman's. "You think I'm kidding around? You and your friends tried to kill me. Their pathetic attempt was all recorded. I could break your neck or throw you out an airlock and nobody would ever question it. I want answers!"

She pushed back, but then used the suit thrusters to stop just a couple of meters away. She didn't say anything, but glared at the woman.

"Ashur is the man you murdered after he beat you at cards at Aluna."

"That's a little better, except I still don't know what Aluna is. Some kind of casino I take it? Also, if I killed everyone who beat me at cards, I'd have to murder half the Belt."

As she said it, she wondered if it was really true. Could she have killed someone, then suppressed the memory? She'd been to a lot of tiny bars and card rooms throughout the Belt. One of them might have been named Aluna. She didn't know most of their names. She doubted most of them had names.

"Who was this Ashur person that three people would be willing to come all the way out here and risk their lives to avenge him?"

"He was Felix's husband."

And she finally had a motive.

"Who told you I killed him?"

"Felix."

"And who told Felix?"

"I don't know. Felix was the only one who spoke to him."

"Spoke to him? Him who?"

"Somebody approached him in Aluna and said you were the one who killed Ashur and he would finance our trip here if we'd take you out."

"Why did this guy want me dead so much?"

"I don't know. Only Felix ever talked to him."

"All right then, I'll ask Felix."

Her head snapped up. "He's alive?"

"They both are. I left them over on that rock."

"Why?"

"Why what?"

"You said they tried to kill you," she replied. "Why didn't you kill them?"

There were several answers she could give to that. The question wasn't which was correct, but which one would be most useful.

"Because I don't kill people needlessly," she could say.

"Except when the voices tell me to," she probably shouldn't add.

Best not to let her prisoner get too comfortable, though.

"I wanted information," she told her.

"What...?" Del could tell she didn't want to ask the question. "What happens when you get it?"

"That depends on the information," she replied.

"If we tell you everything, will you let us go?"

Which was an awfully bold thing to ask. She pretended to think about it. "Maybe," she said. "Though you're all guilty of attempted murder and, since I was the target, I hope you understand if I'm taking it a little personally."

The other woman had no answer.

Del continued. "And what reassurance do I have that you won't just try again later? Maybe with some more competent help."

"You said you didn't kill Ashur. Is that true?"

"It is. But that didn't stop you from trying to kill me anyway. The fact that you were so eager to go to all this trouble to commit a murder purely on the say-so of a stranger doesn't exactly speak well of either your integrity or your judgment." It was the kind of thing Jie would say.

Her prisoner again had no answer.

She had passed a couple of pressure doors on the way up here, which she assumed led to crew quarters. Most likely, the corridor going down the starboard side of the ship was the same. "Which room's yours?" she asked, pulling her along.

When the woman indicated one of the doors, Del hit the button next to it to open it. She pulled her prisoner in with her and checked quickly around to make sure there were no weapons in the room.

"Where's your vacsuit?" she asked.

Again, that wide-eyed terror. She really wasn't cut out for this kind of work.

"It's in its locker. Next to the bridge."

Good. That meant she couldn't get to it from here.

"Here's what I'm going to do." She grabbed the other woman and pushed her gently toward the back of the room. "I'm going to lock you in here for a bit. That's a good pressure door leading to your quarters here. Since you refused to open the airlock door to me when I so politely knocked earlier, I had to cut it open. Which means, this entire corridor is now the airlock. When I open the outer door, there won't be anything outside your room but space. So, I highly recommend you don't try to open your door until I get back and give you the all-clear. Got it?"

She nodded and Del proceeded. The airlock refused to pull the air out until it had confirmation the inner door was closed. Of course, it could never get it because Del had cut it off. She hit the emergency override and a great rush of air blew her out the lock.

She tumbled into space, turned, and saw the large metal inner door heading straight forward. With a burst from her suit thrusters, she managed to dodge the door. It was going fast and in space would never slow down until it hit something. Just one more object flying through the Belt.

She used her suit thrusters to return to the ship and travel up the hall. On her way, she peered in through the window of the room where she'd left the woman.

She was floating near the edge of her bed, still bound, the very image of misery.

Del made the "no air" gesture across her throat with her hand.

If the pressure door followed the standard protocols, there'd be a light on the inside confirming the lack of air pressure on this side.

The woman on the other side of the window nodded her understanding.

Del brought up the interface to the restraint cuffs and released them.

Inside the small room, her prisoner rubbed her wrists and looked to her with gratitude, which Del accepted with a nod. She would still be scared, trapped, surrounded by vacuum, with no way of knowing if, or even when, Del would ever return, but she didn't need to be uncomfortable, too.

When she got back to the asteroid, Del pulled the helmets off of both her captives and tossed them into the airlock before closing the inner door. She realized she didn't know which of the two men was Felix. Probably should have asked for a description. They were both still out and would be for several more hours.

She chose one at random and hit him with the antidote. She was careful to aim his mouth away from herself. He didn't vomit, though he did wince when Del shone her light in his face. She'd had both the knockout drug and the antidote herself, during training. The effects were similar to a nasty hangover, only far more intense. Thankfully, though, not as long lasting. He would fully recover within a couple of hours. It did tend to make suspects being interrogated a little more compliant, as every enforcer knew. Perhaps there was some sort of "make the pain stop" subconscious assumption if they cooperated. Of course, it wouldn't matter. The only thing that would do that was time.

"Welcome back," she said as the man woke up.

He blinked, winced again, and looked back over at his friend, bound hand and foot and likewise missing his helmet.

"Are you Felix?" she asked.

His eyes grew wide, and then he nodded.

"Oh, good," she said. "I wanted to talk to you about a mysterious stranger and a place called Aluna."

"I got nothing to say to you," the man responded.

"That would make this an awfully boring conversation."

The man just glared at her.

She continued anyway. "You met some guy at Aluna, right?" His face registered surprise. Guess he didn't need to speak for this to work after all.

"He told you I was responsible for the death of your husband, Ashur. I wasn't. I don't know who he was, or where this Aluna place is, but I didn't kill anyone there. Someone suckered you into trying to kill me. Which means there's someone out there who wants me dead. Somebody who's not above hiring extremely gullible people who'll rush across the system to commit murder based on nothing more than his word.

"Now, since you're not the only stupid people out here, he's likely to try again. So, I hope you can understand why I want to find out who this is, and why he wants me dead. Or, at the very least, stop him before he gets more people like you killed. You gonna tell me what I want to know, or do you want to just sit here on this rock until you rot?"

"Get spaced."

"Wrong answer." She pushed herself over to where Felix was floating, planted her feet on a nearby wall for leverage, then pushed him toward the back wall, giving him a slight spin as she did so. As he bumped against the far wall, helpless to resist, she grabbed his friend by the back of his collar. She pulled him with her to the airlock.

"What are you doing?" Felix cried out.

"Don't worry. This one's still asleep. He'll never know what happened. The one on the ship on the other hand...Well, I'll have to figure out a way to bring her over here so you can watch." She hit the button to open the inner airlock door. "Let me know if you change your mind in the meantime."

She pushed the unconscious man into the airlock then followed him in. Felix glared at her the whole time, but kept silent.

She closed the inner door, and stepped aside, out of view of the remaining occupant of the asteroid. She counted to ten, then looked back in through the window.

Felix was facing away from the door, but she could tell he was crying. She supposed threatening to space his friends didn't go a long way toward proving she was no murderer. He had called her bluff, but he felt bad about it.

Did he even realize she was bluffing, or did he just assume that she was going to kill them all no matter what he did? She suspected it might be the latter.

She opened the inner door again, pitched the unconscious man into the room, then closed it without a word.

She took her bike back to the *Zheng He* and parked it in the cargo bay. After re-pressurizing the port hall from the bridge, she went back down to Nurayda's room.

The woman was still there, looking nervous.

Del opened her door. "All right, get your suit on," she ordered.

"What? What are you going to do to me?"

"Giving you a choice," she said. "Your friend, Felix,

wouldn't cooperate, but I have his and your confessions on record now. So, up to you. I can haul you over to Ceres where you can get a fair trial from Zono Mastro, followed by a long indenture. Most likely you'll end up mining antimatter on Mercury, though it could be anywhere where hard labor is needed. You might even end up back in the Belt. Or..."

"You're going to suggest something even worse."

"Or you can go join your friends over there, and I'll let you all off with paying a substantial fine. Say, this ship."

"And there's the shakedown," Nurayda said. She was getting bolder now that she realized Del wasn't going to kill her. "I can't make that decision."

"You're gonna have to make that decision. You're the only one."

"It's not my ship."

"You're the only crew member on it. It's your ship if you say it's your ship. As a Zono Mastro employee, I can't claim salvage rights. You can. So, claim the ship and transfer ownership to me. Since your mis-aimed vendetta was against me personally, I'll accept it as sufficient compensation and the matter's dropped."

"This is extortion!"

"If you want to file a formal complaint with BeltSec..."

The woman knew she was beat.

While she filed the necessary claims and transfers, Del filled a crate with food from the ship's pantry. They might be there for a while, and she didn't want them to starve. When they got back to the asteroid, she took the other woman's helmet.

"If any of you idiots changes your mind and wants to help me track down the guy who set you up, now's your chance," she said, stepping into the airlock.

Nobody answered.

"Have it your way. I'll just make a general announcement of where you are. It'll be interesting to see who turns up here first - any friends you have, any enemies you have, or me." She waited a couple of seconds, and when nobody said anything, closed the door behind her.

She left the helmet floating outside the airlock, near the other two. If any of their friends showed up they could probably find and return them. Or they'd have to bring them new ones. She really didn't care. She hit the release on the restraints and kicked back over to her bike.

Del headed to the bridge after securing her bike in the cargo hold of her spaceship. She liked the sound of that. It looked like she'd be finishing this patrol in style.

From the bridge, she found the protocol to pressurize the cargo bay. It would take a while to refill it, and it was a colossal use of air. But why not? The air was recycled, and it wasn't really hers, anyway. As much as she liked the idea of owning her own spaceship, there was no way she'd be able to keep it. Nothing she'd done was technically illegal, but if she suddenly showed up with a cargo ship there would be questions, and she didn't want to answer them. Plus, there was no way she'd be able to afford to keep it in fuel and repairs. She would stop by Kenny's before returning home. She could probably get at least six months, if not an entire standard's, rent out of it.

FIVE
MESSAGES AND MEETINGS

While Del waited for the cargo bay to pressurize, she sent a message to Bilan asking if she'd ever heard of a place called Aluna in the Hygiean sector. She was far enough away that a message would take a few minutes to get to her, and there was no telling how long it would take her to respond. She checked the time on her suit, but then realized she had no idea when Bilan would be working, or asleep. Most Enforcers had some kind of definable schedule, though they varied widely. Del herself spent so much time traveling, and then meeting people according to their schedules, that her own was chaotic at best. She rarely slept more than a few hours at a time anyway, so it worked out.

She could wait for the return call, but she had no idea where Bilan would direct her to.

She sent a message to the man who had told her he'd spotted Dario. The reply came back fifteen minutes later that Dario had moved on. Her contact thought he might have been heading to the Pallas sector. That was too far away to pursue.

She swore at the screen, but realized she had to let the man go. She thanked the informant and forwarded the offered credits to his account, then changed course for Hygiea. It would take another four days to get there.

Hygiea had several corporate offices and she planned on spending at least a few days there meeting with them. She hated corporate meetings, but they had to be done. They had local Enforcers of course, and even a branch office on Hygiea itself, but BeltSec felt the need to send representatives of the home office from time to time. It was necessary to remind them all that BeltSec existed and why they were paying for it. On the plus side, each meeting had the potential to end with some "little favor" they wanted her to do. Things they didn't want to officially request but could ask in person. They would always have corporate bonuses attached to one degree or another. It presented good opportunities for networking, too. Not everything they needed could be officially requested. It helped to let the corps know she was willing to cooperate and could be contacted directly.

While the ship piloted itself toward Hygiea, accelerating at about half a G—the most she could make it do—she set out to explore her new acquisition. It wasn't that large. Two corridors led from the bridge, with three rooms branching off of each before both corridors ended in airlocks leading to opposite sides of the same large cargo bay. There were a total of four crew quarters, including the one she'd locked Nurayda into earlier.

The kitchen/dining room combination that she'd raided for supplies for her prisoners branched off the port corridor, and a medical bay, complete with doc table, branched off the other. She was delighted to discover one of the starboard quarters had a separate attached bathroom with an actual tub. One of the luxuries of her asteroid apartment was the genuine shower, but this was the first real tub she'd seen since she left Mars. She pushed down a feeling of homesickness and decided to move into the room. She almost reconsidered selling the ship at the end of her patrol.

She returned to the bridge and was looking at the console when the reply from Bilan came through.

"What the void, Del?" the message started. "After the other night, you take off without a word? You finally send a message after three days, and all you do is ask about some bar?"

That seemed unfair. Del had told her, along with Jie, about the patrol. Should she have called while still in realtime range? She had been pretty miserable then, though, and had really only been thinking of getting onto her bike and setting the course so she could pass out again.

"How are you doing?" Bilan continued. "Anything..." She trailed off.

Del appreciated her not saying anything more specific. It was an old aphorism that there was no such thing as secure communication on the net. The chances of anything being seen were slim, but if someone had reason to look...

"I've been worried about you, okay? I hope you're well." Then her expression changed again. "I looked into that place you mentioned. I hadn't heard of it myself, so I asked around. Don't worry, I left your name out of it. It's not far, actually, from where you're supposed to be. It's on one of the asteroids in the Hygiea family itself.

"It's weird. The net's silent on it, but there are a few Enforcers who've been there. You can get there from Hygiea, but I couldn't find out how. It seems to be by invitation only. It's primarily a gambling spot, card tables and the like. Alcohol, of course, and—get this—a smoking room. Also, an attached brothel. And lots of underground activity going on. I'm surprised you haven't heard of it; it sounds like your kind of place. I'd be careful if you do go there. Probably want to leave your uniform behind. Anyone there isn't likely to welcome the presence of Enforcers."

That would be perfect, then. She could fit in figuring out how to get there around the rest of her meetings, and continued on course to Hygiea, settling into her usual routine of running, weight training—another pleasant surprise had been the set of free weights secured in the cargo bay—and taking breaks for meals, naps, or watching vids.

When she arrived at Hygiea, port control directed her to a gaping pit already full of ships of various sizes. It was an obviously artificial hole cut with perfectly smooth, straight walls deep into the rocky terrain of the dwarf planet. She wondered if it had once been a crater or if the entire cylinder had been dug out. When she had set the *Zheng He* down on a rather flimsy-looking deck protruding from the wall, a docking tube extruded and connected to her port airlock. She managed to piece together an outfit from amongst the wardrobes of her ship's former crew and headed out to get the lay of the land before deciding what to do next.

DEL STEPPED out of the docking tube and into a busy port. The gravity was barely noticeable.

People around her were moving up and down by pulling themselves along vertical cables or ladders as much as they were walking. A number of people were carrying cargo up and down lifts set into the walls.

One man peeled himself out from the crowd and looked like he was rushing to meet her, but then stopped for a few seconds, before approaching more slowly. He glanced around as if he was waiting for someone. Or scoping out possible escape routes.

"Did you just get off the *Zheng He*?" he asked her.

Damn. The transponder would have given the name, and anyone could have been watching for it. This man - whoever he was - was obviously here to meet the ship. If the crew frequented the area, their other contacts might all know their ship was now docked. This could just be the first of many people looking into what was going on.

"That's right," she replied with a practiced, easy smile. "Name's Del." When the man looked past her, she asked, "Were you expecting someone else?"

"Nurayda?"

"She's...uh, not on the ship."

The man's eyes grew wide with sudden fear. "Is she...?"

"She's fine," Del said quickly.

His relief was palpable.

They must be close. A lover, maybe? Or a brother? If this man was close to Nurayda, Del might be able to get information from him.

"What do you mean? Why isn't she on the ship?" he asked.

"It's kind of a long story," Del responded.

When she'd downloaded the map of this place, Aluna wasn't marked anywhere on it. A search of the net didn't turn up anything, either. She wondered how Bilan had even found out it was here. If this man knew the *Zheng He* crew and they did business there, he'd likely know about it.

"Why don't you buy me a drink and I'll tell you all about it?" she offered.

"Nurayda and I are monogamous," he said.

So, a lover then. And once again, for all the reputation of Martian prudishness, a Belter was even worse.

"Fine. No mashing, then, but I could use a drink and a chat," she replied.

"Where?"

"How about Aluna?" she said, trying not to look too eager.

"Why there?" he asked.

"I haven't been there before," she replied. "Nurayda recommended it."

The man stopped and fixed his gaze on her. "Who are you, really?"

"I'm Del."

He scowled at her. "Nurayda hated that place," he said. "She'd never have recommended it. Tell me where she is. What have you done?"

"She's safe. She's not harmed, and I want information. I suggest we trade. Over drinks. At Aluna."

"Why there specifically?"

"Do you know how to get there?"

"Yes, but—"

"That's why."

"You don't know where it is? Then why do you want to go there?"

"I'm looking for someone."

"Who?"

"Don't know yet."

"Then...then how do you think you're going to find them?"

Del shrugged. "Still working on that part. You gonna take me there, or am I gonna find someone else and leave you wandering the docks wondering where your girl is?"

He didn't say anything for a long moment.

"Okay," Del said, and walked past him, with no idea where she was going.

"All right, you win," he said. "Don't do anything stupid, though, and don't call attention to us. It's an exclusive place." He lead her deeper into the docks.

"What's your name, anyway?" She asked as they walked. "How come you weren't with Nurayda on the ship?"

"I work here," he said, and then added, "Here we are." He stopped at what looked like a maintenance hatch. He opened it and ducked inside. "Coming?"

Del followed, tentatively, into the bottom of a dimly-lit narrow shaft. A ladder rose up into darkness. If this was a trap, she'd need a lot of luck to make it out of it.

The gravity here was even lower than on Ceres. Her guide moved up the ladder in great bounds, grabbing both sides and pushing himself upward several rungs at a time.

Del followed, copying his technique.

They passed by half a dozen other small hatches similar to the one they had used before they reached the top. Del guessed they must be close to the surface of Hygiea by now.

"Diogo," he said, answering her question. At the top of the ladder was another hatch. Diogo undid the double latch and swung the door open, and they stepped through into an immense airlock.

An older model from before Hanzhong Construction arrived in the Belt with their cheap standard devices. *A manually operated door into the middle of an airlock.* There was no way that could be safe. No wonder she'd never seen one like it before.

He hit a button beside one of the airlock doors. There was a red light next to it, indicating vacuum on the other side. Del suspected that her guess was right, and they were on the surface.

After about a minute, the light turned green and Diogo opened the door, manually turning the large wheel. The other side led to an elevator—a large, glass-walled room with seats around the perimeter for maybe ten people. This at least was familiar. Most tethered asteroids in the belts had elevators similar to this riding the cables between them. Even Del's had one, though she'd only been on it once, and used the airlock that led to it as a closet.

Bilan had said that Aluna was part of a tethered pair, not attached to Hygiea itself. She tried to do the calculation in her head. Hygiea had a fourteen hour rotation, which meant something tethered to its surface would have to be sixty thousand kilometers away to have even a tenth of a G. That was too far. An elevator traveling along such a tether would take days to get back and forth.

Her unspoken question was answered when the miniscule gravity disappeared altogether as the cabin they were in detached from the tether and was flung off into empty space. She looked to her guide in alarm, but he just gave her a smug smile.

Several minutes later, another tether caught their box and reeled it in toward another large asteroid.

"Neat trick. How's it know when to let go?"

"If you're allowed in, there's a code you send the elevator when you board."

"Can I have it?"

He looked hesitant for a while, then shrugged. "Sure," he said, and sent it to her.

He didn't like the place they were going, she remembered, and apparently had no reason to keep their secrets for them.

Eventually, the elevator came to a stop. Her suit read the gravity at 0.19G, just over half that of Mars. The doors slid open onto a raucous affair. Music blared throughout a huge central chamber. Tables were scattered about the lower level, surrounding a large dance floor in the center of the room. More tables sat on platforms protruding from walls throughout. Catwalks connected several levels of balconies about the immense chamber.

People were drinking or playing cards around some of the

tables, while barely-dressed men and women carried trays of drinks around in the low gravity, between the tiny pools of light at each table. There were half a dozen doors in addition to the one they came through. Some undoubtedly lead to other rooms, but she guessed at least one if not more lead to separate docking bays. This many people couldn't have come the same way she and Diogo had. There must be other ways in.

"Shining Stars," she said, borrowing Bilan's phrase. "This place is incredible." She understood why Bilan had thought she'd like it. She wanted to learn all of its secrets then bring Bilan and Jie both here. How could they keep something like this in the Belt secret? And why?

"How about up there?" she suggested, pointing to a narrow table near the top of the room. It had seats only along one side, allowing a good view of most of the rest of the room.

Del caught the attention of a well-toned man wearing tight shorts that left nothing to the imagination. "Do you have whiskey?" she asked. When he answered in the affirmative, she asked for a flask, with ice.

When Diogo didn't reply to the server's questioning look, she added, "And one for him, too."

Diogo nodded and paid for the drinks, then followed Del up the ladder to the table she'd indicated.

Several minutes later a woman dressed exactly as the man brought them the drinks.

"You have your drink," Diogo said as soon as she'd taken her first sip. "Now spill. Where's Nurayda?"

"Last I saw her, she was on an asteroid. Her two friends from the ship are there with her. They have air and enough food and water for a couple of months."

"What? What asteroid? Where?"

"Nuh-uh. Your turn. Answer my questions and I'll give you

the coordinates so you can arrange to get them off of it again. They were on a mission. Who hired them?"

"I don't know. I told you, I'm not involved in that. They haul freight for most of the corps."

"This wasn't freight. This one was special."

"I don't know what you're talking about."

"When they're doing less honest work, who gives it to them?"

"I'm sure she'd never be involved in anything illegal."

"Uh huh. We both know her better than that." When he didn't respond right away, she continued. "I'm not looking to cause trouble for her. Just the opposite, in fact. Whoever hired her is going to be upset when they learn she's failed them. If I can get to them first, I might be able to protect her, and the rest of the crew."

Diogo was silent again for a long moment.

Del took another sip of her whiskey. It was surprisingly good.

"I don't know. She never shares that side of things with me."

Del wasn't sure whether to believe him. Don't long-term lovers share everything with each other? She'd always assumed it was so. "You're going to have to give me something."

He was silent again for a long while. "I might know someone who knows someone. I can ask him to meet you here tomorrow."

"Nowhere near good enough."

"It's the best I can do, I swear. I happen to know a few people, but I don't have any position there. I swear I'll do my best to get him here."

"What's this guy's name?"

"I don't know. They just call him the Rabbit."

Del looked around. For all the secrecy surrounding this place, it didn't seem like a very violent crowd. If this was a setup, she wondered how much attention a murder would bring. Not much, she decided. They might try it. Well, she'd have a day to prepare.

"All right. If they don't show, or if they try to pull anything, I will find you. This rock isn't that big."

Diogo nodded, relieved. "So, you'll give me their coordinates?"

"Not quite yet. I'll hold on to that information as my insurance policy. You want to see your girlfriend again, you'll make sure I don't end up dead."

"Can you at least tell me why? Why would they agree to that? How did you bring their ship back without them?"

"I didn't give them much choice. Someone set them up. Hired them to kill me, then to ensure they didn't back out, told them I'd murdered one of their crew members."

"Ashur."

"That was the name."

"Del...you're Delokita, the Enforcer."

"That's right."

"You killed Ashur."

"I didn't."

"Then who did?"

"No idea. The first I ever heard of any of you people was when your friends lured me to the asteroid and tried to kill me."

"And you...what, locked them in and stole their ship?"

"That's the short version, though I didn't steal it. It was lawfully given to me as the penalty for their attempt on my life. It was the alternative to formal charges, which would have sent them, most likely, to spending the rest of their lives as indentured servants on Mercury."

"That ship is their life."

"No, their lives are their lives. You know, the thing they

wanted to take from me. Without the ship, they'll have to get real jobs like the rest of us."

Del could tell he didn't like it. Inside, he was seething. But he knew she was right.

"If they tried to kill you, how come you let them live?"

It was the same question Nurayda had asked.

"Because, unlike your girlfriend, I'm not a murderer," Del answered this time.

"Nurayda's not..." he started then trailed off. Del guessed he was right, but he himself wasn't so sure. They'd have a lot to talk about if they ever saw each other again.

"They failed," Del said, "and gave me their ship in penance. As far as I'm concerned, we're even. I'm just worried that either they're going to try again, or the guy who originally hired them will. If someone's willing to go to this much effort to have me killed, I want to know why. If it's an actual mistake, I want to get myself taken off his list."

"What if it's not a mistake?"

"Either way, I don't plan to have a threat hanging over me," she answered.

He understood. "I'll make sure he comes tomorrow."

"If he does, I'll send you the coordinates."

Her host nodded, accepting it.

"One more thing..." She felt the need to add, just to make sure, as he stood to go. "I took out all three of your friends and managed to do it without injuring them. If they'd been more competent, I'd've likely been forced to kill one or more of them. You don't know what my capabilities are, or how many people I have working for me. Think long and hard about that before you think about setting me up tomorrow."

He nodded again, and left, sliding deftly down a nearby ladder.

She raised her hand to a nearby server and ordered another

drink and was pleasantly surprised to find Diogo had left the tab open. Whether it was by generosity or by oversight she didn't really care.

She spent the next hour drinking and watching the patrons below. She probably shouldn't drink this much, but the booze was good, and free, and she'd had a hard day.

Eventually, she decided nobody was going to try to kill her tonight. She spotted a man she liked the look of amongst the dancers on the floor. She slid down the ladder to a lower level, then vaulted the balcony. She might have misjudged the gravity a bit and landed clumsily next to him, collapsing to the floor. She climbed unsteadily to her feet though and made a joke of it.

He laughed once he realized she was unhurt.

It took another hour of dancing, talking, and letting him buy her more drinks before he invited her back to his place.

They were walking, arm and arm, and laughing over some inanity when all the whiskey caught up to her and she fell to her knees in the hallway and retched onto the floor.

The man was gone by the time she stopped. At first, she thought perhaps he'd gone for water, or a towel, or something to help, but realized he'd abandoned her. She wanted to curse his name, but couldn't remember what it was.

She stood up, looked around the empty corridor, and pulled up a map on her suit's interface.

A cleaning bot was already heading her way. Either her erstwhile companion had summoned it or sensors in the hallway had determined the need. She didn't feel like being charitable, so assumed the latter.

She got back to the ship, and in the minuscule gravity of Hygiea, passed out in the bridge's central seat.

THE NEXT MORNING, Del was still in the chair in her vacsuit. The clothes over it were stained with vomit, and she had a splitting headache.

With no idea how to clean the outfit out here—normally she'd use the laundry facilities on Ceres—she shoved them in a garbage chute in the corridor outside her new quarters before washing up. She put on her uniform for her meetings that day, starting with the local office of BeltSec's parent organization, Zono Mastro.

"Delokita?" the administrator asked when she showed up at his office. "I'm Administrator Ales. I was expecting Johanka this visit." He seemed disappointed.

"She canceled," Del told him. "BeltSec dispatch asked me to take the patrol."

"Why you?"

She shrugged. "Probably just next on some list somewhere."

"But aren't you under investigation?"

That took her aback. "Not as far as I know."

He checked his display again. "Regarding an attack at a Rimedo office? On asteroid 1327-27?"

"Oh, that."

"Oh that?" he repeated. "That doesn't exactly inspire confidence."

She sighed, then fixed a stern gaze on him. She didn't answer to him. At best, they were co-workers. He could still cause trouble for her if he was sufficiently motivated, so she bit back her first thought. "I'm aware of the investigation," she said. "The person in charge of it has already spoken to me. I'm not the subject. She's looking into a man who attacked an office, at the request of his family."

"This Jeremy Bartran?" Ales said, looking at his display.

"Yes."

"Are you planning on discussing this incident with Rimedo while you're here?"

She hadn't been. She hadn't even thought about it until he brought it up, but she was meeting with them in just a few hours. "Amongst other things," she said.

"I would be very interested to hear what they have to say on the matter. Or anything else you discuss."

"No problem. I'll stop by before I leave and give you a full report." Because why not? It could certainly be to her advantage to be seen as cooperative. Ales seemed surprised. *Was Johanka not as helpful? Or was he just expecting other people not to be as forthcoming as she was?* She suspected it was the latter.

THREE HOURS LATER, after finding a decent breakfast and some seltzer water and analgesic, Del was feeling somewhat more human as she entered the Rimedo administrator's office.

"Delokita! Pleased to make your acquaintance! I'm Nadia Chen." She held out her hand. Everything about this woman said Earther. The handshake, the pale skin, and the two names, but she moved with the practiced ease of someone used to low gravity. "We were originally expecting someone else for our regular visit," she said.

"I've been hearing that a lot," Del replied. "I've been with BeltSec for a couple of years now, based out of Ceres. This is my first patrol to the Hygiean Sector."

"I'm glad you could make it then," the other woman said. "I can thank you in person for your actions at 1327-27."

"You wanted to...thank me? For what? I'm sorry, but I was too late to save anybody."

"But you did stop the madman who was attacking. No telling where he'd go next."

"Or maybe I just killed a man and wasted a missile I can't afford to replace," Del replied bitterly. She caught herself as she said it. *Never let anyone know how broke you really are.* It had been one of her primary rules since childhood. It was a mark of stress that she let slip something like that.

"BeltSec doesn't pay for your equipment?" Chen asked.

"Just the basics. They provide the bike, but modifications like the missiles I have to pay for. It's fine. I order them through BeltSec. I'll get a replacement when I get back to Ceres. I just didn't have time when I was there last."

"What kind of missiles do you use?"

Del gave her the name and model and Chen punched something into her display.

"There. The cost of the missile has been added to your account."

"Thank you," Del said. "You really didn't have to—"

"Nonsense. You used them defending our property. Rimedo Corp is grateful. If you ever expend resources on our behalf in the future, let me know directly and I'll see what I can do."

Del knew there was a reason she liked these long patrols.

"Looks like upper management decided against a third-party bonus. Sorry about that. I see you've already discovered Aluna. Are you planning on going back?"

"You were watching me?"

"Everybody watches everybody on Hygiea," she said with a smile. "I'm afraid everyone here knows your every move, and who you've been talking to."

"Oh. Um...." Del flushed, thinking of her embarrassing performance the night before.

"Relax," Chen said. "Just be careful. Not everybody here is your friend."

"Thanks," Del said, looking downward.

"Here." Chen tapped her display once more. "I gave you some starting credit in the casino. Have some fun."

"Thank you," Del said again, meaning it. She wondered, though, if a corporate executive not only knew about Aluna, but had direct access to their accounts, how they manage to keep the place so secret away from Hygiea.

"You're welcome. And if there's anything else I can do for you, please let me know. Rimedo Corporation desires a much closer relationship with BeltSec, to our mutual advantage."

"Thank you," Del said once again. She knew exactly what the other woman was doing. Chen had just purchased an asset in BeltSec. At some time, she'd ask a favor, or for some information, and Del would be obligated to provide it. There would be limits, and it went both ways, so along with the obligations came many new possibilities. This could be a big first step in expanding her meager network of contacts throughout the Belt.

She found a small plaza near the corporate offices where she was able to find a good lunch, including fresh vegetables. It was a luxury, but she had the money Chen had just given her. It was intended for replacement missiles, but she should easily be able to cover those from the sale of the ship.

She headed to the bridge to compose a new message to Bilan. She could have sent it from anywhere, of course, but thought it would look most impressive from the bridge and wanted to show off a bit.

"Hi!" she started. "Thanks so much for your help! I found the place we'd mentioned. How did you know it was here? Even with your information, I only found it by pure luck. Great place, check it out." She switched the image being sent to the recording from her suit, showing the bar from her seat on the balcony, then the woman who had brought her her third—or was it her fourth—drink of the evening. "I think you might like it here, too. They've got great whiskey. I'm going back later tonight, supposedly to meet with someone who knows the guy who wanted to kill me."

She knew she was rambling, but she was in a good mood, being somewhere familiar after the meetings of the day. She couldn't think of any way to explain what had happened in a way that nobody else seeing the message would understand, so she decided to just say it plainly. "Oh, wait, you don't know that part yet. Well, suffice to say someone tried to kill me, but they failed—obviously—and now I have a ship. See?"

She switched the image back to the ship's camera and panned around the bridge. "Nice, huh? It's a long story, and I'll tell you when I get back. Oh, so...uh...you're maybe thinking now that I went crazy and killed a bunch of innocent people and stole their ship, but I didn't, I swear. Other than the people trying to kill me nothing, uh, weird has happened." That part she still didn't want to say out loud. Bilan would understand what she meant.

"Here, I'll just attach the footage after this message, you'll see. Oh, and, um, I'm sorry about not saying anything when I left. I was a little hung over. And when I say a little, I mean a lot. Like, horribly. Oh, and speaking of the people trying to kill me, I know they were hired by someone they call the Rabbit, at Aluna. This guy," she attached an image of Diogo, "is supposedly going to introduce me to someone who knows him tonight. Don't worry, I'm being careful! But, in case the whole thing's an ambush and you never hear back from me again, you know where to start if you can scam BeltSec into paying for an investigation."

She paused again, not sure what else to say. "Still more meetings. You know how much I love talking to corporate execs. Though Rimedo gave me a bit of a bonus after all, so that was nice, and a bunch of casino credit which I'll be throwing away sometime after my meeting with Ministoj. Though I'll probably stop back here and take a bath first. That's right, my spaceship has a bathtub. You may be jealous now. I'll talk to you later. Unless everything goes wrong tonight, in which case it's been an honor to work with you and all that. Bye!" She finished and sent the message without reviewing it first.

SIX
A GAMBLE ON HYGIEA

“We were expecting someone else," Harailt, Chief Administrator of Ministoj, said when Del had entered his office.

"A lot of that going around," Del responded as cheerfully as she could muster. "It was Johanka I take it, who you were expecting?"

"Yes. Why are you here?"

Del was determined not to be cowed by his manner. "She couldn't come. They sent me instead."

"No, I mean why are you here, now, in my office?"

"Uh...we had an appointment?"

He looked at her as if she were unbelievably stupid. "What business do you have here?"

Unaware of what he wanted, Del fell behind the company line. "BeltSec wanted to check in and see if there was anything needed or any actions we could take on behalf of our corporate partners."

"Ha! And remind us you exist, I'm sure."

Del shrugged. "That's pretty much it, yeah. But if there is

anything you need—"

"I needed Johanka," he said.

"I'm sorry," Del said. "If you don't want to talk to me, I'll go. I checked in, strutted around in uniform, and that's all BeltSec requires of me. If you don't want anything more than that, no worries. I'll just enjoy the amenities of your lovely outpost here, then be on my way in the morning." She bowed and turned toward the door.

"Wait," he said. He nodded toward the door behind him. "Shut that, will you?"

She hit the button beside it and a pressure door slid down, closing them in. She turned back to him.

"Can you be discreet?" he asked.

"Absolutely," she replied without hesitation. That question always held the promise of lucrative work.

"I'm not sure this actually involves BeltSec, but I could use a favor."

Bingo. She took another step toward his desk and lowered her voice. Not that it was necessary. With the pressure door closed she'd have to scream to be heard outside this room, and even then it was iffy.

"What is it?"

"I want to track down a missing indenture."

"That's not a problem," she said. "BeltSec enforces indentures for its members all the time. It's part of the standard—"

"This isn't for Ministoj."

"Oh."

"And I'd like to leave BeltSec out of it as well."

"Got it," Del said, taking a seat. Not that she needed to sit down in the low gravity here, but changing stance subtly reinforced that she was taking on a new role. The conversation was now relaxed, informal, off the record. Except they both knew they were both recording it.

"BeltSec doesn't care what I do in my off time, and I don't bother to tell them."

The administrator visibly relaxed. He'd probably worked off-book with Johanka before and wasn't sure if another Enforcer would be willing to do so.

"Who's the indenture? And who owns the contract?" she asked.

"I hold it personally," he said. "Her name is Amelia. She had two years left when she decided to skip out."

That raised several questions, starting with: how much did Ministoj pay their administrators if he could afford to purchase an indenture contract directly. Or, more likely, how much he was skimming off the top. Unless someone higher up at Ministoj asked her to look into it, though, that wasn't any of her business.

"Any idea where she was heading?"

"Venus, eventually, I imagine. I know she has family there. But I have no idea how she'd get there. I believe she may have stowed away on a cargo ship heading to Ceres."

"How long ago?"

"Three days."

"I'll see what I can do. There's only so many ways out of the Belt. Easiest is to catch a Hohmann from Ceres, if she's not in a hurry."

“She may have enough cash to pay for passage. I believe she was embezzling before she left.”

“You believe? You’re not sure?”

“She’s a skilled accountant. That’s why I had her doing the books in the first place. I thought she had learned her lesson the first time, but apparently I was wrong. I know,” he said, waving away Del’s next comment. “In hindsight, it was stupid.”

“To me, it’s just information. The more I have the better I can do my job.”

"Thank you. I hope you understand she has to be apprehended before she leaves the Belt."

Del understood. Like Mars, indentured servitude was illegal on Venus. They were likely to give her sanctuary once she got there, especially if she had family there already.

"More eyes might be better," she said. "Mind if I contact a couple of others about this? Your name won't come up of course."

"As you see fit." He nodded and she knew she was dismissed.

DEL HEADED BACK to the *Zheng He* to prepare for the evening. She was disappointed to discover that the bathtub wouldn't work in Hygiea's low gravity. The computer informed her it wouldn't fill it in anything less than one-sixth G, the acceleration produced by a single engine firing at half power.

She cleaned up the old fashioned way, running her suit's hygiene routines, then put together a new outfit to replace her damaged one from the previous day, and headed back out.

The code Diogo had given her the night before still worked. She was the only one in the elevator as it made its throw-and-catch maneuver to dock with the asteroid housing Aluna. Aluna itself was just as crowded as on her previous visit. She headed up to a balcony that contained a few tables that people were sitting around playing various card games.

She found an empty seat at one and when the dealer saw she already had credit, he happily passed her a large stack of physical chips of various colors. Since the credit had gone directly to the casino, Del never saw it, and had no idea of the value of the chips she was gambling with.

The table was playing some variant of poker, but not one

that she was familiar with. She had to have the dealer explain the rules to her, which involved a combination of face-up and face-down "hole" cards, as well as special rules for the jokers. The explanation of course marked her as a novice to everyone else at the table. She'd have to be careful.

After the first hand, which she lost after she continued when her instincts had told her to fold, a woman approached carrying a tray of drinks and wearing only a loincloth and body paint. All the servers were wearing similar outfits. She guessed they changed the uniform throughout the day.

The woman passed out drinks to nearby patrons, then took orders from the rest. Del decided to stick with beer tonight, and only a few of them. After the transactions, the server nimbly vaulted the railing to the balcony several meters below.

Del recorded the whole transaction then told her suit to forward it to Bilan. She included Jie as well with "Having fun!" in text floating over the images. It was then she discovered her suit wasn't connected to the net. She tried it again. Nothing.

"Is there a problem?" the dealer asked.

"No...it's just...I was messaging a friend and my suit seems to have forgotten the net."

There was a snigger from one side of her and an audible sigh from the other.

"There is no net connection from inside Aluna," the dealer told her.

The only other place she'd ever heard of that being done was Kenny's asteroid. She looked around again. She wondered how many of her fellow patrons were quietly arranging clandestine deals. Most of them, she decided. Of course they wouldn't want anything broadcast. This place could be the platinum asteroid if she could figure out how to get in.

There was an "Ahem" from her right and Del turned her

attention back to the cards. The man to her right had nothing showing, but had just raised.

The man to her left had two kings showing, which already beat her pair of tens, one of which was still hidden. She could stick with it and hope for another ten in the next two rounds, or just give up now and cut her losses for this hand.

She flipped over her face-up cards and pushed them all across the table to the dealer. "I'm out," she said in case he didn't understand the obvious gesture and stood to stretch, while they finished the hand without her. She looked around the bar again. She didn't see either of her friends from last night, or anyone looking like they were looking for her.

After a few more hands, only one of which she won, she was at about half her original stake. Both the men at the table had left, and two others had replaced them. The fourth slot had been taken by a woman who smiled broadly at every card she was dealt. The effect was unnerving, which Del guessed was the intent. She had two jacks showing and Del had two sevens.

She looked down at her cards, then found herself awash in a strong memory of the previous night, talking to Diogo. The flash of memory lasted only an instant before it was replaced by another image. She was sitting at a table high up overlooking the dance floor when a door opened and she could see herself step out of it. It passed so quickly but was so strange, she looked down to find the door.

Trying to figure out the angle, she looked up and spotted a table that looked to be the right size and location. There was a short man sitting at it drinking alone and she could swear he looked away as soon as she glanced in his direction.

"Do you wish to make a trade?" the dealer asked, and she turned her attention back to the game. It was the last round of cards and he had just dealt her the red Joker. It would let her take a card from any other player, which would have been perfect if there'd been another seven anywhere on the table.

HER HOLE CARD. TAKE IT!

The imperative was so strong, Del almost followed it without thinking. She had picked up the joker and was reaching toward her opponent's cards with it when she realized what was happening. *No, not now,* she thought. She tried to activate Kenny's protocol only to be greeted with an error. Offline. *Dammit, NO!*

"Are you taking my jack or not?" the woman next to her asked.

The jack made the most sense. Disrupt the pair, and her sevens would be the winning hand. Unless there was another jack amongst the two face down cards.

THE TOP ONE! TAKE THE TOP HOLE CARD!

She tapped the top card, then dropped the joker on the table next to it.

"The hole card?" the woman asked.

Wasn't that what her mind had been screaming at her? Del nodded. She didn't trust her throat enough to form words. Black spots were forming at the edges of her vision.

The woman pulled it out and handed it to Del. It was another seven. She was as shocked as anyone and didn't bother to hide it.

Seeing she was beaten, the other woman folded, then got up from the table, scooping her remaining chips into a cloth bag.

The two men on her left remained.

"She shoulda done a better job of keeping her cards out of sight," one of them said.

"Is that what happened?" the dealer asked. "You caught a glimpse of her card?"

Del shook her head, then realized that it would have been

the most logical explanation.

From long practice, she started speaking quickly, deciding what to say as she said it. "Truthfully, I thought she had a third jack, and I had a fifty-fifty chance of snagging it. I'd forgotten that the card would be face-up when it was swapped."

The others seemed satisfied with that explanation.

Del thought of leaving. She stood up. If she was having another episode, this was the last place she wanted to be.

SIT DOWN. RELAX.

The server brought her another beer. She took it and sat back down. The episode seemed to have passed. When the dealer asked if she was in, she pushed a chip into the center.

So far, there'd been no sign of this "Rabbit" or of Diogo. She could just count her losses and flee. The problem was, she did need to solve the issue. If they'd tried once, they might again, and might not confine themselves to the Hygiea sector. She didn't want to spend the rest of her life looking over her shoulder.

She continued the game. A few more beers and a few more hands, and she was just below her original stake. She was again thinking about quitting and going to claim a high table where she could sit alone and scan the crowd for Diogo or his unknown friend. The table the short man had been sitting at was empty now.

They were again on the last round and Del had a pair of queens showing, and a third face down. All four of her remaining opponent's cards were diamonds. The woman had been pushing the betting with every round, and she and Del were the only ones left. There was a good chance at least one of her face-down cards was a diamond. If it was, she would beat Del's three queens. Half of Del's money was in the pot. She looked her opponent in the eyes and saw nothing there to give her away.

Del relaxed, took a deep breath and suddenly she knew—knew beyond any doubt—that the woman was bluffing. She had two clubs in her face-down cards. Del knew this as clearly and as certainly as if she'd seen them. She pushed most of her remaining chips into the pot, calling the raise.

As she pulled her hands back from the chips, she found herself lost in another memory. For just a second, she was back in school, on Mars. She was seven Martian years old, and had stolen some money. Her teacher had called in her foster parents, and they were all gathered together in the school office. Del stared out the large window over the broken, red rock of the Ister Chaos. She didn't know how much proof they had and had tried a bluff. She failed. They already knew about the money and had recovered it from her backpack. They had given her a chance to do the right thing, and confess, and were all expressing their disappointment in her that she did not.

The memory faded as quickly as it had come on, and she was back in Aluna, at the table.

"Stars!" the other woman said. "I was certain you'd fold after that last raise. You have the third queen then?"

Del flipped over her two cards to show that she did.

Then her breath caught in her throat when the other woman turned over her cards to reveal the six and eight of clubs.

She just stared. She'd known what they were. She didn't understand. Did she catch a glimpse, too fast for her conscious mind to see, then her subconscious filled it in? This was too weird. She could feel her mind slipping away again. There was too much confusion, she had to get out.

YES! GET OUT!

The thought reverberated in her mind. She scooped up her chips, leaving a few behind as a tip for the dealer, and hastily stood up. "Thank you," she said, barely gasping out the words, to the woman she'd been playing against and stepped away from the table. She headed back toward the hallway to the docks.

NO! THE AIRLOCK!

Again, that overwhelming urge. And somehow, again, she knew there was an external airlock behind a curtain on one side of the room. She pulled back the curtain and hit the button to open the inner door.

LEAVE YOUR HELMET! STEP THROUGH!

She stopped. The helmet was part of her suit. It couldn't come off. She turned back.

Behind her, the short man from the high table had been following. He'd been watching her this whole time, she was certain of it. She looked right at him. He didn't react but she knew, suddenly, he was afraid. Terrified.

RUN! FLEE! GET OUT NOW BEFORE IT'S TOO LATE!

A cold sweat covered her and the room seemed to spin. She wasn't sure what direction the gravity was going. She hit the control for Kenny's special protocol as confusion overwhelmed her and it failed, again. It still couldn't find the net.

She was back on Mars, sitting on a stone floor crying alone, waiting for her family to come back from the hospital with news of her little brother.

She was running in a championship race in the Big Dome in Bradbury Point. She vaulted a boulder and her ankle gave out underneath her when she landed and she fell.

She was relaxing with a friend from school in a warm shallow pool in front of a high window with Valles Marineris stretching to the horizon below them.

She was on a train speeding over the dull red sands of Argentea Planum, on her way to a concert she'd been forbidden from going to.

She was on her bike, firing a missile at a fleeing suspect.

She shook her head vigorously. She was on Aluna, standing in front of an open airlock, and there was a short man with light brown skin not ten meters away staring at her with a mixture of horror and disgust.

Whoever this man was, whatever was going on, he was the cause. Del took a single step toward him and again was hit with an overwhelming thought, awash in fear and panic.

THE AIRLOCK IS SAFE. GET TO THE AIRLOCK!

She turned and fled into the airlock and slammed the button to shut the inner door. As soon as it was closed, she hit the emergency override to release the outer doors without waiting for it to depressurize. The rush of air blew her out and away from the small asteroid. Sensing the sudden pressure drop, her helmet automatically deployed from its collar, and she found herself drifting into space. She felt a profound sense of relief, and it seemed to come from outside herself.

As the asteroid swung away from her on its kilometers-long tether, she saw a number of ships hanging about it, each connected by a docking tunnel, snaking out like Medusa's hair.

DEL LET HERSELF RELAX. Far away, she saw the lights of Hygiea. If she accelerated constantly, it would take almost all of her suit's fuel to reach it and she had no way of refueling until she got back to Ceres. She'd have to be careful. She shot toward it, at maximum thrust for about fifteen seconds before cutting power and drifting. As long as she did the same on the other end, but in reverse, she'd be going slow enough to land safely. It would just take her a couple of hours to get there.

The man who had been watching her had to be the Rabbit. He had tried to kill her. She was sure of it. She had no idea what he'd done, but it wasn't a coincidence. He had somehow triggered an episode, a major one, and he had done it intentionally.

She drifted alone through space. The image of watching herself entering Aluna was vivid and real. She'd learned while still on Mars that not everybody experienced memories that way. While they spoke of being lost in thought, or of reliving a memory, they didn't really mean it. They weren't completely shut off from the rest of the world, but for her it had always been so. She assumed it was somehow tied up in her voices. But that memory of watching herself from his seat wasn't her own. It wasn't her imagination, either. It was his memory. Somehow, the Rabbit's memory got into her mind.

This could also explain how she knew about the assassins she'd taken her ship from, and the cards. *Why now, though? Why did she choose now to suddenly start reliving other people's memories?* Or did she? Could the flashes of imagination she'd always had been other people's memories? She wasn't imagining what they said or did, but remembering, from their mind? It was impossible, and yet the only thing that made sense.

Away from Aluna and whatever they'd been using to block the signal, Del's suit found one of the relay nodes scattered throughout the solar system and notified her that it had connected to the net. The message she'd sent earlier went out, and she got a notification of an incoming message from Bilan. She played the message on her faceplate as she drifted.

"Depths of the clouds, Del!" Bilan said. She looked like she was in bed in an apartment on Ceres. "You can't just say things like that! 'I might die, so nice knowing you?' What is going on? Do Jie and I need to mount a rescue mission or not? And why do you have a spaceship? What kind of trouble are you in?" She heaved a deep sigh. "We really have to work on your communication skills here. I'm not surprised Rimedo went well. We'll talk about that when you get back. Watch out for Ministoj, though. I want to talk to you as soon as you return. We have a lot to catch up on."

She gave another short thrust with her suit, then turned back from where she came. She still couldn't see the rock that held Aluna, which was good. Eventually it would swing back around to where it had been when she left. She wanted to be as far away as possible by then.

She didn't want to think about what had happened. She played Bilan's message back again, then realized how her last message would seem if it followed the one Bilan just sent. With a deep breath she prepared to send one back. She switched the camera to the view in front of her, the tiny sliver that was Hygiea visible in the distance.

"Hi!" she started her message. "Sorry - I just left Aluna. They have some kind of weird net blocker there, so I didn't get your message until just now. As you can see, I'm taking the long way back, but please don't worry. I'm fine. More or less. Um... remember how earlier I said nothing weird had happened? Well...something weird happened."

She switched the view back to show her face inside the suit.

"It's...um..." She fought back panic as she spoke. "It's weirder than I expected and I'm not sure what to think about it or what to do and I really want to talk to you, too."

She took a couple of deep breaths to calm herself.

"But right now, I'm okay," Del continued her message. "I got a good look at who I think is trying to kill me. If my guess is right—and no reason to assume it is, but it is—he's known as the Rabbit. This guy." She scanned through her suit footage, found an image of him glaring at her and froze it, attaching the frozen image to the video stream for several seconds.

"Still have no idea why he wants me dead. Well, I have an idea, but it doesn't make any sense." She took another deep breath and said, all in a rush, "And I hope I don't scare you away or piss you off too much because I don't think I can unravel this on my own."

She wanted to wipe her eyes, she felt tears threatening to come. She'd only made two real friends out here in the Belt and she was on the verge of losing one of them. If Bilan left her, Jie would almost certainly follow, and then she'd be left with no one while slowly going crazy.

"But I am okay, now, really. I'll be back in a week and would really like to talk to you then." She sent the message then spent the next hour floating gently through space.

When she got to Hygiea, she turned feet-first toward it and activated the suit thrusters and landed softly on the top of a large boulder. She could see the shaft for the elevator she'd taken to Aluna not too far away. Normally, she'd hop from boulder to boulder, using suit thrusters as needed, but wanted to conserve the fuel, so jumped down instead. She slid on the loose rocks as she went, but in the low gravity it hardly mattered.

Before she got to the doors, she sent a quick message to Diogo. "Your friend failed in his attack. Just thought you should know. I warned you what would happen if you set me up." She paused then for a few seconds, just to let him worry. "But your friends don't deserve to die for your stupidity, so I'm sending you their coordinates. Fortunately for you, I have urgent business elsewhere." That sounded better than saying she didn't want to bother actually trying to find him again. "Pray that our paths never cross again."

BACK ON THE bridge of her extorted ship she prepared to leave. She wanted to get away from this whole area as quickly as she could. Realizing she was still carrying the bag of chips from Aluna, she stuck them in a cupboard and latched the door. As she started up the ship, she noticed several messages to the ship waiting on a console. Services offered by the dock.

She scanned through the list of recommendations. Air was at seventy percent, which seemed a little low, but not in the critical range. The water tank was about half full. The capacity was astounding, though, and a half was still two orders of magnitude more than her bike carried when full. The fuel, though, which unlike air and water could not be recycled, was slightly below one percent—a critically low amount. It would still be enough to use the ship to finish her patrol and get her back to Ceres, but not much further than that.

She checked the price of a refill and was stunned by how much it cost. Far more than she could possibly afford, even with her recent windfalls. She might double the value of the ship if she filled the tanks. Any thought she had of keeping it vanished. No wonder the former crew was desperate enough to commit murder to pay their bills.

Speaking of...

Once away from Hygiea, she settled into a seat on the bridge and composed a new message to Bilan.

"Hi! Well, that was fun. And yes, I did mean that sarcastically. I'm only a little scared now. Things have mostly settled down. I'm away from Hygiea and not planning on going back any time soon. I didn't mean to make you worry. I hope you still want to talk to me when I get back cuz there's lots I want to talk to you about. I wish I got your message about Ministoj before I went, so I would have paid more attention. But whatever you're thinking about them is probably right.

"Also, I can't wait to hear your thoughts on Rimedo. I wish I could just come back there now. It's only one more week. I still have to make stops at a couple more corps who don't have offices on Hygiea for whatever reason. Don't worry, I'm not planning on doing anything dangerous, and if I do get any more distress signals, I'll be very, very careful. For now, since I have real gravity at last, I'm going to finally try out my new bathtub."

DEL WAS in said tub when the console on the wall chimed to let her know she had a message. She told the wall console to play the message. To her surprise, it was not from Bilan, but from Jie.

"Hello, Delokita," he said seriously.

She slid further down into the water, so she was visible only from the shoulders up. Not that he could see her at all, of course, from the recorded message. She was much too far away for realtime communication.

"Bilan suggested I send you a quick note," Jie continued. "She's on patrol and then a stakeout until morning but seemed to think you couldn't go that long without knowing that she's not mad at you and is looking forward to seeing you in person. She's worried about you and wouldn't say why so now I'm worried. Hopefully, one of you fills me in before I go completely out of my mind."

Del laughed out loud.

"Bilan tells me you have a new ship. Then she felt the need to tell me that you obtained it legally and didn't kill anyone. Then she told me you sent her proof of that last, which I'm not sure makes me feel better or worse about the whole thing. Personally, I'm dying to hear the story of how you got a ship. If you're going to turn pirate now, I'm going to be very sad you didn't invite me along."

Del laughed again, this time at the idea of Jie as a pirate.

She resisted the urge to splash water at the screen. "Return message," she told it.

"Please select video," the console replied.

"What?"

"Please select video," the console repeated in exactly the same cadence and tone.

Del rolled her eyes. "What do you mean by that?"

"This access point does not display its own video by default," it said. "You can choose to display it or any of the other feeds from set locations within or without the vessel."

That was interesting.

"Show me."

A series of views from both inside and outside the ship appeared on the screen and Del found she could use standard gestures to switch between them. She lined them all up along the bottom of the screen so she could choose quickly, and started with an outside view of space, the Milky Way prominent across the center.

"Hey, Jie," she said, keeping her tone light and cheery with an effort. "Good to hear from you! Don't worry about me. I'm good. Well, mostly. Well, maybe not entirely. Void." This wasn't what she meant to say. She thought for a second about starting over but decided to continue. "It's a long story. Maybe you can get Bilan to tell you." She realized why she hadn't. "Oh, except I swore her to secrecy. But you should know, too." *Should he?*

She forced more cheer into her voice to hide her terror over what she was about to do. "Go ahead and show her this and tell her it's okay. I was a little freaked out, but I've thought it over now..." Did she mean that? Did she dare tell him about the voices? What if he decided she was a danger and reported her?

Slag it. Like she told Bilan, she could either trust someone or go through life never trusting anyone. That would be worse than risking betrayal.

She shifted the video to herself, slunk down in the bathtub, and waved to the screen. "Hi, Bilan! If you could, go ahead and tell Jie everything we talked about, then we can all three get together when I get back and have a horrendously awkward conversation. Oh, yeah, I'll explain about the ship then, too. In the meantime, check it out." She shifted the picture around to show the crew quarters, cargo space, exterior, bridge, and finally back to her.

"So, yes, I'll see you both in a week. In the meantime, I'll be flying in the lap of luxury. And thank you for your message, Jie. It did help. Really. Everything's good. I'm gonna go work out now."

Just to tease Bilan, she pushed herself up out of the water. Just before her chest cleared the bubbles, though, she cut the video feed back to an exterior view, then ended the message.

She did get up then and headed down to the cargo bay to work out. She liked the weights. There was something more satisfying about them than the resistance bands she was used to. She thought briefly of keeping them, once she'd sold the ship, but didn't really have enough room for them in her asteroid apartment. Perhaps they'd make a nice gift for Jie, as thanks for introducing her to the concept in the first place.

After several sets, she had to power up her bike to use its treadmill. She'd never been on it without her suit on before, it was strangely disorienting.

Her bike had everything she needed to travel with - the ship was just extra luxuries and didn't even have anything like the bike's treadmill or interfaces. She found she much preferred seeing Mars unrolling beneath her when she ran to just being in the cargo bay. She wouldn't miss the ship when it was gone, she decided.

An hour after sending her message, she received a reply

from Jie: "Bathtub? Put in a swimming pool, then I'll be jealous."

She looked around the cargo bay. They could easily flood it to a depth of a meter or two. The only difficult part would be containing that much water when not under acceleration. In order to keep it drifting around in zero G, they'd have to rig up an entire door that could close over it. If they did it right, it could be a second airlock that opened into the cargo bay. Past a bunch of water. She had no idea how that would work.

She shook her head. The whole thing was moot anyway. She wouldn't be keeping the ship.

SUITED UP AGAIN and in the center seat on the bridge, she watched the large asteroid housing the main offices of Alba Corp approach. It was part of a tethered pair and there was no way to land the ship itself on it. She parked it a couple of hundred kilometers outside its path, where it would pass by every seven minutes. Letting the computer control the timing, she took her bike over, matching the asteroid's velocity.

She still couldn't shake the feeling there was something wrong. She thought, again, over the events at Aluna. She knew that the woman at the poker table had two clubs. She knew where the airlock was. And she knew that that man, who was almost certainly the Rabbit, was involved.

Her "voices" weren't angels, they weren't demons, and now they weren't even her own mind. They were coming from the people around her.

At the moment, there was nobody around her, so she had no way to test that theory. What about 1327-27? For the theory to hold, there had to have been someone else there. Someone she couldn't see. Which meant...what? She had no idea.

She wanted more than anything to talk all this over with Bilan. Bilan knew about the voices and could help her figure out the rest. She still wasn't sure if she dared trust Jie with this yet, and was having second thoughts about telling Bilan to fill him in about everything else.

Thanks to the spin of the tether, the Alba Corp office was at a nice comfortable one-third G, just below the gravity of Mars.

"Thank you for seeing me," she told the administrator, who had introduced himself as Elias, when he had waved her to a seat.

"Not at all. I'm happy that BeltSec is finally taking us seriously."

"What do you mean? Haven't other Enforcers been here?"

"Not since the last routine patrol."

"I am the routine patrol."

"They didn't send you because of my requests?"

"If they did, they didn't tell me anything about them. They just gave me a list of places to stop at, and you were on it."

"When I learned it was you they sent instead of our usual Enforcer, I just assumed."

"Wait...why me, specifically?"

"Because of your involvement in Rimedo 27-27."

"What does that have to do with Alba Corp?"

"We've had similar attacks here," the administrator said.

"Attacks? Plural? By the same guy?"

"I thought you killed the one at 27-27?"

Del shut her eyes for a second and took a deep breath. *Was this man deliberately trying to drive her mad?*

She reopened her eyes. He was still there, watching her.

"Let's start over. What attacks? BeltSec didn't tell me anything about Alba Corp being attacked."

Elias looked surprised. "So, you're not going to be looking into them?"

"I didn't say that. Just that this is the first I've heard of them."

"I've sent multiple reports to BeltSec."

"Those don't always filter all the way down to me." She wondered if they had been mentioned. She hadn't made it to a daily briefing in person for months and rarely watched the recordings all the way through. Maybe she should have been paying more attention to them. "Tell me everything. Start at the beginning."

"We've had three attacks similar to the ones at Rimedo."

"Rimedo had more than one?"

He looked intently at her.

She tried to calm her mind and listen, beyond the words he was saying, to try to hear what he was thinking.

All she accomplished, however, was to miss what he had been saying. Something about other attacks. She tried to seem thoughtful to cover for her inattention.

"Wait...the attacks on Alba came after the Rimedo one that I was at?"

"One of them did, yes."

"So, it couldn't have been the same guy."

"No. In one of them, we know who it was. The whole thing was transmitted. The other two we are pretty sure both perpetrators are deceased, killed during the incidents."

"Three different people, all go crazy and attack their own people. That seems...weird."

People did sometimes go violently insane in the Belt. With life as close to hard vacuum as it was, it could be especially dangerous when they did. This many all at once, though, was too much to be coincidence.

She still couldn't read the man's thoughts, and felt ridiculous trying. Maybe it could go the other way. *Could she do what the Rabbit had done to her on Aluna?* There was a picture, a still image in a wooden frame, sitting on his desk. She stared at him then and thought, as hard as she could:

GIVE ME THE PICTURE!

She didn't know what to expect, so was shocked when he suddenly sprang to his feet, snatched up the picture, and hurled it at her.

"Take it then!" he shouted.

Del barely ducked in time.

The administrator looked even more shocked than she was. "God! I am so sorry!" he said. "I don't know what came over me."

Del stood up and retrieved the picture from the floor.

"It's all right," she said as she did so. "Is that your family?" She noticed the corner of the frame was splintered. Real wood. He must have brought it with him from Earth. She felt bad about the damage.

He just nodded.

She handed him the picture. "Are they out here?"

"My wife and oldest son are. My youngest is back on Earth studying."

"Something worth protecting," she said. A line she'd heard from old vids. Or maybe it was from Jie. "I don't blame you for being frustrated." She handed the framed picture back to him. "I promise I'll do what I can to get to the bottom of this. I believe you when you say they're connected somehow. Maybe some kind of underground stochastic terrorism we're not aware of. I'm sorry if you didn't get any response on your reports before. You will now."

"Thank you. If there's anything I can do for you..."

"Can you give me access to the sensor logs of the stations where the attacks were?"

"Of course. Here." He activated a screen set into his desk,

and Del's suit interface gave notice of new resources available.

BACK ON HER SHIP, she sat in the center seat of the bridge, held down by the gravity from the ship's acceleration away from Alba Corp.

The administrator had thrown the picture at her when she'd thought at him. It had seemed to him like it was his own idea. What else could it be? Who would ever think their ideas originate from anywhere besides in their own heads? But there could be no doubt about it. She implanted the compulsion in his mind herself, and the effects were dramatic. All it did was raise more questions. *How was she able to do this now, and why hadn't she before? Or had she always been able, and just never tried?*

Would this always work? How far could she push it? Could she make someone kill? That must have been what had happened at 1327-27 and the others. At Aluna, the Rabbit had tried to make her walk outside without her helmet, and had seemed surprised when it didn't work. *How many people had he killed that way?*

FOUR DAYS LATER, she stopped by the asteroid where she'd left her ship's previous crew. She had almost been hoping they'd still be there, so she could test this power of hers, but the asteroid was empty. Both airlock doors were open, and there was no sign of the helmets she'd left outside. She assumed Diogo had arranged something. She found she didn't really care one way or the other. She was tired of this sector and everybody in it.

SEVEN
EXPOSURES AND REVELATIONS

It was another four days before Del returned to the Ceres sector. She was happy to see the familiar lights of her home in the distance and could barely make out the illuminated cable connecting it to its counterpart. When she got close enough, she stopped the ship and let it sit, keeping station a couple of hundred kilometers away from the tethered pair of asteroids. She suited up and headed to the cargo bay and climbed into her bike's pilot seat.

Two BeltSec vehicles were already clamped outside her airlock: a bike similar to her own and a larger two-seated scoot with an enclosed canopy.

She parked her own bike, using the docking clamps to attach it to the smaller of the two. With the bike in place, she climbed up over the top of the asteroid and over to her back window. Hopefully, whoever was there would be watching the door, and wouldn't see her. She was surprised to see Bilan and Jie sitting on her couch, both looking toward the airlock. She signaled Bilan for realtime communication.

"Del, where are you? Is everything okay?"

"You tell me. I'm outside," Del replied and switched her feed to show the view in front of her.

Bilan, recognizing herself in the image, gave a start, then turned to the window, pointing to direct Jie's attention there as well.

Del waved to both of them.

"What are you doing out there?" Bilan asked.

"I was wondering who broke into my apartment while I was out," she answered. "But now, I'm wondering how, and why?"

"Come inside and we'll talk about it."

"Why don't you tell me first?" She wasn't sure anymore if she could trust them both, after everything that had happened and been said in their messages back and forth over the last two weeks.

Bilan gave her a strange look through the window. "'How' is that you gave me access to your suit, so when your last message said you'd be back tonight, we came to see you. When you weren't here, I used your suit to unlock the inner airlock so we could wait for you inside instead of hanging around on your front porch. And why is because I wanted to talk to you. You know, like you said you wanted to?"

"Good enough. See you in a second." Bilan's explanation made sense, and Del was trying hard not to be paranoid.

She climbed back up, walked across the top of the asteroid again, and climbed the handholds back down to the front door, using the suit's thrusters for balance. At this point, she wasn't afraid of using up the remaining fuel. She could recharge it inside.

Once the airlock had finished cycling, she stepped through the inner door and lowered her helmet back into the collar. Her couch occupied, she took a seat on the edge of her bed. "I think the gravity's increased since last time I was here," she said.

"How much longer 'til it's at a full one G?" Jie asked.

"Not sure. I thought it was a few more months. I believe they're planning on dialing it up to one-point-one."

"So..."

She didn't say anything.

"Um..." Bilan started.

Del was trying to think of what to say, too, but couldn't come up with anything.

"So, you hear voices now," Jie said, "and you have a ship."

Direct and blunt. Good.

"And those two facts are not as unrelated as they may seem," she said.

Jie and Bilan both looked surprised.

"Before we go into that, though, I want to know why you're here."

"Because we wanted to talk to you," Bilan said. "Isn't that what you wanted?"

"I had been hoping to do so at Rokoj, after I'd had a chance to shower and change and where I could have a beer or several."

"I thought you'd switched to whiskey now," Jie said with a smile.

"I've sworn off whiskey for a while."

"That's too bad."

"Why is that too bad?"

"It means you won't want this," Jie replied and pulled a beautifully crafted bottle out of the bag at his feet. "Perhaps you can store it until..."

"Oh, give me that." Del got up and took the bottle from him. She pulled three of her four flasks out of the cupboard and added ice before pouring the whiskey into them. She noticed the writing on the bottle as she did so. "Is this from Earth?"

"That's what the guy who sold it to me claimed."

Del took a sip. "Damn, that's good. Okay, you're forgiven for breaking into my home and keeping me from Rokoj." She handed them the other two flasks.

"Cheers," Bilan said, raising her canister. It was a tradition she'd picked up from somewhere.

Del had no idea what it was supposed to mean, but raised her own flask in the appropriate response.

"Everything good, then?" Bilan asked, after taking a sip of her own. "I really want to hear how your voices have anything to do with your ship."

"I'll tell you, but you have to honor the pact."

Her eyes widened. "I will."

"The pact?" Jie asked. "Is that something I need to know about?"

Bilan looked uncomfortably to Del, so Del answered. "I'll be honest, and she has to be as well. My sense of what's real might be...off sometimes. When it is, I have to rely on hers."

Jie nodded. He looked scared. She didn't blame him.

"Bilan filled you in, right?"

"She told me you sometimes hear voices, and they tell you to do things."

"They're not really voices. And...it's really more information than compulsion. Although sometimes there's compulsion attached. I'm sorry. I'm not good at explaining this. It...it never occurred to me I might have to. Normally, if someone finds out they just disappear. I wasn't prepared for anyone to know but still be there."

"Kenny knew," Bilan said.

"He's a special case. He doesn't care what's wrong with me as long as I make him money." She hadn't really meant *tell him everything* to include Kenny, but she supposed it was too late to clarify that now.

"These compulsions. Sometimes they're dangerous, right?

Like when they told you to launch a missile at the Rimedo offices?" Jie asked.

"Yes." His tone was accusatory, and she didn't like it. "And I didn't."

"Then where did the second missile go? I checked the records. You purchased two. You fired one at the fleeing scoot. But both ports on your bike are empty, so where did the other one go?"

"Jie..." Bilan started, with a warning in her tone. They must have talked about this while she was out.

"No accusations," he said. "I just want to understand."

Del had used the same line on suspects she was interrogating. She stayed quiet, gathering her thoughts. Bilan, she had decided she could trust. She was more friend than cop. Jie, though...she wasn't sure how far she could trust him not to play the Enforcer.

She looked up at Bilan, who gave her what she hoped was a reassuring smile. "I dumped it."

"Dumped it? Why?"

"I hadn't had an episode in a while. I was freaked out and didn't want to do anything stupid, so I deactivated it and disconnected it from my bike."

"But if your episode had passed by then, why dump it after the fact?"

"I was afraid it might come back stronger, and that next time I wouldn't be able to resist."

"Is that a possibility, then?" Jie asked.

"I don't think so. Not anymore."

Bilan perked up. "What's changed?"

Jie raised a finger. "Before we get into that, I'd like to ask one more question."

Bilan nodded.

Del took another sip of her whiskey and squirmed at the edge of the bed where she was perched. She didn't like this. It seemed too much like an inquisition, and the other two seemed to have worked out some kind of rules between them before she got here.

"Go ahead," was all she said out loud.

"When you fired the missile at Jeremy Bartran..."

"Yes?" She was getting annoyed.

"Was there a...compulsion...to do so?"

"You mean, did I kill him because the voices told me to?" Her anger must have been obvious despite her attempt to keep it hidden, as Jie visibly recoiled.

"I don't think that's what he—" Bilan started. She set her flask on the floor.

"It's okay." Del looked at her. "And it's not a bad question." She looked back to Jie and continued, "I've asked myself the same thing a dozen times since then."

She hated the look of concern and fear in both their eyes now.

"It's not the right question, though. It's not like that. Not really. When I say 'compulsion,' I mean..." She fumbled for the right words. "It's like I know what I should do. But you of all people know that I don't always do what I should."

That elicited a wry grin from Jie.

"But the real question you're asking," she continued, "is if I'm going to hear a voice that tells me to hurt you, and then listen to it."

"Or yourself. Or some innocent." *At least he was being honest with his concerns.*

"I don't think so," she replied.

Bilan looked relieved.

Jie did not. "But you're not sure."

"I didn't do it the other times—"

"Other times?" Bilan startled.

"Yeah. That's one of the things I wanted to talk to you about," she said. "So, how I got my ship..."

"Wait, no, go back to the other incidents," Jie said.

"They're related," Del said. "All of it is. And I have news and a question for you."

"Related how?"

"I'll get to that. It started when I got a distress signal on the way to Hygiea."

"I saw the video," Jie said. "Bilan showed me. You were very lucky."

"I wasn't," Del said. "The part I didn't tell you, and the part that freaked the hell out of me at the time, is that I knew the assassins were there."

"When you launched yourself into the room and shot them both," Bilan said.

"How?" Jie asked at the same time.

"I could 'hear' them planning their ambush."

"How?" he repeated.

"I think...when I hear voices..." She didn't want to say it. She knew how it would sound. "They're not always, if they are ever, coming from my own head."

"You think you were hearing their thoughts?" Jie asked.

Del just nodded, and looked back and forth between them.

"Whoa, whoa, whoa, hold on," Bilan said. "You wanted me to tell you when what you believed wasn't real. That's not real."

Del walked back over to where she had left the bottle, picked it up, and turned back to them. "Are you sure?"

"Yes. You're talking about telepathy. There's no such thing."

"I think there might be. There's more." She noticed Jie hadn't said anything. He just sat there, upright on the edge of the couch, watching her intently.

Del told them of Aluna, and the poker game. "I knew exactly what card to take, and that the other woman had clubs."

"You could have caught a glimpse. Too fast maybe for your conscious mind to process, so your subconscious interpreted it as voices," Jie suggested.

"I've played poker with you," Bilan said, "and no offense, but I've never seen any evidence that you could read anyone's mind."

"I think...I got the impression that he was doing something in my head. Like he was trying to read them through me. Maybe that did something, opened something up. I don't know, but something happened."

"He?" Bilan asked. "Who's he?"

"The Rabbit. He was there. What about the airlock? It was hidden, but I knew exactly where it was."

"Same thing as the cards maybe. It was just a curtain—" Jie started.

"You don't believe me?"

"I don't know what's going on," he replied. "I don't understand it, but I am concerned, so know it comes from love when I tell you this. You should go back to Mars."

"That's not an option."

"They have facilities there that can help you."

"It doesn't matter. Even if I wanted to go back—which, for the record, I don't—I can't."

"Earth, maybe?"

"They'd burn me as a witch."

"It's not all like that."

"But enough is. With all due respect to your wives, I'd rather go crazy and die out here than get sent to Earth." She'd lost them both. She could tell from their expressions. They thought she was crazy, and as soon as they learned her secret, they wanted to send her away. She let anger well up just to keep from breaking down and crying.

"Then it's up to us to help you," Jie finally said.

"What?" Bilan and Del both said at once.

"You can't go to Mars. You can't go to Earth. Venus won't take you in without family there. You can't tell BeltSec because their only solution would be to send her to Earth, and they wouldn't be likely to pay for it." He turned to Bilan. "We're all she has, so it's us."

Del felt the tears coming now and fought to hold them back.

"We're not professionals," Bilan said.

"Do you know where to find one? Outside of Zono Mastro?"

Bilan shook her head. "I could probably get a black market surgeon within a couple of inquiries, but I've never even heard of a black market psychologist."

"Then it's us." He turned to Del. "Whatever is going on, it seems worse when you're alone. So, I don't want you going on any long patrols for a while."

"I don't get to choose those."

"You chose the last one. But for others, I can pull some strings..."

"Don't." That earned her a startled look from both of them.

"Whatever this is, I have to live with it. I appreciate your help." She tried to keep her voice steady and her eyes dry as she said it. "A lot. But I can't reorder my whole life around this. I won't. I go where they send me, I do what I need to do. If I can't live my life on own terms, I might as well just walk out and take a big breath of vacuum now."

There was a sharp intake of breath from Bilan. "Please don't do that. Ever. A lot of people live perfectly full lives even with severe restrictions."

"Speaking of..." Jie started.

"What?" Del snapped.

"I will do everything I can do to help you, to be there for

you, and to keep BeltSec from learning about your condition. As long as you don't endanger innocent people."

They were still talking about it as if it was a condition. Could she be that wrong about reading people's minds? Delusion was the more likely answer.

"I won't do that," she said.

"I mean it. I worry about you sometimes. Even before I knew about this. You can play fast and loose with the rules. You're careless, and such carelessness can get people killed out here. You don't think like a Belter, Del. There are dangers everywhere here, and you've never seemed to appreciate that."

"That's not true. I—"

"I have seen you close an airlock door behind you while your helmet is still down."

"It self-deploys when the pressure begins to drop," she said.

"Which is something no Belter would ever say. It fails once, you're dead. You forget to put it on, you're dead."

"I get it, but..."

"No buts. I won't belabor my concerns, except to say this: if you endanger innocent people, I will report you and have you sent to Mars, or Earth, or wherever will help you. I won't do it out of malice, I won't do it in anger, and I will mourn you. But my priorities are clear: your freedom is not more important than the lives of everybody else in the Belt."

"I understand. Promise me one thing, though."

"What is it?"

"That ever comes, don't even bother reporting me. Shoot me in the back and shove me out the nearest airlock. It'll be the kinder action."

"Nobody is spacing anybody." Bilan jumped to her feet. "Or reporting them. If you endanger someone, we'll stop you, and do everything to help you."

"I—" Jie started.

"No." Bilan whirled on him, her hand up. "She needs to know she can trust us. And I need to know I can trust her. And none of that can happen with a bunch of threats hanging in the air."

Jie fell silent for a moment, then asked: "Do you have a deck of cards?"

"What?"

"Cards. I'd like to see a deck of cards. Surely you must have one."

"I don't, actually," Del said. "Unless you count a tarot deck."

"That'll do."

That'll do. Such a small thing to say. Del had left superstition behind her long before she left Mars. She didn't believe the cards had any kind of magical power. Nonetheless, she hesitated. This would be the first time in four standards she let anyone else see them. The first time since she was seven that she had taken them out without doing the simple ritual of banishing her third fosters had taught her.

She left the silk cloth they were wrapped in in the cupboard and walked back across the room to hand Jie the deck.

"Thank you," he said, and shuffled them in a high arch, bending their backs as he did so.

Del suppressed a wince.

He pulled out a card and looked at it. "Tell me what card I have."

"What?"

"What are you doing, Jie?" Bilan asked.

"Two things. One, I am not willing to completely dismiss Del's earlier assertion that she can read minds. To some degree isn't that what the neural interface in your suit is doing? Or a prosthetic limb? Is it completely impossible that a human—an orphan from Mars no less—may have somehow evolved the ability to do so over a short distance?"

"Pretty darn close, yeah. I don't think indulging in fantasy is doing her any favors."

"And that's the other reason. If the experiment fails, hopefully that will be enough to convince her that she is not telepathic, and we can focus on more likely scenarios. But why not eliminate the impossible first?"

"I'm right here, you know."

"Yes. I apologize."

"But even if I can read minds sometimes, I have no idea how it works. Failure in your experiment won't prove anything."

"I suppose not. Still, a positive result will tell us something, and a negative result will lose us nothing but time. So," he held up the card again, its back to Del, "what card am I holding?"

Del concentrated. Nothing. No image formed, no knowledge appeared. "I'm sorry, I got nothing."

"Guess. It may not be conscious knowledge."

"The clubs were."

"But the seven was not."

He had her there. She tried to relax, and said the first thing that popped into her mind. "The Six of Glavoj."

He flipped the card over. The name was spelled out in Old Martian: Jugo, one of the major arcana. It had a painted image of an ancient rocket launching near a blue ocean as a crowd of people clamored to board. It was an appropriate card for this moment, as it signified judgment and, regardless of what Bilan said earlier, she felt that's what was going on tonight. One way or another, they would each make a decision before leaving here.

Jie handed the deck to Bilan. "Just try it. Please."

Bilan turned the deck over in her hand and looked at the cards. "These are beautiful, Del. Where did you get them?"

"One of my foster brothers gave them to me when I was six."

"What is that in human years?" Jie asked.

She scowled at him but appreciated the attempt at humor to lighten the mood. "About twelve standards. He was nine - eighteen standards. Despite our age differences, he always treated me well. It was a good year." They were her favorite of her fosters, and she thought they'd all bonded to a point where they were going to keep her, but at the end of the year they hadn't renewed the contract.

"You must have been fond of him. I thought you didn't bring anything with you from Mars."

"I brought a few things. These. A book."

"What book?" Bilan asked.

"The Martian Chronicles."

"By Ray Bradbury?"

"Yeah. It was required reading at one of my schools," Del replied. "During my tunnel rat days, I mentioned I liked it, so a friend gave me his special sesquicentennial printing. Then he laughed at me for not realizing it wasn't a history."

Bilan laughed, but then held up a card, its back to Del. "How about this one? What did I choose?"

Again, Del tried to unfocus her mind and let the card come in. "Seven Glavoj?" she guessed.

"Sorry," Bilan said, and dropped the card face up on the couch beside Jie's. The image was of a woman sitting on a throne holding a book. Behind her, a great window looking out on Mars. She was wearing light robes, the same red as the landscape, with one breast exposed and one covered. The words *Alta Pastrino* were written along the bottom.

"Why did you choose that one?" Del asked.

"I thought she was pretty."

The card represented intuition or secret knowledge. They'd each chosen appropriate cards. She shook her head to clear it. Telepathy, she was almost ready to believe in. Tarot cards would take a while.

"What does that mean?" Bilan said.

"It doesn't mean anything," Jie said. "It's not evidence either way."

"No, I mean, what does the card mean?" she asked. "All the cards have a meaning, right?"

"It depends a lot on context," Del said. "Draw one more at random and we'll see. It takes at least three to do a proper reading."

Bilan pulled a card from the middle of the deck and dropped it face up on top of the other two. It showed a single crystal goblet. It was full of water, overflowing and splashing onto the red rock it sat on.

Tasoj was written across the bottom.

"Cups?" Bilan asked. "But there's only one."

"You know Old Martian?" Del asked in surprise.

"It's Esperanto," she said. "I took a couple of semesters in school."

"Esperanto?"

"It's an old Earth language. Earth has thousands of languages. When the early settlers hit Mars, since they spoke so many different languages, they tried to choose a single one they could all learn."

"Damn. I always thought Old Martian was originally from Mars."

"How long ago do you think Mars was settled?"

"I dunno. Thousand years?"

Bilan chuckled. "More like two hundred. But even a thousand wouldn't be enough for a language to develop on its own. Didn't matter, though. By the time they got there, English was pretty much entrenched as the lingua franca for Earth."

"What's *lingua franca* mean?" Del asked.

"It's Latin for French," Bilan said.

"That...doesn't clear anything up."

Jie stopped them before they could go any further. "The rather enormous gaps in Del's formal education are fascinating and all, but can we get back to planning how we're going to help her with her issues?"

Her issues. She did not like that at all.

"What about pushing?" she asked.

"About what?"

"I didn't tell you about Elias, the administrator, and his picture. Also, the Rabbit. I'm positive he was the one implanting the suggestion on Aluna that I jump out the airlock."

"Or he was following you because he was concerned when he saw a woman behaving erratically heading for the airlock with no helmet on," said Jie.

"I'm a little concerned that you jumped out of an airlock just because you heard a voice," Bilan said.

"I went to get away from him," Del replied.

"With no helmet," Jie added again unnecessarily.

"It automatically deployed when the pressure dropped. And, I might add, I knew it would do that because that's what it does. If this compulsion came from my own brain, how come it didn't know that?"

"You know that some helmets do come off," Bilan said, gesturing toward Jie's, currently deflated and hanging from his belt. "Yours can, too, you know, so you can replace it, just not while wearing the suit."

"Administrator Elias practically threw that picture at me."

"Try that, then," Bilan said. "Make me do something right now."

Del thought for a second. Bilan had the same model suit she did. She wouldn't be able to take off her helmet. Del looked at her and thought as hard as she could:

TAKE OFF YOUR SUIT AND STEP INTO THE AIRLOCK.

She didn't say anything out loud.

The effect was startling. Bilan leapt to her feet. "Here," she said. "I'll make it easy for you." Like Del, she wore her uniform over her vacsuit. She began taking it off.

When she had finished, she looked at Del who still didn't speak, watching her in fascination.

Del glanced over at Jie who was looking rapidly back and forth between the two of them.

"Nothing?" Bilan asked. "Okay, try it now." She undid the clasps on her vacsuit. Releasing the magnetic seal, she peeled it off and stepped out of it.

"What...what are you doing?" Jie asked her.

"Just making sure I have nothing in the way of whatever power Del has," Bilan said, laying her vacsuit carefully on the couch where she'd been sitting. She walked across the room to the airlock and hit the button to open the inner door.

When she stepped into it, Jie leapt to his feet and ran after her.

Bilan turned back to face Del. "Anytime," she said.

Jie took hold of her by the shoulders and tried to steer her back into the room. "Bilan, stop this," he said.

She pulled away from him. "Relax," she said. "I'm not going through it, I'm—"

"Del!" Jie called back, still trying to pull Bilan out of the airlock. "You've made your point. Let her go."

Del stood there, staring at them both.

"Delokita!" Jie yelled again.

COME BACK IN AND SIT DOWN.

Bilan strode back in and over to the couch, pushing her suit to the side to make room to sit.

Jie closed the airlock door and turned to Del. "You could have killed her!"

Del shrunk from his fury. She'd never seen him truly angry before. "I'm sorry. I didn't mean to—"

"It's fine," Bilan said. "She didn't do anything." She looked up at Del, who turned her attention to her.

"I'm sorry," she said again. Her eyes grew moist and for a moment, she was back on Mars, crying alone on a red stone floor beneath a high balcony. Then, she was back in her asteroid apartment, sitting on the edge of her bed, with Bilan and Jie both watching her from the couch.

"You didn't..." Bilan started, then realized: "You did."

Del nodded.

Jie was standing, staring in speechless horror.

"Can you describe what it was like?" Del asked. It was a trick she'd learned from one of her first psychiatrists. Describing the experience would reduce the emotional impact of it, make it seem more external and easier to process. At least, that was the idea.

"It didn't feel like I was being controlled," Bilan answered. "I just...knew I should step into the airlock. It felt perfectly natural, like that's what I should do if I wanted Del to try to control me. Then, when Jie was upset and panicking, I knew I should go sit down. I wasn't thinking about being commanded, I just wanted to calm him down. This...this is terrible. How can you ever trust your own thoughts again? Is that what it's like for you all the time?"

She had asked that question before, though the circumstances were very different. The answer was the same. "Not all the time. But sometimes."

"This is what you were explaining to me before you left, when you told me how we met."

Del nodded again.

Bilan turned to Jie. "I wasn't going to open the outer door. I didn't intend to go out."

"But you did intend to be sitting naked on Del's couch, in front of both of us?"

Bilan looked down. "I...uh...yeah, I think I'll get dressed." She got up pulled her vacsuit back on, then her uniform. She spoke as she did so. "But to answer your question, yes, it did seem like a perfectly reasonable thing to do at the time, and it still feels perfectly natural. I mean, it is natural. A lot of people don't bother with clothes at home, even when their friends are there.

"But no, stepping out of the airlock doesn't feel that way at all." She turned her attention back to Del. "Could it have? Could you have told me to open the outer door, and would I have done it?"

"I...I don't know," Del said. "I'm not going to try, obviously. But, yes, I think it's possible. In fact, I think that's the connection between the attacks. I think that's what the Rabbit is doing."

"Do we even know these attacks are related?" Jie asked.

"I'm almost positive they are," Bilan answered. "I was originally thinking it was some kind of stochastic terrorism effort, but I couldn't find a source."

"I thought the whole point of stochastic terrorism is that it doesn't have a single source," Del said.

"Coordination and planning of the specific attacks isn't centralized. But the rhetoric and encouragement to violence usually is. If not a single source, then a variety of sources who echo and amplify each other. But in general before it outbreaks into widespread violence some prominent figure encourages their followers, knowing that some few will take them up on it. Usually it's a politician or a religious figure. Very frequently both, which is why Mars has such strictures against religion in its politics. But you can't really keep that sort of thing secret. If you do, it doesn't reach the edge cases you need to reach for it to work."

"If Del's theory holds true—" Jie began.

"I'm now convinced it does," said Bilan.

"All these attacks could be coordinated, by the Rabbit or someone he's affiliated with," Del said. "What's the official word from BeltSec? I haven't seen anything in the briefings."

The other two glanced at each other.

"What?" Del asked. "What's going on?"

"Official word is there are no attacks," Bilan said.

"But Alba Corp—"

"Never happened."

"He sent reports."

"I'm sure he did. But officially, there is no such report," Bilan said.

"At Bilan's request, I finally asked the top brass about them," Jie said. "I was told to stay away from it."

"That's interesting. BeltSec knows something, but they're trying to keep it quiet. Why?" Del asked.

"Maybe they don't want to let whoever is doing it know that they're being investigated?" Bilan suggested.

"Whoever's in charge must know BeltSec would look into it. And the corps are demanding it. Why shut them out when their fears could be allayed just by claiming there's an investigation?"

"You're saying there is no investigation?" Bilan asked.

"Even if there was one, would it be possible that they'd even know about the Rabbit?"

"Say we tell them about him," Jie said. "I could do so, I suppose, but how would I explain how I know? Or how he's doing it?" He turned back to Del. "Are you willing to go before Zono Mastro and demonstrate what you can do?"

"Void no," Del replied.

"I didn't think so," Jie said with a wry smile. "If you were, I'd advise against it."

"Really?" Bilan and Del said simultaneously, which made Jie laugh.

"I thought you trusted Zono Mastro," Del said.

"Not in the slightest," Jie replied. "BeltSec, I can trust to a certain extent. The Belt needs some degree of order, and they—we—are the only ones willing to provide it. Without BeltSec, the Belt devolves into chaos and violence, as the larger corps fight each other to rob the rest, employees become slaves, and disputes are resolved through armed conflict. Nobody wants that, but, no, I have no illusions that they are overly trustworthy, or that they would see Del's ability as anything but a resource to be exploited."

"So, once again I'm keeping secrets."

"Only this time you have friends to share them with," Bilan said.

Jie nodded his agreement.

Del finished her drink and tossed the flask into a corner of the room. She could place it in a bin to be cleaned, but didn't feel like walking right then. The bot would get it whenever it got around to running. She was fairly certain it was on some kind of schedule.

"Thanks," she said. "I mean it. You have no idea how much that means. I'd love to just walk away and leave it to BeltSec, but since whoever it is is trying to kill me, I don't think I can."

"Then we need to stop them. I'm already investigating Jeremy Bartran, so that gives us cover and resources to look into it."

"What, seriously?"

"Someone's trying to kill you. It turns out you're not sick. I got one implanted compulsion and I don't know if I'll ever be able to trust anything I think ever again. I'm onboard for stopping whoever has done this to you throughout your life."

"Wait...you think the earlier episodes might be related?"

"Unless there's more than one of these people. Maybe there were some on Mars, and you just now ran into your first one out here."

"Also," Jie said, "whoever is doing this is causing problems throughout the Belt. I don't know what their agenda is, but it's unlikely to be in our best interest. And as far as I know, we're the only ones who have an inkling of the real problem."

"So far it seems the Rabbit's our only lead," Del said.

"Or the assassin's boyfriend," Bilan suggested.

"And would-be assassins themselves," Jie added.

"No idea where I could find them again, though."

"I'm not sure how wise a decision it was to just let them go like that," Bilan said.

"I don't know what else I could have done. The alternative, other than killing them outright, would have been to send them back here for trial."

"They'd be safely out of the way then."

"As indentured servants, slaving away in the antimatter mines on Mercury or some equally hellish labor, most likely for the rest of their short miserable lives."

“Antimatter isn't actually mined, you know,” Bilan said, at the same time Jie said, "They did try to kill you."

"And hopefully I've convinced them not to anymore," Del responded.

"I will never fathom you, Delokita," Jie said. "You'll let someone go free after they tried to kill you, because you don't want to ruin their lives, but you'll sell prohibited drugs back to your home."

Del turned to Bilan. "You showed him that, too?"

Before Bilan could answer, Del turned back to Jie. "One, Mars isn't my home. Not anymore. Two, nobody uses those who doesn't choose to, and cosmo is basically harmless unless they do something stupid."

"Except for the ones who end up as permanent vegetables."

"They should know better than to take that much. Even so, that almost never happens."

Bilan interrupted before that discussion could go any further. "Now these people have a vendetta against you directly and likely realize that coming after you is a way of getting their ship back as well as being paid."

"Yet another reason I'm planning on getting rid of the damn thing as soon as I can."

"All right, then, let's start with the Rabbit," Jie said.

"Do you have any footage of him?" Bilan asked.

"Yeah, here." Del searched through her suit's video archives and found the part from Aluna. She had edited it on the trip back from the Hygiean sector and was planning on giving it to Kenny when she went to sell him the ship. She displayed the video on her wall screen.

Together, they watched as Del scrambled in panic toward the airlock. Del winced when she saw it. She had thought at the time that she was doing a good job keeping it cool, at least externally, but now saw from the shocked looks of everyone staring at her how obvious it was.

"Hold it. Back up a few seconds," Bilan said, as on the video playback Del hit the emergency airlock open button.

Del froze the image and backed up three seconds.

"Stop there," Bilan said. "Turn it around, I want to see behind you."

The "image" on the suit of course was composited from thousands of tiny sensors embedded throughout the fabric. The display on the flat wall screen had a field of view roughly what she had seen with her own eyes, but all the data was captured. With the image frozen, she spun it around to see behind her. She saw the inner airlock door, closed, with the Rabbit's face pressed against it. He wore a broad wicked smile that turned to wide-eyed surprise when the outer door opened and Del was blown into space.

"By Heaven rebuilt," Jie said, seeing the man. "I think that confirms my evolved trait theory."

"What? What do you mean?" Del asked.

"He could be your brother," Bilan answered. "Look at him. He's maybe a couple of centimeters taller than you at most. Same brown skin, same little nose, same eyes."

Now that she pointed it out, Del did notice a resemblance.

"You don't know who your parents are, right?" Jie asked.

"No. I don't know anything about them."

"It might be worth contacting the Martian Authority and finding out. I wonder how many siblings you might have, and if you all have these abilities."

Del shook her head. "They won't have any information. MA Protectors found me on a derelict ship that had entered Martian orbit. I was unregistered and nobody else was aboard. Even the ship had been stolen decades before, probably changed hands a dozen times since then. No way to find out who had it last."

"That's...definitely significant, I'm just not sure how. Perhaps this Rabbit himself would know. If we could find a way to capture and question him." Jie said.

"Far too dangerous," Del said. "He can kill people by thinking at them."

"There must be a way. Bilan and I, perhaps, could spend a few days there, and needle him unconscious and arrest him."

"Arrest him for what?" Del asked.

"Whatever we want. You're the one who taught me that. We're BeltSec, nobody's going to question us."

"Somebody might in this case. The guy's pretty well connected. Even if nobody directly interferes, there's going to be a lot of people who would pay attention to what happens to him."

Jie sighed. "Perhaps we should continue this discussion tomorrow night. We are agreed now that we will do something about this menace, yes?"

"Agreed," Del said.

A moment later, Bilan nodded in response.

"So," Del said, "who wants to see my new spaceship before I get rid of it forever?"

"I'm afraid I'll have to pass," Jie said. "I'm meeting someone for dinner in a few hours."

"You have a date?" Del asked, amused.

"Just a preliminary meeting. We'll see how it goes."

"Do your spouses know about this?"

"Of course. My husband met her before I did." He seemed genuinely offended.

"Sorry."

"It's okay. We don't cheat. I trust them, and vice versa."

"Must be nice."

"It is."

EIGHT
LAST VOYAGE OF THE ZHENG HE

Half an hour later, Bilan and Del were flying toward the *Zheng He*, each on their own bike.

Del set up realtime communication. "This idea that the Rabbit is so well connected gave me an idea..."

"You think Kenny might know him?" Bilan finished for her.

"I could ask. I'm going there anyway."

"Good idea." That surprised Del. "Just be careful, okay?"

"I will."

"Don't get too eager to try out your new-found abilities," Bilan said. "We don't know how reliable they are, or to what extent they can be used. For that matter, what kind of damage you might be causing your own brain by using them."

"I hadn't even thought of that. It doesn't seem to be doing anything, but..."

"But how would you know?"

"Exactly." Nobody said anything for a second, then Del changed the subject. "When I visited the Zono Mastro office on Hygiea, the administrator was surprised to see me."

"Didn't you mention that Johanka usually does that patrol?"

"It wasn't just that. She told me I was under investigation. Not Jeremy, me, and it seemed to be an official BeltSec investigation, not a side job. What's going on, Bilan?"

"Oh, hey, is that your ship up ahead?"

"Fine, we can talk onboard," Del said.

Del sent the code to open the large cargo door and it swung silently out into space. The hold had already been in vacuum so there was no visible puff of air as it did so.

Bilan surprised her by not heading in. Instead, she swung wide around the ship.

Del followed her past the cargo bay and toward the bow. The name *Zheng He* was painted in bright red letters just below the large windows that lined the bridge, followed by some characters in a language that Del didn't know how to read.

Bilan continued past the port airlock, then toward the back to take a look at the large engine array behind the cargo bay. "Looks like you've got some damage to the engines here."

"Yeah, only two of the six function at all."

"I think I know why." Bilan switched on an external spotlight.

Now that she could see it clearly, it was obvious. There was a large hole in the engine pods. "What would cause that?" Del asked. "A big rock?"

"Something definitely hit it. Too rough to be weapons fire and wrong position for containment loss."

"Must've been a terrifying experience for the crew."

"Probably," Bilan agreed. "From what I've seen of the state of this thing, they likely had lots of terrifying experiences in it."

"Probably lots of good ones, too."

Bilan didn't say anything in response.

Del continued. "This wasn't just transportation for them. This was their home for probably a very long time."

"Don't feel sorry for them. They tried to kill you, Del."

"And I took away their home." Less than ten meters away, both of them drifting without acceleration, Del could see her face clearly.

"They were planning on taking a lot more than that from you. Of everything you could have done, taking their ship was just about the kindest act possible. I watched the vid you sent Jie."

Del got an image, just for a fraction of a second, of Bilan and Jie in civilian clothes with no vacsuit underneath, sitting in a small room with a curved wall.

Bilan picked up a console and said, "I really want to see the rest of that."

Jie looked concerned.

The vision faded and Del realized this time it might not just be her imagination conjuring up images. *Had it ever been her imagination? Was it possible that every time she'd ever imagined what people did when she wasn't around, she was actually experiencing their memories?* She could find out if this one was.

"What?" Bilan looked concerned. "What is it?"

"Did you...?" Del started. "How many times did you access my suit?"

"What? Why?"

"Just...just answer the question!" Del felt her heart racing. She tried to calm herself. "Please. It's important."

"I..." Bilan started.

"I'm invoking the pact," Del said and tried to keep the rising panic out of her voice.

"A few," Bilan said immediately.

"Was one of them with Jie?"

"Yes. Right after he showed me the vid where you got your ship. I'm sorry. I had to see the rest of it." Which was almost exactly what she'd said in Del's vision. She wasn't sure if it was a relief or not.

"Why didn't you just ask me?"

Bilan again was silent for a moment before answering.

Del tried to see what she was thinking of but couldn't.

"I didn't want to let you know I was looking," Bilan said. "I'm sorry."

"For just a second, I think I saw your memory. You were sitting on a floor next to a curved wall, wearing a blue shirt with a high collar, but not your vacsuit. Jie was there showing you the vid, and you picked up a standard console to see the rest."

"Depths, that's freaky. But it sounds right. I don't actually remember what I was wearing at the time...except, I guess I do. How can your memory of it be clearer than my own?"

The image was real. "C'mon," Del said. "Let's get inside."

After securing their bikes in the cargo bay, Del led her toward the starboard airlock. "Let's use this one," she said. "I had to cut through one of the doors in the exterior airlock from that side."

Once they had passed through into the interior corridor, they both opened their helmets.

Del pushed away from the airlock without activating the controls that would have pressurized the cargo bay. "There's a slow leak in there. If we pressurized it now, it'd be mostly vacuum again by the time we got to Kenny's, and I'm not sure how much we've got left to spare."

"The air supply is low?"

"And fuel. And every other consumable. These guys were right on the edge. I can see why they might take a contract and not look too closely."

"Careful. Don't project too much of yourself onto these people."

"I'm not," she said. "Don't worry. Even back on Mars, when

things were at their absolute worst, I never stooped to murder for hire."

"That's good to hear," Bilan said. *Did that mean she was surprised to hear it*? "Does the doc table even work?" Bilan asked, pausing to peer into the room as they were passing.

"No idea. Haven't tried it. Don't plan to."

They'd pushed a little further up and after a quick stop at the captain's quarters, Bilan turned to her and asked, "Can you tell what I'm thinking right now?"

Del tried to clear her mind, relax, and let the thoughts come. Nothing happened. "No. I'm sorry. I have no idea how it works. I don't seem to be able to do it on command."

"Unlike projection, which you seem to have down pretty well. No! Don't do it. Please, it's horrible. Please don't ever do that to me again."

"I won't. I'm sorry...I—"

"It's okay. Seriously. I won't hold it against you. Stars, listen to us. We need to stop apologizing to each other every other sentence."

"I'll try not to read your mind anymore," Del said, a little taken aback.

"And that's definitely the weirdest promise anyone's ever made to me," Bilan said. "And if I'd ever thought it was something someone might say, the last thing I'd expect to respond with would be no. But, no. Don't promise that. You need to understand this, how it works, maybe you can learn to do it when you want to."

"Does that mean you want me to read your mind?"

"It's probably safer than anyone else's. Just..."

"What?"

"I'm torn between wanting to know, and never wanting to know what you see."

"I'll tell you then. I'll need you to verify if what I see is real, same as before," Del said. "And here's the bridge." She was grateful for the change of topic.

The airlock leading to the bridge had three pressure doors—one each to the two corridors and one into the bridge itself.

"No air in the port corridor?" Bilan asked, indicating the red light next to the door leading to it.

"It should hold it, but I never bothered to pressurize it after I used it last."

"Mind if I take a look?" Bilan said once they'd passed through onto the bridge. She slid into the center seat without waiting for an answer.

"Yeah, here, gotta give you access from the console," Del said. She approached one of the other stations and pulled up the security interface. It recognized Del and seeing Bilan in the central seat, offered to give her authorization as well.

Del confirmed.

"I couldn't get anything but the coms to interface with my suit," Del apologized.

"That's probably by design," Bilan said. "Partly for security - you wouldn't want someone outside the ship steering it into a planet or opening all the pressure doors at once and venting you into space."

"Makes sense, I guess," Del said. She shuddered at the thought, and wondered if her parents' ship had had that same safety feature. Might their demise not have been an accident?

"An even more important reason might be crew psychology," Bilan continued. "Ships like this can spend a lot of time drifting through space. They'll head to, say, Earth, by burning for a few hours, maybe, then cutting back to zero, or very low thrust, for most of the trip. It could take weeks or even months before they get there. Having tasks that can only be done at certain stations forces the crew to interact and move around.

There probably aren't any cleaning bots either. Everything would have to be done by hand."

"That sounds awful. Speaking of mindless time-wasters, though, when you were researching Aluna did you happen to come across anything telling you what these might be worth?" She pulled the bag of chips out of the cupboard she'd stashed them in and tossed one to Bilan.

"How many of these do you have?" Bilan asked, indicating the bag Del was still holding.

Del gave the bag a shake. "Dunno. Couple hundred?"

"You never even counted them?"

"Was kinda preoccupied at the time. Besides, with no idea what they're worth, what difference does it make how many there are?"

"Do I even want to know how you got them, then?"

"Perfectly legitimately!" Del said indignantly. "The administrator of Rimedo gave me some casino credit, as a thank you for 27-27."

Bilan laughed at her indignation. "But how is it possible you never knew how much you had?" Her tone was more amused than patronizing, or so Del hoped.

"I was planning on keeping one if I lost everything, and win or lose I'd find out how much when I cashed out. Then I ended up winning a lot, but obviously didn't get a chance to exchange them."

"Shining stars. I'd be terrified."

"That's why I didn't ask. If it was a lot, I'd be too nervous to risk them. If not much, I wouldn't care, and it wouldn't be any fun."

"You know, this gift could be pretty lucrative. Even if it only worked once in a while, it could tilt the odds enough to win more often than not."

"Cheating at cards for a living?"

"Is it really cheating if—"

"Pretty sure it is. They may not be able to figure out how, or to prove anything, but it'll be obvious once I start winning that I'm doing something."

"If you only do it occasionally—"

"Besides, the only casino I know in the Belt large enough for it to work would be Aluna, and I don't think they'll let me back in there any time soon."

"Good point," Bilan conceded. "Let's check out the rest of the ship."

A FEW MINUTES BEFORE TURNAROUND, they were both on the bridge again. "Getting a message from Jie," Bilan said, then added, "oh, hey, it's for you. Here."

The center pane of the great window that wrapped around the bridge turned opaque for a second, then Jie's face appeared. "Hey, Bilan, is this the person you're looking for?" he asked.

The image switched to a video of Amelia, the escaped indenture the administrator of Ministoj had hired her to retrieve. She was sitting at a table with a man Del didn't recognize at what looked like a pretty fancy upscale restaurant.

"Is that Amacio's?" Bilan said. "She must have money if she's eating in a place like that."

"Harailt thought she might be stealing from him," Del replied. "Guess he was right. Is that on Ceres?"

Bilan nodded. "In Center city. You haven't been? You should try it. They have their own vegetable gardens. They make an amazing spinach and mint lasagna with white prote."

"Not really my kind of place," she said.

"Wanna tell Del to come grab her?" Jie said on the screen. "I assume this is for her, right? You two anything resembling sober? Dressed?" He said the last with a disturbing leer.

Bilan rolled her eyes.

Del laughed out loud, partly to cover her sharp pang of jealousy. The comment seemed so out of character for Jie. Certainly, he had never said anything like that around her. It was a sign of the completely different relationship he and Bilan had that Del wasn't part of.

They were only half a million kilometers from Ceres, which was still too far for realtime communication. The ship would be turning around any minute now. Even if they wanted to return now, they were already going over a hundred thousand meters per second the wrong way. With four of the ship's engines out of commission, it wouldn't even be possible to push enough to carve any time off that.

Del used the ship's com to reply so she could show him where they were.

"Hi!" she called and waved at him.

Beside her, Bilan raised her hand as well and smiled.

"I've taken Bilan with me for the last voyage of the *Zheng He*. Yes, we're dressed, pervert!"

Bilan laughed.

"And mostly sober," to which Bilan responded with a shrug. "But we're a little way away right now. I don't suppose you'd be willing to stash her somewhere for me for about ten hours, would you? I'll cut you in for half the bounty."

She sent the message. A minute passed, then another.

"Oh, come on, you're only a couple of light-seconds away," Del grumbled at the empty screen.

"He's probably with his date," Bilan said.

"Oh, right. Hell of a place for a first date," she said.

"After Noah raved about her, I think he wanted to make a good impression."

"You knew his husband had already met her? How come I didn't know this before today?"

"I guess when we're all together, we mostly talk about you."

"I...I'm sorry. I don't mean to—"

"It's okay. It's not your fault; you're just usually the most interesting topic. Half our conversations when you're not around are about you, too."

"Now I'm really not sure what to think about it."

"Then don't. Seriously."

"And there's his reply message, finally," Del said as the screen lit up again. She flipped the incoming message onto the big screen.

This time the video was of Jie himself; he was standing in a hallway full of tiny alcoves, the restaurant visible behind them. All the really fancy restaurants on Mars had those, too. As a child, she never really thought about it, but this was probably exactly what they were for - keeping the atmosphere in the restaurant pleasantly quiet by redirecting such conversations out of the dining area.

"Greetings to the crew of the *Zheng He*," Jie said with a smile. Then his expression sobered, and he looked uncomfortable. "I looked into this bounty. I'm a little concerned about it. Are you sure it's legitimate? I've tagged her in the net, so I'll know if she tries to leave Ceres, and I guess I'll decide what to do then. I'll let you know where she is when you get here, so hurry."

"Oh, sure, he'll decide. I hope he doesn't decide to just let my bounty walk out the door," Del complained.

"Don't be mad at him," Bilan responded. "It's a lot to ask. Especially of Jie."

"What, just grab one little girl and shove her in a closet for ten hours. How hard can that be?"

Bilan laughed.

Del had to admit it was a lot.

"Do you know what his concerns with the bounty are about?" Bilan asked.

"Probably because the contract's held by Harailt directly instead of by a corp," Del responded.

"That sounds a little shady. What exactly is he doing with her?"

"Whatever it is, she agreed to it. It's a valid contract, whoever the owner is."

Bilan shot her a look. It didn't take a telepath to tell what she was thinking.

"Well, if Jie lets her get away, at least I've still got the ship to sell so I can make rent."

"I can take those chips and see if I can find someone interested in them, if you'd like," Bilan offered. "Probably get a better rate for them from Johanka or someone who has business on Hygiea than you could from Kenny."

"Probably. Don't mention the girl, though. I got the impression Harailt wanted to give her the bounty and I don't want it to seem like I was sniping."

"No worries. We've still got a few hours left of this ship. I'm going to check out this vaunted bathtub."

"Enjoy. I'm gonna head down to the cargo hold and get a last workout in. Think Jie would be interested in a set of dumbbells and a bench?"

"You don't want them?"

"Don't have any room for them anywhere. I tend to do most of my exercising on my bike anyway."

"Yeah, I think he'd like it. We can bundle them up and clip them to my bike when we cut acceleration. If you wanna talk before we get there, you know where to find me."

THREE HOURS LATER, they were approaching a cluster of asteroids, one of which housed Kenny and his workshop.

"I'm getting a transponder code," Bilan said from her station.

Del was reclining in the center of the three chairs, looking up at the stars. "The whole cluster's tagged and registered to some shell company."

"Ardana Corporation. Never heard of it. That's interesting."

"What is?"

"It's based on Venus. It doesn't look like they have anything else out here, but they have extensive Venusian holdings."

"I wonder if they even know they own a worthless asteroid cluster?"

"Somebody knows. This is probably a good place to drop me off. Should I listen in, in case you need me, or wait for your call?"

"Neither. The place is shielded, like Aluna, so no signals. Don't worry. I've dealt with Kenny lots of times before. Nothing's going to go wrong. If it does, I'll deal with it."

"So...I'll just sit out here and worry, then?"

Del chuckled. "Don't worry. You won't have long to wait."

That turned out to be a more accurate statement than she expected. As Del approached the hidden entrance to Kenny's asteroid home, she saw a light. There shouldn't have been any light out here. Kenny deliberately did not have any external lights, or windows. Then the debris field came into view. Devices, tools, and parts, all the small items that habitually floated around Kenny's workshop were hanging, illuminated in space by the light spilling from the open airlock.

"Something's wrong," Del messaged back to Bilan. "Airlock's open. Both doors, I mean. Looks like it was blown. I don't see any bodies, though."

"On my way," Bilan replied.

When she got there, they both set their bikes to keep station next to the asteroid and proceeded inside using suit thrusters.

The outer door was standing open, and the inner door had a huge hole in it. The jagged oval that had been cut out of it floated inside the airlock.

"Breaching cord," Bilan said. "Either it hit the outer door and bounced off, or there was air in here when they cut it."

"They closed the outer door before blasting open the inner one? That was polite of them."

"It means they might have been looking to take prisoners," Bilan said. "They would have kept the air while they were working, and only vented it when they left."

Inside there were no signs of Kenny or his assistants. All the pressure doors leading to the inner warrens stood open. They were placed at seemingly random locations in the floor, wall, and ceilings. With no gravity, it didn't matter the direction.

"No sign of any bodies in here, either," Bilan said.

Del understood what she was saying. "Whoever did this might have taken them. They could all be alive somewhere."

"But where?" Bilan asked.

"No idea. Let's get the void out of here."

"Are you...sensing something?"

"Not unless you mean sensing an urgent need to get as far away as possible before they come back."

"Do you think they're likely to?"

"Do you think they're not?"

"I still want to look around a bit first. For instance, what's behind those cupboards?" She indicated a large column along one wall.

"Is there something?"

"They're moving. Something must be making them move."

Del flew over to the indicated cupboards and saw they

weren't fully attached to the wall. She pulled on them and they swung open, revealing the seam of a large pressure door, with a tiny hole, half a centimeter wide, cut into it. Del tried to shine her light through it, but the hole was too small to look through at the same time.

"Here," Bilan said. From a pouch, she pulled out a tiny metal sphere. It was the perfect size to fit through the hole.

"What is that?" Del asked.

"Sensor probe. It'll let us see what's on the other side."

"Convenient how well it fits."

"There's a cutter that goes with it," Bilan said. "I'm guessing that's exactly what these people used."

"Is that from the Zono Mastro catalog?"

"That's where I got mine. Are you thinking it might be BeltSec that did this?"

"You didn't give anyone else the location, did you?" Del asked.

"I didn't, but that doesn't mean they couldn't have found out elsewhere. You're not the only one who knew of this place."

Del tried again but still couldn't see what Bilan was thinking. It was frustrating that it wouldn't work when she wanted it to. She decided to believe Bilan was telling the truth. "What's on the other side?"

"Here, I'll share the feed."

The chamber beyond the doorway was immense, far greater than the workshop. A vast warehouse full of crates, boxes, and bags of all sizes secured to walls and shelves around the room. She couldn't even guess at the value.

"Yeah, they're coming back," Del said as they watched. "This wasn't what they came for, but there's no way whoever did this is leaving all this behind. Hey, it's my missile!" Del said, as a familiar weapon caught her eye. It was sitting alone on a rack, secured with two straps.

"Why does Kenny have your missile?"

"Part of the salvage of 1327-27, remember?"

"No, I mean...you threw away two pistols because you didn't want to be responsible for them being used against innocent people."

"Right. So?"

"But then you went ahead and gave the location of a ship-to-ship missile to a smuggler. Who do you think he was going to sell it to?"

"I was hoping he'd be selling to me."

"What?"

"I dumped it and didn't dare go back for it. I couldn't risk BeltSec finding it there, and they were about to be on the way. The only way I could think of to get it back was to ensure that Kenny's salvagers got there first and sold it to Kenny who could sell it back to me."

"Sounds like a pretty dangerous gamble."

"Best I could do at the time. Let's see if we can get this door open."

She pushed another row of cupboards back and found the controls to the door. It slid open and they drifted into the room. Across from them was an immense cargo door, which she assumed opened into space.

Bilan scooped up her probe and returned it to her pouch while Del found her missile in person. She couldn't figure out how to undo the bindings and eventually just sliced both straps open with her cutting torch. She pulled the missile out and wrapped both arms about it to move it. It was about as long as she was tall, and she took it with her toward the large exit door.

"Now I'm ready to go," she said.

"Hold up," Bilan said. "This is the salvage from 1327-27?"

"Yeah. There's my old engine over there." She pointed to a large chunk of metal with a meter-long scorch mark in it, netted with a jumble of other loose or damaged objects against one wall.

"Stars, Del, you're lucky to be alive."

"It's just the engine," she said. "It's like half a meter away from where I sit."

Bilan just shook her head. "Think the data core is around here somewhere, too?"

"Kenny told me he sold it almost immediately." She thought about it for a second. "That doesn't mean he actually delivered it, though."

"Help me look."

"No problem," Del replied. "What does it look like?"

"Should be a shiny metal cylinder, about this big." Bilan held her thumb and forefinger about four centimeters apart.

"Crap. That could be anywhere," Del said, looking around at all the detritus of the room.

Half an hour of searching turned up no data core, though Del did find several other potentially valuable items, which she stuck in a box to take with her.

"Anything we don't take with us now will fall into the hands of whoever did this when they get back," she said when Bilan raised her eyebrow.

"Excellent point," Bilan said and grabbed a bag herself. She poured out the contents and rummaged through them as they floated away. "You know, we could ensure that they don't get any of this."

Del didn't like the way Bilan was eyeing her missile. "I just got that back!" She protested.

"I'll get you another one when we get back to Ceres," Bilan said.

"All right," she conceded. "I still have to get it back onto my bike to arm it, though." She pushed it gently toward the doorway and they continued their search.

Bilan floated over to the controls by the door. "I'm going to evacuate the rest of the air, so it doesn't all get lost to space."

Del didn't see the point, but didn't object as she was chest-deep in another large box she'd cut open.

"Hey, is this it?" she asked. By now there was a large cloud of small items that they'd discarded, tossing them in random directions.

Bilan took the small metal cylinder Del was holding up. "Almost certainly." She tucked it into a pocket in her uniform. "I've got everything I need here. You done looting?"

Del gave a short snort of laughter. "Yeah, let's go."

BACK ON THE *ZHENG HE*, they again parked their bikes in the cargo hold and made their way to the bridge.

"Now what?" Bilan asked.

"I dunno. Gonna need a new fixer. I guess I can sell the ship on the open market. I was just trying to..."

"I mean, what about Kenny? Who would do this? Do we have any leads?"

"No idea. He dealt with a lot of people. No telling which one got pissed enough to eventually launch an attack."

"This is something more. Let's get out of here."

Del set the course and a big red warning light lit up.

"Void! There's not enough fuel to get back!"

"Relax. We still have the bikes."

"If I leave the ship here, it'll just get stolen by whoever..." She stopped, then looked over at Bilan with a big grin.

"A trap?" Bilan asked.

"We could either hide on the ship or leave a transponder on it."

"It could be a long time before they come back."

"I have a feeling it might not."

"I don't think it's a good idea to risk being here. We both go on duty in about ten hours, right?"

"We could make it official. Call it a stakeout of a criminal organization."

"Wouldn't work unless we were ordered to. Unless he interferes with the registry BeltSec isn't going to care one way or another about someone like Kenny."

"How much of all that in there," Del waved vaguely in the direction of the asteroid, "was stolen from our corporate clients?"

"Even so, do you really want to wait here for however long it takes for them to come back? And what about your bounty?"

"Void. I almost forgot. Great, maybe I won't end up homeless after all."

"You could always move back into BeltSec housing on Ceres."

"Never."

"Would it really be that bad? You know I live there, right?"

"You rank high enough for a private room. Me, they'd stick in quarters with three other people and a mist shower at the end of the hall."

"You—"

"Let's just say I like my gravity and leave it at that, okay?" How could she explain that moving back to Ceres would feel too much like regression? Especially now she was just starting to get used to this new ability—to the idea that it even was a new ability. She had to keep moving forward.

"All right," Bilan said, taken aback by her tone. "If you want, I can still try to sell those chips for you. Maybe that'll tide you over until you find something better."

"Half-and-half, whatever you can get for them."

"Sounds good. You know I'll have to sell them below face

value."

"Whatever that is. Anything you can get for them will be more than if I just left them here."

"You know the ship better than I do. Help me write a new protocol for surveillance."

"A protocol? Like the one Dario put in my suit?"

"Exactly like that, except the ship has a lot more capabilities so it'll be a little more complex."

They spent another half an hour on the ship designing and testing it. Any movement and it'd start sending its entire sensor feed to them along with transponder location. They could write the suit half on the six hour trip back to Ceres, then upload them once they'd had a chance to put the vacsuits on their manikins.

Taking a page from Dario, they had it automatically turn itself back on if it was turned off, and reply with a false status code.

"What if they just find it and delete it?" Del asked.

"They probably will, but we should be able to see who they are first, if not where they're going."

"Where they're going is the important part," Del complained.

"I agree, and they may just delete it if they find it. I would."

"Which is what I didn't do with Dario's." Del sighed.

"Don't feel bad. This is all new to you."

"It shouldn't be. I'm pretty sure we actually covered this in school."

"You moved around a lot. There are bound to be some gaps."

"Or I just wasn't paying attention. I went to the rich people's schools, being prepared for a life I knew I would never lead. Who knew any of that stuff I was supposed to be learning in school would turn out to be useful later?"

Bilan laughed. "You're learning it now. That's what counts."

"Maybe. Stop me if this is a stupid idea, but can we make it not delete when told to?"

"Not stupid, but it won't work. The delete function's built in and can't be changed. Probably specifically to stop people from doing that."

"Void! I don't like the idea of just losing the ship if we can't even get anything useful for it. Let's just leave. If BeltSec doesn't care about this, why should we?"

"I thought Kenny was your friend," Bilan chastised.

"Friend might be a bit of a stretch. Even if he was, why are you so interested?"

"I think it's related. Jeremy, the other attacks, the Rabbit. It just seems like too much of a coincidence that Kenny gets attacked at the same time."

Del thought for a moment. "Protocols don't have to say what they are, right? I mean, you can call them anything? And they can have hidden functions, like you were afraid my med module might?"

"Still worried about that, but yes."

"What if we have it do something like that, say, monitor life support, or show the pressure in various compartments but also send images and locations?"

"That might work. Then we can just lock most of it away. They might not trust it, but they won't dare delete it."

"How are they going to move the ship? It doesn't have enough fuel to get anywhere."

"They could tow it, or bring fuel, or just do a ballistic shot."

"Like a Hohmann ship?"

"Kind of, only instead of being set on a low-energy orbit, they accelerate in the right direction, let it drift for a while, then decelerate when it gets there. The same thing it normally does, actually, only instead of a couple of minutes in turn around, it's at zero G for most of the trip. That's probably what this ship usually does traveling between planets."

In the end they got the protocol working how they wanted it. It would read the air pressure of each compartment and show a graph of how they were changing.

"Beautiful," Del said. "If I'd actually had this on the way here, it would have saved me a great deal of air."

"Perfect then. Let them discover that themselves and worry about the rest of it. Now let's get out of here."

Del sent the signal to close the cargo door as they left on their bikes. She didn't expect to see the ship again, but it was their best bet at catching whoever was behind all this.

They flew along in silence, while Del watched her empty ship getting smaller in the distance. She already missed it.

"I want to try to get into that data core," Bilan's voice said in her helmet. "How're you holding up?"

"I'm fine. Just taking a last look at my ship."

"You know it could be days—or never—before anyone shows up."

"I know. I'll eventually figure something out. If nobody comes for it before I can sell it..."

"That's not really what I meant. You've been through a lot..."

"I've been through worse."

"That doesn't make me feel better."

Del smiled. "I'm okay. You know me."

"I also think we should try to learn more about your ability when we get back."

"Fancy strutting about my little asteroid naked some more?" she said, still smiling.

That was greeted by a gentle laugh from Bilan. "I'd rather not. Especially with Jie there. But if that's what it takes..."

"You're serious, aren't you?"

"About testing your ability? Yes. Aren't you?"

"I have no idea how it would work. Or even how to learn."

"I have a few ideas on the second. As for the first...I have a couple of ideas on that, too."

"Can't wait to hear them," Del said. "But for now, I need to do something physical. I'm gonna go for a run."

"What?" Bilan seemed alarmed.

"My bike has a treadmill?"

"Oh!" Bilan laughed.

"You thought I was going crazy, didn't you?"

"No! Well...yes. I didn't know what to think. I'm sorry."

"It's okay. Sometimes I'm not sure myself."

Bilan was silent for half a second too long, then said, "I actually thought about that upgrade when I saw it in the catalog. Didn't get it though. Too expensive for something I wasn't sure I'd use. Have fun."

DEL WAS BREATHING HARD, running at full speed while the uneven Martian terrain unrolled beneath her feet. She nearly tripped over an illusory boulder when she received the realtime call notification from Bilan.

"Sorry to interrupt," she said, "But I think you'll want to see this."

Del accepted the offered feed, dismissed the Martian terrain she'd been running through, and continued at a fast walk on flat ground while she watched the recording.

"What am I looking at?"

"That's the cafe at 1327-27."

Del recognized it. When she'd been there, it was empty, airless, with a large hole cut into its ceiling with a mining laser. On the screen, it was full of people, laughing and talking, eating and drinking. These were the bodies she'd seen floating in space after answering their distress signal. The thought sent a chill down her spine.

"Why am I watching this?"

"Hold on..."

She watched the image of the people, clustered around small tables, eating in the low gravity environment.

"Here." Bilan froze the playback, then zoomed in on one corner.

Sitting at a table, talking to a woman Del didn't recognize, was the man from Aluna. The Rabbit. He was wearing a BeltSec uniform over a vacsuit.

"He was there!" she said. "He's BeltSec?"

"Might be stationed in one of the outer regions," Bilan answered. "He could also just be wearing a stolen uniform to give himself cover for being there. I've never seen him at any of the briefings. I could do an image search..."

"But they'd know you did it," Del finished for her. "Which is the last thing we'd want if he is part of BeltSec. Void. Do we know who he's talking to?"

"No idea." The image in front of Del started moving again. She felt tired and had the treadmill change configuration back to a seat.

In the vid, The Rabbit stared intently at the woman.

"I know that look," Del said.

Without speaking, the woman rose from the table and walked over to a screen set on one wall. When she got there, she shouted into it frantically.

A second later a column of light, air made incandescent by a powerful laser, split the chamber. The column continued moving across the room in a wide arc. People, tables, chairs, all flew upward, the feeble gravity of the asteroid no match for the air rushing toward vacuum through the ever-widening puncture.

Bilan stopped the playback. "I'm sorry you had to see that again."

"It's okay," Del replied, trying to keep her voice steady. "I don't know any of those people. My only connection to them was finding their corpses. Is there any recording of what she was saying?"

"She was begging Jeremy Bartran to stop, I'm guessing."

"Do you have that footage, too?" Something strange had caught her eye.

"Yeah, here."

"May I?"

"Go for it." Permission to control the video feed on both screens popped up briefly. She noticed it was only video control, not full control of the suit like she'd given Bilan when Bilan had asked the same thing.

She started the two vids side-by-side, with their timers synchronized. The unknown woman went to the screen and shouted into the console. "Jeremy! Jeremy stop! Listen to me! Please, we're not in suits down here!"

Del stopped the recording. "How'd she know?"

"Know what?"

"Who was operating the platform? How did she know what he had planned?"

"Maybe he threatened before? Or she saw him out the window."

"Let's see where the Rabbit went."

Since she still had control over the video, Del backed it up to where the woman and the pale man had been sitting. She started it again, only this time, she stayed with him.

When the woman stood up, the Rabbit did as well, and left the room. He headed for a hallway that Del remembered led to a small docking bay. He had deployed his helmet as soon as he stepped out of the cafe. He knew what was about to happen. Jeremy Bartran continued his attack as the Rabbit left the docking bay on a scooter.

"He was controlling them both, wasn't he?" Bilan said.

"I think so. He must have been still hiding somewhere nearby when I got there."

"Why the woman? Why have her beg Jeremy Bartran to stop?"

"Because he wasn't really attacking," Del said.

"What?"

"He wanted people to think Jeremy was attacking. The sensors in the mining platform were all disabled. Even so, if Jeremy had been on that platform, we would have found out about it eventually. It's misdirection. The only reason to make people think he was there would be if he wasn't."

"We recovered his body from the wrecked scoot, though."

"He pushed him, but maybe couldn't force him to attack. He could force him to...I don't know, maybe wait for someone to show up, attack them, then flee?"

"Who was controlling the platform in the initial attack, then?"

"Remote maybe? Carving the asteroid didn't need any particular skill. In fact, I'm willing to bet if you asked a miner about it, they could tell you the cuts weren't made by an expert."

"I might look into that." She was silent for several seconds.

Del cleared the displays on her helmet and looked across the empty space at her. The other bike was too far away to see her as much more than a figure lying against a tall-backed seat, facing upward. It seemed to hang motionless in space, a weird illusion for something accelerating fast enough to impart gravity three times that of Mars.

Bilan's voice returned to her helmet. "You didn't missile that room."

"Right," Del said, not sure where she was going with this.

"And Jeremy didn't kill those people."

"Also right."

"Which means whatever mind control this guy is doing can only go so far. It's not all-powerful."

"Seems like it, yes, so that's good. Also, the airlock. He was trying to get me to leave my helmet behind."

"That didn't work, either."

"I would have if it had been possible. He did get me to jump out the airlock, so it's not a sure thing."

"You think it can be learned? Practiced?"

"Resisting the power? I don't know. If it can, I'd have no idea how to even begin."

"From what we've seen, trying to get someone to do something against their nature might work. A command you know someone doesn't want to do."

"Did you want to be naked in front of Jie and me in my apartment?"

"I..." Bilan started, then trailed off. "The fact is, this guy's not going to be happy that we're looking for him. He already wants you dead, and it's only a matter of time before he learns about me."

"Void. I'm so sorry I dragged you into this."

"You didn't drag me into anything, Delokita. I took the Jeremy Bartran investigation all on my own."

"Then get out of it. Send your final report. He went crazy, killed some people, and now he's dead. Sorry for your loss. Rich Earthers should stay out of the Belt. The end."

"You just said a minute ago that he didn't."

"It doesn't matter what I said. I don't know what I'm talking about."

"I'm pretty sure you do."

"What are you going to tell them? A BeltSec officer killed those people, then took over Jeremy's brain and forced him to flee so he could frame him for the deaths?"

"If he didn't kill anyone, his parents should know that."

"Why? What difference does it make? He's already dead."

"If it were you, wouldn't you want people to know you weren't a crazy mass murderer?"

"Half of Mars already thinks I am," Del said with a bitter laugh. "But if I'm dead, who cares? I can't leverage a reputation for anything once I'm gone."

"That seems a rather cynical way to look at it. How about this? I'm getting paid a whole lot of money by his parents to look into this and if you help me, I'll cut you in for a substantial portion. It'll be more than enough to cover the bills for the next few months."

"I still don't know what we're going to say."

"Let's find the truth first, and then figure out how to tell it."

"All right. Fine. I'm in."

The turnaround warning chimed, and because Del was already in her seat, she let it proceed. Unlike on the *Zheng He*, turnaround was a simple affair. The engines cut out briefly and the maneuvering rockets fired, fore and aft, for about a second. The main engines started up again with the bike pointed the other way as it began its long descent toward Ceres.

"Let's talk in person at your place after our next shifts are over."

"Sounds good. You still in on the bounty?"

"Sure. Jie says he wants to talk to us when we get there first."

"Yeah, he said he had misgivings. Fine, tell him we'll be there in about three hours."

NINE
MUTINY OF THE BOUNTY

"She's still in the room. Hasn't left since I last spoke to you," Jie said when he met them outside the docks. "You two had fun yesterday, I take it?"

As they walked, Del filled him in about how she and Bilan had taken the ship to Kenny's and found that he'd been abducted, and about their plan to use the ship as bait.

"What if they don't come back?" Jie asked her.

"Then I'll go back in a few days and figure out something else to do with the ship."

"I mean, what happens to Kenny?"

"This is my only lead to find him. If it doesn't work out..." She gave a sort of apologetic shrug.

"Tell us what you know about this bounty," Bilan changed the subject. "And what's so sketchy about it?"

"For one, she's not reported anywhere as skipped."

"Harailt said he wanted to keep it quiet," Del said.

"And that didn't strike you as suspicious?"

Del shrugged again. "He's a corporate administrator. If he was an honest person, he wouldn't be in that position."

"You know her indenture was bought by Harailt personally, right? Not by Ministoj? What kind of work did he have her doing?"

"He told me accounting. Does it matter? She agreed to it and signed the contract."

"Is she even old enough to make that decision? She's only nineteen standards. On Mars, she'd still be a minor."

"As you like to remind me, we're not on Mars. She was old enough to be an employee of Ministoj before she did whatever she did that got her in trouble."

"You don't even know what she did?"

"I know she agreed to a three-year indenture to pay for it, then skipped out after less than one."

"You're okay with this?" He asked Bilan.

Whatever Bilan said in reply, Del didn't hear it as she found herself briefly lost in another memory.

She was sitting across from Jie at a table in Rokoj.

"What do you think?" she asked him, and Del realized this memory was Bilan's.

"I've seen too many like her," Jie replied. "It's always all or nothing. They come to the Belt to die and sooner or later the Belt will accommodate them. Just promise me you won't get roped into any of her schemes. I couldn't stand it if I lost you, too."

The memory—and she was certain that's what it really was—was over in a second. A flash of anger followed it. That's what he thought of her? Wanting to die? Schemes? Did Bilan feel the same way?

She realized she had stopped walking and the other two had pulled ahead of her. She hurried to catch up. "You don't have to come," she said to Bilan. "I can do this on my own."

"I'm in," Bilan said, taken aback at her sudden switch in tone. "I already said."

Del took a deep breath. "I'm sorry. Thank you." She turned back to Jie. "Where is she? Did you want to come along?"

"I don't," he responded. He was looking at Bilan as he said it. He turned back to Del. "You won't need me. Promise me you'll at least listen to her before sending her back. And that you'll take her yourself, not just bag her and dump her in some unmanned cargo transport."

Which was exactly what Del had intended to do.

"It's forty hours each way," she said.

"I'll clear your schedule for the next four days. Better yet, I'll arrange to send you on a follow-up patrol to Hygiea."

"You can do that?"

"Level Four Inspector," he said. "The title comes with a few perks. I'll pull a couple of strings. But that's my price. You talk to her first, and escort her personally, and I'll tell you where she is."

"Ugh. Fine. I'll take her. I don't have a passenger compartment on my bike, so she's gonna be in a bag the whole time."

"Check a two-seat scoot out of the BeltSec pool. Your bike's not designed for trips that long anyway."

"It works for me. Scoots won't have the treadmill system and there's no way I'm sitting in one place for forty hours."

"Just make sure she doesn't suffocate."

DEL BRIBED the watchman at the hotel Jie had sent them to and got the key to Amelia's room.

Bilan stood to one side of the doorway, her needler in her hand, while Del stood on the other and had her suit transmit the key.

The door slid upward into the ceiling. Just as it reached the top, there was a *click*, and something dropped to the floor.

Before either of them had time to react, there was a bright flash of light and smoke filled the air.

Del's helmet automatically deployed itself and for a second she thought the atmospheric containment had been breached. They were too far underground for that, though. She rushed into the room, despite not being able to see through the thick smoke. Her shin struck something, and she flew forward across a bed which had been pushed against the doorway. She face-planted into the mattress harmlessly in the low gravity and turned her momentum into a roll to land on her feet on the other side. After three more steps she came to a large hole in the back wall. Made by breaching cord, similar to what Bilan carried, maybe. She'd have to remember to order some of that.

"Watch out for the bed," she called back to Bilan.

"Found it. Thanks," Bilan said with a tone of frustration.

Del guessed she probably should have said something sooner. "She went out the back. Smoke's clearer over here."

She stepped through the jagged opening in the back of the room, her right arm with its mounted needler held straight out in front of her. Something heavy slammed down and a jolt of pain traveled up her arm.

She turned in time to see her quarry, holding a metal pipe that she'd just smashed into Del's arm. She swung it back up toward her face, and Del leaned back to avoid the blow. It slid harmlessly off the front rather than smashing the faceplate.

Before the woman swinging the pipe could bring it down on her again, Del bent low and launched herself forward, tackling her at the waist. Assisted by suit thrusters, she pushed up off the ground and carried her forward to slam into the far wall.

The metal bar fell to the floor.

"Hold her there, I got her," she heard Bilan say. "Three... Two...One..."

Her assailant went limp, right on time.

Del stood upright and let her fall to the floor. She resisted the urge to kick her. In the corridor, the smoke had mostly dissipated, and Del could see her clearly. There was no doubt it was Amelia. Her bright red hair was the same as in the picture. She looked even younger in person, sleeping peacefully on the floor.

Del quickly looked around. There was no crowd gathered. It wasn't that kind of place. If anyone heard the commotion, they were hiding in their rooms, avoiding any entanglements with the authorities. Good for them.

"That's gonna be some paperwork," Bilan said, indicating the damage to the room.

"We'll add it to her bill," Del said, nudging her unconscious prisoner with the toe of her boot.

"You wanna secure her while I check out the room?" Bilan asked.

Del nodded. "Careful. We don't know what else she may have set up in there." She marked the area off limits on the net. Anyone approaching would get an alarm on whatever interface they used, warning them to stay away.

Then she attached a pair of binding cords to Amelia, hand and foot, and slung her over her shoulder, an easy feat in Ceres' low gravity. She took her back into the room. The smoke had mostly cleared in there as well.

"Nothing else in here," Bilan said when she came in.

The smoke was already dispersing. Del handed her the pair of grenades she'd taken from Amelia.

"She had these on her, but nothing else."

"How's your wrist?"

"I'll have a bruise to remember her by, but nothing's broken. Needler still works."

"Not surprised. Those things are tough. What are you gonna do with her?"

"Just what Jie said. Stick her in a bag and fly her ass back to Hygiea."

"Don't you want to talk to her first?"

"Not really."

Bilan gave her a look, even through the smoke and two helmets Del could read it.

"Fine. You wanna do it here? I've already marked the place off, though Forensics and Salvage will be here any minute."

"Can we take her back to your place before waking her up?"

"Yes. Let's. I'll send in my report on the way. I don't feel like staying around and answering a bunch of questions anyway."

THE ANTIDOTE INJECTOR hissed against Amelia's neck as Del applied it. Like the needler projectiles, it had built in sensors to monitor the subject so it could deliver the exact amount needed to be effective.

When it had done so, Amelia blinked her eyes open then winced in pain. She tried to bring her hand up to shield her eyes only to discover they were still bound and trapped inside the bag. The space bag was commonly used to transport prisoners or rescue civilians who had to be moved through vacuum but weren't wearing functioning suits.

After bringing her into her apartment, Del had opened the end enough to let Amelia's head poke out, but nothing else.

It was possible to live in the Belt without a vacsuit, using only commercial docks, and only visiting places, such as Ceres, that had their own contained atmosphere. But it was rare not to own at least one. If Amelia had one, though, she'd left it behind when she fled.

"Fuck you," she said as she tried to wriggle free from the restraints.

"As opening lines go, I've heard better," Del answered.

"'Where am I?' Is traditional," Bilan added.

Amelia's head turned to look at her. "I assume you're the scum that Harailt sent to get me."

"That would be us," Del said. "We're the scum."

"Pretty sure you're the one who skipped out on a lawful contract," Bilan added.

"Lawful, ha! That's rich!"

"You signed it."

"I was set up. He didn't want an engineer, he just wanted another girl for Aluna."

"I thought you were doing bookkeeping for him," Del said. "That's how you embezzled the money."

"What are you talking about? I didn't embezzle any money. If I'd stolen anything more than those grenades you took off me I'd've made it back to Venus by now."

"You get the idea that there's more going on than you were told?" Bilan asked.

"What were you doing in Aluna?" Del asked, afraid of the answer.

"What do you think?" She sneered.

"He had you doing sex work?" Bilan asked, a note of anger in her voice.

"I thought you Venusians didn't have a problem with sex work, unlike us repressed, prudish Martians," Del said.

"When it's voluntary, I don't. That's not what this is."

"No indentured work is voluntary," Del said. "How is this any different?"

"It just is."

"I'm not going back," Amelia said.

"I'm sorry. You are," Del replied.

"I'll die before I go back there. Even if I have to take both of you with me."

"That'll make a fun forty hour trip."

"Del..." Bilan started.

"I know. Void. This is why I didn't want to talk to her. Damn Jie anyway."

"Who's Jie?" their prisoner asked.

"He's the asshole responsible for your freedom."

Amelia looked confused.

"Here," Del said and sent the code to release the cables binding her prisoner.

"Wait, you can't just let her go," Bilan protested.

"If I'm not sending her back, what else can I do?" Del said, then turned to Amelia. "If you attack me again, you'll wake up bound in a space bag halfway to Hygiea, understood?"

"Yeah, got it," She replied and crawled out of the bag. "Binding me while unconscious wasn't enough, you had to stuff me in there, too?"

"Didn't have any other way to transport you," Del said. "The bike doesn't have an enclosed area so no other way to bring you across open space."

Amelia looked over at the window, and back at the airlock doors. "Where are we? This isn't a ship."

"It's a tethered asteroid near Ceres," Del replied.

"Why am I here?"

"Like I said, I promised I'd talk to you before sending you back. I take it you've arranged passage to Venus already?"

Amelia looked down again. "I had a ship. I thought."

"You thought?"

"I paid for passage and was supposed to meet my contact from the ship at Amacio's. He never showed up and now I don't know what I'm going to do."

"You paid in advance?" Del asked.

"He said that's the way it's done."

"It isn't. Nobody does that unless they're just taking the

money and running."

"How were you planning on getting them to let you land on Venus?" Bilan asked.

"I have family there."

"Family? Who? What settlement?" Bilan asked.

When Amelia looked surprised, Del explained, "Bilan's from Venus originally, too."

"Really. They're nobody you've heard of, I'm sure," Amelia responded. Then, when nobody said anything, added in a quiet voice, "Armstrong."

"Oh," Bilan said, in a tone that indicated she was sorry that she'd asked.

"Why? Which one are you from?"

This time it was Bilan's turn to look embarrassed. "Berbera," she answered.

Del looked back and forth between them. "What am I not getting here?"

"It's nothing," Bilan said. "Back on Venus, on Berbera, Armstrong has a certain...reputation. It means nothing out here, though."

"It's where the poor people live," Amelia added. "It's one of the oldest and least safe of the floating cities and nobody wants to live there."

"I thought everybody on Venus was rich," Del said.

"Ha! Somebody's gotta do all the work required to let all the idle rich sit around by their pools all day."

"It's not quite that bad," Bilan said. "But yes, not everybody's rich."

"No, not everybody," Amelia agreed. "But everyone in the great houses are. If you're from Berbera, what house are you from? And what are you doing out here playing assistant bounty hunter?"

"It's a long story," Bilan said.

Del was curious, too. This was the first she'd heard of any "great houses." *Just how important was Bilan's family? And why would she be out here if she had those kinds of connections on Venus?* "We can get into it at a later time," she said out loud. "Right now, I have some questions."

"You'll take me back to Ceres if I answer them?"

"Yes."

That seemed to surprise her. She was most likely expecting to have to bargain harder.

"Okay, then."

"First, you were at Aluna. You ever see this guy?" She put the still image of The Rabbit on the big screen.

Amelia scrambled backward on the couch, bumping against the back wall, and pulling down one of the colorful scarves Del had hanging along the wall, revealing the uneven black rock behind it. She came to a stop sitting on the back of the couch as the scarf fluttered to the ground.

"I take it that's a yes."

"The fuck you want with him?"

"You know who he is?"

"Everybody knows who he is."

"I don't. Enlighten me."

"He's...void. I don't even know how to explain it. He's the Rabbit. He knows people and people do what he says."

"Sounds like he's a fixer, like Kenny," Bilan said.

"You know Kenny?"

"Yeah," Del said. "What do you know about him?"

"He's like the one guy the Rabbit stays away from."

"Kenny?" The idea was baffling. Del would have thought this Rabbit's reputation was all smoke except that she knew what he could do. "Why would a man like the Rabbit be scared of someone like Kenny?"

"No idea. I don't know anything about Kenny and it's just

gossip says he's afraid. Maybe they just agreed to stay out of each other's business."

"What can you tell me of his business?"

"Nothing, really. He comes into Aluna a lot and talks to people, but I was never involved."

"You never overheard him say anything?"

"I've never even heard him speak. Literally never. Like, he'll just sometimes sit and stare at you for minutes at a time without ever saying a word. It's creepy. Sometimes he'll go with one of the girls, but he never did with me. If he spoke to them, they never told me what he said."

Del glanced over at Bilan. She could see on her face that she was thinking the same thing. He was reading their minds. For what reason, she couldn't fathom, but there was no doubt what was happening.

"What?" Amelia asked, seeing their looks.

"We'll explain later. Right now, just say it fits with what we know of this guy."

"What later? You said you'd take me back to Ceres if I answered your questions."

"We will," Del reassured her. "Assuming that's still where you want to go."

She looked up sharply. "What do you mean?"

"Where will you go from there?"

"Venus. Like I said. Where else?"

"I have an idea about that. You said you were an engineer?"

"Del, no," Bilan interrupted. "You can't."

"Why not? You know we can't send her back, not without ensuring she makes it to Venus somehow. Even then, if they find out I talked to her then let her go she won't be safe. Whoever these people are, they're going to want to know what we talked about. I wouldn't put it past them to send someone to Venus to find out."

"What? Who are you?" Amelia knitted her brows.

"That's a good question," Del responded with a slight smile. "Who I am to the Rabbit, I have no idea, but he's tried to kill me twice."

"Are you related to him? You look kind of like him."

"I don't know that, either. It's possible, and I suspect he knows a lot more than I do about it."

"Del? Remember what we said about projecting?" Bilan said.

"I'm not," Del replied. She turned back to Amelia. "I've got a spaceship. It's got some, uh, issues."

"You sure you want to do this?" Bilan asked.

"Why not? It'll solve both our problems. I can't afford to fix it, and even keeping it fueled would be a full-time job and I've already got a couple of those."

"What are you proposing? I fix your ship up for you and you give me, what? Room and board on it?"

"Plus a fair percentage of anything we make from using, or selling, a working ship."

Her eyes grew large.

"Or, once we know it can make it, passage to Venus."

"Void. What kind of ship is it? And what kind of shape is it in?"

"Most of the compartments will hold atmosphere."

"Engines?"

"Two of them work."

"Out of how many?"

"Six."

"What's wrong with the rest of them?"

"They don't work."

Amelia gave an exaggerated eye roll. "Anything else I should know?"

"Fuel's almost empty."

"Don't forget the registration," Bilan added helpfully.

"Oh, right, it's going to need a new transponder. The Rabbit might be looking for it."

"Don't tell me you stole this ship from the Rabbit."

"No. I stole it from the assassins the Rabbit sent after me."

"Great. A deal this good, how can I refuse?"

"That's what I was thinking."

"So, you gonna take me to this ship?"

"Er...yeah, that's one more problem."

DEL DISABLED the outside communications from her apartment before heading to Ceres for her walking patrol.

This particular patrol tended to be uneventful and today was no exception. In the bazaar, a vendor offered her a whole fresh apple, which was sufficient to distract her from asking where he'd obtained them. A ship that had reported a large theft of cargo had already departed. The produce was insured, and she saw nothing to be gained by pursuing the matter. She was making her way back when the notification came through. The *Zheng He* had been boarded.

Del quickly made her way to the side of the giant natural cavern that housed the majority of the bazaar, trying to get out of the way of the bustling crowd. When she got to a safe spot, she brought up the feed. She watched as four space-suited figures entered the ship through the port airlock.

"Bilan? Are you seeing this?" she asked over her com.

The message came back about three minutes later. By then, the intruders had made their way to the bridge.

"I see them," Bilan's message said. "Doesn't look like they've gotten it moving yet. My shift ends in three hours. Want to meet back at your place and come up with a plan then?"

"Sounds good. I'll be done in an hour. I'll check on our friend and see you there."

"Might want to stop by supply and pick up your new missile," Bilan said. "Just in case."

It couldn't hurt, and two hours later Del was back in her apartment.

Amelia was still there, sitting on the couch watching the view screen. She sat up when she heard the airlock cycling.

Del smiled and waved at her through the airlock window, making sure the lights on the inside of her helmet were on so Amelia could see her face.

"Oh good, you didn't just strand me here to starve to death alone," Amelia said when she entered.

"This is my home," Del replied.

"It was a joke. I've been going out of my mind with boredom. Seems you disabled the net from here?"

"Didn't want you calling out."

"What did you think I was gonna do?"

"I don't know. Maybe change your mind and go back to Harailt."

"That'll never happen."

"Good. I also didn't want you deciding to maybe buy your freedom by telling the Rabbit where I live."

Amelia was quiet then for a second.

The thought had crossed her mind at least. Del didn't blame her. She'd have thought the same in her place. At least they understood each other.

"I heard from the ship," she said. "They found it. I'm going to wait a couple hours for Bilan, then head out there to see where they're taking it. Four people, heavily armed. If you want in, now's your chance."

"Sounds awfully dangerous."

"Probably is."

"What other choice do I have?"

"I could take you back to Ceres. You'd be no worse off than you were when I found you."

"And no better, either. I'll come with you, help you deal with the bad guys, and see what I can do with this horrible ship of yours."

Del tried to pull up the signal from the *Zheng He* while they were waiting, only to discover it had stopped transmitting half an hour ago.

"Void," she said. "They disabled the transmission." She backed up the recording.

The four figures remained together while they were searching the ship. Del wished she could hear what they were saying, but they remained in vacsuits even in the pressurized sections. She assumed they were speaking over their own coms.

They made it to the bridge, and one of them went to a console and popped open a panel. The figure reached inside and a second later everything went dark. Del couldn't see what he had done inside the console.

"If only they'd waited til they were underway before turning everything off. We might have been able to tell which way they were going. Too bad my backup didn't work."

"No offense, but what you described wouldn't have tricked anyone but complete amateurs," Amelia said. "Looks like they just reset the ship to its default settings. That's what I'd've done if I was planning on stealing it."

Del raised an eyebrow.

"Engineer, remember?"

"Any idea how we can ever find my ship again?" Del asked.

"You're BeltSec. Can't you just flag it so it gets stopped when it docks?"

"Wouldn't work if they change the transponder before they

dock. Also, I don't really want BeltSec to know about this. It'd raise too many questions that I'm not interested in answering."

"And you can't access it remotely?"

"The only system I could access were the coms. Bilan says that's by design."

"Makes sense. Wait, if it's a different system, can you try sending a signal through it? Enable your console, let me log in and I'll see if I can see anything."

Del looked at her skeptically.

"I'm not going to try anything, I swear. Look, you didn't sell me out when you could have, I'm not going to sell you. We might be able to trace the origin of a signal."

"All right, but if you..."

"Yeah, yeah, shove me in a bag and sell me back to Harailt. I know."

Del released the console, giving Amelia access under her own identity.

"Give me a few minutes to set this up. I want to make sure everything works before we try the ship, just in case they notice anything."

Fifteen minutes later she was set up and Del sent her a simple message. "Hi! This is a message. How long does it have to be?"

"That should be good."

A second later, the console pinged and Del saw her message, relayed through the ship.

"And there it is! Excellent!" She pulled up an analysis of the message she'd set up, showing all the nodes it had been relayed through.

"Beautiful. Let's keep doing that every half hour or so and each one should give us a bit more accuracy. We should leave soon to find it, though."

Del called Bilan to fill her in on the situation. "Any chance you can get here earlier than planned?"

"Sorry, no. Go ahead and go, though. I'll just do a high-G burn and catch up to you."

"Right." She turned to Amelia. "Ready to get back into your bag?"

"It's my favorite way to travel," Amelia said with a resigned sigh.

Del unlocked the interface in the bag itself. "You can talk to me, or whatever you need to, now."

An hour into their journey, Del got a message from Bilan that she was accelerating at over two G to catch up to them.

The *Zheng He* hadn't made it more than half a million kilometers before they caught up to it. It was no longer accelerating.

"There she is," Del said when they got close enough for visual.

"Whoa! That's a long-haul freighter," Amelia's voice sounded excitedly in her helmet. A cable ran from each end of the bag to Del's bike. With both ends attached it made a passable hammock as the tiny craft accelerated. "Ship like that's designed to have entire families on it for years. Even in its current condition it's worth a fortune."

"I'll be glad to have it back then. Of course, it'll be another fortune to fuel it up."

"How do you want to do this?" Bilan asked from her own bike that was still decelerating to match their speed. "Chances are, they're armed, and they'll see us coming before we get there."

"Yeah, and I probably won't be able to open the cargo door from the outside if they've reset the security," Del replied. "So... go in through the port airlock like I did last time. Breach any door we have to and worry about repairing and re-pressurizing anything later."

"Great. More damage for me to fix," Amelia complained.

"What do you suggest?"

"If you're gonna burn your way in, go through doors. They're both easier to breach and easier to repair than the hull and they never have important subsystems routed through them."

"The smoke bombs probably won't be any use, since we'll mostly be in vacuum." Del said. "Aside from them, I've got my needler and my...uh...you know."

"Can we rely on that?" Bilan asked.

"No."

Bilan continued. "I've got the snake rifle, my needler, and about twenty meters of breeching cord."

"What's a snake rifle?" Amelia asked with a barely-suppressed laugh.

"Fires a bunch of mechanical snakes," Del answered. "They're kind of a longer, slightly smarter version of the restraint cables you're familiar with."

"And what's this secret weapon?"

"It's not important. It may help, it may not. It's never been tried in combat before."

"With any luck, the ship'll be empty and it's just on autopilot to wherever they're sending it," Bilan said.

"Wanna bet that's the case?" Del asked.

"Not a chance."

Amelia didn't press about the "secret weapon," so Del continued. "Not a lot of resources, against four heavily armed people. The ship's not accelerating, so that makes everything easier. I'll hit the airlock with Bilan and drag you along with us. I'll send the bike around on remote - if they're still there, they'll likely be on the bridge. Either way, that's our destination. I'll have the bike ready to missile it if we need to."

"They'll almost certainly see us before we reach them,"

Bilan said.

"You still have access to the coms, right?" Amelia asked.

"Yeah, but we know where they are now," Del answered.

She could almost hear Amelia's expression from where she was. "The coms include sensors. We're close enough to operate in realtime now. Give me a minute and I'll see what I can do."

"All right," Del said and increased the engines to slow down even more.

Bilan did the same.

A few seconds later, Amelia responded. "Yep, there they are. Two on the bridge, fully enclosed in their vacsuits. The other two lounging in the starboard cabins. Both wearing vacsuits with their helmets off."

"Excellent. So, what do we think? Port airlock?" Del asked her two companions.

"I might be able to set up a feedback loop to overload the sensors so they can't see us," Amelia said.

"That should help," Bilan said.

"Of course, we won't be able to see them either."

"We know where they are, so it still gives us the advantage," Bilan said. "I say go for it."

Del nodded, then said "Yes," realizing they wouldn't be looking at her.

While Amelia worked on the sensors, Del released the bag from her bike and got a longer towline to clip one end to her belt, letting the other drift behind her. She could reel her in as they went, but still keep her out of immediate danger.

"Of course, they still outnumber you two-to-one, and have better weapons."

"Don't worry," Del said. "If we both get killed, they'll probably need an engineer, too. Tell them you were a prisoner. Maybe they'll let you join them long enough to escape, or decide you want to stay. Whatever."

"Or maybe they'll open up the bag to see what's in there without making sure it's surrounded by air first. Or just leave me in there until I run out of food and water and die."

"Best hope that doesn't happen, then."

Amelia sighed. "Sensors are offline. Now's the time to go."

"*Shanso, Estu sinjorino,*" Del said, in an invocation to the Martian goddess of luck, then activated her suit thrusters. Bilan followed a second later.

Bilan laid the breaching cord around the door.

One more repair to make, Del thought. When she sent the signal, the door flew silently off into space, which meant that whoever took the ship had pressurized the port hallway but had not repaired the inner door.

"Well, they're gonna know something's going on," Bilan said.

"Let's get to them before they figure it out," Del said, and pushed her way into the ship using her vacsuit thrusters. "Maybe we'll get lucky, and they'll come checking one by one."

"That's what they usually do in the vids," Bilan said.

Del pulled the bag into the corridor, then left it to drift behind her again as she made her way upward. The port pressure door to the bridge was closed. She peered in through the window and a figure in a large vacsuit pointed a weapon right at her face.

"Gun!" she shouted as she ducked to the side. As soon as she was out of view of the window, she pushed herself up toward the ceiling, hoping that it was the least likely place for him to aim if he was stupid enough to shoot through the wall. Assuming the weapon he was using was even powerful enough to do so. It was, unmistakably, another slug thrower and that more than anything convinced her these people were tied to the Rabbit.

"Blow it?" Bilan asked, approaching the door low and close

to the wall, the spool of breaching cable still in her hand.

"Hold on. I wanna try something first."

Bilan pushed back and readied her weapon.

Del peeked through the window and again faced the suited figure. This time, she could see him clearly. His helmet was pressed up against the window, looking out. He pushed away from it and raised his weapon. Del thought at him as strongly as she could:

DROP THE GUN. OPEN THE DOOR!

She pulled away from the window again before he finished aiming his weapon and again launched to the ceiling.

For a long second nothing happened.

"I don't think that—" She was interrupted by the door sliding open.

A rush of air blew the man right past Del, where he slammed into the opposite wall and careened down the corridor, flailing limbs and bouncing off walls. His weapon, along with a cloud of loose debris, blew out of the doorway behind him and followed the only direction to go.

The bag holding Amelia was buffeted at the end of its tether and slammed against the wall.

"Hey!" she shouted. "What the void?"

"Hold on!" Del replied.

"What's going on out there?"

Bilan was quickest to recover. She leveled her rifle at the space-suited man desperately trying to regain his balance.

He grabbed a hand-hold in the wall and grasped it tightly against the wind.

Bilan fired and half a dozen long cables flew toward him. As they hit, they wrapped around him, seeking limbs and torso to hold tight. His hand was pulled free from its hold, and he bounced again and shot out the airlock, both arms held tightly against his side.

"One down," Bilan said. "We can pick him up when we're done."

"Or not," Del said.

Nobody responded.

"Going in. There's at least one more."

"Wait," Bilan started, but it was already too late.

Del shot forward, setting her suit thrusters to maximum and moving as erratically as she could.

A second man was in there, and fired his weapon. The shot missed her and knocked her assailant off balance.

Del twisted, extended her arm, and sent three needles flying into his midsection. All three hit and in the vacuum, she could see the unmistakable signs of gas escaping his suit. They'd have to get the bridge pressurized soon, or he'd lose too much air.

He flailed in panic for a few seconds, then went limp.

Bilan floated into the bridge and shot him with another round of snakes. Del found it creepy how they worked. One end twisted itself around an ankle and the other end flailed around seeking something else to grab. When it had it, it looped around that as well and pulled the two ends together until the man was held tight. One of the snakes found a handhold on the wall and anchored their unconscious prisoner to it.

Del reeled in the line connecting to the space bag.

"What's happening?" Amelia shouted as she started to move.

"We've got the bridge. Bringing you in."

"If the bridge is clear, I'll bring the coms back online," Amelia said.

Once she had the bag inside, Del shut the door and tapped the control to pressurize the bridge.

"We got two people left," Amelia said from inside the bag. "They're both in vacsuits, heading this way. Where the hell are they getting all the slug throwers? Is the bridge pressurized yet?"

"No. In fact, we'll probably have to open it again in a minute here."

Del slid over, grabbed an end of the bag holding Amelia, and tugged it toward the back of the room and pushed it behind a large bank of machinery.

"Here. Stay down."

"There's no maneuvering in this thing," Amelia retorted.

"Good."

"They're at the door. They've got breaching cord," Bilan called out.

"Are they deploying it?" Del asked as she shot back over to a console, trying to keep an eye on the door.

Bilan had taken up a position on the ceiling, her snake rifle in one hand and needler in the other. The rifle didn't need good aim to work.

Del shot herself back over to the center console. "Tell me when they're about two seconds from finishing."

For a second, she'd thought about just letting them blow the door, but didn't want to damage it. They already couldn't seal the port corridor now. They were running out of pressure doors.

"Also, hold on to something." The bridge pressure was up to about half an atmosphere, enough to generate some significant force when Del opened the door with the emergency override. This was exactly what she did when she saw the face appear in the door's window.

"Now!" she shouted, then hit the button.

"You know, you don't need to shout," Amelia said.

Del fired her needler at the center of the figure now tumbling away from the door.

She was about to fire a second time, but Bilan flew in front of her. She was riding the rushing air and her own suit thrusters to land on the man hard with both feet.

He spun and flew away from them, smashing face-first into the wall.

Bilan fired her rifle at something out of Del's line of sight, then pushed back, flying against the rapidly diminishing wind, back into the room.

The man she kicked spun around, turned toward them again, flailing in panic as air rushed out of his helmet. He must have cracked it when he hit the wall. The hand that he had pressed against it was pulled back and down by the snake wriggling around it. He went limp as his eyes boiled and Del couldn't suppress her urge to look away. He would be dead in seconds and there was nothing anyone could do about it.

In vacuum now, Bilan pulled the other man, squirming but held tightly by the snakes, into the bridge and closed the door behind them. Del started pressurizing it once again. The air reserves were getting dangerously low.

At last, she opened her helmet and let Amelia out of her bag.

"You're up. Can you figure out where we're going?"

Amelia moved to the console.

"I can see the logs, but navigation's locked out."

"Can we do the same trick they did? Reset the protocols?"

"If we just wanted to control the ship, sure, but not if you want to read what's already there."

"Dammit, now what?"

"Can't you convince one of your new friends to help us out?"

Del flitted over to one of their captives, held tight to the wall with Bilan's snakes. She undid the clasps on his helmet. Less versatile than the one Del wore, but better suited to combat, with its reinforced armor. Her needler wouldn't have penetrated it if it had been set to anything less than maximum power.

Bilan checked the other one. "Still alive. Though he'll be out for a while. Should we antidote him?"

"Nah, let him sleep," Del said once she'd pulled the helmet off the conscious one. "Let's see if this one wants to cooperate. If not, we've got a spare."

"I know the drill," her prisoner responded. "You don't have to bluster."

"Good. Then you can answer some questions," she said.

"Let's start with turning over access to the ship's systems," Amelia said, from her center seat. She turned to Del, "That way, I might be able to tell if he's lying about the rest."

"Sounds good. Here." Bilan released the snakes holding the man to the wall and Del pulled him over to a console. "I'm sure I don't need to bluster about what'll happen to you if you do anything wrong."

Her prisoner released command to Amelia.

"That did it," she said. "I'm in."

Del pulled the man away from the console and left him floating in the middle of the room.

"Good. Now, who do you work for, and where is this ship going?"

"Before I answer that, what are you planning on doing to us once you have your information?"

"That depends on the answers."

"I don't know what you think you're onto here, but the Rabbit's not looking for a fight with BeltSec. Let me go, and I can set up a meeting. You could profit from this. A lot."

"So, you work for the Rabbit."

The man winced.

Del smiled. "What kind of profit? What does the Rabbit want with this ship?"

"He doesn't care about the ship. That's just us."

"What about the people from the asteroid? Are they still alive? Where are they?"

"We took 'em to the Factory. Same place we were taking the ship."

"What is this Factory?"

"Salvage yard, mostly."

"What kind of salvage?"

"The kind of salvage you don't want registered anywhere."

"I've heard of it," Amelia said. "It's got everything. Ships, parts. People. If you don't care where it comes from, you can buy pretty much anything there."

"Sounds like fun." Del turned back to her prisoner. "Do they know you're coming?"

"No, like I said, the salvage was a side job. We were just hired to take in the guy who ran the asteroid."

"Are you thinking of posing as a customer there?" Bilan asked.

"Got a better idea?"

"Get out. Cut our losses?"

"Not if the Rabbit's still trying to kill us."

"Nah, he doesn't want you at all. Like I said. He's after somebody named Delokita."

"Why?" Bilan said, before Del could say anything. She realized her mistake quickly, though, and recovered. "What does he want with this...Delokita person?"

"No idea. He wants her bad, though. Apparently, she's already attacked him a couple of times."

"Was taking...uh...the people from the asteroid supposed to be bait? Draw her out?" Del asked.

"I think so. He had some kind of score to settle with them, though, too."

"The way I heard it, the Rabbit didn't mess with this Kenny

guy," Amelia spoke up. Del wished she hadn't.

Their captive looked over at her skeptically. "I thought you didn't know his name."

"I never said that." Del drew his attention back to her. "What was your plan? Did you have a buyer lined up for the ship?"

"Not the ship, no. We were going to sell the cargo and use the money to repair the ship and use it ourselves."

Del raised an eyebrow. "Cargo? What cargo?"

"We found some stuff in your friend's warehouse."

Del turned back to the com system and brought up a view from the cargo bay. Last time she had seen it, it had been empty. Now it was full of materials, some of which she recognized from Kenny's stores.

"You people were busy."

"For all the good it did us."

"You wanted to make a deal. I think we can still work something out."

"What do you mean?"

"You got the connections on this place, right? You sell the cargo, I'll let you keep half. Drop you off there, I keep my ship."

"Half seems overly generous," Bilan said.

"You won't get near what I can for those goods," said their prisoner.

Del shrugged and looked to Bilan.

"Fine. Half," Bilan responded. "You can decide how you want to split it between your friends."

"They're still alive?" he asked, apparently surprised. Del was sick of everyone being surprised every time she didn't commit murder.

"This one is," Del said, indicating his friend who was still bound and unconscious. "And there's another one outside who should be fine. We just have to go get him."

"We still have a couple of problems," Amelia said.

Del looked up.

"His suit has a slow leak. I don't have a suit. I can't leave the bridge unless I get one. And, most importantly, it's still going to be four weeks at the current rate of travel before we arrive at our destination, and we don't have the fuel to speed that up."

Del wasn't sure what to say to all that.

"I also have some solutions," Amelia said. "I stay with the ship. It's as good a place as any. You guys meet us a few hours before we stop. We put our friends here in the port quarters. With the coms disabled and no atmosphere in the corridor, they'll be safe enough there."

"What about you?"

She turned to their prisoner. "I'll take his suit. That'll let me move around the ship."

"Sounds good," Del said. "I'll go get their friend, and a couple more bags. That'll make sure they don't cause any trouble, and leaky here won't die on us while the cabin's pressurizing. Just be careful. Call if anything happens and we'll get here as soon as we can."

Flying back, side by side, Bilan opened a channel to Del.

"It's a good plan," she said. "Except aren't you worried that she'll just cut a deal with them and fly off with your ship?"

"Not really," Del said. "If she does, what have I lost? A ship I can't get rid of anyway? Besides, I have almost ninety hours. That'll give me enough time to get to the Factory first, scope it out, and see if I can locate Kenny."

"You plan on doing that now? Let me come up with some excuse to join you."

"Don't. I'll probably be safer on my own. This Factory seems more my kind of place. Between it and Hygiea, I'm beginning to suspect the Ceres sector is the most boring part of the whole Belt."

TEN
DELOKITA AND THE ASTEROID FACTORY

Almost forty hours later, again in the Hygiea sector, Del was on final approach for the Factory. It was easy to spot. A kilometer-long asteroid with at least four more good sized ones tethered to it maybe fifteen to twenty kilometers out. Depending on how fast the whole system was rotating, there could be some decent gravity in the outer asteroids. Multiple other asteroids either orbited it, or co-orbited with it.

"Attention approaching craft" she received a message in realtime when she got close. "This is a restricted area, under control of Zono Mastro. Please state your business."

She sent the code that her prisoner had given her, hoping it worked. There was silence on the other end, and she was getting nervous until the voice came on again and replied, "Welcome back. Please accept landing instructions. You're in a smaller craft than before so we're sending you to a different bay. I hope this is acceptable."

From the tone she guessed he didn't really care if it was acceptable or not. On the off-chance he might recognize the voice the code was supposed to belong to, she sent an automated acknowledgment and fed the offered course to her bike.

Her bike dove into the inside of the asteroid, down a large tunnel to a small docking bay barely bigger than it was. A pressure door closed behind her and the bay began filling with air. Fancy.

She didn't want to walk around in her BeltSec uniform. She assumed port control was lying about being under control of BeltSec's parent corporation, Zono Mastro. The problem was, she had nothing else to wear over her vacsuit. The suit was skintight in all the wrong places.

Should have thought of that before you got here, Del, she decided. Jet black with silver piping, it wasn't exactly hideous, and certainly people frequently wore less on Ceres. It was just Martian prudishness that kept her from being comfortable in it, she tried to convince herself, as she headed out. She stashed her uniform in the small compartment under her bike's seat.

The man who greeted her on the other side of the airlock didn't seem to think anything was unusual. He was wearing a simple reinforced jumpsuit and had a needle gun similar to the BeltSec standard issue strapped to his waist.

"You're the new representative from the Rabbit, I take it?" he asked.

"That's right," she replied.

"What happened to Gim?"

"The others are still on their way," she replied, trying to think fast and not knowing what pronoun to use for this "Gim" person. "He wanted me to come early and pick up one of the prisoners."

He looked apprehensive for a moment, then nodded. "Of course. Come with me. Are you going to be able to transport him in that thing?"

"I've got a space bag."

The man laughed. It was not a kind laugh.

Could it really be this easy? Del tried to relax her mind, sense what the other person was thinking. Maybe have a flash of memory like she had with Bilan. There was nothing. It was so frustrating to have this power and no idea how to make it work.

He led her down a long, curved corridor lined with irregularly distributed pressure doors. The walls seemed made of metal. She guessed it was an iron-rich asteroid that they'd extracted most of the interior from and hollowed out instead of just chopping the whole thing apart. A sparse crowd wandered up and down and in and out of the doors, which always shut behind them. Del caught glimpses into a couple of rooms that looked like storage holds with people looking through the materials therein. Shops for stolen goods maybe? Would they let just anyone in, or was it by invitation only? She didn't want to betray her ignorance by asking questions. She wasn't sure how much an actual representative of the Rabbit would know about the place. *Did he own it? Or was he merely one of its customers? If he was a customer, was Kenny?* She would have loved to talk to Johanka, who most likely knew all about this place.

What other gems did the Hygiean sector hide, she wondered. For that matter what was hidden in the Cerean sector? It would be easy to keep your secrets when your nearest neighbor was likely to be half a million kilometers away. Not having sought these places out before made her feel like she'd wasted a year of her life out here.

The corridor continued to curve and rise until it ended in an airlock. They went through it without cycling and emerged in an elevator. She looked to her host.

"Prisoners are on B," he told her.

She just nodded in response, as if she wasn't being escorted two asteroids away from her transportation.

This elevator, like most, had the standard panel showing the gravity as it traveled. Elevators between tethered asteroids usually had a zero-G spot in the middle where the passengers could turn around so as the gravity grew again their feet would be facing the right direction. The arrow in the panel never changed direction, though it shrank to a tiny fraction of its original size. She looked up at the immense central asteroid approaching. Of course. They weren't passing through the middle, they were stopping in it. Her guide had said the prisoner was on a different rock. She wondered if the one she had landed on was all docking bays and the others had to be reached through different elevators.

The elevator went up into a short tunnel and stopped. The door opened up into the largest space dock she'd ever seen. Above a transparent ceiling, a dozen ships, most of which were larger than the *Zheng He*, were being worked on by scores of vacsuited workers.

"Impressive, isn't it?" her guide said. "I forgot you hadn't been here before."

"Yeah, it really is," she replied. She suspected this place could easily supply her with all the parts she needed and refuel her ship to boot. If she could meet their price, which she almost certainly could not.

She followed, pulling herself along the rail as her guide did instead of using suit thrusters. Crossing under the shipyards through an open marketplace with perhaps another hundred people in it they wound their way up to another elevator.

They were joined by a few other passengers, only a couple of which were wearing vacsuits. Nobody commented on the fact she wasn't wearing anything over hers and she began to relax. The elevator sank into an interior shaft in the asteroid at the end of the tether. The doors opened and a pair of the people riding with them got out. She was surprised when her guide did not. It went down again and everyone else left. Again, her guide held her back.

It stopped a third time and he said, "This is us." This time the door didn't open until he stepped near the panel beside it, his face in front of a lens set into the wall. There was a short friendly beep and the door slid open.

"Right this way."

He led her down a long, empty corridor carved from black rock, left rough in a similar style to that of her own asteroid home. She decided she'd made the right choice with the colored swaths of fabric. Without them, the look was oppressive. The lack of people, and of any markings on the pressure doors along both sides, added to the effect.

He dropped back as they reached the pressure door at the end of the corridor.

Del turned just in time to see him drawing his weapon.

She finished the turn, spinning to face him, and heard the door slide open behind her. She had to act quickly, without taking time to check who was coming up behind her. She stepped forward into her guide before he could finish the draw. He stood nearly forty centimeters taller than her. She struck upward with all her strength with the heel of her hand.

He tried to pull back and she connected with his jaw, not the nose she was aiming for. Before he could do anything more, she grabbed his weapon with her left hand and cut down hard with her right, smashing hard into his elbow.

She felt a sharp sudden sting in the back of her neck. She spun, turning her guide at the same time, trying to move him between her and whoever had come through the door.

Two men were there, dressed similarly to her guide, and both holding needlers. That must be what hit her in the neck, which meant she had less than three seconds.

She sent a mental command to her suit to deploy the

helmet, then brought up the medical module's interface while dancing behind the struggling man, trying to keep him in front of her. She had the suit deliver the antidote. She could only hope that the dart she'd been stuck with used the same drug as her own.

The two men beyond the door were both trying to draw a bead on her without hitting their friend. He twisted away from her but dropped his weapon in the process. As he reached for it, she kicked it away and shot him twice with her own.

She dropped her helmet again, reached up, and pulled the dart out of her neck and dropped it to the floor. Two more needles slammed into her chest, piercing the thin armor mesh of her vacsuit. She rolled to her side and came up onto her knees. On the way, she fired at one of the men. Then she thought as forcefully as she could at the other:

DROP THE WEAPON! GET RID OF IT NOW!

They both fell back into the room as a needle gun clattered to the floor. She heard one of them shouting something, but then the door slammed shut in front of her, cutting off all sound. She pulled both the needles out of her suit and gave herself another dose of the antidote.

The man who had led her here lay unconscious on the floor. Her head felt like it was going to split open. In training, they'd been warned against giving a subject more than one dose of the antidote in a single day, and she'd just given herself three in less than a minute. She fell to her knees and barely got her helmet open in time to vomit on the floor.

Long after there was nothing left to throw up, her gut kept spasming. Finally, she pushed herself up slowly to her feet.

These people had set her up as soon as she got here. Someone was going through a lot of trouble to try to kill her, and she wanted to know why. According to Jie, that's what she wanted, right? She thought bitterly of his words. *She came to the Belt to die.* She would have to confront him about that when she got back, assuming she survived that long. Or maybe she never wanted to talk to him again.

Right now, she wanted through that door, and it wasn't opening. That was plenty to focus her anger on right there. Remembering the elevator, she picked up her former guide, fighting vertigo as she did so, and tossed him over her shoulder. It was easy in the low gravity—about that of Mars. *When did she start thinking of that as low?*

When she got to the door, she held the man's face up and pointed it at the console. A second later, the door slid open. She wasn't sure what she was expecting on the far side, but it wasn't a large, lavishly-furnished office. A sturdy desk that may have been made of real wood stood in the center of the room. Behind it, a transparent dome stretched across the entire back wall.

One of the men she'd fought seconds ago was slumped unconscious just inside the door.

The other stood behind the desk with his weapon in his hand, pointed at her.

She pointed her wrist at him, hoping he'd recognize the needler tube as a weapon, while turning to get as much of his colleague blocking a clear shot from him as she could. "Drop it," she said out loud.

He set the weapon down on the desk and raised his hands.

She crossed quickly over to it and snatched it up, dropping her burden on the desk. Then she stepped back to the door and closed and locked it.

Her head hadn't gotten any better and her stomach was threatening to escape.

"Why?" she said, still pointing her weapon at him.

"Orders."

"Whose?"

"I think you know."

"Tell me anyway."

"The Rabbit."

"I keep hearing about this Rabbit. Who is he, and who am I to him? Why's he want me dead?"

"If you know of him," he said, "you're either very brave or very foolish to come here."

"Probably one of those. But that doesn't answer my question."

"He doesn't want you dead, if that's of any comfort. I was told to bring you in alive."

"That's interesting. The first group he sent didn't seem to have any such instructions."

"I don't know anything about that. The first I heard about it was when you showed up here."

"What does he want me for?"

"I don't know. He's paying a lot, though, so you must be pretty important to him."

"Where's Kenny, then? Did you ever actually have him, or was that a ruse, too?"

"No, he's here. He's upstairs. I'm expecting someone tomorrow to pick him up."

"Good. Take me to him."

"I'm afraid I can't do that."

"Oh, I'm pretty sure you can." She gestured with her weapon.

"No. Even if I wanted to, I couldn't. In just under a minute, four armed Enforcers will be coming in through that door. I'm afraid they won't have orders to keep you alive at all costs like I do."

She looked to the door.

"They're on the elevator now." He swiveled a console on his desk around to face her.

On the screen, four figures in what looked like combat

vacsuits had just stepped into the elevator. They all carried handguns at their side.

"I suggest you not be holding a weapon when they get here."

"I've got a better idea." She reached into the pouch, where she was carrying the spool of breaching cord, and pulled up the interface for it. She took about half of it, three meters long, and went over to the large window.

"Can you address the whole station from here?" she asked, sticking the cord to the window in a large circle.

"Why? What are you doing?"

"Do so now. Put me through to everyone."

"This won't work. You have nowhere to go."

"Am I live?" She again thought hard at him:

DO IT!

"Fine. Here."

The elevator was at its second stop; they'd be stepping out of it soon.

She spoke loudly for the station. "Attention! In about twenty seconds, all air will be evacuated from all corridors on this asteroid. I strongly suggest seeking safety inside the nearest pressure sealed room. This is your final warning."

She snatched the unconscious guard from the table and carried him to the door. Opening it, she dumped him unceremoniously on the other side. She looked back toward the administrator who was standing, frozen in place, staring at her in wide eyed horror. "Last chance to breathe," she said, gesturing toward the door.

He ran through it without another word.

The door on the other end of the hall opened and the four figures she'd seen on the monitor stepped through it. She shut the office door and sent the activation signal to the breaching cord. Soon, the circled cord glowed white hot. In the second and a half before it blew, she stepped to the desk and snatched up the monitor.

The window blew and a sudden rush of wind carried her toward it. Her helmet instantly deployed over her head and she had a brief flash of memory of Jie chastising her over it. She was almost certain that one was her own memory.

She was expecting the window to shatter as everything hit it, but whatever it was made out of was sturdier than that. A one-meter diameter hole blew out into space, but the rest of the window remained intact, even after the heavy wooden desk smashed into it, splintered, then streamed out the opening. The force of the wind pushed her into the hole, and despite trying to right herself, she slammed into it lengthwise and was bent almost double before popping through. She was still sick from both the needle's poison and the antidote, bruised where she hit the sides of the window, and she was pretty sure she pulled a muscle going through. All in all, Del had had better days.

On the other hand, her suit was intact, and she was out of the asteroid and away from the four soldiers.

She tumbled in space, just one part of the long arc of debris spewed out of the asteroid as it sped away into the darkness.

If this footage didn't bring in some good views, she didn't know what would.

"Well," she said out loud for the benefit of her future audience, "that could have gone better." Then, with a broad smile, she said, "Fortunately, I have transportation. No, not the *Zheng He*. I'm not going to just hang out here for four weeks. I can't access its controls through my suit anyway. My bike, on the other hand..."

She brought up the interface for her bike, where it was parked in its bay. She fired up the engines and directed it out of the docking bay, down the tunnel, and out into space toward her location. Whoever was running this place hadn't locked the bay doors, so they opened when her bike sent the appropriate signal. While she waited for its arrival, she checked the feed from the console she'd stolen from the administrator's office.

The video feed showed the same corridor completely empty. She panned down the corridor and saw the door to the office stood open. There was no sign of other people there, conscious or not. She backed the recording up to where her pursuers had emerged from the elevator.

The administrator approached them, but they walked past him. He was shouting, but they all had their helmets up. They approached the office door as he followed, yelling, trying to get in front of them. With the vacuum of space between her and the console, she couldn't hear what he was shouting.

When he physically interposed himself between the group and the door, one of them took hold of him and held him back. He continued to struggle and thrash until the door was finally opened. Somehow the four vacsuited people had anchored themselves so they weren't blown through the door.

The two men she had rendered unconscious earlier weren't so lucky. She shifted the view to the room and saw them both fly through in the wind from the corridor, smash into the hole she'd cut, then blow out into space.

A second later, the administrator did so as well, trying desperately to grab hold of anything he could. He slammed into the window, bent horribly, then passed through into space and flew out of view of the asteroid's sensors.

She looked away from the console then, and toward where the asteroid had gone. With the naked eye she could see nothing. But somewhere out there three dead bodies were floating, and likely would be for all time. Those bastards had just killed three people–people who, although trying to capture her, had taken some pain to keep her alive—just because they didn't want to take the time to stash them in a room before opening the door. There was no reason for it. *Who was she to them?* Any possible answers just went out that window.

No, not all of them. There was at least one person who may have answers. She just had to find him and break him out of whatever cell he was in while eluding four armed, armored, and murderous people.

"Upstairs," the recently departed administrator had said. So, the first or second level of this same rock.

She realized she was still holding the console, and it was still showing the sensor feed from inside the asteroid. She moved the window showing the soldiers into a corner so she could keep an eye on them while searching the rest of the rooms.

She started on the second level. The corridor there was empty. Either it didn't get much traffic, or it had been deliberately evacuated. She hoped it was the latter. There were a number of rooms, each with its own pressure door. Checking each in turn, she found Kenny lying on a bed in what looked like a small apartment. His bulk holding him down, he was unused to so much gravity. She scanned the controls on the console interface. She had to find out how much control she actually had.

Her bike arrived before the asteroid had finished swinging back around. The four soldiers were still there, upstairs at the top floor, in a large room that looked like a cafe of some sort. There was no way she could take them in a fight. Her needler wouldn't pierce the reinforced suits, even on its highest power. For a moment she regretted not keeping one of the slug throwers. Maybe when this was all over she'd look into getting one, just to have handy in case of emergency. Maybe a snake rifle like Bilan had used as well. Del assumed it was something she could order through the Zono Mastro catalog. Last time she looked through it, she was more interested in upgrades to her bike than in weaponry. She'd have to check what else was available once she was on her way back to Ceres. Probably nothing that would make her a match in a fight with four armored soldiers.

For now, she had a rescue to perform. The soldiers were still upstairs. They had their helmets on, and everyone around them gave them a wide berth.

On schedule, the lights of the approaching asteroid became clear. While waiting, she sent a request from her suit to the console, then used the console to grant it to herself. Now she could access all the systems from her suit.

On the bike, she got ahead of the asteroid, matching its speed. The middle floor had the same layout as the bottom one. She pulled up to its office window and was happy to see it empty. Through her interface, she checked that the corridor outside it was as well. She clamped the bike down to a pair of handholds at the bottom of the window. There were none on the window itself, of course. Standing on the bike, she laid out another crude circle with the last of her breaching cord, as far up as she could reach.

Checking that the corridor was still empty, she opened the door to the office and sent the signal to activate the cord. She ducked as a circle from the window blew away in front of her, followed by everything that had been in the room. Furniture splintered or broke as it flew through the window, leaving a long arc of debris behind her. She clipped a space bag to her belt, then dove in through the hole in the window.

She sprinted through the open door and used her suit interface to close it behind her, then checked the feed as the hallway re-pressurized.

The four soldiers from upstairs were reacting to the sudden loss of pressure and were headed her way.

Before the elevator could get to them, Del overrode their

call signal, sent the elevator to the bottom of the shaft, and took it offline. That'd delay them, but not for long.

They were already cutting through the door with a handheld torch by the time she got to Kenny's room. The pressure in the hall wasn't full yet, but it would have to do.

She opened the door.

He was already sitting up, and she rushed in to help him, dropping her helmet as she did.

"Kita! You've come to rescue me, I hope?"

"What do you think?" She pulled the space bag from her belt and activated it. It expanded out to its full size, open at one end. She handed it to Kenny. "Get in, we're on a tight schedule."

"You can't be serious," he said, eyeing the bag.

"It's gonna be vacuum soon. You wanna be in the bag or not when that happens?"

It took him longer than she expected to get him into the bag.

It took the armored guards less time than she expected to get to the room.

On the stolen feed, she could see they'd cut their way through the door from the elevator shaft, and were about to do the same to the door in the room she was in.

She deployed her helmet and opened a com to Kenny's bag. "Change of plans. Hold on."

"There's nothing to hold on to in here!"

She opened the door to the office again, hoping the sudden rush of air would blow her friends away. It did nothing. Of course. The corridor was in vacuum since they cut through the elevator door to get in here. At least she hadn't left anyone in the hall this time.

These men had already killed three innocent civilians trying to get to her. She had no illusions about what they'd do when they got that door open. Kenny would likely be stuck in the bag until he was delivered to the Rabbit. Almost certainly, he'd survive longer than she did.

She brought up her bike's interface, released it from its mooring, brought it up and turned it to face the corridor. From its sensors she could see straight down to the four men at her door. A solid pressure door that was designed to take a lot of punishment.

Pulling Kenny's bag back against the far wall, she ducked down on top of him on the other side of the bed. Just as the door opened, she armed, aimed, and fired the starboard missile from her bike.

The screen went white, then didn't return. She could feel the thud of an explosion and was tossed into the air.

"What in the void was that?" Kenny screamed. "What's going on?"

"Little bit of trouble. I'm on it," she responded.

The screen was still white. The sensors weren't coming back online.

And, she noticed, she hadn't fallen back down.

"We're still in my cell," Kenny said. "Why are we weightless? What did you do?"

"That's...uh...a really good question," she said.

She could still interface with the asteroid's systems, there was just nothing on the sensors in this corridor. She switched to the bike's sensors. It was still operative, and floating outside, keeping station with the asteroid. It was no longer firing main engines to do so, though. She looked through it and into the hallway. Scorch marks now lined the walls, all the way to the elevator shaft.

The elevator.

The elevator which rode the tether connecting them to the main asteroid, which they spun around to give them gravity.

She had aimed specifically at one of the men outside the room. His mass wouldn't be anywhere near enough to slow the missile down, though. It must have continued all the way down the corridor, and slammed into the elevator shaft, the explosion ripping right through the tether. They were now flying free of the Factory. The asteroid was heading out into the Belt on a Scio-alone-knew what course. If these people weren't angry at her before, they would be now.

ELEVEN

ANSWERS IN THE VOID

Del clipped Kenny's space bag back to her belt and headed back to her bike, still hanging outside the window. She pushed off the doorway and used her suit's thrusters for more speed.

"We're moving again!" Kenny called in a panic.

"It's okay," she told him. "We're free. We've just got to get really far away from here before any of their friends show up."

"Whose friends?"

"Whoever it was that was trying to stop me from taking you. I killed four of them in the escape."

He didn't have a response.

She slung the bag behind the bike, making a hammock the way she had with Amelia. "Comfy?"

"Not really."

"Sorry. I'm gonna burn hard at three G for a while, then turn and go dark for a bit. Hopefully they won't catch us."

"This is the worst rescue ever."

She laughed.

A minute later, his face appeared on her screen again, flattened grotesquely by the gravity. "Why...ugh...why did you come? How did you even know where to find me?"

"I wanted to ask you something."

He gave a short barking laugh. "Must be Jupiter's own question if you risked your life just to ask it."

"Maybe."

"Ask away. It's the least I can do. How long do you plan on crushing me like this?"

"About another thirty minutes. Can you handle that?"

"As long as you don't expect me to do anything involving moving. I think your friends back there helped by keeping me in gravity fields for the last week. What's your question?"

"What do you know about a guy called the Rabbit?"

There was a sharp intake of breath, then several seconds of silence.

"What?" Del asked. "What is it?"

"It was you," he said.

"What was me?"

"They kept accusing me of sending agents into the Hygiea sector to disrupt his operations there. I swore I would never do such a thing. But, it appears, I did."

"Me? I'm not your agent. I never intended to disrupt any operations. I don't even know what they are."

"You weren't in the Hygiea sector recently?"

"On BeltSec business. It was just a routine patrol."

"Why did you go?"

"The Enforcer who was supposed to go backed out at the last minute. I was next on the list. When I got there, the Rabbit sent some rather incompetent assassins after me. When they failed, he came himself. I still have no idea why."

"Did you do anything at all unusual before they attacked you?"

"I did interrupt an ambush he set up on a Rimedo corporate office, but that was in the Ceres sector."

"Oho. That's interesting. You sure he was involved in that?"

She was about to say that she had seen the video herself, but that would reveal that not only was she in his warehouse before it was looted, but that she knew he was lying when he told her he no longer had the data core from 1327-27. It would also skirt too close to the fact that she currently had a ship loaded with goods stolen from his warehouse inexorably heading toward the very place she had just rescued him from.

"Yes," she replied. "I'm positive. Why? Why is that interesting, I mean?"

"It means he violated the truce first. The one he claimed I violated."

"There's a truce?" She thought about it for a moment. "Who is he, really? I've heard that you're the only one he's afraid of. What makes you so scary?"

"That's more than one question."

"You got thirty-eight hours to answer them."

"We're that far away? Crap. Where are you taking me? For that matter, where are we?"

"You didn't know? We're in the Hygiean sector. You were on some place called the Factory."

"Void."

"You know of it?"

"I've dealt with it from time to time. Half the stolen cargo in the Belt goes through it."

"Including you, apparently."

"I wouldn't be the first."

"Get ready, we're gonna drift for a bit, then change course."

"If you let me have zero G for a while, I'll tell you the whole story."

"Thought you were going to do that anyway."

"It's not a trade, I just think better when I'm not being crushed."

"Fair enough. Here you go." She cut the acceleration and turned the ship slightly. She gave it another brief burst then shut off again. Anyone trying to track her from her initial trajectory would have no way of knowing where she went anymore. With the engines off, the tiny craft would be nearly invisible in the darkness of space.

"You planning on taking me to my asteroid?"

"Unless there's somewhere else you'd rather go."

"No, home's good. I need to check it out at least. I can arrange a move from there, assuming there's anything left to move."

Now that he had enemies who knew where he lived.

"You gonna give me your new address?"

"You'll be amongst the first to know, after me."

"So..." she prompted. "The Rabbit?"

"I don't know where he came from," Kenny started. "I first heard of him a little over a year ago."

"One standard? That's it? He seems awfully well established."

"And quickly becoming more so," Kenny agreed. "He seems to have connections everywhere and influence in every powerful organization in the Belt."

"But not you."

"No. We fought—he was involved in some illegal salvage that I'd sent people after, and even managed to pull a major heist that I was nearly blamed for. Our agents clashed several times. There were some deaths, and when things escalated to the point where BeltSec would have to get involved, he agreed to meet."

She looked out across the vast expanse of open space while he was speaking. Somewhere out there all this was taking place.

Probably the debris from their clashes still floated in the Belt, as well as the bodies of their victims. The only thing she could see were the stars, and the nearest of them was still impossibly far away compared to everything that was happening unseen around her.

"How come I never heard anything about this?"

"Neither of us is really in the habit of telling BeltSec our business," Kenny replied with a chuckle.

"I knew you by then. How come I wasn't involved?"

Kenny laughed again. "You were. Remember that big smuggling ring? Or the tip I gave you about who was stealing from Alba Corp? Those were his agents."

She couldn't fault him for not telling her. Keeping her ignorant of the bigger picture protected them both.

"You fought him back and forced a truce. Why's he want me dead now? Has he been targeting anyone else who's worked with you?"

"Not as far as I'm aware. And if there were a widespread attack on my agents, I would be aware."

"What makes me so special? For that matter, what makes you so special? Surely there are other fixers in the Belt. Why are you the only one this Rabbit is afraid of?"

He was silent again for a long time. "I'm...afraid the answer to that is difficult to give in a way that you would both understand and believe."

"Is it because you're a telepath like...him?" She almost said "me," but switched at the last second. If he didn't know what she was talking about, she could play it off as a joke.

"What...what do you know about telepaths?"

"Only that they're more common than one might think," she said.

"More common..." He started, then was silent for a moment. "Your voices."

Dammit. She didn't want to admit it yet.

"We were talking about you," she said.

"Then no," he answered. "I'm not one. It would be an awful handy ability in my line of work, though, and I've recently begun to suspect that's why the Rabbit has been so successful so quickly."

"So, why is he afraid of you?"

"I believe he is, as you say, a telepath. I think not only can he read people's minds, but he can implant suggestions, and do it in such a way that people think the ideas are their own." He paused for a second. "Is that how it works?"

She thought for a moment before answering. He obviously knew, or suspected strongly enough that he was willing to discuss it openly. She'd always been straight with him in the past and so far, it had worked out. "I think so," she responded. "I'm still working on figuring it out myself. I've had more success implanting suggestions than reading minds."

"Are you still taking your meds?" he asked.

She realized she had been.

"Void! Do you think they interfere?"

"Almost certainly."

"But they're for neurotic asynthesis, not telepathy."

"They seem to block your telepathy, though. If I had to guess, and assuming you didn't know about this last time we spoke, the reason you heard him suddenly isn't because there's anything wrong with the meds you're on, but because you finally encountered someone projecting through them instead of the usual background murmur that you always hear."

"You're making some pretty detailed assumptions here for someone who didn't know anything until pretty recently."

"Not really. The clues are all there. The missing piece to assemble them is merely accepting the existence of telepaths to begin with. I wonder how many other people grew up on Mars with this same ability and were treated with the same drugs? Or, more to the point, figured out what was going on and learned to hide it?"

"Void. And you think that's what this Rabbit is?"

"Maybe. Though I'm not sure Mars is the only source of such people. They have rabbits on Earth, too."

"Isn't that where all animals come from originally?"

"And possibly telepaths. But this one, and you...is it possible you have relatives you've never heard of?"

She had never told him anything about her past, about how the Martian Authority found her as an unregistered infant, alone on a stolen ship that had entered Martian orbit.

"Very likely. Do you think this guy might be related? That it's genetic?"

"I'd be very surprised if it was not. Which means there may not be that many of them. But look at him. He could be your twin brother."

“Yeah.” She almost said Bilan’s name but decided to leave her out of it. “I noticed the same thing. I don’t know of any other genetic relations, but it’s possible.”

"When you get me home, I'm going to give you coordinates for an asteroid. I've never been there myself, and everyone I know who has gone has died, but you might want to check it out."

"Sounds mysterious. Perhaps I'll do that. Speaking of mysterious, you're still dodging my question. We've still got almost forty hours together with nothing better to do, so I'm not going to be dissuaded."

He laughed out loud. "You're going to have to remind me. What question?"

"Why's he afraid of you?"

"Ah, yes. His power to control people..."

"Yes?"

"I seem to be immune to it."

"Immune? Like he tries to control you and it doesn't work?"

"Exactly that. With other people, his—it's weird to say, but telepathic suggestions—seem to be overwhelming compulsions. To me, they're merely suggestions. Suggestions which I easily ignore. I have no idea why."

"Interesting. I have an idea about that."

"I'd love to hear it."

"I was describing it to...a friend...recently that when it works, it's like you just know the right thing to do."

"Yes?"

"When was the last time you did something simply because it was the right thing? Regardless of how it benefited you?"

"You're saying I'm safe because I'm an antisocial criminal."

"That's one way to put it."

"Ouch. But you're not wrong."

Neither of them said anything for several seconds, then she asked, "Could his network be splintering?"

"With someone like that in charge, I don't see how. Why?"

"There seemed to be two different factions on the Factory. Both of whom were after me, but with contradictory orders."

"That is interesting. I'll have to look into that."

"The ones that were trying to kill me were wearing BeltSec uniforms. Could BeltSec actually be involved?"

"Gee, if only I had someone in BeltSec I could ask to look into that for me," he replied.

"Hah! They barely tell me what I need to know, let alone anything beyond. If there's a conspiracy within the corp, nobody's tried to recruit me into it."

"Would you tell me if they had?"

She thought about her answer. "Probably. Might as well profit from both sides."

"That's my Kita," he laughed.

They were silent for some time as they continued drifting through space.

When he spoke again, it was in a different tone altogether. "Can you give me access to the net back here? I want to talk to a few people, and check on the status of the world since I've been out of it."

As he spoke, the request showed up on her interface. She immediately granted it.

"Thanks," he said.

"No worries. I'm gonna do the same, then get some sleep. Let me know if you need anything. I'm going to turn the acceleration back on in a couple of hours. I'll keep it down to one G."

"Still too much. I look forward to getting home."

"I can give you a ride to your new place if you need it. I suspect we both have a vested interest in dealing with this guy."

"Agreed."

When they'd closed the connection, she recorded a message for Jie. "I just wanted to let you know I'm still alive, and on my way back to you." She paused for a moment and looked over her shoulder as if Kenny would be listening in. In a bag, surrounded by vacuum, hanging back by fifty meters of cable, there was no way he could hear her without the coms being attached.

"Also, that thing you insisted I do?" she continued. "I did. I admit, you were right. So...uh...the package was not delivered. Everything's good. See you soon. I owe you a drink." She sent the message and then opened a new one to Bilan.

"Hi!" She started the message as cheerfully as she could manage. "I'm heading your way. Gonna make a quick stop first to drop off our friend at his place. Wanna meet up for drinks when I'm done?" She hoped that would be enough to let her know she had found Kenny.

When that was sent, she realized she needed to warn Amelia what she was heading toward.

"I've retrieved the package," she said in the message, "Unfortunately, there were some...issues." She didn't know how to say it so that Amelia would understand what happened but anybody else who saw the transmission would not. She decided to just say it plainly. "They were not quiet issues. They, uh, know I was there and aren't very happy about it. What would it take for you to change course, and go somewhere else?"

About ten seconds after she'd sent her message, the reply came back. Amelia was in the same space suit, floating in the cockpit in zero-G.

"Change course? It's possible, it's just a matter of how fast we can go. The question is where? I could take the ship all the way to Earth if you want, but it'd take the better part of three years to get there. We can sell our goods at the Factory and refuel as well. Know anywhere else that that's true? Because I don't."

Del didn't either, of course. There was only one solution that she could think of, and she didn't like it.

"If that ship docks with my name attached in the registry..."

"That's what I was thinking," Amelia replied a few seconds later. "I didn't want to be the first to suggest it, but do you want to transfer ownership to my name? They may not check at all. But there's a good chance they do, especially now."

Either way, there was a risk she'd lose the ship. But one way put Amelia in less danger. She sent the codes to the appropriate places and transferred ownership.

"Good luck," she sent back. "You sure you want to do this, though? It's not too late to just come pick you up and abandon the ship, or set it on some slow course somewhere else until we decide what to do with it."

"I think we can do it. I've been talking to Cor—that's one of our prisoners. He's done business at the Factory, and I think we can work with him."

Great. Now Amelia had an ally on the ship that Del had just given her. She would be surprised if she ever saw either of them again.

She was about to call Kenny again when she got a return message from Jie. He was walking along a busy corridor on Ceres.

"If you aren't escorting your bounty, what are you doing in the Hygiean Sector? I hope you aren't causing any trouble. That's not why I arranged for you to go."

Oops. She had forgotten that she'd never filled him in on their plan.

"It's related," she messaged back. "It's kind of a long story, though. I'll tell you the whole thing when I get back. What about Johanka?"

"I look forward to talking to you when you get back then," the reply came ten minutes later. "You might want to hold off talking to Johanka, though. She wouldn't tell me anything and seemed pretty angry at you for stealing her patrol. I didn't mention the bounty, though she seemed to be expecting one and would probably be annoyed at the least to think you not only poached it from her but then let the subject go."

"Hey, it was your idea to let her go," Del started her reply angrily. "And I didn't 'take' the patrol. She canceled, and dispatch offered it to me." She was perhaps a little more curt than she'd intended, but she hadn't forgiven him yet for the memory she'd seen in Bilan's mind.

IT WAS NEARLY ten hours later when the message from Bilan woke her up. She'd been sleeping, lying in her seat, after a long run then a quick lunch, floating at zero-G to give Kenny some rest as well.

"Sorry I took so long to get back to you," Bilan started. "Things have been a little...interesting around here recently. Let me know when you've reached our friend's place. I look forward to sharing a glass of your favorite rum at Rokoj."

That was confusing. Del hated rum. Bilan had to be trying to tell her something, but Del had no idea what. Perhaps the message was simply "beware."

She just replied with a quick "Sounds great! See you there!" to let her know she'd at least received the message. She still had nearly twenty hours to figure out what it meant and what to do about it.

"How are you thinking of taking down this Rabbit once you do get back?" Kenny asked the next time she spoke to him.

"I could take a few people to Aluna. Once he sees me walking back in, he'll probably show up again to see what's up. Then I'll pop a couple needles in him and haul his ass halfway back to Ceres."

"Halfway back?"

"Accidents happen."

"That sounds a little out of character for you."

"That's why nobody will question me."

"Seems a waste."

"What - to dispose of him? Got a better idea? I'm not real keen on the unnecessary killing thing, but I'm not convinced it's unnecessary."

"You're probably right. It may not be that easy, though. What'll you do if he has backup?"

"I'll have backup too. Hell, we can flash our badges and that might be enough to convince them to back off. Certainly, it'll keep any of the bystanders from trying to be heroes."

"I'll leave the planning up to you. I'll supply whatever intel and support I can."

"Speaking of, this might be of some use to you." And she sent him the access permission.

"Access? To what?"

"Administrative systems to that asteroid I pulled you out of. Sensors, doors, and so forth. Dunno if it extends beyond that, or if it's any good now that it's floating freely through space."

"Seriously? Do you have any idea what this is worth?"

"To someone who knows how to use it? I imagine quite a bit."

"How did you even get it?"

"Administrator gave me access. Didn't have time to give it back before they spaced him."

"They spaced him? Not you?"

"Remember what I said about factions? You have access to the video feed. Check it out yourself."

She looked up at the screen and he was already doing just that. Still didn't trust her.

"While you're playing with video, here," she sent him her suit's sensor feed along with the bike's. "This should provide some fun for whoever you sell that to if you want to edit it."

"You sure you want to make this public?"

"Why not? The deaths were clearly self-defense, and since the whole Factory's illegal, I didn't break any laws there."

"What about the Rabbit?"

"I'm sure he's getting a complete report soon if he hasn't already. There were a lot of witnesses, even with his goons' attempts to cover them up."

"He's going to be pissed at you."

"He's already trying to kill me. How much angrier is he going to get?"

"I thought you said the administrator wanted you alive."

"But the other group didn't."

"You sure they were working for the Rabbit, too?" he asked.

She had assumed that. Unlike the administrator, they never said so. "Come to think of it, no. They didn't do a lot of talking."

"You might want to look into whatever internal resources you have," Kenny said. "If they were actually BeltSec, this could spell trouble for both of us. I would be very interested in any information about them." Which meant he'd be willing to pay a good deal. Good to know, especially since she wanted the answer, too.

HE PASSED her the edited video half an hour before they arrived at his home. He'd spliced in the surveillance video with that from her feed. He'd also cut it into three pieces, which he explained he planned on pricing consecutively higher.

"Home sweet home," she said, cutting the acceleration.

"Finally!" Kenny said. "Thank all your gods."

When they were inside, he checked his inventory and found the warehouse chamber had been picked through. He led her through the door.

She pretended to be surprised at its existence. She still wasn't sure if she should tell him where everything really was. He'd probably pay a fair bit to get it all back, and it would be safer than dealing with the Factory. The problem there was that the ship didn't have enough fuel to make it back here, at least not in any reasonable time. And the only place she knew of to get the amount of fuel they needed was the Factory.

"Fortunately, I already moved everything of real value," he continued.

Like the data core, she thought. *And my missile*. Neither of which he'd mentioned to her. Suddenly she didn't feel bad about not telling him where all his thrice-stolen merchandise had ended up.

He was searching through one of his many cabinets and finally pulled a small metal cylinder that Del recognized as a data core. He tossed it over to her and she caught it, then looked it over.

"What is it?" she asked.

"Logs from a former agent of mine. It's the location of someone known as The Veteran."

"The Rabbit? The Veteran? Doesn't anyone use names?"

"Good question, *Delokita.*" He stressed her name.

"All right," she conceded the point. "But why do I want to find this Veteran?"

"Because there have been rumors about him since I first arrived in the Belt. And because whatever you have heard about me, the Rabbit seems genuinely afraid of him. His agents have strict instructions to never approach his location under any circumstance. When I tried to talk to him, he refused to meet with me, but I have a feeling he might be willing to meet you."

"And why is that?"

"One of the rumors, which I paid no heed to until recently, is that he can read minds."

He was silent for a moment to let that sink in.

Del didn't say anything. The implications were obvious.

Kenny continued. "Also, as you'll see when you review the footage, the last thing the original owner of that data core did was to leave the Veteran's asteroid, and after a short period of high-G acceleration, stop and open the canopy to his small craft. He was not wearing a helmet at the time."

Whoever this "Veteran" was, he definitely had the same power as the Rabbit, and as Del herself.

“It took nearly a year for this footage to make its way to me,” Kenny finished.

"A year...?" she asked, astonished. "How old is this?"

"I've had that core for three years now."

"Three years? So, even before the Rabbit. Why?"

"I don't like there to be anything in the Belt that I don't know about. When I first heard the rumors, I looked into them. He made it clear he didn't like visitors, so when it also became obvious that he had no interest in interfering with me, I decided to leave him alone."

"But you held on to this for three years."

"Look around you, Kita," he said, gesturing with both hands. "I hold on to everything. You never know when something may become relevant again."

Back on her bike and heading toward home, she sent a message ahead of her to Bilan, letting her know she had just left Kenny's. She had no idea what she was going to say when she got there.

TWELVE
TRUTH AND BETRAYALS

Del directed the treadmill to match her speed, brought up her Martian landscape program, and ran. She ran fast, heedless as always to time or distance. It was maybe an hour later, possibly two, when she stopped, collapsing in happy exhaustion to the now still platform. She moved her seat back into its normal position for the rest of the journey.

When she arrived back at her own little asteroid, there was another BeltSec bike clamped outside her airlock. Inside the airlock, she peered through the inner window.

Bilan was sitting on her couch, console in hand. She waved, and waited for the airlock to pressurize.

"Welcome home," she said when Del entered. "How was your vacation?"

"The usual," Del responded. "Daring rescue, thrilling escape, ran out of missiles again. Freed an asteroid tethered to an illegal shipyard. How about you?"

Bilan's eyes grew wide, but she quickly regained her composure. "Oh, pretty much the same, except mostly correlating records over the net and doing a lot of in-depth data searches. Then I was ordered to back off."

"Wait...what?"

"Zono Mastro closed my investigation."

"Zono Mastro themselves? Not BeltSec?"

"Yep."

"What did they say about why?"

"They claimed it was a waste of corporate resources."

"Wow. So, what are you going to do?"

"What would you do? I'm going to be more careful."

"You're going to continue the investigation?"

"Yep. Here, may I?" A request to access the large screen appeared on Del's interface. She granted it, and a grid of images appeared. Each image showed a different attack, including the one Del had interrupted on the Ministoj offices at 1327-27.

"I'm including everything originally reported as a deliberate attack or an act of sabotage to BeltSec in the six months," Bilan started.

"So many?"

"I had to crawl through raw reports, corporate memos, and closed records to get all these. I'm also including those that were immediately ruled as accidents by BeltSec, which is most of them."

"Immediately? You mean without any investigation? Why would they do that?"

"Official statement: 'We do not have the resources to investigate every accident in the Belt.' After all, our original mandate was only to prevent claim jumping and piracy."

"What about disaster rescue?"

"That was added later, after they realized we're the only ones flying around out there with nothing better to do. Plus, I think someone wanted to make a killing selling us space bags.

Now, check this out." She swiped the screen so all the images showing the attacks shrank and gathered at the top of the screen.

Then another series of images took their place. A dozen different corporate logos. The tiny "attack" images flew back down, each settling in one of the boxes.

"Notice anything?"

"Ministoj," Del replied. The box containing the logo for Ministoj was otherwise empty.

"Yep. No attacks there."

"You would think somebody would have noticed before now that none of the attacks happened to Ministoj."

"Officially, almost none of these attacks occurred at all."

"Good point. So, they're behind them somehow?"

"Coordinated with the Rabbit. They tell him who to hit and he finds some patsy and forces him to attack."

"Like Jeremy."

"I'm afraid so."

"I killed an innocent man."

"You had no way of knowing."

"Exactly. I should have made sure. Instead, the voices told me to fire, and—"

"Not the voices."

"No. Not voices. Voice. The Rabbit." She filled Bilan in on what she'd learned from Kenny. "Somehow, he's involved with Zono Mastro."

"That's what else I was going to say," Bilan agreed. "Ministoj was involved, which means Harailt was involved, and he directly owned the contract on Amelia's indenture."

"You think she knows something?"

"I'm sure of it. A whole bunch of messages had been exchanged between Harailt and Lakshminarayanan. I wondered about that, so I asked him."

"What'd he say?"

"That's about the time they ordered me to drop the investigation."

"Pretty damning."

"There's one more thing. Johanka didn't give up her patrol."

"What do you mean?"

"Two hours before she was scheduled to go out, she got a message from dispatch telling her that you'd already claimed it."

"That's fek," Del replied. "They told me she'd had it scheduled for weeks then canceled at the last minute."

"Not according to the logs."

"The logs are wrong!"

"Relax. I believe you."

"But if someone in BeltSec wanted me to take that patrol, and then altered the logs..."

"That means someone in BeltSec is working with the Rabbit," Bilan finished for her. "And you were sent on that patrol deliberately to set you up."

"And the Rabbit is working for Harailt."

"The question is why? What do they want?"

"Who cares? The fact that he wants me dead is enough reason for me to want to stop him. Kenny offered his help in taking him down. Seems like they're old rivals."

"That's great. Does he have a plan?"

"No, but he did give me a data core that he says will lead to someone who might be able to help." She tossed the core over to Bilan.

"What's on it?"

"No idea. I was hoping you could read it."

"You really should get a core reader. If you don't want to go through BeltSec, you can pick one up in the Ceres market. They're not expensive."

"This is the second time in my life I've needed to read one of these things, and both times you've been there."

Bilan sighed. "Let's see what secrets your friend is giving out." She pulled back her sleeve and opened a small slot on the wrist of her vacsuit. She dropped the core into it and a second later a star field appeared on Del's screen. "Looks like you have the whole ship's log here. Hold on, I'm jumping to near the end."

The image cut to the inside of a scoot, a small craft similar to the bike Del used but with an enclosed canopy. A man sat at the controls, wearing a familiar uniform.

"Kenny never told me he was BeltSec," Del said.

"Looks like there's something there," the man in the recording said. "My information may have been right after all. Good to know I haven't just wasted a trip."

Bilan switched back to an outside view and in the distance Del could see what looked like a cluster of small asteroids around a large bright object. An almost round ball of ice.

"How big is that thing?" she asked. "That much water could be worth a fortune."

"Lemme check," Bilan said. There was a loud *thunk.* At first Del thought it was part of the playback, but then Bilan shouted, "There's someone in the airlock!"

Del looked, there was movement, but nobody at the window. She hadn't heard it cycling, but also no sound of the air it contained being blown into space.

She jumped up from the couch, crouched beside the airlock with her arm-mounted needler pointed at it, waiting for the door to open. Bilan ducked behind the couch, her weapon in both hands aiming at the center of the door. On the screen, the unknown BeltSec agent continued his journey toward the slowly growing ball of ice.

The airlock door flew inward, torn out of its mount, accompanied by a billow of white smoke that filled the room. The door slammed into the window on the far side and fell to the bed.

"There's no transponder," the agent on her screen said. "It's huge, though, at least a couple hundred meters."

She got just a glimpse of four figures emerging from the smoke before there was a sudden flash and a loud repeated booming noise. A bright strobe turned the white smoke opaque, blinding and disorienting her.

She knew which way these assailants had come from, though, and fired rapidly toward them, heedless if she hit anything. She deployed her helmet as she dropped to the ground, hopefully under any return fire. Her visor polarized itself in rapid succession to precisely counteract the strobe and internal sensors filtered out the repetitive booming. She could still feel it through her suit, though. An odd sensation.

Three hazy space suited figures made their way toward her through the smoke. She tried to swing her arm around to point her needler at the one in the lead holding a rifle and found her arm wouldn't reach. She looked and saw the end of a metallic snake wrapped around her wrist, indistinct in the haze. The other end was wrapped around her thigh and slowly contracting. With her free hand she fumbled for the pouch with the cutter before remembering she'd already taken it off. It was on the couch at the other end of the room.

She felt the impact of two needles, one in her side, one in her left arm. She pulled out the one in her side and gave herself a shot of the antidote as she rolled away from the advancing figures. Coming up to her knees, she spotted someone holding a rifle. She lowered her head and launched herself at them, assisting with a boost from her suit thrusters. She connected center mass, sending them backward to slam into the wall next to the open airlock. She reached for his weapon and wrested it from his grip. It was a snake rifle like the one Bilan had used.

Pushing away from him, she turned and fired it point-blank. Instead of the mass of snakes flying out the front as she was expecting, two sprung out of the side, both grabbing her wrist, then flailing about for something to attach their other ends to. It must be a failsafe in case the weapon was taken from its owner, and she had triggered it like an amateur.

A wave of nausea washed over her from the antidote, and she doubled up. She managed to avoid heaving into her helmet, but the motion brought her left wrist too close to her ankle and the other end of the snake found purchase, wrapped around it, and constricted, pulling the two ends together, holding her fast.

One of the figures stepped forward, pushed her arms in front of her, and slapped a restraint cable across them both.

Another wave of nausea hit her as she fell to the floor. The strobe had stopped, and the fog seemed to be dissipating. On her apartment's big screen, a video was playing of someone floating through a giant cavern of ice.

Bilan was lying on the floor, motionless. Del hoped she'd been hit with needles too and was merely unconscious, not dead. There was one needle still stuck in her own arm. She rolled across the floor to try to get it out. She succeeded in snapping it in half, preventing it from pumping any more poison into her system, but there was an agonizing pain as she drove the broken end of the needle deep into muscle.

As she turned again, a boot landed on her chest, arresting her motion. Both her arms were bound with snakes, and together with a restraint cable. She couldn't move under the weight of the boot. Her wrist mounted needler was held tight to her side and even if she did get to where it was pointing the right way, she'd be more likely to hit herself with it than anyone else.

She sent the command to open her helmet. There were no toxins in the air and the pressure was solid, so it slid open without complaint. She looked up at the person standing over her and caught, just for a second, a memory of Bilan. She was walking down a corridor on Ceres.

"I am not being mind-controlled!" Bilan yelled.

She couldn't catch the response, but Bilan answered with, "Yes, this is something I would normally do, because someone did actually try to kill her."

The memory passed, and Del looked up at the man standing with his boot on her chest.

"Jie?" she asked.

She didn't know if he could hear her inside the suit or not, or maybe he just saw the expression on her face.

He reached with his free hand up to his helmet. With a snap and a twist and a brief hiss of escaping gas he lifted it off his head. Jie looked down at her but didn't move his boot. He looked angrier than she'd ever seen him.

"Don't," he said and pointed his needler at her face. "Don't even think, Del. This time you went too far."

"What...what's going on?"

"Did you really think you could rob a Zono Mastro facility, and nobody would notice?"

"What are you talking about?"

"Four Enforcers are dead. There's no coming back from that."

As angry as he seemed, the gun didn't waver in his hand. Behind him, on the screen, someone was approaching a door in a wall of ice.

Four dead?

"The Factory?"

"So you called it in your broadcasts. Did you really think nobody at BeltSec was going to see those?"

Del looked back over at Bilan. She was lying still. Nobody was attending to her.

"She's fine," Jie said, following her gaze. "She'll be asleep for a while."

"I never controlled her," Del said. "Anything she did was of her own free will. Her investigation..."

"Is over now. She'll be questioned, same as you."

Questioned. But if they think she attacked a BeltSec base and killed their people, there was only one way such questioning would go. She couldn't very well tell them she had attacked their secret facility in order to free her fixer from legitimate imprisonment.

One of the other Enforcers who had come in with Jie followed his lead and removed her helmet. She scanned the room and caught Del's eye, from where she lay on the floor under Jie's boot. Del still had a couple of tricks up her sleeve.

She looked the woman in the eye and tried to project:

SHOOT HIM! SHOOT HIM NOW! HURRY!

The woman's eyes grew wide, and she turned, raised her needle gun at the one person standing in the room still wearing a helmet, and fired.

"What the hell?" Someone barked over an external speaker.

He turned toward her, raising his own weapon, another snake rifle.

The woman who'd shot him was already moving, dove forward, rolling behind Del's overturned couch.

"Del, you're doing this! Knock it off!" Jie screamed.

When she didn't react, he swung his weapon down to her chest and fired. There was a shock of pain as the needle slammed into her sternum, barely a centimeter from his boot.

She tried to twist away from him, but her limbs were still constrained by the cables. With only a second or two of consciousness left, she pulled up the medical interface again and gave herself another shot of the antidote. Another wave of nausea overtook her and she heard a very satisfying thump from somewhere behind her. One more down.

Jie took his boot off of her as he moved toward the downed enforcer, an injector in hand. He was planning on reviving the ones she'd put down.

"Cole?" he asked. "You okay?"

"I'm good." A voice came from behind Del somewhere. "Don't revive him."

Jie paused for a moment. "Why not?"

"I think he's working with the suspect."

"That's why you needled him?"

"He was about to shoot me."

Jie nodded. "I'll leave him for now. Help me with the prisoner."

He turned back to Del. "Fine, you have the antidote in your suit. Are you going to behave, or do we have to take your suit?"

"Oh, you'd like to try that, wouldn't you?" she snarled back.

On the screen was space again. Her unknown colleague was heading back toward his scoot.

To the void with Jie. She owed him nothing. She lowered her head and activated her suit thrusters. They weren't intended for use in gravity, but she set them to maximum for a short burst. She deployed her helmet again halfway there, as much to hide her tears as protect her head. Then slammed into his shin as she'd hoped.

He fell to the ground, and she rolled toward him, assisted by another short thrust from her suit. Despite her arms being held, she tried to get back to his dropped needler before he did.

She almost made it.

He snatched it away from her reaching hand, just as she was about to close around it. Instead of using it again as she'd feared, he reattached it to its magnetic holster, then rolled her onto her stomach and held her there. The front of her helmet was pressed against the floor. She felt another set of restraint cables attaching, holding her tight.

"Get the case from one of those pillows," she heard him his voice through her suit's external sound sensors.

"From what I can tell," he said on a private channel to her, "you need to make eye contact to use your powers, right?" As he said it, one of her own pillowcases slid over her helmet. A crude but effective way of blinding her. She felt herself lifted and set on her feet. The cables holding her legs together fell off and slid to the floor.

"Go forward," Jie commanded her.

She thought of deliberately falling forward, maybe pulling him down and getting another chance at his gun, but blind and bound, she didn't have much chance of succeeding. She trusted Jie to make good on his threat to take her suit. Aside from having no desire to be dragged naked through the tunnels of Ceres, the suit gave her options she might be able to use if she got a better chance later.

She decided to try a different tack.

"Listen to me," she said on the same direct channel. "Whatever's going on, somebody in BeltSec is involved."

There was no answer. She continued.

"I'm not mind-controlling Bilan. She was helping me because she found the same thing through her investigation. The Rabbit. He's a fixer in the Hygiean Sector, but he's working on taking over Ceres."

There was no reply.

"Are you even there still? Gods and fishes, Jie! You have to listen! The Rabbit, he's like me, but far more. He can control his powers and he's expanding his reach."

She paused again, and he pushed her forward. They were walking through a docking tube. She could feel the soft give of its floor under her feet. They'd attached it, then over-pressurized the tube. That's why the door blew inward.

"Wait," she said, and stopped again. Again, someone pushed her forward. She leaned back into it, refusing to move. "No! Bilan! If you take the docking tube away - her suit's punctured and she's unconscious."

"Bilan's not your concern," Jie finally spoke.

"Void, Jie, stop being a cop for two seconds and listen! You wrecked my door. There'll be no air when you withdraw the tube. She'll die!"

"She won't die," he said, then after another long pause, during which she didn't move, continued, "I know what I'm doing Del, it's taken care of. Keep going." He pushed her again.

"Listen to her, then. Ask her about the Rabbit."

"You killed Enforcers."

"Don't be so sure they were actually Enforcers."

"They were wearing BeltSec uniforms!"

"And they'd just murdered a bunch of civilians!"

"I saw the video. The civilians died when you blew open the administrator's office."

"What? No - watch it again, that's not what happened!"

"I saw it. I saw it directly. It had been heavily edited, but the timestamps make it obvious."

"Look more carefully. I put them in the corridor, then the mercs opened the pressure door into space."

"I don't know what you're trying to do, but it's not going to work. Nobody can hear you but me. I suggest you walk the rest of the way in silence."

"The rest of the way where?"

There was no answer.

"Fine. I know you're still listening. If you don't want to talk to me, talk to Bilan. Ask her what she found. People are dying, Jie. All these attacks that BeltSec's keeping quiet are connected, and it all comes back to the Rabbit and Ministoj."

Another minute went by in silence. She was led to what seemed to be a ship and strapped into a chair. The gravity gave way, then a moment later resumed in a different direction. Jie had not spoken the whole time.

"You'd better not be leaving her there to die, Jie, or I will find a way to make you pay."

There was still no response. She couldn't see anything around her still, then realized she was being an idiot. The pillowcase covered her head. The suit had sensors embedded in every square centimeter of its fabric. She brought up the direct feed and looked around. She was strapped into one of five seats along one wall of the spaceship. The other four were all occupied, with Jie to her immediate left. They were all strapped in like her.

Jie seemed to be talking to someone on a channel she wasn't on. He likely hadn't even heard the last few things she'd said. She realized she could do that, too, and opened a message.

"Hi, Bilan," she started. "I'm not sure what's going on. It might be a while before you see this, and I'll probably be either in a prison cell or halfway to the antimatter mines when you do. You need to talk to Jie. I know he thinks I've implanted everything into your mind, and I have no idea how to convince him otherwise. But if you don't stop him, the Rabbit is going to keep expanding and I'm afraid there's going to be a lot more deaths before he's done. I may be unavailable for a while. Possibly forever, and they'll probably take my suit away as soon as I get to my cell, so you may not hear from me again for a long time.

But find a way to make Jie listen." As an afterthought, she added "Kenny seems immune to the Rabbit's power, so you might be able to use him, though I have no idea how to contact him now."

She sent the message.

THIRTEEN
BETWEEN LAW AND ORDER

Having never been past the booking area before, Del was surprised at how well they treated her at the prison. They did take her suit, of course, and gave her a sort of gray pyjama pants and top to replace it. The only adjustment was at the waist of the pants, but once she'd figured out how to change the size, it was comfortable enough. Jie warned them of possible unauthorized modifications to her suit and told them to send it to the lab for analysis. So much for all her secrets. Even if she was able to prove her innocence after this, her career at BeltSec was over. They'd find the med module and the medicine she used to control the voices. Ironically, only after she learned she didn't need them.

He didn't trust her not to use her power and wanted to accompany her the whole way through intake. They wouldn't let him. Score one for mindless bureaucracy. She wondered if all the suspects she'd dropped off here over the last couple of years had been treated this respectfully, or if she was getting special treatment because she'd been an Enforcer.

They took her to a simple room, of which she was apparently to be the only occupant. The mattress on the bed was thin, but in the low gravity of Ceres it didn't much matter. A pressure toilet was in an attached tiny room. No shower, of course—that was a luxury few on Ceres had—but the standard hygiene systems were available. There were no windows.

They even gave her a net console, which surprised her until she learned how strictly limited it was. She could request books or vids on it, but not send messages or access those sent to her. She tried searching for the vids she'd uploaded—or rather, Kenny had uploaded on her behalf—but wasn't surprised to find them unavailable. There was a request process she could go through to ask for other material, but she didn't want to let anyone else know she was looking. Kenny had always given her a copy of the edited version before he sent the vids out, but she had never watched them. She didn't even know how to find them on the net. She could just hear Bilan's admonishment about that.

The lack of messaging grew frustrating after her first day. An autovendor in her cell let her get food from a variety of sources, though nothing fancy. She checked but wasn't surprised that Amacio's wasn't one of the sources. Overall, they did everything necessary to keep her comfortable and alive, but that was it. She was grateful she'd already gone off her medication. The side effects of quitting them now would have made everything even more unbearable.

She wanted desperately to know how Bilan was. She trusted Jie not to just let her die—not that she'd ever tell him that—but hated not knowing if she had been arrested or was out free or how much trouble she'd gotten herself into because she'd made the unfortunate decision to befriend Del. She never should have dragged Bilan into this. Her actions had destroyed the career of her only true friend, just like they had on Mars.

She'd give anything for a treadmill or a set of resistance

bands right now. There wasn't enough gravity to make pushups worthwhile, not that it stopped her from trying. She tried to find the old pre-spaceflight vid serial that Jie had told her about but all she could find was the 2057 "negative bicentennial" remake, which he'd said wasn't worth watching.

Why was she still taking any advice from Jie now, anyway? Void, she'd thought he was her friend.

You're not more important than the whole rest of the Belt, he had told her. Guess he proved that. Not even important enough to sit and listen to for one minute, slag him.

She spent most of the second day scanning news sites. There was no mention of her, or Bilan, or even Jie that she could find. There was no way to tell if that was because they weren't in the news feeds, or because all mention was blocked from her access. She didn't want to search for the *Zheng He* or Amelia. No reason to alert BeltSec to their existence.

Of course there was nothing about Kenny or the Rabbit. They both worked hard to stay unknown to all but a select few people.

The news she could find from outside the Belt was the same as it always was, which was why she never bothered with it. More wars on Earth, more talk of forming a new all-nation organization. That sort of thing had come up every few years as long as she could remember and always quickly fell apart over infighting, arguing over religion or resource allocation, or allowing people to move from one region to another. Whichever region was doing well at the time was always against it, fearing being flooded by people from the rest of the planet. Then, when the isolated pockets of prosperity shifted again, the same arguments sprang up again with everyone on different sides.

On Mars, yet another group of terraformers was petitioning the Martian Authority with their newest plan. Such plans seemed perpetually "under consideration." Mars had about as much chance of ever being terraformed as Earth did of being united.

Belt news was always the same as well. Some corporation had made a big find. Some scientist had found evidence for microbial life, but it was inconclusive. It was always inconclusive. Somebody else wanted to set up a public school on Ceres, but nobody wanted to pay for it. She thought Jie might like that last. He talked about making the Belt into a paradise, or at least a place where he could raise his children in peace. How was sticking her in this pit all alone with no clue what was happening supposed to help toward that goal?

Del had been fine when she was on her own. She'd had her network of contacts, and people she could drink with, or dance with, or have sex with. She didn't have to care about any of them. It was only when she started caring about Bilan, and allowing Bilan to care about her, that everything fell apart. She should have stuck with her original plan: grab whatever happiness you can out of life, because eventually you die and none of it will mean a slagging thing.

She hated being alone with her thoughts, without even her unknown vid fans to talk to while narrating her activities. She wondered if she could get ahold of a sensor system on Mercury, or wherever she got sent, and if she could find a way to sell her content. Maybe eventually even make enough to buy her way out of indenture.

Ten, maybe twenty years, slaving away in the antimatter mines and if she somehow survived that, she'd eventually be free. Free, broke, homeless, unable to find legitimate work...

She wondered what the Belt would be like in twenty years. Would Jie's dream of it becoming a real society have come true by then? That would be nice. Maybe he would be an administrator, and she could come back and cause trouble. Pull together whatever contacts she could find. Become a fixer like Kenny. Kenny would most likely be dead by then. There's no way he'd last two more decades out here. The Rabbit might. How much would he control by then? Would she have to fight him, or eliminate him to build up her own little criminal empire before she died? It would be fun trying.

Life wasn't over here. This was just another new chapter. One more change in a lifetime where the only constant was change. "God is change," she remembered a school friend once saying. Apparently, it was one of the central tenets of her religion. Del always liked that.

She was dreaming about running across the surface of Mars, being chased by something she couldn't see, and knowing that Valles Marineris was getting closer ahead of her when she was awakened by her cell door opening and the room blazing into light.

Two uniformed BeltSec Enforcers entered.

"Come with us," one of them said. They did not apologize for waking her.

They slapped a restraint cable across her wrists, binding them together in front of her.

"Where are we going?" she asked, not expecting an answer.

"Administrator Lakshminarayanan's office," the Enforcer replied.

"Then where?" Normally a criminal had a right to a trial before sentencing, though she didn't know if that was a universal rule. One more thing that she probably should have paid attention to. She'd testified at over a dozen trials in the last year. She'd never known anyone to be found innocent. Trials seemed to be mostly just to determine the size of the fine.

When she got to the administrator's office, she was surprised to see Jie there. He nodded to her escorts, and they left the room, closing the door behind them. Both the administrator and Jie wore their needlers at their belts.

"You've been offered a deal," Lakshminarayanan said, sliding a console across his desk to her. "I suggest you take it."

"Where's Bilan?" she asked, ignoring him and looking at Jie.

"This is a much better deal than you're likely to get at trial," the administrator said, as if she hadn't spoken.

"Is she alive?" She continued to ignore him. "Or did you leave her to die after you destroyed my home?"

The administrator reached forward to tap the console to draw her attention to it. She fixed Jie with a hard glare.

"She's fine," Jie finally said. "She's not been charged with anything."

"Yet," Lakshminarayanan added. "That depends on you."

The threat, as well as the promise, was clear: take the deal, confess to whatever we want you to, or we go after her, too. Cooperate, let us blow everything out the airlock, and we'll leave her alone.

She tried to think of a way her power could get her out of this and came up with nothing. She should have had the guards shoot each other on the way over. She could have the administrator shoot Jie. That might give her enough time to...to do what? She had no idea. Without a suit, and without her bike, there was no way off of Ceres for her. Every square meter of Ceres was occupied. It wasn't like Mars with its networks of abandoned tunnels where you could hide out. And if she did run, she didn't know what would happen to Bilan.

It was over. What choice did she have? She picked up the console, careful not to touch the screen anywhere it might look like she was signing. Of course, it was an indenture contract.

"Ten years?" she said, reading the contract. No mention of the exact monetary amount. She scrolled quickly through it. Having never seen one before, she had nothing to compare it to.

"What about monetary damages? There's no mention of them here."

"It's a time-locked contract," Lakshminarayanan said. "Room and board are included at no extra charge."

"What if I want to buy my way out early?"

"It's a time-locked contract," he repeated.

"That's a good deal for you, Del," Jie said, finally looking at her.

She didn't look at him.

"It means you're free after ten years no matter how much you make for them, or how little."

She kept reading it. The nature of the work was unspecified, but subject to change at the discretion of the contract owner. Amelia's probably had an identical clause there. There were further paragraphs spelling out her rights: adequate food. A safe sleeping place. Reasonable hygiene access. Treatment of injuries. All had to be provided at no additional cost. Those were usually the things, she knew, that trapped people into longer terms. A paragraph outlining punishments for misbehavior, refusal of any work, or attempts to escape could all be punished by additional time. There it was. All they had to do was tell her to do something they knew she wouldn't and she could be stuck in it for life. There was no definition of what constituted misbehavior. She would have the right to appeal to a judicial review board. She could guess how that would go.

Then she saw the clause on corporal punishment. She shuddered. Corporal punishment had been illegal on Mars since its founding, and for good reason. She had no idea it was even legal in the Belt.

"They can beat me if they want? Whip me if they don't think I'm working hard enough?"

"Only if you violate your side of the contract," the administrator said. "Or obstinately refuse to work. These are all standard clauses, and considering what you're accused of, it's incredibly lenient."

There was something about the way he said it.

"You have a buyer already, don't you?" she realized. Ten years. This had to have been worked out with a client. She had an idea who that might be.

"That's unimportant. There will be a purchaser."

"Who is it?" she asked. She set the console back down and looked him in the eye. She could read nothing from him. "Is it Harailt? Of Ministoj?" It had to be. It made sense. She wouldn't last ten years. Either he'd kill her, or she'd escape. She realized what kind of work he would have her doing and wanted none of it. This was the same thing he'd done to Amelia.

"Take the deal, Delokita," Jie said gently. "Ten years isn't that long. You'll only be thirty-two when it's all over."

Sixteen, asshole. He could shove his Earth-based years.

But if she didn't sign, they were going after Bilan. For all Bilan's strength, ten years under Harailt would break her. Better Del confess to whatever they wanted and spare her that.

Once she was out of here, maybe she could find a way to escape. Escape or die trying. She could understand Amelia. She was glad she'd transferred ownership of the vessel so BeltSec couldn't seize it. She hoped Amelia was doing well. Maybe if Del managed to escape she could look her up and join her crew.

She picked up the console again and looked at Jie. He frowned and didn't meet her gaze. She felt a new wave of anger toward him.

"Will you come visit me?" she asked. She only wanted to hurt him.

He narrowed his eyes.

"At Aluna. That's where he puts his indentures, you know. You can come watch me prancing around with almost nothing on, serving drinks. It'll be nice to see a familiar face once in a while."

Jie squirmed uncomfortably. Not enough.

"Maybe you can rent me for a night," she said. When he scowled, she added with a bright smile, "Oh! You should bring Bilan and we can have a threesome! I bet Harailt will give you a good discount for being the one who sold me to him!" She paused, just a second to twist the knife a bit more. "Better hurry, though. After his first two attempts to kill me failed, there's no telling how long he'll keep me around once he has me."

She picked up the console once again and looked for where to press her finger against it to sign.

"Wait," Jie said quietly. He looked down and took a deep breath.

She paused, not sure what he was going to say. If he tried to justify himself or tell her she was overreacting she was prepared to slam the console into his face. *How much worse could it make anything at this point?*

"Is what she says true?"

"What?" Lakshminarayanan asked.

"Did you negotiate with Harailt from Hygiea for this contract? Is he already a confirmed buyer?"

"Jie, we talked about this..."

"And since then, I've learned that certain records have been altered and that someone at BeltSec has been working with the Rabbit. I am beginning to suspect that that someone is you."

"Everything I've done has been with the full knowledge and support of the Zono Mastro board."

"I see."

"Good."

Jie turned his attention back to Del. Now she wasn't sure what to do.

"Is he telling the truth?" he asked.

It took Del a moment before she realized he was talking to her.

"I..." That was a good question. She looked into Lakshminarayanan's eyes.

He looked back and forth between her and Jie.

She tried to relax her mind, remember how she'd done it before. Nothing.

"No. I can't tell. I'm sorry." *Why in the void was she apologizing to Jie for? And did they both just reveal in front of the administrator that she could read minds and...*

"It's okay," Jie reassured her. "I believe him."

Great. Glad that was settled. Whatever it was.

Jie drew his weapon and fired it point-blank at the administrator.

"What?" Lakshminarayanan said, looking down at the needle protruding from his chest.

Del shared the sentiment.

The administrator lurched forward, trying to snatch the console away from Del, but merely succeeded in knocking it to the floor. He went after it, and she kicked it out of his reach.

Jie snatched it up.

"Void," he said. "They're coming."

Lakshminarayanan lay slumped on the floor, the drugged needle having finished its work.

Jie typed something into the console furiously. "There. Take his weapon."

She was still confused. She looked at the weapon. This could be an elaborate setup. They burst in. She has a weapon in hand. They kill her in self defense. But she couldn't imagine Jie going along with something like that. She snatched the weapon off the administrator's belt.

"Get ready. Also, you better be telling me the truth about everything."

"I am," she said.

"And not mind-controlling me."

"I'm not. I swear."

"Good. Stand on that side of the door." Finished with the console, he tossed it to the other side of the room where it landed next to the administrator on the floor.

"Three seconds," he said and plucked his helmet from his belt. At a touch it inflated, and he put it on.

Del took a deep breath. The door slid open, and they both went into action.

Jie fired his needler into the Enforcer on his left, who responded by turning and firing back.

Del launched herself at the other one, grabbing his arm, lifting and twisting, trying to push his elbow back into his nose as Bilan had taught her. The maneuver didn't work as well as she'd hoped. In the low gravity, the man's mass wasn't enough to work against him. She tried turning it into a joint lock instead, focusing just on the wrist of the hand that held a needler.

That ended up lifting her from the floor, supporting herself from the man's wrist as she tried to bend it. Finally, the pain made him drop the weapon, and Del kicked off the wall, swinging behind him. A quick glance showed that the other man and Jie both had injectors in their hands.

She almost laughed.

Both shot each other, then injected themselves with the antidote, then shot each other again. She continued her swing, then leapt in a flying kick, aiming for the other man's weapon. He pulled it away from her, but she kicked upward, connected with his other hand, sending the antidote injector flying.

Jie shot him again and he went down as Del hit the floor, flailing for balance.

The man she'd originally attacked had recovered his gun, rolled into a sitting position, and fired at her.

She felt two needles strike her abdomen and thigh. Instinctively, she sent the mental command to her suit to pull up her medical interface. It wasn't there, of course. Damn Jie for taking it away from her.

Jie was moving toward the man on the floor, his needler in one hand and the antidote injector in the other. Del struggled to her feet, found one of the needles stuck in her thigh and pulled it out. As she was reaching for the other, everything went dark.

SHE CAME to with a wrack of pain, like a crude fist had seized her from the inside and squeezed. She bent double, dry-heaving painfully, then looked around. She was in a corridor in BeltSec HQ on Ceres. Not far from the administrator's office, she guessed.

"Let's go," Jie said and half-helped, half-pulled her to her feet.

He let go and she immediately fell over in another spasm of pain and nausea.

"We don't have time for this," he said and lifted her up again, slinging her over his shoulder, which did nothing for her stomach pain.

"Leggo, I can walk!" she yelled, squirming out of his grasp. She put an arm out to steady herself against the wall as she landed on her feet.

"Walk fast, then. We need to get out of BeltSec before they get here."

"Before who gets here?"

"Everybody."

"Where are we even going?"

"This way," he said impatiently, and walked ahead of her down the hall.

"If we want out of here, shouldn't we be going the other way?" she asked.

"We need to get to my office first."

"Because they'll never think to look for you there."

"If it gets to the point of them looking for me, it's too late," he replied.

"What in the void is going on?" she asked. She hurried to catch up with him. The needle drug antidote was still wreaking its havoc with her system.

"I am rescuing you from certain doom at the hands of corrupt corporations," he said.

His office door slid open as he approached it.

"When did you decide to do that?" she asked.

"You were there."

"You shot Lakshminarayanan."

"Yes. I suppose I'm unemployed now."

That brought her up short. She'd been angry at him, even wanted to hurt him, but not like this.

"And a fugitive," she started. "Your daughters—"

"Safely on Earth. Out of reach of Zono Mastro."

When she followed him into his office, he said, "Your suit. Get it on fast."

It was there, hanging on a standard service manikin, the same kind Kenny had.

He didn't have to tell her twice. Without hesitation, she stripped off her prison garb as she raced across the room to it.

Jie sent a command to release it and she stood next to the

manikin, waiting for it to retract into itself enough to release the suit.

Jie had crossed to the desk and picked up several pieces of what looked like actual paper, folded them, and stuck them into a pouch. She stood captivated by the sight for a second, then he looked back over at her.

"What are you waiting for? Hurry."

Suddenly she felt embarrassed, standing there naked in his office, next to her vacsuit, which had slumped to the floor. She stepped into it, and pulled it on, closing seams and activating the seals. When she had finished, she looked back over at him where he'd been standing and watching the whole time.

Before she could say something rude, he put his helmet on and indicated she do the same. Then he touched a wrist control and the door to his office slammed shut. She could hear the unmistakable sound of air being sucked out of the room and deployed her own helmet.

Del opened a private channel. "What's going on now?"

"I'll explain once we're away."

Away? She looked at the window, set into the side of Occator Crater. Was he planning on blowing the window and escaping that way? What, on foot across the surface? She stood in silence for another long minute, as the external pressure fell to zero. When it had done so, the window opened. *It was designed to do that already? To what end?* That seemed like an extravagant option to build in just in case a quick escape was ever needed. *How long had Jie been planning this?*

She followed him out the window and onto the surface of Ceres. Behind them, the window swung back down. He touched his wrist again. If he re-pressurized the room, and nobody else knew about the window, nobody would have any idea where they'd gone.

Jie leapt down into the small crater. Boulders littered the

ground which was covered in broken rock. "Watch your step," he told her. "Use your suit thrusters to steady yourself if you start to fall. We're not going far."

Lights from other windows in BeltSec offices dotted the crater's steep side wall. She expected Jie to lead her to another airlock, but instead, he headed downward into the crater. He stopped behind one of the larger boulders, where a tiny space craft sat. His scoot. About twice the size of her own bike, it had a small cargo space and an enclosed cockpit with two seats.

At another touch of his wrist, the cockpit swung open, and he climbed into it. A second later, she did the same, using the handholds set into the side to pull her minuscule weight up and into it.

As soon as she was in her seat, without even waiting for the cockpit to close, Jie pushed forward on the control yoke. Acceleration pushed down on her, and Ceres shrank behind them.

When the cabin had pressurized, he took off his helmet.

She opened her own and turned to him. Before he could say anything, she asked, "Why?"

"Because you were right. Because you were innocent. Because Bilan was able to convince me that the timestamps embedded in the footage I saw were fake, not the edit itself, and because you are my friend."

She almost wanted to reach over and hug him. He'd sacrificed everything to get her out of there. They were both wanted fugitives now. She wanted to forgive him for everything he'd done. But she couldn't. She wasn't over being angry at him yet.

"You weren't being much of a friend when you led a team to arrest me, or when you were trying to sell me into a lifetime of servitude!"

"No," he said. "I'm sorry."

"You're sorry?"

Without speaking, he reached into his pouch and pulled out the paper he'd taken from his desk and handed it to her.

She unfolded it and saw it had writing on it. She hadn't tried reading handwriting since she was in school. She read it out loud as she struggled through it. It was a long list of things that had happened, ending with:

- Enforcers killed Admin? Watch Del's reaction to claim of seeing video. If she's innocent, she'll look confused.

- May not be able to salvage ZM

- Can't talk on Ceres w/o being heard

- If ZM is hopeless, they'll offer a deal - play along

- May have to flee if they catch you freeing Del

"What in the void is this?" she asked them. "If you knew I was innocent, why go along with this at all? Why leave me in the hole for days then let me believe you were selling me to be a sex slave to Harailt before my murder?"

"I didn't know. I suspected."

"How come my word wasn't good enough for you? And why is all this on paper? You had to have written this before going in there."

"I...I wrote it on paper so I'd later know it wasn't altered. I couldn't trust net records, and I couldn't trust my own memory."

"And you didn't trust me." She remembered the flash of memory she'd had the night she was arrested. "You thought I was mind-controlling Bilan."

"Some of her actions seemed out of character for her."

"Or maybe you just didn't know her as well as you thought you did." She could feel the anger rising again. Good. This was easier to deal with.

"I'd considered that, too, but truthfully I was more worried about myself."

"You? What do you mean?"

"You don't seem to understand just how terrifying your power is, Del. Ever since...ever since I watched Bilan go into your airlock, I've been scared."

The thought that Jie even could be scared startled her.

"She wasn't going to open it!"

"That's not the point. I realized then I can't trust my own mind. I've been second-guessing and third-guessing every thought. Every action. Do I believe this because it's my own conclusion, or because it's what's been implanted in my mind?"

"I didn't put anything in your thick head!" Del shouted from her seat right next to him.

"And you're not the only one with this power."

"You mean the Rabbit."

"And Scio only knows how many others. If it was just you then the power might be unique. But if there's two of you, there's probably thousands."

"I hadn't thought of that," she said.

He gave her a look.

"Oh, don't be so smug about it. If there were, how come we haven't heard of them before now?"

"Maybe we did, but..."

"We're getting off topic here anyway. Why were you so eager to sell me—"

"I was never eager. I was under orders."

"You should have broken them then! You could have refused!"

"If I hadn't gone, they would have sent someone else."

"Then you should have let it be someone else!" Why was he so damn calm? She didn't want to be the only one screaming here.

"Someone else wouldn't have brought you in alive."

"What?"

"How much restraint do you think anyone else would have

shown when you gave yourself the antidote? Or when you attacked after being restrained? How do you think most of your fellow Enforcers would have reacted?"

She looked hard at him. "I don't know, Jie. Maybe they would have wrapped me in restraint cables, stomped on my chest, and threatened to shoot me in the face."

He was silent. Then, quietly, "I'm sorry."

She folded her arms in front of her, slumped back in her seat, and stared out the window away from him without saying anything. She couldn't think of anything else to say.

"Someone else would have killed you."

She continued to stare out the window. Finally, without turning to face him, she said in a quiet voice, "You should have let it be someone else."

Neither spoke for a long time, and they flew in silence through the darkness of space.

"How does breaking me out of jail and going on the run support your vaunted rule of law?" she asked.

"There wasn't going to be any justice there. Not for you or, I am beginning to think, for anyone else."

"If the Rabbit's working with Zono Mastro, he's probably increasing their power in the Belt. Did it occur to you that that might be a way to get what you want? It could lead to a more stable Belt, and more power for you. You could do a lot of good with that kind of power."

He dismissed the notion with a grunt of disgust. "It would be tyranny."

"They say the same thing about the Martian Authority, and despite what the old songs say Mars is exactly the kind of place to raise your kids."

"I want peace, yes, and prosperity. But also freedom. If the Enforcers of the law aren't following it themselves then there is no law."

Del squirmed but didn’t say anything.

"No peace. No justice. And you only have as much freedom as you have wealth, influence, and power to take."

She shrugged. "That's how it is everywhere."

"It doesn't have to be."

"What are you going to do?"

"I'm not sure yet. I still want the same thing for the Belt, but it seems further away than ever before. I might end up taking a more direct hand in it. In the meantime, though, I thought I might petition to join your crew."

"My...my what?"

"I believe Bilan said something about you turning pirate?"

"Hah! I had a ship. I doubt very much I still do. I'd be surprised if I ever see it again."

She filled him in on the whole story with Amelia.

When she was done, he had a strange thoughtful expression on his face that she couldn't read. She couldn't read the thoughts behind the expression either, and not from lack of trying.

"Wait..." She recognized the approaching asteroid. "What are we doing here?"

"Picking up your bike and whatever else you might need."

"You don't think they'll think to look there?" she said.

"Eventually. Bilan's been keeping an eye on things, though, and so far, nobody seems to be heading this way. She's still helping them search Ceres."

Del felt guilty about not asking about Bilan yet. "You left her back on Ceres?" she demanded. "We have to go back for her!"

"She's not a prisoner," Jie said. "And aside from visiting your home, she's not tied to you closely enough for her to be in any real danger."

"They know she's connected enough to use her to threaten me with!"

"She's not involved enough for them to move against her."

Del didn't know if he was trying to convince her, or himself. "What about the assassins? She's still in danger."

"Probably less than she'd be in if she ran. This is Bilan we're talking about. She knows the risks and she's not reckless. She won't take any stupid chances." Unlike you, he didn't say. He didn't have to.

"Will the manikin fit in your hold?" she asked when they'd entered the apartment.

Her inner airlock door still lay on her bed, and she felt a twinge of anger at him for that.

"Yes," he replied, as if he couldn't tell how much this hurt her. "The hold's made to fit a person if it needs to. I've put prisoners bigger than you in there."

She went to the cupboard next to the bed and withdrew her tarot deck and its silk wrapping, and her sesquicentennial special printing of The Martian Chronicles. The two things she'd brought with her from Mars. She hoped that exposure to vacuum wouldn't hurt either of them. She tore a long silk scarf from the wall to take with her as well, wrapping it around them to make a bundle with an easy handle. She opened her back airlock, pulled out a suit of civilian clothes, and put them on over her vacsuit.

"Let's go."

"That's all you're taking?" Jie asked.

"Nothing else here anymore but bad memories."

The bundle she stashed in the compartment under the seat of her own bike, which she was happy to see hadn't been touched. Jie put her manikin inside his own small cargo hold. He tossed her a small box.

"What is this?" she asked.

"Gift from Bilan. She thought you'd need it."

Del opened the box. Inside was a data reader, and a core already inserted in it. She had an idea of what it would be.

"What's your plan now?" Del asked.

"Try to fight back. Help you stop this Rabbit guy somehow."

"You don't have to. Why not just go to Earth? Be with your daughters and their mothers?"

"Earth wouldn't let me land. Besides, the Belt is my home. I still want to help make it a place where people can live. We have the resources. It could become the kind of place to raise your kids."

"Not my kids, thanks. I shudder at the thought. If you're looking for a place to go, I probably don't have a ship anymore, but you might be able to catch up to Amelia."

"You think she'd take me on?"

"She'll be looking for crew and knows she owes you."

"Didn't she steal that ship from you?"

"If she did, I can't fault her for doing so. I have no grudge. I might look her up myself. But I want to make another stop first. If this core is what I think it is, it leads to someone called The Veteran, who both the Rabbit and Kenny seem to be scared of."

"What makes you think he'll want to talk to you?"

"Call it a hunch. But the fact that all I want to do is talk should buy me something. Kenny and the Rabbit were both trying to enlist his aid in something he wanted no part of."

"And you don't want backup?"

"No. I think bringing anyone with me will do more harm than good."

"Good luck, then."

"One more thing before we go." She found the record she wanted and sent it to him. "Here's the coordinates of an abandoned house asteroid I encountered earlier. We can use it as a rendezvous spot if all else fails."

"Thanks. I'll talk to you in a few days."

It was only nine hours later when she got the message from Jie. All it said was, "Primary destination not found. Proceeding to secondary."

The ship wasn't where they expected it to be. At some point, Amelia had changed course. Del wasn't at all surprised at that. At least Amelia could get away from all this. Del couldn't even find it in herself to be angry. Amelia had made the wisest choice. She wished her the best of luck wherever she ended up.

She didn't dare contact Bilan. She didn't want to draw Belt-Sec's attention. She'd have to settle for meeting her at Jie's asteroid. She missed her, but this wasn't nearly as bad as when she was in her cell. This time, she knew she'd see her again.

FOURTEEN
NO BELOW

After her bike turned around, Del went for another long run and then a nap. She was awakened by the alarm telling her she'd arrived. She stood, stretched, and ordered the seat to resume its usual form.

"Beneath" her small craft was a large, icy ball that she was heading straight toward.

"Looks like my calculations were right," she said for her suit's recorder.

There was no transponder signal, and at this range there should be, but there was no mistaking the asteroid. She left her own transponder on as she approached, not wanting to startle whoever was there. The asteroid itself was covered in dust and rocks and pitted with craters, but there was an ancient-looking airlock visible on one side, illuminated with a dim light. From the asteroid's trajectory, it was either a newcomer to the belt, or had been recently moved. She suspected the former. A Centaur perhaps, traveling on some long spiral path inward. In another hundred thousand years or so it would be gone, boiled away as it got too close to the sun.

For now, it seemed it was somebody's home.

She tried to send a message as she approached, but her ship's computer didn't recognize any receivers in the vicinity. Nobody tried to contact her, either.

At less than two hundred meters across, the surface gravity of the asteroid would be negligible. She set her bike to keep station just outside the airlock and leapt across open space. The light on the outer door was green and started blinking when she hit the controls to depressurize it. No reason to anger the inhabitants by dumping any of their air into space. Also, the sound of it cycling would make it plain she wasn't trying to sneak in.

When the light had turned to a solid red, the door slid open. As it refilled, she looked in through the window in the inner door and two people looked back at her, floating at the end of a large central chamber. Tall and thin, both in their late forties perhaps, they wore similar gray smocks. They looked curious, but neither frightened nor angry. She smiled and waved to them, waiting for the airlock to fill.

Another dozen or so people of similar build and dress fluttered about in an immense chamber on the other side of the window. The walls were made of ice, polished but left uneven. It may have been a natural cavern within the asteroid, sealed and filled with air. The people inside seemed unconcerned with her presence. At least there were no weapons in evidence.

At last, the door slid open, and the woman tossed a gray smock, similar to the ones they were wearing, into the airlock, then quickly shut the door again.

Del hit the button to open it, but nothing happened.

"Put it on," a voice said over a speaker. "Leave your suit there."

"I'm not taking off my vacsuit," she answered.

"Then you may leave," the voice responded. "Do not return."

To have come this far. She didn't even know what questions she had here. Would the answers be worth it?

"All right. Give me a minute to change," she said, and stepped to the side, out of view of the window.

The couple on the other side stepped back as well to where she couldn't see them.

She released the seam and pulled her suit off, well aware of the danger. She was standing in an airlock, without her vacsuit. Anyone on the other side of that door could kill her with the push of a button. She was literally trusting her life to strangers, at least one of whom had murdered her colleague.

She was immensely relieved when, after she stepped back up to the window, the inner door slid open, allowing her access to the large central chamber.

"Welcome," the woman who had tossed her the smock said, "The Veteran wants to see you. Don't worry," she added when Del glanced back toward her discarded vacsuit. "Nobody will touch it. As I'm sure you've guessed, this airlock doesn't get much use."

She kicked off toward the other end of the room and her companion followed her. A second later, Del did the same. She was surprised at how warm the room was, with its icy walls. When she got to the end, her two guides stopped, and gestured toward a tunnel leading further in.

"It's the last door at the end," the woman said. "He knows you're coming."

Apprehensively, Del pushed down the long corridor, passing a half dozen pressure doors on each side, set in all directions. There were hand-holds in the wall in all directions as well. This place was never designed to have gravity. At the end a heavy pressure door slid open, and she entered.

She wasn't sure what she was expecting. What she saw was a middle-aged man floating alone in a room filled with wooden furniture and crates of all sizes strapped to the walls. She wondered if this was where Harailt's desk came from. The man was staring out a huge window, his back to her.

"Please come in," he said. "Close the door. We have much to discuss."

"Umm," she started, then hit the button next to the door, which slid shut. He turned then and seemed to look toward her, but not at her.

"Tell me," he started, then seemed to look even further past her when he said, "Why are you here?"

Before she could respond, he asked, "Who told you I knew any answers?"

She realized he must be reading her mind. She clutched her smock tighter to herself, checking it was really closed.

He chuckled. "I'm sorry, but I don't allow weapons in here. All I wanted was to be left alone, but there are too many who just aren't happy with that."

"Who...who are you?"

"Nobody that you'll recognize. But you didn't come all the way here to ask about me."

She was afraid to ask the other question. Afraid at what the answer might be. She asked anyway. The question she'd been avoiding asking herself.

"Who am I?"

"You are Delokita of the Belt. Are you not?"

She clenched her fist. She hadn't come all this way to play games.

"It is a truer answer than you credit it," he said in answer to her thoughts. "Though perhaps you aren't ready to understand that yet."

"You know what I mean."

"You're a telepath, though you've already figured that out. One of the lost ones, I assume."

Lost ones? Now they were getting somewhere.

"You really had no idea," he said sadly.

She found herself thinking, in rapid succession, of the first time she'd heard her voices, and the reactions of those she'd confided in. Her foster family at the time, and how hard it had been to find others after that. When they did, each in turn had their own ideas of how to "fix" her, up until she finally opted herself out of the system and lived the next two years among the "tunnel rats"—the homeless youth of Mars inhabiting the disused tunnels near Burroughs and Bradbury Point. Until a friend helped her fake a profile that ended up landing her a job as an Enforcer with BeltSec. A job she no longer had.

The memories flashed through her mind, ending with her discovering what she really was. She was helpless to stop them, and she knew then that he was experiencing them all as well.

"You poor child," the Veteran said. "You had no idea. Yes, a large number of you were kidnapped, twenty-two standard years ago, as infants. Many scientists were killed by the terrorists. Until now, we had no idea any of the missing infants survived."

Kidnapped? Scientists? Terrorists? There was too much to unpack. She looked at him and tried to relax her mind, to feel his. Out of nowhere, it coalesced around her.

In her memory, she was standing outside what seemed to be a maternity ward. Rows of infants, dozens of them, each in a crib, as a couple of people, covered head to toe in some kind of protective suits moved amongst them.

"*Idiots.*" She could hear his mental voice. "*The children don't have anything contagious and environment suits won't do anything for what they do have.*"

The memory vanished and was replaced with a roiling red sea with black pools exploding across it, closing in on her from all sides. She was floating free in the middle of it all and tumbled, trying to keep her bearings. She bumped into an icy wall and the room she was in appeared around her again. She looked across to the Veteran, who was still floating in front of the window, glaring at her.

"Stay out of my mind," he said. "Those memories are not for you."

"Please," she said, still stunned. "What was that? Was I one of those babies? Was this...some kind of experiment?"

He had already been an adult, she realized.

"Yes," he answered. "I was part of the first batch. I grew up in the facility and assisted the scientists when I was old enough."

That hardly seemed fair, reading her mind immediately after attacking her for reading his.

"I'm not concerned with fairness," he again answered her thought out loud. "You came to my home. If you don't like it, you can leave at any time."

Again with the arrogant dismissal. She shrugged it off. "I was told my parents died when their ship depressurized."

"That may have been true, except they weren't your parents. You were taken from the facility by activists trying to put an end to the project."

"What was the project?"

"To make telepaths, of course."

"Why? Who?"

"Some corporation. I don't even know the name. As for why? Why does anyone do anything? Profit. We were for sale to the highest bidder, mostly various nations on Earth."

She was about to say that you can't just sell people, then thought of Amelia, and what Harailt and BeltSec had conspired to do to her. The Veteran shot her a knowing look, which she acknowledged with a mental shrug.

"What does Earth want with telepaths?" she said.

"Same thing Earthers want anything for. Wealth. Power. War."

She was about to ask how reading occasional memories would do any good when people were lobbing missiles from across the planet when her mind was hit with a barrage of images and feelings.

She was wearing a coat made of explosives, and was terrified, not wanting to hurt anyone and not understanding why she was about to as she reached for the detonator.

Then she was standing, watching without feeling anything as the fireball engulfed the distant crowd.

And again, she was at the controls of a rocket that she decided to push into a hard turn right as it was launching. She had half a second to be terrified as the ground approached...

She was standing over the body of a young man, holding a bloody metal pipe in her sore hand when a man approached her and explained what she needed to do to keep video of the incident quiet...

"They made us do horrible things," the Veteran was saying to her as her surroundings emerged into awareness around her. "We fled. Eventually, I wanted nothing more to do with fighting and with war."

"We? You mean the Rabbit." They had to be working together, she realized. *But how...?*

"Not at first," the Veteran answered. "He was sent to the Belt to further their plan of control. There's an untold abundance of wealth out here. Even more than on Earth, even if it was possible to reach it all."

Enough wealth that there'd be plenty for everyone.

He laughed. "Enough wealth that it'd be worth killing for, and waging a war amongst the corporations. Ministoj may have been the first, but you can be sure more are following. Why sell to just one side when you can make so much more selling to both?"

It wasn't just telepaths, she knew. Guns, missiles, anti-matter bombs. They'd all be coming to the Belt in massive numbers as well.

"But...why try to kill me? I never would have known any of this if you'd have just left me alone. I wasn't a threat to you."

"When you interfered with the attack on Rimedo, he thought you were working for a different corp, so arranged to have you killed. He had his connections in Zono Mastro assign you to a patrol where he could arrange an ambush. If it had worked, you would have just quietly disappeared, and nobody would ever know what happened."

"But why? How does that benefit you?"

"If you were working with an enemy, you'd be dangerous. They would just send another eventually, but at least it would be a delay and a disruption in their plans."

"Whose plans?"

"Whoever sent you."

"Nobody sent me!"

"We didn't know that at the time."

"You keep saying we. How do you fit into all of this? Was getting me here just a setup? If so, why didn't you just kill me in the airlock?"

"We have no desire to kill you."

"All those people shooting at me indicates otherwise!"

"That was before The Rabbit knew who you were."

"What about the Factory?"

"Then, he wasn't trying to kill you. We wanted to talk to you and didn't think you'd come willingly."

"Maybe it was all the lethal weapons being waved in my face that gave me the wrong idea."

"That fiasco on the Factory was not our doing." He gave a

deep sigh, in answer to her thought. "I had already convinced the Rabbit to join me by then. Those men you killed on the Factory weren't his. They were sent by BeltSec, and it may already be too late for them. It's possible they may have been completely infiltrated."

"Infiltrated? By who?" She thought of Lakshminarayanan. *Everything I've done has been with Zono Mastro's full knowledge*, he had said. They didn't need to be infiltrated, they were already cooperating.

"Too bad you aren't part of BeltSec anymore. If you were, we might have been able to use you."

She felt another flash of anger. She wasn't some tool to be used, especially in some game she didn't understand.

"It's more than a game," the Veteran said. He was still reading her mind, which did nothing to cool her anger. "There are two possible futures for the Belt. It could become a battleground for Earth corporations, with most of its resources squandered supporting constant warfare. Or it could gain its independence and eventually become a major power in the Solar System. With the resources available to it, there's no reason Ceres shouldn't rule the whole system within a year if it puts its mind to it."

Del shuddered at the thought.

"I know," the Veteran said. "You could have been a great asset, but I can see with things the way they are you would never cooperate with us. In time, you'll come to understand that the status quo is unsustainable and serves nobody."

As he spoke, Del began falling slowly toward one wall.

The Veteran had planted his feet on a railing and was holding on. "I'm afraid you'll have to be staying for a while," he said. "You may eventually come to see things correctly, but for now you're still too young and naive. You want everything to be perfect and are willing to scrap good progress because it's not. You don't understand how bad things can get."

Del tried to scramble back up to where he was standing, far above her now.

He was still speaking. His voice seemed to echo from a distance. "You've never known true hardship. You think you have, but you haven't. And we almost lost the Rabbit because of you. You would be his undoing, and you've never cared about anyone else enough to worry about whether they suffer or not."

She almost reacted to that last. It was so offensive she nearly missed the message in the rest of it. *What are you saying?* She thought at him. She knew she was failing to keep her anger and fear out of the thought.

"Things should be in place within a year - yes, a standard year..." His voice seemed to fade again, and she found herself sitting at a table with four other people. Across from her was the Rabbit, with a broad smile on his face that she wanted to wipe off with her fist. The others she didn't recognize, though they could all be her brothers and sisters. Maybe they were.

She caught only snippets of their conversation and their thoughts, all jumbled together. The terrorist attacks were just the beginning.

"Fear will bring them crawling to BeltSec, demanding they take more power..."

"Belt resources for the Belt..."

"Don't fuel the engines of our own destruction..."

"Corporate warfare. They'll demand someone stop it..."

"A wealthy, prosperous asteroid Belt, the beneficiary of its own resources..."

"Enough to reach for the stars..."

"They're all mad..."

She was brought back to her own senses with a loud *clang*. A pressure door slamming shut. Somehow, she was outside the room, drifting in the long corridor. The gravity was gone again. Had it ever really been there? The light by the door was flashing green - the air was being removed from the room.

She had to get to her suit.

She turned from the door and pushed as fast as she could down the hall in a near panic. The main chamber was empty. Where had all the people who were here earlier gone?

They were never here. She didn't know if she knew that because she'd figured it out or if the Veteran had put the notion in her head, but she knew with a certainty everything she'd seen since coming here had been an illusion. Placed there by her host.

She made it to the airlock. The light on the control panel was solid red. She looked through the window. The outer door stood open and her suit was nowhere to be seen.

She cycled the airlock anyway, waiting impatiently for it to fill with air and the inner door to open. It was empty of course. She screamed in rage and frustration and spun and kicked off as hard as she could away from it. By the time she got back to the room he'd been in, the light by the door was a solid red.

"I am sorry," a voice said from some nearby speaker. "I truly am. But don't worry. No harm will come to you. There are provisions - enough food, air and, of course, water, to last you for years if you need them to. Somebody will come for you long before they run out. I promise you, once everything is over, there will be a place for you in the new order. There will be a place for everyone."

"To the Void with you and your new order!" she screamed.

There was no response.

SHE RUSHED into the room once it had finished pressurizing. The large cargo door was visible now, behind the torn wall hanging. She peered through the window and saw no sign of a ship. There must have been one, though. Gone now. To the void with these people and their false walls, just like at Kenny's workshop. How much of this was real? Was the veteran even here? Was there even such a person? Or was all of this an elaborate ruse on the part of the Rabbit? He'd been trying to kill her for weeks. It looked like he finally succeeded.

She wanted to cry. She settled instead for screaming. She pulled the rest of the tapestry from the wall, tearing it and throwing the pieces into the room. She kicked off the wall, twisted around in mid-air, and smashed feet first into his desk. She yanked at it until it came loose from its holdings, and threw it against the wall where it splintered, the shrapnel drifting about the room. She grabbed a chair, smashed it into another wall, and used the broken leg as a club against everything else she could reach.

Each act of violence and destruction sent her tumbling across the room, where she found something else to rip or tear or smash. She yelled, she screamed, she destroyed everything she could find in the room. When a jagged piece of wood tore into her arm, she sent her screams after it, following the long arc of blood from the wound.

She cursed the Veteran for stranding her and Kenny for sending her here and Jie for running off to play pirate on a ship stolen from her and Bilan for abandoning her to save her own career and, above all, herself, for making all the decisions that had brought her to this in the first place.

Finally, exhausted, cut, and bruised, she curled into a fetal position and cried, floating alone amidst the aftermath of her destruction.

SHE WIPED the tears from her eyes and looked over at the large cargo door standing between her and the void, its controls now clearly exposed. One push of the button and it would all be over. All of the debris from her tantrum would be blown out into space and her along with it. They'd already won, why not just stop?

For a long time, she floated, drifting, staring at that button.

She drew back. She hadn't seriously considered such a thing since she was nine years old and on her own in the tunnels of Mars. Her answer now was the same as then: spite. Anger and hatred would see her through. A poor substitute for hope maybe, but it would do. They hadn't won yet. As long as she was alive, they hadn't won.

If they did manage to build their new order by the time she got out of here, then she'd just dismantle it. They were so scared of war in the Belt, that's what she'd bring them. She'd find a way of bringing the wrath of all of Earth and Mars and Venus and herself. She would rip apart their new order until the entire asteroid belt was nothing but a bunch of lifeless broken rocks floating in the silence of space.

She pushed herself out of the room, leaving her cloud of debris and the too-tempting door behind her. She wondered if one of the doors in the corridor led to an infirmary. She should probably do something about some of these cuts.

She recognized her thoughts for what they were—a continuation of her earlier tantrum. There was no other word for it. She was alive and in no immediate danger. Her captor had told her there were provisions here. She hoped that they included medicine to prevent bone and muscle loss from too much time in zero G. Her own supply was in her suit, probably kilometers away by now.

Once she knew she wasn't going to starve to death, she needed to figure out a way to get out of here. This place had been inhabited, and not too long ago. She'd seen no evidence of any console here, but she intended to check. If she could reach someone, she would let them know where she was. And if she did that, hopefully, they could get here before someone else intercepted the message and got to her first.

She'd have to prepare for either possibility. She had plenty of time, and a dozen rooms to search through. She hoped if there was one, it hadn't been in one of the boxes she'd smashed in the cargo bay.

Three days—or as near as she could guess—and two dozen frantic searches and half a dozen minor tantrums later, she had despaired of ever finding a net console. She had found a store of food—more than enough to keep her alive for a year, or even five. Also, a full supply of medication. Starvation or deterioration would not be problems.

She'd torn the rooms apart, giving in to her anger each time, until the hall was full of floating debris.

Over the next couple of days, Del cleaned up, moving up and down the corridor, throwing all the heavy, hard, and sharp bits toward the office. Throwing clothes and linens toward the entrance chamber. The food, she left where she found it, which she now designated the kitchen.

In one of the sealed boxes, which had taken her the better part of a day to open, she'd found materials for taking core samples. She thought briefly about how she could use them. Maybe drill to the surface and release some of the air to steer the asteroid. She laughed at the notion. Steer it to where? It would have been given its current trajectory through the use of temporarily attached antimatter-fueled engines. How would any mere gas release make any difference? Even if it did, how could she possibly know where she was going?

The materials didn't completely go to waste, though. She hauled the box back to the office and dumped the contents out. Throwing drill, tubes, metal containers, and finally the boxes themselves, randomly into the air. It wasn't senseless destruction, this time. Lacking gravity or any kind of exercise equipment, she had to come up with a way of slowing muscle loss. All the debris in the office would serve as her obstacle course. Pushing off hard from one end, she could travel, twisting, turning, dodging, or grabbing at the heavy items, trying to avoid injury as she went, before hitting the other end and repeating the process in the other direction. It wasn't a perfect exercise, but it worked. There were a large number of very small, sharp pieces along with the heavier ones. The minor danger kept her awareness present where it should be as she ran the ever changing course over and over. Even being careful, she picked up a few new cuts and bruises with almost every session.

The lack of net access, or even any books, was what was most likely to drive her crazy. There was also no day/night cycle. No access to the net. No chronometers. No way at all to tell the passage of time. She ate when she felt like eating, slept when she felt like it. She had no idea if she slept an hour or ten. Washed, changed clothes, ran her obstacle course, whenever the whim struck her. She couldn't tell if that was multiple times per day or once every few days. She found switches just inside the corridor that controlled the lights embedded in the ice. Day was when she turned the lights on. When they were off, she slept in the main chamber, drifting amongst all the cloth items she'd tossed into there, the only light being that of the stars peeking in through the airlock window.

She wondered if her bike was still outside somewhere, faithfully keeping station as she'd instructed it to. She opened the inner airlock door and peered out the outer window. She couldn't see it, but it could be just around the corner, out of her sight. She looked again at the wall button on the door. If her bike was nearby, she could override the safety, spot it, leap through open space, and drive it right back through the open airlock, then close it again before she passed out and died. The more she thought about it over the days, the more plausible the plan was.

She could do it. She was nearly there—ready for one last, desperate, literal do-or-die rush for her bike when she stopped, backed away, and left the airlock. It couldn't work. Even if the bike was there, the blast of air would blow her right by it. Without a suit to send any commands, it would sit there, unmoving as she sped by, spending her last remaining seconds of consciousness watching it recede into the distance.

She closed the door and pushed away from it. The idea had been so tempting. What happened when it was too much? She wished she could lock the doors at least to make it more difficult for her to open in the future. She didn't think she could last a year. Eventually, she was going to hit one of those buttons, either out of desperation, delusion, or despair.

She was floating in the middle of the front room again when she decided to try something else. Jie had put a bag over her head to keep her from using her power on him. He thought it depended on making eye contact to use. She realized now that was probably why she'd been in solitary confinement the whole time, and that Jie must have been the one to order it. She felt another wash of anger at him over that.

She put that thought aside for now. He'd rescued her and had lost everything doing so. She'd eventually have to find a way to forgive him for making it necessary.

The important thing now was that he was almost certainly wrong. The Rabbit had been in a corridor of an asteroid while Jay was operating the mining platform. Direct sight wasn't needed. Did the power have a range? The fact that the Rabbit had traveled all the way out there instead of staying safely home in the Hygiean sector seemed to indicate that it did. It was also possible that the range was millions, but not hundreds of millions, of kilometers. Or even that the Rabbit may not know the limits. Perhaps proximity allowed finer control, or perhaps he wasn't very good at it, and she'd turn out to be better. Or maybe a compulsion to murder someone's friends required being closer for a stronger signal than a call for help would be. Or maybe she needed to stop over-analyzing and just do it.

Still floating in the middle of the room, she drew herself into a sitting position, arms and legs crossed. She had no idea how to proceed and drew upon the lessons of her youth once again. She took three deep breaths to calm her mind and reached "up," visualizing a field of glowing energy all around her. She took hold of it and pulled a luminescent strand "down" to, and through, herself.

Intoning the names of the six deities as she'd learned, she visualized the pentagram formed of lines of energy around her, as she traced it into existence in the air. For the last intonation she extended it in a great column before and behind her.

She hadn't done the full ritual for years, but wanted to be fully focused, eclipsing all other distractions. She sent her mind out. She didn't know where or how it would work. None of it made sense. It didn't have to.

"Come. Help me. I'm trapped," was the thought she repeated, while visualizing Bilan's face. Over and over as she floated, eyes closed, concentrating on every deep breath. In. "Come. Help me. I'm trapped." Out. "I'm trapped. Help me. Come."

At last, she grew tired of the exercise. She looked at the airlock door. Nobody came. She wasn't expecting anyone to do so. Even if it worked, she was days away from Ceres.

She recognized her actions for what they were. A way to keep her mind diverted. Something to keep her focused enough not to open the doors. She added it to her regular routine, repeating the pattern: sleep, eat, obstacle course. Meditate.

She let herself believe it would work, because without hope, even false hope, she was lost. She didn't think her anger would be enough this time. She wondered what Bilan was doing now. Trying to find her? Were she and Jie still in touch? Did Jie ever find Amelia? She hoped they were all right.

With such thoughts, she once again drifted off to sleep.

FIFTEEN
VIOLENCE AND RECONCILIATION

Del woke to the sound of an airlock cycling. She opened her eyes, and looked around to orient herself, searching for her tiny window of starlight. She found it and thought she saw a shadow. In a panic, she spun around, looking for the pants she'd been wearing the day before, or for anything at all when the inner door slid open. What had she been thinking, sleeping like this in the middle of the chamber? Without her suit thrusters and without gravity she couldn't get anywhere quickly. For days, it had been a game, seeing how close she could get to the center of the room with one push from the wall, then when she woke up, trying to get back to another wall without the aid of suit thrusters. Now it looked like it would be her undoing. If whoever was entering was armed, she'd be helpless.

No, not quite helpless. She still had one weapon, but no idea if it could be effective against the invaders.

The inner door slid open and a bright light played across the room. It stopped when it hit her, shining in her eyes and she raised a hand against it, trying to see the person holding it.

There were at least two vaguely humanoid shapes behind the light. One of them launched toward her.

In a panic, she thought toward the figure.

DROP THE LIGHT!

It continued straight toward her, but pointed the light downward. In the sudden darkness all she could see were shadows. Then the other figure raised its own light and in it, she could see her assailant more clearly. It was someone in a vacsuit much like her own, wearing a BeltSec uniform over it.

They found me, was her first thought. Then the figure opened its helmet.

It was Bilan.

Del stared, blinking in disbelief. She was suddenly flooded with a series of memories, and she recognized them as Bilan's.

She was searching through records, searching for Del's name.

She found them: arrested, escaped with help. Warrants out. Armed and dangerous.

A supervisor she didn't recognize, yelling, "You will cease and that's a direct order."

Then, on the net, sending a message. "I'm on my way and by the depths you'd better be there."

Then, hanging in space, looking at the approaching *Zheng He*. "There's nothing here. How can there be nothing here?"

Then finally, "Depths! Her suit! I still have access, unless she's changed it by now."

Jie's voice in her helmet, laughing in response to that, "What're the odds of Del taking proper security measures?"

Then they were both on the bridge of the *Zheng He* with Amelia and a man who looked vaguely familiar.

Amelia turned to her and spoke. "Of course we're in. Let's go now."

Then she was back in the middle of the main chamber and Bilan was there, holding her in a tight hug.

"You're here!" Del said, squeezing her back. "It's really you! I never thought I'd see you again!"

"You reached out to me, didn't you?" Bilan asked. "Across the void, you reached my mind."

"I tried. I tried so hard. I was so desperate and scared and I didn't know if it would work."

"It did. I felt it. I came as soon as I could. Jie owes me a bottle of whiskey."

"I never actually agreed to that," Jie said with a laugh, coming up behind Bilan.

"Don't care. I'm still holding you to it."

"Here," Jie said when he caught up to them, and she saw he was carrying her suit. He tossed it gently to Del. "Found it outside. Thought you might want it. Is there anyone else here?" He asked as she pulled it on.

"Nobody. Nobody at all," she replied.

He put away the needler he'd been holding.

She pulled up her suit's display, and she'd never felt so relieved as when it came up. She checked the time. "Twenty days?" she exclaimed.

"I'm sorry," Bilan responded, "It took a while to determine you were even missing and then..."

"It felt like months! I had no clock, no reference, no way to know how long it had been..."

"What happened? You look like you've been in a dozen fights!"

"It's nothing. Just...wait, you found the ship?"

"Yes," Jie said. "They had to change course, but Bilan tracked them down."

"How?"

"Same way we did before. Same way we found you. I still

have access to your suit. I traced its location, and when we found it, traced its trajectory back to here."

Del glanced at her suit's interface and the access link. She thought for a second about updating it, locking it back down, then thought better of it. So far, Bilan had only ever used it to help her. If she hadn't had the access, Del would almost certainly have died on this ice ball.

"That's what Jie was talking about. When he laughed about me not updating security."

"You saw that in Bilan's mind?" Jie asked.

She nodded, but turned back to Bilan, "When you first got here, I saw a whole flash of memories. You must have been thinking of all the things you had gone through to get to me." She paused for a second, then said gently, "Thank you."

"You're welcome. And...I think there might be a hint there about how your power works."

"What do you mean?"

"Every time I felt that you were in trouble, was when I was thinking about you. Something about...I don't know exactly... synchronizing wavelengths in the brain? I never studied any biology in school. But I knew you were in trouble - I had an image of you sitting with arms and legs crossed, floating in the air, you were surrounded by glowing light, and desperately trying to reach me."

"That's...almost exactly right," Del said, then realized what the one vision meant. "You were ordered to back off. But you defied orders to come find me."

"You're worth it."

"You can't go back. I've cost you your career. Both of you. You're now wanted fugitives because of me."

"No," Jie said. "You can't blame yourself for that. BeltSec was thoroughly corrupt. There was nothing more I could do from within it."

"And hey, I already told you, no fair running off to become a pirate without me," Bilan added with a smile.

"I hate to be the one to put a damper on things," Jie said, followed by a snort of laughter from Bilan. "But shouldn't we be getting out of here before anyone else shows up?"

"I don't think they're coming back," Del said. "The Veteran said he'd come back after a year, though I don't know if he was actually planning on doing that."

"He really was here?" Jie asked. "This 'Veteran' was a real person?"

"I don't think this was set up to be a trap originally. He definitely knew I was coming, though, and started messing with my head before I even came in."

"Did you learn anything at all?" Bilan said. "Where you came from? What The Rabbit's up to?"

"Both of those things," Del answered. "He wanted me to join them at first, before deciding they couldn't trust me."

"And then he stranded you here?"

"Yeah." She told them the story while they went, about the corporate program to create telepaths, about the activists who stole a bunch of them, including her, and about the mysterious project's attempts to control the Belt, and how the Rabbit turned against them. Also, about the Veteran's ability to make her see people who weren't really there.

"Void. Was anything real?" Jie asked. "Was he even here?"

"I think so," she said. "I...felt, if that's the right word, his mind. I think my two escorts were real, too. I don't know if they were telepaths, too, but I suspect so."

"This illusion worries me," Jie said. "If he can make you see things that aren't there..."

"You and me both. I think the people are a memory of his own. I got the feeling he's been here for a while, and those people used to live here with them. Certainly, a large number of people lived here until relatively recently."

"Why would he tell you his plan?"

"I'm not sure he wanted to. There was a lot of mind-reading and mental grappling going on. I'm still not sure how much of it is real, how much he implanted, and how much I read from him without him wanting me to. Or maybe he couldn't gauge my reaction until the idea was in my head."

"But why trap you here? Don't take this the wrong way, but wouldn't it have been pretty easy to just kill you at that point?"

"I think he was still hoping to recruit me. Possibly he thought I'd come around to his side once I saw this stable future already accomplished. Plus..." She hesitated. She wasn't sure of the implications of the Veteran's thoughts. Finally, she said, "He may have been keeping me alive for leverage. Use me against the Rabbit if he needed to."

They stepped into the airlock and waited for it to cycle. When the others had put their helmets up, she did as well and continued over the coms. "Did you bring Amelia, too? And, more importantly, the tall man with the broad shoulders and deep eyes?"

"I'd leave that one alone if I were you," Jie said.

"Why?" Del asked. "What's wrong with him?"

"Amelia's claimed him. And I don't think she likes to share."

"She has?" Bilan seemed surprised.

"You didn't notice the way they keep looking at each other?" he asked.

"Isn't he awfully old for her?"

"Maybe by Venusian standards, but this is the Belt. Here, she's an adult. If it's what she wants, I'm not going to interfere, and I suggest nobody else do so either." He looked pointedly at Del.

"I got it," she replied. "No touching. Give me some credit.

I'm perfectly capable of keeping my hormones in check for the sake of professionalism." She looked at Bilan. "And stop remembering that! That was a completely different situation!"

DEL PARKED her bike along with Bilan's and Jie's scoot in the *Zheng He*'s cargo bay. There was no gravity when she entered, but while it was underway it would be hanging upside down, secured to the ceiling. The three of them went up to meet Amelia on the bridge.

"And you thought I'd stolen your stolen ship!" Amelia laughed in mock-offense.

"It wasn't an unreasonable guess," Bilan said. "Show of hands: Who here hasn't stolen this ship at least once."

Jie raised his hand, laughing.

A large man who'd come onto the bridge with Amelia looked down at the floor and kept his down.

"Captain - this is Cor," Amelia introduced them. "Cor, Captain Delokita."

She was the captain now? How did that happen?

"We've met," Cor said.

Del realized why he looked familiar. "Last time I saw you, you tried to kill me."

"You were trying to steal my ship."

"It was my ship first."

"And how'd you get it?" Cor's foot was set against a wall, ready to spring either toward her or away if need be.

"Point," she nodded.

He bowed, then looked up and met her gaze. "Thank you for not killing me when you could have."

"You're welcome. We're good, then?"

"Amelia says you're the captain, you're the captain."

Del nodded acknowledgment. That was good enough. He was declaring he'd follow her orders, but his loyalty was to Amelia. She could live with that, and it answered in one sentence two of the questions she had for him.

"What about the others?" she asked the third.

"My partners, you mean?" Cor asked, a bit of edge to his voice.

"I mean, are they in on this, too? If not, what do we do with them?"

"We talked about that," Amelia volunteered. "They did do all the work of stealing the cargo before we stole it from them. What do you think about giving them a fair share then letting them go?"

"It's up to our captain," Jie said with a smile. "But how do we know they won't sell us out as soon as they're free?"

"I think I can convince them to keep quiet," said Cor. "Especially if we don't pay them out until we're ready to leave. They're professionals. If they're being paid for the job, they're not going to hold a grudge. Just business."

"I can live with that," Jie replied, which seemed unusually pragmatic for him. "Captain?"

Again, with the Captain. She didn't want to say anything about not being sure of the title, not with Cor there. She didn't know him well enough to dare show any sign of weakness.

"They did try to kill me," she said.

"Are you going to hold a grudge?" Amelia asked.

Del looked at her, then at Cor. Then, rather pointedly at Jie. Of the four people present, Bilan was the only one who'd never offered her violence.

"No," she said. "Like you said, just business. As long as they don't try anything again, I'm happy."

The port corridor still couldn't be pressurized because of all the damage to the airlock. A direct vacuum outside their doors made the perfect seal ensuring their "guests" couldn't get out. They had enough food and supplies to last them until they got to the Factory. Using the internal coms, Amelia explained the situation to them - there was no reason to let them know that Del was involved, or that their colleague was free—and they seemed happy enough with the arrangement, if not the captivity.

Del agreed to let Amelia and Cor keep the captain's quarters until they got to the Factory. Without gravity, there was no need for a bed, and she took to sleeping in the cargo bay, floating freely.

"WE'RE GOING to need a plan for how to handle the Factory," Del said when everything had settled. Her crew, as she'd already began thinking about them, were gathered about the bridge. She was "sitting" loosely in the center chair. She could have strapped into it but there was no need.

"You can't set foot in the Factory. They'd mark you immediately," Amelia said.

"Agreed."

"So, when we get there, you hide. Let me and Cor make contact. He's the one who knows people here anyway. We'll sell the stuff, make the repairs, then come pick you up." When nobody responded, she looked to Del and said, "I'm not going to steal your ship!"

Del couldn't read anything from her mind. How come it never worked when she wanted it to? If Bilan's theory was right, now was the time. Amelia should have been thinking about Del right then.

"I trust you," she said. "It's a good plan. I'll zip off on my bike when we get close and wait for your signal."

"I agree, except I want to go with you," Bilan said to Amelia.

"You don't trust me either?"

"It's less that than I don't trust this Factory. I want to be nearby if something goes wrong."

"What do you think?" Amelia looked to Cor.

"Fine with me. Probably best if you let me do the talking, though," he replied. "Only because I've done business here before. Frankly it'll help in negotiations if I'm being flanked by a pair of bodyguards. You should both visibly carry firearms. Slug throwers, not needlers."

ON THE FIFTH DAY, shortly before the engines were set to fire for the final deceleration, Del and Jie climbed onto their respective crafts and departed the *Zheng He*.

Amelia and Jie had been able to work together during the flight to install a switch on his scoot's transponder, as Kenny had done to Del's. With the transponders off, they could just hang in empty space nearby and be nearly invisible to anything but a directed scan.

"Remember, priority one is fuel," Del said over her suit's com as she headed out on her bike. "Repairs we can always do somewhere else if we need to, but without fuel we can't get there."

"Yes, captain. Thank you. Go away now," Amelia responded. Del could hear Bilan laugh in the background.

Once they'd reached their determined rendezvous point, close enough to move in quickly if need be, but far enough away that they shouldn't be spotted, they settled in to wait. Del flew over to Jie's ship so they could open their helmets and speak without any chance of the communications being intercepted by anyone over the net.

"What are your plans about this Rabbit?" Jie asked her.

"I don't think he'll be coming after me anymore, and he seems to have fallen out with both the Veteran and Ministoj. As long as we stay out of his way, we should be fine."

"And just let the rest of the Belt hang, then?" Jie asked.

"I don't know what else I can do about it."

"From what you've described, there are two large and well-funded factions waging a covert war for control of the Belt. Neither of them has the Belters best interests in mind."

"It won't be covert for long. Eventually, one side will start losing and have to act openly. Then they escalate to exactly what you've always feared: open warfare in the Belt. Corp against corp."

"Thought you said that's what the Veteran wanted to avoid."

"Yeah, but he's not going to. You don't prevent a war by starting one," Del answered.

"So, what, just...accept it? There's going to be a war and there's nothing anybody can do about it?"

"You think I don't care? You just pointed out yourself how powerful these groups are, even without the telepaths working for them. What in the void do you expect me to do about any of that?"

"What can anyone but you do? We're the only ones who know what's going on, and you're the only one in the whole Belt who can fight back against the telepaths."

"How? You think we can expose them? Announce it all over the net? Without any proof it's just another fringe conspiracy theory, no different than the insect people secretly controlling all governments from under the clouds of Jupiter."

He was quiet for a moment.

Del tried to look into his eyes, but he was looking past her out the window. She couldn't read anything in his mind.

"I don't know," he finally said. "I've spent my whole life

trying to make things better for the Belt. I'm not going to stop now."

Del stared out into space as if she could see their machinations amongst the distant asteroids. "I don't like it any better than you do, but they have entire governments behind them. If we're very, very lucky, in a couple of days we will be five people in a stolen spaceship. We can run. Hide. Stay alive. Figure out how to live under whichever one of them eventually wins."

Again, Jie was silent for a long moment before speaking again. "What about joining them? You could be a great asset to either side. It would be a lot safer than being on your own."

"I'm used to being on my own. I like it. I got a taste of what working for them is like and I'm not interested."

"They could make life very comfortable for you. Riches, booze, men..."

"Men forced into indentured servitude? No thanks. Why are you playing tempter anyway?"

"I want to know where you stand."

Her anger welled up again.

"You've never had a high opinion of me, have you? I've always been just little Delokita. Can't be trusted. Too flighty. Too immature. Too unreliable. That's it, isn't it?"

"You—"

"You didn't even stop to hear my side of things back on Ceres. You just saw some doctored video and assumed I must have murdered people."

"I—"

"Or is that I, how did you put it, 'came to the Belt to die'?"

He stiffened. "Did Bilan tell you I said that?"

"You did say it, then."

"I did," he admitted. And for a brief moment she was in another memory of his.

They were in his room on Ceres. "It's important to be

honest with her," Bilan was saying. "No matter how painful. It's the only way she'll be able to know what's real. She has nobody, Jie, she has to be able to know she can rely on us."

Then Del was back in the cockpit of Jie's scoot. "I..." She started. She didn't know what to say. Finally, she spoke again.

"Do you still believe that?"

Jie lapsed into silence again, gathering his thoughts. Why couldn't she see them? Bilan may be right. It seemed only to be his memories, and only his memories involving her. It had to be possible to do more, though. The Veteran had seemed to see her every thought.

"No," he answered.

"Are you telling me the truth? No matter how painful, like you promised Bilan?"

"Did Bilan tell you that, or was it something you read in my mind?"

"I asked you first."

"Then yes. I'm telling you the truth. I will always tell you the truth, no matter what."

"Because it's the only way I can sort fact from fantasy," she finished for him.

"Bilan didn't tell you."

"No," she affirmed.

"I was remembering that conversation just as I said it."

"So was I."

He stared at her for a long moment then, pondering the implications.

She stared back.

"The other thing you said...about me wanting to die..." She started, then trailed off.

"I already told you I don't believe it's true anymore," he interrupted.

"I read that in Bilan's memory. She was thinking of that argument. She was angry."

"Thank you for telling me the truth," he said.

"Why?"

"Why thank you for telling me the truth?" Jie almost seemed amused, but that wasn't her intention.

"No. Why did you change your mind?" she snapped.

"I think the first thing was Amelia. When you set her free instead of returning her. It was the first time I'd seen you do something purely for someone else. You went out of your way to help her, sacrificing a great deal of money, and incurring the wrath of a powerful corporate head. I thought then maybe you'd found something to live for after all. At the very least, the capacity to find something to live for."

"That's...that's kind of confusing."

"Keep reading people's minds, I suspect you're going to be confused a lot. We're not as rational as some people like to believe."

That was patronizing. But it was not meant unkindly. She decided she could let it go.

"Speaking of..." He hesitated.

"Yes?"

"The Rabbit has the same power as you do."

"Yes."

"But he's better at it."

"Yeah. A lot better."

"Is that because he's stronger? Or just has more practice?"

"I'm...I'm not sure what the difference is. He's had all his life to practice. He's always known what he is and has had people to guide him since childhood."

"It'll be hard enough fighting someone like that..."

"If you want to take him on, don't fight him. Find where he

lives and put a couple of missiles through his window while he sleeps."

"There are others like you. Some of whom may have different agendas." Jie didn't even react to her suggestion, which scared her in itself.

"What are you getting at?"

"It might be helpful to practice using your gift."

"How?"

"You've got four people on your ship who can assist you."

She had a flash of memory of Bilan walking naked to the airlock and wasn't sure if it was her memory or Jie's.

"I want to learn how to resist it," Jie continued.

"I'm not even sure that's possible."

"You've done it."

"Only because what he wanted me to do was impossible, and he didn't know that."

"Not then. Earlier. When you didn't launch a missile into the Rimedo offices."

"He was too far away."

"I think there was more to it than that."

"Missiles are expensive?"

That brought up a bark of laughter. "There may be something to that, actually. Somehow, you recognized it as a compulsion."

"Thanks to years of therapy."

"And that it was wrong."

"And a lifetime of not doing what I should."

"You give yourself too little credit. I think part of what helped you resist was because you knew it was wrong to kill innocent people."

"I don't know. When you arrested me, your lackey knew it was wrong to shoot her friend, but she did it anyway."

"Maybe there is more to it than that. I think with practice we might both learn to get better at it, though."

"And of course, I might be able to resist it just because I'm a telepath, too."

"Perhaps. Didn't you say your friend Kenny was considered immune?"

"Maybe. I mean, I did say that, but I have my doubts about him. If he is, it's a count against your 'knowing what's right' theory. He might not be a telepath, but he could be something else related. I think the power—or whatever it is—works by hitting exactly that spot in the brain. It changes what you think is right."

"Is it possible it changes what you think is the right reaction, but can't touch your actual sense of right or wrong?"

"I have no idea. I don't even know what the difference is."

"Put it this way. We don't have anything better to do for the next couple of days at least while they're fixing your ship."

"You do make a compelling argument," Del responded.

"Excellent. How do you want to start?"

"I'm in charge now?"

"It's your power. The whole thing centers around you."

"All right. How about if I start with implanting a compulsion?"

"Sounds good. Just don't make me walk naked out an airlock."

Something that he would know was wrong. Something she knew he didn't want to do. She thought about it for a second, then directed the thought at him:

SLAP HER

Without hesitation, he drew back his hand and slapped her hard across the face. The blow sent both of them tumbling, without gravity to hold them in place. There wasn't far to go in the small cockpit.

"Oh god, I am so sorry," he said, horrified at what he had just done.

"Why'd you hit me?" she asked.

"I'm sorry, I..."

"No. No apologies. No judgment. Don't even think about your answer. Just tell me why. Be honest."

"You just...after all we said you looked like you weren't taking the idea of practicing seriously and..."

While he was talking, she directed the thought at him again:

HIT HER AGAIN

This time she was expecting the blow and rolled with it, turning all the way over until her feet were resting on the canopy.

"I am so sorry. Oh my god, I've never..."

He trailed off and Del confirmed his suspicions. "It's not you," she said. "It's me."

"You...you wanted me to hit you?" he said incredulously.

"I didn't exactly want you to," she said, rubbing the side of her face. It hurt a lot. "But that was the suggestion I put in your head."

"Void. And it seemed so...natural. As if—"

"As if it were entirely your idea. Yeah. How do you fight something like that?"

"You did. Kenny did. There must be a way."

"I'm a bio-engineered freak and Kenny is either the same or just a total sociopath."

"Still there must..."

HIT HER!

This time his fist flew forward and struck her full in the face. She pulled back and spun head over heels in a complete circle, leaving a long arc of blood droplets.

"Goddammit," she said.

"I am so sorry," Jie said.

"Not your fault," Del said, holding her hand to her injured nose.

"Here, let me look at that." He pulled a med-kit out from one of the cockpit's many cabinets. "Doesn't look like anything's broken. Can we call a truce now?"

"Sounds good," she laughed, holding the bandage to her nose. "Now tell me why you hit me. What were you thinking about?"

"I was angry. I knew you wanted me to hit you and you were just sitting there smirking about being able to control me and I got so angry about it I just wanted you to stop."

"You hit me to stop me from making you hit me?"

"When you say it like that it sounds silly." He laughed, but quickly sobered.

"You know none of your actions here were your own, right?" she said.

"Weren't they? I was the one doing them. Maybe you implanted the suggestion, but I should be able to not do things even when I feel like doing them. I'm not a toddler."

"It's a telepathically implanted suggestion, Jie. Nobody knows how it works."

"Void, Del. If someone has no idea this is being done to them, how many times would they have to commit a violent act and justify it to themselves before they start doing it on their own?"

"No idea. What are you getting at?"

"Could they create a violent person out of anyone?"

"We've already seen they can."

"I mean, they could convince somebody that violence is their very nature, and release them..."

"Not sure what good that'll do. Without aiming them, what, slightly increase the violence in some area? Universe is full of violent assholes already. I don't think a few more would make much difference."

He didn't have an answer to that. "Why did you want me to hit you, anyway?"

"I thought it would be easier if I had you do something you didn't want to. And, for the record, I know you were telling yourself in your head over and over after the second time not to hit me anymore. You don't have to be a telepath to read that."

"It didn't work. Maybe you're right and there's no way for a normal person to stand up to this. If that's the case, we have a problem."

"Or maybe you're right and it just takes more practice," Del said. Then thought at him:

TAKE OFF YOUR VACSUIT

She suppressed a smile as he did so. "And now you're naked," she said once he'd finished. "Why?"

"If I had to hit you again, I wanted to make sure I didn't have the power assist from the suit."

"Good justification. Did you use the power assist before when you hit me?"

"Well...no. It's not usually active outside of gravity. This wasn't you, though. This was a logical decision. It makes sense and..."

She looked down for a second then back up to make eye contact, trying, and failing, to keep a straight face.

"Dammit, Del." He pulled his vacsuit back on.

"I deliberately chose things you wouldn't ordinarily do, specifically so we could tell when you were following suggestions as opposed to taking normal actions. But you managed to justify them. I don't know how you can learn to resist it with your own mind working against you."

"I hate this."

"Hey, this whole thing was your idea."

"We may have to work up to it. Your power seems pretty well developed, though. Did you try any compulsion that I didn't do?"

"No," she replied. "You dutifully complied with all of my suggestions." She looked him up and down again. "This could be fun."

"No. Please. I'm serious. This is a terrible power you have. You...you take away someone's free will and convince them it was their idea. It's horrifying."

"But you want me to keep using it on you. And you want me to learn to use it better."

"Yes. I'm willing to endure this because it might mean learning to resist it when other people do it."

"You endure. I'm the one with the broken nose here."

"It's not broken, and it's your own fault. You shouldn't have made me do that."

She laughed out loud. "That's one of the first phrases they taught us to watch out for in the Martian foster system. We were supposed to report it if an adult ever said something like that to us."

"Report it? Why?"

"'Any action an adult takes is their own responsibility,'" she quoted from her long-ago classes. "'You are never responsible for what they choose to do.' It never occurred to me before that they could be wrong."

"They weren't," he said after a moment of thought. "But... could they be sometimes? I mean, is it possible that you've used this power before without realizing it?"

"I...void. Probably. How many times have people around me done exactly what I want? I..." Could she have forced him to break her out of BeltSec headquarters? She shied away from mentioning that. "I can remember times when I've been playing cards and really wished the other person would fold and they did. I don't know if that's because they should have or because I made them."

"Of course, everyone's done that at some point."

"Any suggestions on how to proceed then?"

"Maybe if you tell me ahead of time what you're going to suggest, I can concentrate more on not doing it."

"The Rabbit's not going to give you a warning ahead of time."

"When you learn math, you don't start with vector calculus. Let's start simple and see if we can work out any basic concepts."

"I'm just worried that we may not have time to get to the advanced stage."

"Think like a Belter. Rushing's more likely to get you killed than to save time."

"What do you suggest, then?"

"Something that comes from you. You'll have to decide."

"Flip upside down. I mean, that's what I'm gonna try to make you do."

"I won't do it then."

"That's it. Unleash your inner petulant child."

Another memory flashed. His anger consumed her as she was squirming beneath his boot. But beneath the anger was anguish. Sorrow. He was snarling to hold back tears.

It was over in an instant, but there was an immense gulf there. This memory was still painful, raw, and it gave her an idea.

But first:

FLIP UPSIDE DOWN!

A second later, Jie had swapped head for feet.

Del raised an eyebrow.

"Oh, wait..." Jie said. Then, "Void!"

"Why? Tell me why you did it. What was your thought process?"

"I...I thought for a second that you were playing some kind of word game, and that I already was upside down. I switched so I wouldn't be. Void, this is so weird. Keep going! Try this same one over and over until I get it." He flipped back to his original position. Then looked up and saw her. "Void!"

"I didn't do anything that time. That was all you."

"I don't know if that's better or worse."

FLIP OVER!

He reached toward the seat back to push off from again, then stopped. He floated there, staring at the seat back, his hand trembling until he pulled it back. He made a fist, and pounded it into the seat, then looked over at her where she was sitting peacefully watching him.

"No," he said through gritted teeth. "The Void with you. No flipping for me today. I won't do it."

"It worked," she said.

"Yes!" Jie said with a broad smile. "It did. Good! That's a good step. Finally, we're going in the right direction!"

"Maybe. Let's try it again."

For the next couple of hours, they continued to practice. She could tell Jie was getting frustrated, as was she. Almost every time he knew what was coming, he was able to resist the compulsion she'd send him. But every time he didn't know what was happening, he'd fall into it.

"You rely too much on thinking you know what's right," Del told him. "Think about your actions. Consider the consequences. Ignore if the action's right or wrong, think about what will happen if you do it."

"Somehow I don't think that thinking carefully about the consequences of your actions is the secret to your success here."

"Maybe not, but I also don't convince myself that every thought I have is gospel truth, either."

"Let's take a break for now," he said. "We're both on edge."

"One more," she said. "If you're willing."

"All right. One more."

She had an idea. He had said it himself: she knew killing innocents was wrong. Everything she'd made him do so far was something that in certain circumstances were within his character. Even hitting her. He wasn't usually a violent person, but his job did sometimes call for the use of violence, and he was capable of it when necessary. She needed something big, and something completely against his character, not just his current wishes.

Contrary to his earlier statement, she thought of the consequences, but she sent the command anyway.

The change was obvious. His whole face hardened, staring at her.

"You're gonna like this one," she said, knowing he most certainly would not.

He turned toward her. "You think so, huh?" he asked. His anger was obvious. Did he know what she had compelled him to do? Was he fighting it?

He grabbed her shoulders and pushed her back into the seat, swinging himself over in front of her. The cockpit seemed very small. She fought to keep her mind blank. *Focus on reading his, not on sending any more commands.*

"I know what you're doing," he said. He let go and grabbed the front of her shirt and tore it open, the magnetic snaps ripping open as he pulled it apart and down over her shoulders. "You think this is what I want?" he cried. But his eyes were on her chest, not her face.

She said nothing.

It was just a matter of which way his anger pushed him, and of surviving it.

The vacsuit was designed to be opened from the outside in case of emergency. It was one of the subsystems that didn't require any security access. His fingers found the shoulder tab and pulled, releasing the lock on the seam that ran all the way down the right side of the suit. The air in the cockpit was cold against her bare shoulder.

She pushed his hands away from her then and sent the commands to close the suit. The fabric of the suit crawled across her skin as the two sides of the seam sought to join back together.

"You don't get off that easy," Jie growled and grabbed her front collar, his fingers curling over the projectors that let her see her interface, knuckles digging painfully into her neck.

"This is what you used, isn't it? To give yourself the anti-dote? I should have taken your suit from you then and let the needle do its work. It would have saved everyone a lot of trouble!"

She tried to push back against him, but he had nowhere to go; he was already braced against the console behind him, and pinning her to the seat.

He twisted, pinning her right arm to the wall then again pulled the vacsuit open again, and down. She gasped for air as he moved his hand from her throat. She tried to reach with her left arm, but he caught it easily and held it to her side and continued pulling at the vacsuit, freeing her other arm and pulling it down to her waist.

She thought of stopping him then. Instead, she kept silent and kept her mind as blank as possible. He had to be able to break out of it himself. He pulled her violently from the seat and her head hit the back wall as he ripped the front of her uniform trousers, loosening them to where they would move with the vacsuit as he tried to peel it the rest of the way off.

He slid his hand inside the suit, keeping it from closing back up, and continued opening the seam, pushing the suit downward.

When his hand was on her thigh, he whipped his eyes up to meet hers and snatched his hand back as if burned. He pushed off her and into the far window, as far from her as he could get in the tiny cockpit.

"Get out," he told her, flatly. "Pull your suit back on and go back to your own bike."

She sat there, unmoving for a moment, watching him.

He was turned away, as if he couldn't stand to see her.

"You resisted," she said, as she adjusted and resealed her suit. When it was in place, she reached over to him, pulling his shoulder gently to turn him to her.

He jerked away from her and back toward the window, using one hand to wipe at his face. Drops of moisture floated in front of him in the cockpit.

"Hey, Jie, no," she said in a soft voice. "You didn't do anything."

"I was going to," he said in a small voice she'd never heard from him before.

"No. No, you weren't. And you didn't. Look. You're not trying to do anything now. You stopped yourself."

"But I nearly—"

"No! You didn't. Look at me! You didn't even get my suit all the way off."

He turned back toward her. "Not through lack of trying."

"Exactly through lack of trying! You stopped yourself!"

"You don't understand. I never wanted to touch you like that before. Now I do."

"Still?"

"Yes!" he cried out. "Oh, Del, why did you put that in my head?"

"It had to be something I knew you didn't want to do. Something you would never do."

"This...this is a terrible power you have. Please never make me do anything like that again."

"You didn't do anything."

"You should see your face."

"A few bruises. I've had far worse than this. You would have stopped as soon as you got the suit off. That's as far as the suggestion went."

"Are you sure about that?"

"I was the one who implanted it."

"You just implanted the compulsion. That's what makes your power so terrifying. It was my own mind that justified it. Around that core you put there, my mind had to build up an entire system to fit it. There was only one reason to forcibly remove your suit like that, so that's what my brain convinced myself I wanted. That's what I was going to do."

She didn't know what to say to that for a moment, then realized the implications of what he said.

"And you still want to?"

"Yes," he said, looking again at the Milky Way stretching across the sky outside the window.

"Look at me," she said.

He turned back to her, his face hard.

"I'm right here. There's nowhere I can run to. We both know you're stronger than me and there's no way for me to stop you. You even have justification. You can tell Bilan I used my power on you, and you'd be telling the truth. It would be the one time in all of human history where it would actually be my own fault. So, why aren't you doing anything?"

"I...I don't know."

"I do," she said. "It's because you're Jie, and that's not the kind of thing you do. There's a huge and important difference between wanting to do something and doing it. You pointed that out yourself. Think of how you're feeling now, and how you felt earlier. That's the secret to resisting the Rabbit. Harness those feelings and use them against him."

He gave a mirthless bark of laughter. "You're telling me I should give in to my anger."

"Maybe. Anger is never about doing what's right, and if the power tricks you into feeling like it's the right thing to do..."

"This has been exhausting. I think I'd like to sleep now. If they haven't contacted us by morning, I'd like to try seeing if you can practice reading my mind. I think that'll be an easier exercise on both of us."

"You sure you want to keep exposing yourself to my terrible power?"

"In the morning." He reached for his helmet.

In a deliberate show of respect, she deployed her own helmet before he evacuated the air from the cockpit.

Once she got back to her own bike, she inflated her balloon so she could open her helmet. She couldn't remember when the last time she ate anything was. While the balloon was filling, Jie sent her a message.

She stared at the message notification a long time before opening it.

"Don't feel bad, Delokita," Jie's face said on her screen. "I know you're going to blame yourself, but it's not your fault. And you're not a bad person at all. In fact, you're one of the best people I've ever met." He paused, as if trying to think of how to put it, to reassure her of what she knew wasn't true. "If it comes to it, I would die for you."

Tears threatened to form in her eyes. They were still close enough for realtime communication, but she hit the message button. "Don't you dare ever die for me, Jie," she said in reply. "The universe needs people like you in it." She paused just a moment before finishing. "Far more than it needs people like me."

Before she could think it over, she sent the message then turned off the coms, so she wouldn't have to face his response.

A moment later, she turned off all interior lights and floated there for a long time, unsleeping and bathed in starlight.

SIXTEEN
REUNIONS

Del was awakened by a bright light shining through the transparent balloon. Disoriented, she put her hand up and squinted into it. The light was coming from Jie's scoot. She pulled up her interface to open a realtime channel to him and remembered that she'd turned it off the night before. She turned it back on now to see a dozen message notifications.

"Oh thank the sun," Jie's voice said on her com. "I was about to go over there and knock."

"What's going on?"

"Time to go, Captain. Your crew needs you."

"Where are they? Is everyone okay?"

"No. They got split up. Amelia's captured, Bilan's hiding, Cor's unreachable, and the ship's been impounded."

"Void!" She turned the rest of the ship's systems back on, deployed her helmet and stowed the balloon. "Let's go get them."

"Should we come up with a plan?" Jie asked.

"Amelia's captured? By who? Is she all right?"

"Don't know yet. Bilan was trying to find out but got pinned down. They're hunting for her now."

"Let's go help her first, then. Sounds like she's in the most immediate danger. Maybe she'll have information on the others."

"I guess we know they're not holding them the same place where they had Kenny," Jie said with a laugh.

"Guess not." Del thought of the asteroid she'd accidentally cut free from its tether. "Jie, about yesterday..."

"Later. Let's get our friends first."

There was so much she wanted to say. Instead, she said, "Okay."

"What about the ship?" he asked.

"I'm tempted to say forget it. So far, the thing's been more trouble than it's worth."

"It'll be worth it if they managed to get any fuel or repairs done before everything fell apart."

"Given our history, wanna bet it's in even worse shape now than before?"

"No bet."

"Damn, I was afraid of that," Del said as she checked her feed. "My access to the Factory still works, but it's limited to the one asteroid that's cut off from its tether. Looks like it's abandoned now."

"Another free body flying off through the Belt to probably eventually be used as a pirate base or something," Jie replied over the direct channel.

"You don't think they'll get it and bring it back?"

"Going too fast now to be worth capturing again," Jie answered. "It'd be cheaper to just find another one closer to the relative velocity. They've probably got a couple en route already anyway. Moles will be busy hollowing them out as they go so they'll be all ready to tether and spin up once they get here."

"Having found a couple of free ones in the past, I'm kind of happy to be finally giving back. Fly free little asteroid; go forth and make some little pirate band very happy. Too bad I don't have any missiles anymore," she said, changing the subject. "All I have in the way of weaponry is my needler, and about a dozen restraint cables. How about you?"

"Snake rifle, four smokestrobes, and another handful of restraint cables."

"We're not exactly a walking arsenal here. Without BeltSec, until Kenny shows up again there's no way to replace anything we use."

"You sure he'll be helpful even if he does show up again?"

"After I rescued him? Should be even more so now than in the past."

"I mean, are you sure he's not in league with the Rabbit? He's the one who sent you to the Veteran after all. Maybe that's why they knew you were coming."

"Faking a whole signal, just to lure me there? Seems like a lot of trouble to go through."

"I don't think the Rabbit found out about your presence at 1327-27 from BeltSec. From what I could tell, you were assigned Johanka's route only after he contacted them. So, who told him?"

"He was there. He could have read it from my mind."

"I thought it just worked on surface thoughts. At what point were you thinking 'I am Delokita from BeltSec?'" he said with a short laugh.

"It also seems to be flashes of memories. But that's me. What's the Rabbit capable of? *Scio nur li scias.*" Scio the All-Knowing may know, but she sure as hell didn't. "Besides, even if Kenny did sell me out that doesn't preclude doing business with him in the future. He would have been paid for that already. The fact that I got away is on them, not him, and after they betrayed him, they'd have to pay him a hell of a lot more before he'd sell me out again."

"That's...surprisingly forgiving of you."

"Not really. I just choose not to pursue justice. Unless you want to keep fighting forever, sometimes you need to let go of the desire for justice. I figured that out even before I left Mars. Forgiveness isn't any part of it. He owes me now more than ever, and we need him now more than ever."

"Maybe not. I still have some friends at BeltSec. If we have money, I can probably arrange an occasional shipment. We'd have to do it sparingly, though."

"Redirect resources off-book? Why Inspector, I'm shocked. Also, curious who would help."

"What, you think you're the only Enforcer to ever take a bribe? And there's Bilan."

"What about Bilan?"

"I mean I found her. She's in a cargo facility of one of the outer orbiters."

"Sounds easy enough. Let's go pick her up."

"Not as easy as it sounds," Jie said. "She can't just open the doors because there's a bunch of civilian workers in there with no vacsuits."

"Tell them to leave because the doors are about to open?"

"If she does that, the local Enforcers will know where she is. And they do have suits."

"And an appalling disregard for the lives of the people there, as we've seen. This whole place is an illegal facility. What are legitimate Enforcers doing all over it?"

"Probably on loan - another 'favor' from Lakshminarayanan. And the people working there are probably indentured servants - if not outright slaves, so they'll probably care even less."

"Void. They might just open the doors themselves if they find out she's there."

"And we can't get too close without them seeing us. Whatever we're going to do, we better do it fast."

"You still have the docking tunnel?"

"You thinking of punching a hole somewhere? The rock's too thick for anything we have here."

"One of the windows?"

"We'd risk shattering it and killing everyone inside."

"I've done it before. It just made a neat little hole in the glass."

"I saw," Jie replied. "And then the Enforcers," he spat the word, "opened the door and killed everyone in the corridor."

"The elevator!" Del said. "If it's like the others, it'll have a standard airlock on each level."

"You suggest we cut into the elevator?"

"We don't need to. We can just climb down the shaft."

"Risky. Plus, we still have no way to open the door safely."

"If it's a standard model, the wheel should work on the outer door, even if they keep the inner door locked. But the only locked doors I encountered before were the administrator's office and the cells."

"Fortunately, it looks like she's on one of the outer orbiters, not part of the Factory proper, so we'll be outside the exclusion zone, which means we can take the bikes right in."

DEL WAS RELIEVED when she stepped off the last handhold at the bottom of the elevator pit. She had to wait for the airlock to decompress before entering, then pressurize again before leaving the other side, but there was no issue getting through. Jie was waiting with the bikes on the surface. Bilan was in a cargo hold two levels up, with a group of Enforcers searching for her. Del was the diversion.

There were just a couple of people in the corridor when she stepped through the inner door. Neither were wearing vacsuits. What was wrong with all these people? She almost laughed out loud thinking of what Jie would say about the thought. She was lucky he couldn't read her mind. Of course, if he could do that, they never would have become friends in the first place. That thought made her sad.

Focus, Del, she told herself. *Task at hand. You're the distraction, so cause a distraction. Get the Enforcers down here, then find a way to survive it.*

"*Egido, protektu vian infanon*," she muttered under her breath. *Lady Protector, guard your child.*

She lowered her helmet.

"Hey!" she called to one of the people in the hall. "Is that the administrator's office?" She pointed to the door at the end of the hall.

"That's the cafeteria," the man replied disdainfully. He looked her up and down. She had again elected to wear only her vacsuit, hoping it would make her more recognizable. If someone recognized her from her last visit, they'd be more likely to send everybody they had after her.

"Who are you, and what are you doing here?" he asked.

"I'm Delokita, and I'm looking for the administrator's office."

"You've got the wrong rock. She's over on Seven."

Void.

"Who controls this rock then?" she asked.

"The administrator. From Seven."

"Say I wanted to peek into the coms, or open or close some doors. Where would I find a console that could let me do that?"

"Why would you want to do that?"

"I figured it would make it easier to rob the place."

The woman further down the corridor was heading their way.

"You...you want to rob the place?" the man Del was speaking with said. "Why?"

"What do you mean why? For the money of course! Why else does anyone steal anything? I mean, you don't expect me to work for a living, do you?"

"That's what I do!" He snorted indignantly.

This was taking far too long. She needed someone here to set off an alarm.

"Yeah, but look at you. They don't even give you a vacsuit, and you're standing in a corridor that's going to be exposed to space in about a minute."

"What?" He gasped, and was echoed by the woman who'd come up behind him.

"Once I find whatever you jerks have to steal, I'm going to blow all the air out of this hallway while I make my getaway."

The woman took off running down the hall. The man in front of her just stood there looking confused, like he was trying to decide if she was joking or not.

Del stepped to the nearest door and opened it. It looked like an office, with a single occupant, sitting behind a desk.

"Excuse me?" he said. "I didn't—"

"This'll do," Del said, and gestured toward the door. "Get in, explain what's going on and remember, don't open this door for any reason or you'll probably die."

That should keep them for a bit. Hopefully, they'd call someone further up. She hoped the man remembered her name.

She ran down the hall, hitting the buttons to open the doors along the way.

"What is the meaning of this?" the last one shouted.

"You'll see in a second!" she yelled back.

"Del?" Jie's voice came over her com. "Whatever you did down there, it looks like it worked. You got a whole mess of uglies headed your way."

"On it," she said. "Thanks for the heads up. If luck holds, I'll be coming out the window."

"And if luck doesn't hold?"

"I'll let you know."

She opened the door to the cafeteria. The room was the same layout as the administrator's office she'd seen before, with the same window on the far side. Only the furnishings were different, with a multiple-port autochef along one wall and half a dozen tables scattered throughout, most of which were currently empty.

The people inside were already buzzing excitedly as she entered. The woman from the hall must have told them she was here. Good.

"Listen up!" she shouted over the din, raising her rifle for emphasis. "Mealtime's over. I'm going to blow out that window and if you don't want to get blown out into space with me, get into a room up the hall now and close the door behind you."

She stepped away from the open door to give them room to pass.

"I've already called the Enforcers," the woman from the halls said. "They're on the way down here now."

"You'd better hurry, then!" Del replied. "Because that doesn't give me much time."

She went to the window and pulled out three meters of breaching cable and began sticking it in a large circle, while the crowd watched in horror. She pointed Jie's snake rifle at the nearest one and none of the rest moved forward to stop her.

"What are you waiting for?" she asked, then shouted as loudly as she could, "Run!"

She put her helmet up for emphasis then returned to her work. When she had the cord laid out, she turned back to see the room was empty. Good. She stepped out into the hall and saw six people in armored vacsuits. All were carrying rifles. Her friend, still not wearing a vacsuit, was standing in the middle of the hallway, saying something to them. The idiot!

GET INTO THE ROOM NOW!

As she thought it, she fired her snake rifle, twice, in two long, arced shots, once at each of the two lead enforcers. Without checking if any of her actions were successful, she ducked back into the room and slammed the door and locked it from her side.

A request for communication from Jie popped up on her interface, and she accepted it.

"Hey, any chance you can make it back up here? We've run into a bit of a situation."

"Void! I was about to say the same. Can you hold on for another minute? I have a plan."

Bilan popped up in another window. "Is it as good as your plan for rescuing me?"

"Good to see you, too. I thought we were playing taxi. When did this turn into a rescue?" As she spoke, she dragged one of the tables over next to the door and turned it on its side. She heard a loud bang over both their feeds.

"Was that a slug thrower? I thought I had all the Enforcers down here."

"A couple seemed to have missed the memo."

"Just two? Okay, tell you what. Once I'm done with these six, I'll head up there to help you with yours." She pulled off more breaching cord and started sticking it to the sides of the table.

"Ha! Seriously, though, don't get yourself killed down there. We'll—Jie!" Bilan shouted in alarm.

"What—" Del started, but at that moment her door exploded inward, flew across the room, and smashed into the window on the far side.

Four of the Enforcers piled into the room after the door. Her needler would never pierce their armor, so she didn't even try it. She fired the rifle at the nearest one and saw a pair of the snakes grab onto him. Loose ends writhed in the air trying to find something else to latch on to. She ducked behind the table and held it as tightly as she could with both hands, her feet braced against a couch bolted to the floor. Then she activated the breaching cord on the window.

With the helmet on, she couldn't hear the explosion, but its effects were unmistakable. The sudden rush of air nearly tore the table from her hands. She was expecting it and managed to hold on, for one second, then two, then let it go.

As it flew toward the hole in the window, she wished she could see what had been going on on the other side of the table. It would have made great footage to add to the video whenever she got a chance to sell it. Of the four Enforcers who had entered, she could see one outside the window, rapidly receding. Another one had managed to land on his feet and was balancing against the spin gravity and the rushing air to aim his rifle at her. She fired off a shot with her own and was gratified to see one of the snakes catch his rifle and begin wrapping around his arm.

The other two had landed against the window, one of them knocked prone by the flying table. Another table had lodged in the small hole and was blocking anything larger from getting through. Void. She had hoped to sweep most if not all of them out of the room. One was still kneeling on the window, braced against the wind and trying to aim his rifle at her. She sent the signal to the cord attached to the table she'd sent after them. When it blew, the whole window went out, spewing a long plume of debris including all three Enforcers out into space.

It took a few more seconds for the rest of the air in the station to follow.

She stepped cautiously out into the corridor. Two Enforcers were there, entangled together in half a dozen snakes. One was cutting through the mass with a vacuum torch. She used her suit thrusters to aid her leap over them then, bracing against the far wall, kicked the two of them together into the cafeteria. The one with the torch attempted a feeble swing at her, but his movement was restricted by the snakes, and he came closer to cutting his friend than her.

A loose end of one of the snakes grabbed her ankle and she fell hard to the floor as the man began pulling himself toward her again. Using another burst from her suit thrusters, she reached the button for the door, and it slammed shut.

One of the snakes was still wrapped around her ankle. Attached to the other end was the severed foot of an Enforcer. She kicked at it in panic, but it held fast.

Trying to ignore the foot, she gripped the rifle to re-establish the interface on her suit and released the snake. Both ends released their respective feet, and she kicked the other away from her, where it lay on the floor in a small pool of dark blood which quickly boiled away leaving nothing but a discolored spot on the polished floor.

She struggled back up to her feet and reestablished the link to Jie and Bilan. "I'm good," she said. "Where are you? What's the situation?"

"Jie's hurt. We're in the cargo bay but his suit's ruptured. We need to get him back to his scoot to repair it, and him."

"Void. How serious is it?"

"I'll be fine," Jie cut in.

"He may be telling the truth, as long as we can get him to his ship."

"Rendezvous back at the ships, then?"

"Problem with that is the vacuum between here and there."

"I'm in the elevator, on my way up now. There'll be a few Enforcers following me soon, though I think I can slow them down a bit. Where are the ones following you?"

"Neutralized for now. They're both entangled and needled."

"How'd you get a needle through their armor?"

"After the snakes got 'em, I pulled their helmets off."

"Oh, they must've loved that."

"They had a couple of choice words, yes."

Using the last of her breaching cable, Del sent the elevator car back down to the bottom floor and scuttled it there. Any Enforcers who made it out of the office would have to cut through it then climb back up. That should give them a little bit of time at least.

Jie brought his scoot in by remote and Del climbed out to the surface to attach the docking tube to the outer airlock. They climbed through it and pulled away from the asteroid.

"I really gotta get me one of these," Del said as she settled down in the tube. Unlike her own setup, Jie's bike could still be piloted with the tube attached, giving enough room for the three of them in the small craft as long as they didn't try any complex maneuvers.

"Yeah," Bilan replied. "I'm gonna miss the catalog at BeltSec."

Jie directed it to take them back to their original rendezvous spot while Del sent the command to her own bike to follow the same zig-zagging course.

"How are you?" she asked.

"Been better," he said as Bilan helped him off with his suit.

There was a huge angry welt on his left thigh that was oozing blood.

"Tiny puncture, looks like the suit stopped most of it," Bilan said.

"But it made it through."

"Yep. Bullet's still in there. Not deep, and doesn't look like there's a lot of damage. You got a tissue scanner in here?"

"In the kit. Del?"

She knew the one. She unlocked it from the cupboard it was stored in and handed it to him. Bilan found a painkiller and injected him, then pulled out a small device with a screen and set to work on removing the bullet.

"We can't use the passcode that I got from the *Zheng He* crew," Bilan said. "I'm pretty sure that's what got me marked in the first place. They waited for us to get off the ship first, but I wouldn't be surprised if they followed us from the beginning."

"And you haven't heard anything from Cor?"

"Nothing. We were to meet back at the ship if we got split up, or, failing that, at 198-24."

"Too bad we can't remote pilot the ship," Del said. "Should we head there and see if Amelia made it back, or try to find her first?"

"Find Amelia first," Bilan said. "I have a good idea where she is, and if they've locked the ship down, she can help us break into it."

"I thought you were the technical genius here."

"Only compared to you."

SEVENTEEN
PLAN OF ATTACK

Bilan and Del left Jie lying in the tube under sedation and took the two seats in his scoot.

Bilan's eyes widened when Del lowered her helmet. "Wow! What happened to you?"

"What do you mean?"

"Have you seen yourself? Must've been quite a fight. Why didn't you have your helmet up?"

Del pulled up an image of her face on Jie's screen. She had a large black eye, dried blood around her nose, and bruising all over, especially along her neck near the suit.

"Oh! That. It's...uh...it looks a lot worse than it really is."

"What the depths happened?"

"I was...well...Jie thought it would be a good idea if I practiced with my...abilities...while we were waiting for you."

"Jie did this to you? What the—?"

"Not exactly."

"Then what exactly?"

"I sort of made him."

Bilan took a deep breath. Let it out. Took another one. "You mean you were practicing on how to implant a, what, compulsion, is that what we're calling it?"

"Sounds as good as anything."

"And you implanted a compulsion for him to beat you up?"

"More or less."

Bilan looked her over more closely. "Depths, Del, he must feel awful."

"He did. I told him it wasn't his fault."

"Still. Why didn't you just make him strip naked or something like you did to me?"

Del laughed gently at the memory. "I wanted to make sure it was something I knew he didn't want to do."

"But why? We already knew your power works to get people to do things."

As she said it, Del had a flash of memory, of standing naked in an airlock, facing herself and Jie, accompanied by both a feeling of embarrassment as they were both looking at her as well as a thrill that they were.

"I...uh...sorry, your question, or, right, yeah, he was..." She took a deep breath. "That is, he wanted to learn how to resist it."

"I take it from the state of your face he didn't."

"He did. It took a bit...more, but it worked. He could distinguish his own thoughts from mine in the end. We were going to try again after a night's rest."

"After all that, you wanted to try again?"

"Whatever he does to me, and however bad he feels about it afterward will be nothing compared to if, say, the Rabbit catches up to us and makes him kill me."

Bilan didn't say anything for a moment, then, "Do you think he can do that?"

"He came close to making me kill myself. It was only because he didn't know how my suit works that he failed."

"Stars. Maybe we all should work on learning. If we get in a fight with him..."

"There's no guarantee that any of us can learn to resist him. It may not even be possible."

"Jie did."

"No, Jie learned to resist me," Del emphasized. "And even then, only when I tried to get him to do something completely alien to his being. Unfortunately, you, me, him, we're all capable of violence, if necessary, which I think makes it harder to resist. Adding the sexual component was what made it go against his core. And I'm not sure any of us could even resist that if we came face to face with someone like the Rabbit."

"Jie's going to take a while to recover," Bilan said, and it took Del a moment to realize she was referring to the bullet wound. "What's the plan for getting Amelia out?"

"I was thinking we'd just walk in and take her."

"You don't think there'll be guards?"

"Take them out."

"Port defenses?"

"Damn, I wish I had some missiles left. Hm. That gives me an idea."

"Rig up some kind of explosives? We could probably make something out of one of the engines..."

"I was thinking more of the shooting through the void of space thing. You're pretty good at calculating trajectories and stuff, right?"

TWO HOURS LATER, Bilan and Del were both riding on Del's bike as it sped toward the Factory.

Fifty kilometers out, the bike banked sharply away from the station and they both let go. The bike itself flew on the course

Bilan had plotted back to the rendezvous point, where Jie's scoot was waiting for them. Jie would eventually awaken to find himself in his docking tube with a message from Bilan and Del filling him in on their plan, and suggesting he take the time he was waiting for them to repair his suit. If all went well, they would pick him up on the *Zheng He*.

Del's suit thrusters were already low from her earlier maneuvering in high gravity. She used most of the rest to slow down enough to land on the asteroid itself. She landed hard, the impact driving her to the rocky ground. Pebbles and dust scattered in the vacuum around her, settling down quickly in the spin-induced gravity.

She looked over at Bilan, who looked worried so Del gave her a thumbs-up gesture.

Bilan smiled and nodded, pointed to the cable where it descended into the ground, and stretched to disappear into the darkness above. That little cable is all that held them in place. The asteroid was so small that without it, they'd be at risk of bouncing right off. As it was, the asteroid spinning about the factory had a nice comfortable surface gravity just below that of Mars.

They walked together in silence until they got to the edge of the elevator pit. The pit followed typical construction, with regularly spaced handholds set into the rock and the common Hanzhong Construction Standard Medium Airlock, two and half meters on each side, exactly like the one in her apartment.

"*Shanso, estu sinjorino*," Bilan said as they began their descent.

"I didn't think you went in for that sort of superstition," Del responded, amused.

Bilan shrugged. "Figured it couldn't hurt."

Del hadn't been to this asteroid on her previous visit and didn't know what to expect. Instead of the long central tunnel the others had, this one opened into a room. There were seats along one side, and a pressure door beside a half-height window opposite the elevator. Behind the window sat a tall man, wearing a BeltSec uniform but no vacsuit. His eyes widened as Del and Bilan approached his window.

"No weapons allowed," was the first thing he barked at them when they got there, followed by, "Who are you and what are you doing here?"

"We're here for one of your prisoners," Bilan told him. "TL9-372-114."

While she spoke, Del fixed the man with a glare and thought,

LET THEM IN!

"It's, uh, highly irregular, but, well, okay," he said and reached down to his console. A moment later the door slid open. Del wondered how he justified it to himself. What convolutions of logic did his mind have to go through to make this okay?

"Thank you," Bilan said sweetly, and stepped through the door. It closed behind them and they found themselves in the more familiar central tunnel, with pressure doors at regular intervals on each side.

"Any idea which room she's in?" Del asked Bilan.

"I have no idea. Jie was the one who she talked to."

Del found the news disturbing. "I thought he talked to you."

"He contacted me, but I didn't know where anyone was," Bilan answered.

"He was pretty specific about it. You were pinned down in the cargo bay—"

"I told him that."

"Amelia was arrested—"

"He didn't hear that from me," Bilan said. "Maybe Cor?"

"He said nobody had heard from Cor."

"It would explain why I couldn't reach her."

"It would also explain why you couldn't get ahold of Cor, but he didn't explain it that way."

"You're not suggesting Jie's setting us up, are you?" Bilan asked.

It was obvious what answer she wanted, but Del wasn't sure she could give it. "Not intentionally," she said instead. "But there's been a lot of manipulation going on here and I'm not the one doing most of it."

"You think the Rabbit's here?"

"Something's going on that I don't like. We need to be careful."

"Way ahead of you there, but we did just walk into a secure facility, with only one door, that just locked behind us."

Del tried the nearest pressure door. It was locked.

"These are all going to be locked," Bilan said. "Let's try the booth and see if we can get any information out of your friend there." She pulled a length of breaching cord from a spool in a side pouch. "In case he doesn't want to answer politely."

The door they came in through was locked, as they expected.

"Wait, not that one," Del said, and pointed to the first door on the right. "That one there should do it."

"How can you be sure? Can you sense someone behind it?"

"No," Del said, trying not to laugh. "The booth was on the right."

Bilan laughed and laid out the breaching cord on the door.

A console next to the door lit up and the face of the man they'd spoken to earlier appeared.

"What are you doing?" he asked.

"Preparing to open the door if you don't," Del replied.

"I can't do that."

"No worries. We're almost done. Might want to step back, though."

"No, I mean I can't. The whole place is locked down. I don't have access."

That was interesting. She looked to Bilan.

"That doesn't sound good," Bilan said. "We'd better hurry."

Del turned back to the screen, holding up one finger.

"How about you just tell us what cell Amelia's in, and we'll leave you alone?"

"I can't do that."

"Is that because you can't, or you're not supposed to?"

"Uh..."

"Del?"

She'd been trying but failed. "I can't read him from here. Blow the door."

Bilan stepped backward and raised her helmet.

Del followed her lead.

A second later, the cord stuck to the door glowed red hot, then white, and the center of the door fell inward.

Bilan raised her needler and pointed it toward the open doorway.

Del stepped forward, her arm raised in front of her.

The man stood in front of them, holding both hands up, palm outward. His face was calm.

Del lowered her helmet and looked into his eyes. "He's lying," she said. "There's no lockdown. He was told to stall us."

His eyes grew wide, and Bilan leveled her gun at him. "Open her cell."

"No."

Without another word, Bilan pulled the trigger.

Del wasn't sure whether the sudden feeling of shock was coming from the man or herself.

"I...what?" he said, then slumped to the floor.

"What the void was that?" Del exclaimed.

"Follow my lead," Bilan said. "If you can tell if he's lying, or reinforce my commands, that'd be great."

"Okay," Del said, not really sure where this was going.

"Let's get him into his chair," Bilan said, and together they lifted him into the chair.

"Can you read him with your helmet up?" Bilan asked.

"I couldn't even read him with it down."

"I thought you said—"

"I was bluffing!" Del protested.

"Depths. Ready?" She pulled the injector with the needler's antidote out of its pouch. The man came to with a start, seeing the two women with their helmets on, standing over him.

Bilan dropped hers while Del kept her own up, having an idea where she was going with this now.

"Oh good, you're finally awake," Bilan said. "Here's the deal: your friends are dead. Unfortunately, they've got more reinforcements on the way. They'll be here in about two minutes. If we can get out of here in one minute, we'll use the airlock we came in through. If it takes us any longer than that, we'll blow a hole through the back of the station. If we have to do that, there won't be anything to hold the air in, understand?"

The man nodded vigorously. If he was thinking anything, Del couldn't tell what.

"Open our friend's cell."

Del was about to send a mental command at him, but he reached forward and tapped the console on his desk. In the image on the screen, a door opened. Del stepped into the hallway to see if the door had actually opened. It had, but Amelia was nowhere to be seen. She dropped her helmet and told Bilan "I'll check on her."

When she got to the open cell and peeked her head in, it was empty. She was about to turn back and call to Bilan when something flew down and struck her in the face. She moved to the side to avoid most of the blow and a weight landed on her back. Someone had dropped from the ceiling onto her shoulders. They slung what felt like some sort of cloth across the front of her throat and began tightening it from behind.

She turned slightly and threw herself backward, hoping to slam her attacker into the door frame, but they turned with her, pulling her sideways and she hit it with her shoulder. Then the tension on the cloth lessened and her attacker dropped nimbly to the floor.

"Del?" her assailant said in surprise.

Amelia stood before her, holding a pyjama top similar to what Del had worn in the BeltSec prison, tightly wrapped in her hand.

"Gah," Del said, and rubbed at her abused throat. "Not the greeting I was expecting."

"Sorry. I thought you were someone else."

"I gathered. Let's get out of here. Bilan's up the hall."

Amelia unwrapped her shirt and put it on as she followed Del back up the hall.

"You okay?" Bilan asked. "Where's Cor?"

"I was in a cell until twenty seconds ago."

"Aright. Maybe he made it back to the ship. If not, he might still have found a way of leaving a message."

"That's our next stop, then." Bilan picked up their prisoner, chair and all, and carried him down the hall, throwing him into Amelia's cell before returning and closing the door.

Amelia found the guard's slug thrower on the floor and picked it up. Del was a little apprehensive about that but didn't stop her. It would be the only thing they had that might pierce a combat vacsuit.

Bilan checked the console on the desk, and pulled up an image of the elevator, showing six guards incoming.

"Void. They're already on the elevator. I was afraid of that."

"How much time do we have?" Del asked.

"Maybe ten minutes. They're coming up from the Factory."

"You have command access? Let's go up a level or two then and pull the elevator out from behind them."

"I still don't have a suit," Amelia said.

"That's why we brought the bag," Bilan told her.

"Dammit, I hate that thing." But she handed Bilan the pistol and climbed in when they got to the elevator airlock.

They climbed up the two decks to the first level, pulling Amelia in her bag up behind them. By the time they got the door closed the elevator was almost upon them. They let it go by, and when the Enforcers had left, Bilan pulled it back up behind them and they piled in.

"That was far easier than I expected," she said.

"We're not out of the tunnels yet," Del said. "We still have to find Cor and figure out how to get our ship back."

"First, the cargo," Amelia said.

"Cargo?"

"Cor and I found a bunch of stuff we need. It should be stacked and ready for us in a cargo bay on Three."

"You don't think it's dangerous enough without going back to get the stuff?"

"This whole trip will have been for nothing if we don't get it."

"I'll think about it. Still need to get the ship first, or else we won't have anywhere to put it."

"Agreed."

EIGHTEEN
GUNS, FISTS, AND MEMORIES

They didn't meet any more resistance heading back to the docking bay. The port airlock of the *Zheng He* was still damaged, and they had no problem getting through it. When they got to the first door leading to the bridge, though, the door refused to open to Del's code.

"What's going on?" she asked Bilan, as Amelia opened the door manually.

"There're some forces moving our way," Bilan answered, looking at her own display, where she'd been monitoring the factory's coms. They still hadn't shut her out since they'd rescued Amelia. "BeltSec. Two, no, three groups of four. All with combat vacsuits."

"Let me know when they get close. Amelia?"

"Got it. At least we don't have to worry about air pressure," Amelia responded. Since the ship was inside a large docking bay, there was air all around it. Del wasn't used to not being surrounded by vacuum.

The bridge was empty, and all the systems seemed to be offline.

"You two get this going again. I'm going to check out the rest of the ship," Del said.

"Alone? Are you crazy?" Bilan responded.

"I'll be fine. We need to get the ship ready to go, which means I need you up here assisting Amelia."

"Just stay in touch."

"Of course."

"Here." Bilan tossed her the snake rifle. "Just in case you run into anybody we don't like."

Del took the rifle and Bilan transferred command of it back to her.

The door to the captain's quarters slid open as she approached, and she stepped in.

Cor was sprawled out on the bed. "About time somebody showed up," he said, sitting up. "Any longer and I was going to go out looking for you. Are the rest with you?"

"They're on the bridge trying to get it going. Do you know something 'bout that?" Something in the man's mannerisms made her suspicious.

A second later, her suspicions were confirmed.

"Okay, you win," Cor said, as he swung his legs off the bed and came to his feet. "You were right."

"It was never in doubt," a calm voice said. Del's blood froze as the Rabbit stepped out of her bathroom. "Deal with them, and I will ensure you get your full reward and more."

Cor bent to pick up a slug rifle on a nearby table and Del started to swing her own rifle in his direction.

Then she was on Mars, running through the tunnels. Several officers from Burroughs City Security were running after her and she was scared of what would happen if they caught her down in the old tunnels with no witnesses. There was something familiar about this. She had been here before. She had left after her last fosters. There should have been one more, but there never was. She was eight years old. "What is that in human years?" She remembered Jie asking three years in the future.

"Hey, flatface!" Yander's voice came from somewhere behind her.

He'd been following her around for weeks trying to get into her pants. She'd been thinking of letting him. Now it seemed he was distracting the security officers to let her get away. That was very brave of him, she decided. If they both managed to survive this...

Then she was back in her quarters on the *Zheng He* and the Rabbit was in front of her, aiming the snake rifle she'd had in her hands moments before.

Oh, please pull the trigger, she thought, remembering setting off the defense mechanism of Jie's gun.

He scowled and swung it at her instead.

And then Yander was there, and they were alone in one of the empty tunnels, and he had bruises on his face from where the security officers had hit him because they were upset that their prey had escaped, and they couldn't find anything to arrest him for. The party had been a success and she said he deserved a reward for his bravery and the others all laughed knowingly as she took him by the hand and led him away from the party and deeper into the tunnels.

She was undoing the buttons on her shirt. He was about to be her first. She looked up at the bruise on his face similar to the one on hers where Jie had hit her.

This wasn't right.

She snapped out of it and found herself on the floor of her quarters and there was a sharp pain in the side of her head. The Rabbit stood over her, with the rifle, clutched like a club. He raised it.

Cor was heading for the bridge.

The coms were still unavailable. She should have known something was wrong.

She raised her arm to ward off the blow.

She reached for Bilan's mind, trying to do in an instant what had taken her days before, when trapped on the icy erratic.

COR'S A TRAITOR! DON'T LET HIM ON THE BRIDGE!

The rifle smashed down into her forearm. It didn't feel like it broke, but she wasn't sure. She got dizzy for a second, everything went black, then somehow Bilan was there. She was holding the rifle and pointing it at the Rabbit, who was starting to rise from the floor.

"Quick! Give me access to the rifle!" Bilan shouted.

She reached for it, but Bilan pulled away.

The transfer required physical contact between the sensors in the rifle handle and those in her suit's fingers, and she realized Bilan would know that, just as Del knew she couldn't take her helmet off on Aluna.

This had to be another illusion. Fake perceptions being planted into her brain.

If his power worked on her, though, hers should work on him. *Right?*

ACCESS HAS BEEN GRANTED. FIRE!

She directed the thought at the Rabbit who was now standing in front of her exactly where he had been a second ago.

Bilan vanished as Del sprung to her feet.

The Rabbit had dropped the rifle, but it was too late. The snake had a grip on his wrist and the other end was already flailing around in the air seeking something else to grab onto. He glared at her in rage, realizing what she'd done.

There was a loud report from up the ship somewhere. The sound made by a slug-thrower in atmosphere.

She turned and started to step out the door when she heard another gunshot. It was coming from the bridge. She tried to run in that direction and fell on her face.

Something had grabbed her ankle. She looked back and saw the end of the snake wrapped around it, and in the process of constricting. The bastard had whipped his hand around so the snake caught her instead of another of his own limbs or some graspable piece of infrastructure. She raised her wrist-mounted needler and pointed it at his face.

And then she was in her apartment, on her bed, straddling a man beneath her. He'd told her his name was Jay, but she knew that she would later come to know him as Jeremy.

Immediately, she recognized it as another memory he was trying to trap her in.

This is what you did to Amelia, isn't it? she asked with a thought. *This is what you do. Force girls like her into that place, then make them relive their experiences while you watch. Pathetic. All that power you control, and second-hand voyeurism is the only thing you can think of to do with it. No wonder the Veteran was so disappointed in you.*

At that, she caught both the surge of anger and the unbidden memory of The Veteran berating him for his selfishness and his short-sightedness. The memory was like a thread - she followed it to its source. He knew what she was doing, but he was back in control. His memories surrounded her, overwhelmed her in a flood - a childhood spent in a gleaming institution. Dozens of other children his age. Classrooms. Lessons. Harsh punishments. It was not a kind place. The children were pitted against each other, and failures met with punishment. Not all of them survived. She was horrified, and he was disgusted by her horror. It made him strong. *Only the strongest survived the training.*

It's called survivor's bias, she remembered from a long ago class she must have been paying at least some attention in. *You happened to survive. That doesn't make you special.*

A group of children ran across the surface of a bright rocky planet. A giant sun hung in the sky, bigger than she'd ever seen. The children were in full vacuum suits. One boy tripped and fell to the ground. His faceplate cracked open. It was a freak accident to trip in exactly that spot and land exactly that way.

He wasn't weaker or less clever, just unlucky. Whatever this training was, all it produced was a bunch of sociopathic little toadies like you, willing to do their bidding in exchange for occasional praise and reassurance of how special you are.

He raged against her then, and she could feel him pushing back into her mind.

And what have you ever accomplished? She heard his mental voice answer her own. *Wasted your life in trivialities and selfish pleasure-seeking!*

Then she was in another tunnel on Mars, and a boy was fumbling with the unusual fastenings on her pants. It wasn't Yander. Their relationship, if that's what it was, had been over for months. She couldn't even remember this one's name. For a moment, it bothered her that she couldn't remember.

He got the fly open, and then gravity reversed itself and she fell onto the ceiling. The boy didn't react, he continued to tug her pants down, over her hips, like he did when this really happened. But the gravity hadn't changed then. That wasn't a thing that happened on Mars.

She pushed up out of the memory and found herself on the ceiling in the hall outside her quarters. A mechanical snake still held the Rabbit's wrist to her ankle. He was intentionally delaying her. Keeping her in place and helpless long enough for

Cor to take care of her friends then come back for her. She pulled back with her free foot and kicked him hard in the face. He looked at her with a look of fear, then he shifted. The gravity gave way again and she was on the ship heading from Mars to the Belt.

She was floating in zero G, with her legs wrapped around one of the crew. Their clothes were floating all around them in a small cargo bay.

There was something familiar about that. Something that something else would remind her of. She couldn't recall what, though, or what that meant. She felt a strange weight on her mind as she made love. She should be lost in this moment. It should be all-consuming. She went with it.

When they were done, she floated beside him, basking in the afterglow, their hands touching, not quite grasping. He was a kind man and a generous lover, and she was almost sorry that she'd never see him again after this trip.

She fell to the floor. Nothing else but her was affected. That wasn't right, either.

The Rabbit. She could still feel his mind there. *Is this really all you've got,* she thought at him. She still felt relaxed, peaceful, from the memory of happy exhaustion. *It's a good memory. I hope you enjoyed it. How come you don't have any of your own?*

She dove deeper into his mind and found several connections. She stopped when she came across a memory of him crying as a child, from pain and humiliation. He was bent over the knee of an adult, his pants were pulled down and several other children were in the room with him, most of them openly laughing at his tears as the man raised a paddle. For just a second, she felt pity for him, and could feel his scorn at her pity. She had heard rumors amongst the other children in the foster system on Mars about this kind of abuse, but only rumors. Always something that happened to a friend of a friend. She never heard directly from anyone who claimed it happened to them. Nonetheless, they stressed that she should contact her case worker immediately if anything like it did occur.

You were protected. She could feel his scorn. *Coddled. Weak.*

You were abused as a child, she thought back. *That hardly excuses anything you've done since then. How old do you have to be before your life is your own fault?*

The Rabbit tried to pull away from the memory, but she held him fast. She could feel his anger and she gloated in her own strength over him. She held him there, forced him to relieve the memory as he'd forced her to. She felt the sting of the paddle as it came down on her, again and again. Somehow these memories were connected...

And then she was in school, sitting through a lecture on psychology that she knew she should be interested in but she was far more interested in getting it over with so she could go to the track and field class next.

She was seeing how it worked. She felt his disdain. *I will always be more powerful than you here. It's a fight you can't win.*

And then she was lying on her back in her own apartment near Ceres with Jie's boot on her chest. She twisted underneath it, trying to get free. As she moved, she could feel the rough sole of his boot rub against her nipple through the thin suit. She hadn't even been aware of it at the time. *How could he remember this better than she could?*

You're obsessed, she thought at him. *You pathetic little troll.*

It was only a short jump from there to another similar memory. A track meet, and another fight she had no chance of winning. She was running under the Great Dome in Bradbury Point in the five thousand meter Martian Freestyle semi-finals.

It had taken a year of training to get here, and her rival during most of that time, a boy a full Martian year older than her, was right in front of her. One of them would come in first in this race and go on to the planetary championships. The other would come in second and go nowhere.

They were approaching a boulder. If she timed it just right and vaulted it at the right angle, she could get past him. He'd have to redirect his momentum to avoid colliding with her. It was a dirty trick but could buy her half a second. Half a second was all she needed. She prepared to leap.

He slowed, just enough. A tenth of a second if even that was all it took to throw off her timing. She landed hard on her left foot, and it twisted beneath her, throwing her to the ground. She rolled and came back up, but her ankle gave way in an explosion of pain. There was a gasp from the crowd; their pity rained down on her and she wanted nothing to do with any of it.

She climbed back to her feet again and kept going. Other runners had already passed her. Every step was agony. Runner after runner passed her. She didn't know if the Rabbit could feel the pain in the memory like she could, but she could feel his astonishment and that was good enough.

Del could sense his disbelief that she hadn't quit. Her coach tried to tell her to stop, but she waved him off and kept going. More runners passed her.

Why? You had no chance of winning! He berated her. She laughed at him for that and could feel another memory invoked out of that. She pushed it away. She wanted him here. She finished this race, and he was going to see that firsthand.

Her rival passed her again. The final lap, and she was an entire lap behind him now. She continued. By the time she ran her own last lap everyone had passed her again. She continued. For the last quarter kilometer, she was the only one on the track. Half the stadium was empty by now. But the other half wasn't. They all stayed to watch her, alone, continuing through the pain.

She was approaching the finish line now. The other runners were there. All of them. Waiting for her. The yellow tape had long since been broken. There was a stretcher past them, on the ground. Two medical technicians standing next to it. The older boy who she had spent a year of her life trying to beat stood beside them. He was already wearing the blue ribbon with its medallion. He stayed on the far side of the line as she approached. He wouldn't let the others cross the line to help her and was keeping the stretcher where it was.

She fell in love with him then. He understood. He knew this was something she had to do. By now, she had realized that there would be nobody to rely on but herself. She had to prove to herself she could do this.

She stepped over the line, and then, and only then, did she let him help her stand while she demanded the race monitor officially record her time. He did so, after protesting, and the slowest time ever recorded in the Big Dome at Bradbury Point went up on the giant scoreboard and only then did she allow herself to be lowered to the stretcher. As she was, she pushed herself up and out of the memory.

The Rabbit was still there, his hand still bound tightly to her ankle. He was breathing heavily, staring up at her. If he'd been trying to attack her there was no sign of it.

He spoke out loud. "You lost. In spite of everything you still lost. You stupid little girl."

They were lying on the floor of the Zheng He. It was underway under low acceleration. Cor must be taking it somewhere, or Bilan and Amelia were. She'd have to get to the bridge to find out.

"You can read my mind and relive my memories," she

answered him. "And that eight year old boy still understood me more than you ever will."

"Then help me. Help me stop them," he said.

She shot him twice in the face with her needler. He screamed in anger and pain and confusion, and in the two and a half seconds before he lost consciousness, there was another rapid series of memories. Everything he'd won. Every victory, every triumph, every test he'd passed or trial he'd overcome, and it all paled in significance to her one overwhelming defeat.

She sat and stared at him for another full second, trying to process before she could act. She retrieved the rifle and used its interface to release the snake. She had to get to the bridge.

As she approached the door, it slid open.

Amelia and Bilan stood there, holding the limp form of Cor between them. They both looked up.

"Guess you got my message," she said.

"Eventually," Bilan replied. "There was some disagreement about the validity."

"I apologized, okay?" Amelia said. "You were right. I was wrong."

"That's all I needed to hear."

"Great. Now that Del's safe, let's get asshole here to the airlock so I can ask him some questions."

"Why the airlock?" Del asked.

"That's how they always do it in the vids," Amelia said. "Plus, I'm really angry at him right now and may decide I want to kill him."

There was a quick intake of breath from Bilan. "You sure that's something you want to do?"

"No. That's why I said I may decide. He was going to kill all of us, though."

"Even so, are you sure you want to become a killer?"

"I already said I haven't decided yet. I want to talk with him before I do. You've both killed people before and you're not raving psychopaths."

"That's different," Del said. "We've only ever killed in self-defense." It was a lie, though. The men she'd killed on Mars hadn't been a threat to her at the time.

"The one person I've ever actually killed, I didn't mean to," Bilan said.

Del thought of the man Bilan had kicked, with the smashed faceplate, in this very spot, and wondered again if she had accidentally compelled Bilan to do that. Had she made a killer out of her best friend?

"Doesn't matter," Amelia said. "The decision's mine, unless either of you plan on stopping me."

"Not me," said Del. "You know him best. I only request that whatever you decide you don't set him free on the ship."

"I won't stop you," Bilan said. "Just consider it carefully. Please."

"The only working airlock is the one leading to the cargo bay. Before you take him there, though, I want to get the Rabbit off the ship."

"The Rabbit's here?" both women said at once.

"That's what took me so long. We fought. I won. He's lying unconscious outside the captain's quarters."

"Depths. What are you going to do?"

"Toss him out." She had second thoughts even as she said it, then brushed them away. He'd made his choice. If he'd been willing to talk back on Aluna, she might have listened, but it was too late now. "He's far too dangerous to be allowed to ever wake up."

"And you're lecturing me about killing?" Amelia said incredulously.

"It's different. Cor's a normal human, and you cared for him once."

"Once. Up until about two minutes ago when I found out he was trying to sell me back into slavery. But you're right about the Rabbit. I knew him too, remember? And I won't shed a tear at all when he's gone."

"I don't like any of this," Bilan said, and re-opened the bridge door. She moved to the navigation console and cut acceleration.

"We'll catch up to Jie in about fifteen minutes." She turned to Amelia. "Will that give you enough time?"

"I'll make it work."

"Want any help?" Del asked.

"I'd rather do this alone."

"All right. Once Bilan's got communications going again, you should be able to call me if you change your mind."

They got to where the Rabbit had been only to discover he was missing.

"Coms are back," she heard Bilan say over her suit.

"Great. The Rabbit's gone."

"How is that possible? Could there have been someone else on the ship?"

"Must've been. I never checked the other two rooms. Void, I'm an idiot."

"Don't beat yourself up about it. A lot was happening at the time."

"Could he still be on the ship somewhere? Can you see everywhere yet?"

"No, and yes, and so can you, and I know he's gone because the cargo bay door is open and my bike's missing."

"Void! He must have had help."

"Must have. Unfortunately, the sensors didn't record anything while they were out."

"No point going after them now. Let's get back to Jie. Leave the door open, and we'll let Amelia do what she needs to."

She pulled the needle antidote from its pouch and handed it to Amelia.

When she got back on the bridge, Bilan offered her the center chair, which she took.

"No matter how far we travel," she said, indicating the view out the window. "The stars never change."

"You can go ten million kilometers and never see a difference," Bilan agreed. "But turn around and nothing's the same."

Neither of them spoke for a long time, each lost in her own thoughts.

"What do we do about him now?" Bilan finally asked.

"I don't think he's a threat to us anymore. If he was, he would have come after me as soon as he woke up. I think he's heading home."

"Where's his home?"

"Where we're all from. Mercury."

"I thought you were from Mars."

"So did I until a few minutes ago. I told you how I was found, right, in a cargo ship in orbit?"

"Yeah. It came from Mercury? I thought it was a Belt ship."

"It had been stolen from the Belt fifty years earlier, then traveled unregistered. Probably bought and sold and stolen a dozen times since then. Apparently one of its last stops was taking on an infant, and possibly a couple of terrorists, from Mercury. The infant was part of a program to breed telepaths."

"That's why the Rabbit looks like you."

"Same DNA strands. We're all fraternal twins."

"And you're sure he won't be back."

"Pretty sure. I think...I think he's kind of scared of me. And...I know it sounds weird, but he kind of looks up to me. Like I was doing something he'd always wanted to but never knew was possible before. It's complicated, but he definitely hates them more than anyone out here. I don't think he's going to be doing their bidding anymore."

"So, why would he go back there?"

"To explain it to them. Possibly loudly and with much violence."

Five minutes before they picked up Jie, Amelia came back onto the bridge, wearing a vacsuit. Nobody asked her where she got it, or where Cor was now.

JIE DIDN'T NEED any help getting into the cargo bay. He had already woken up, found Bilan's message, and repaired his suit by the time they arrived.

Del flew out to get her own bike and bring it in as well.

With Bilan's com access, they were able to give themselves permission to dock outside the relevant cargo bay and transfer everything on their manifest, while Del and Amelia, both known and wanted on the Factory now, stayed on the bridge, out of sight and ready to take off at a moment's notice.

When they were finished, they headed away from the Factory, in all probability for the last time. Within hours, their access would be revoked, Bilan was sure, and Amelia concurred. The two of them were becoming quite a team, and Del admitted to a pang of jealousy watching how well they worked together.

When they were well away, Del pressurized the bay on Amelia's recommendation, and cut acceleration to a tenth of a G and joined the rest in the cargo bay to unpack.

"ONLY ONE?" Del said in mock disappointment when she opened the box containing Amelia's special gift to her: a missile for her bike. "Could have saved a lot of trouble if I'd had this earlier."

"Don't worry. I'm sure we'll get into more trouble later," Amelia answered. "Help me with the printer."

"You got a printer?"

"Yeah, those four crates. I thought it would be easiest. That way we can just replace all these doors you keep damaging instead of trying to patch them."

"I'm not doubting the wisdom of it, just the possibility. Even with all of Kenny's equipment, how could we afford all this?"

"Not everything here was technically 'purchased,' but we also sold the medical printer and table."

"What if we need those?"

"They weren't working. Table's shot, and the printer's out of materials anyway."

"A broken med table and a printer that won't print can't have been worth that much."

"I also, uh, found a large bag of chips from Aluna in a cupboard on the bridge."

"Oh, yeah, those. My winnings from the casino."

"Hope you don't mind, then, but it's too late anyway if you do."

"No, I'm glad you managed to get something for them."

"I could only get half face value, but I figured it was worth it. That alone was enough for this." She pulled out a small, metal cylinder, similar to a data core but about twice the size.

"Is that what I think it is?" Bilan asked.

"It is if you think it's a new transponder. Clean registry and everything. Sorry, I had to program it at the shop, and nobody else was around, so I hope you don't mind the name."

"I guess that depends on what it is."

"Once this is installed, we're no longer the *Zheng He*. We are now the *Trovita*."

Trovita. Old Martian for Found. Just like Delokita was Old Martian for Lost.

"That's..." She could feel herself choking up. "That's a beautiful name."

Amelia beamed.

AFTER UNPACKING, they met on the bridge for a meal while the printer went to work on a new seam for the cargo bay. They'd have to evacuate it again before they could install it, but they weren't in a hurry to get anywhere.

"Speaking of which. Where are we going?" Jie asked.

Amelia answered. "Anywhere we want. We have fuel. It's still low, but it'll last us a while as long as we stay in the Belt and don't run at full burn most of the time."

"The Veteran's back in hiding wherever he is, and the Rabbit's gone. I haven't heard from Kenny yet, which is too bad. He could probably find us a job."

"I still have Harailt's documents," Amelia said. "There's lots of illegal shipments in there that nobody will report if they go missing."

"You didn't mention anything about any documents before," Del said.

"You were trying to arrest me when we first met," Amelia said. "Obviously, I wasn't going to tell you about them then. Later, it just never came up."

"Fair enough," Del said. "They might be useful now."

"I still have contacts in BeltSec," Jie said. "People who can pass us information or arrange resources. I'm guessing if we all pool our contacts, and their contacts, we may not need Kenny at all."

"He was a good fence, though. Always treated me fairly. Plus, he could probably get some good money for the footage of our daring raid on the Factory."

"Why don't you sell it yourself?" Bilan asked.

"I don't even know where he was selling it to. It's all underground."

"I'll ask Bilquis," Bilan answered. At Del's raised eyebrows, she explained. "My sister. She's a big fan. She was impressed that I know you. I'll find out where she gets it from, and we can reverse engineer from there."

"So, we've got a ship, and resources, and can go anywhere we want with it," Jie said.

"And nobody left to stand in our way," Amelia added. "As of today, the asteroid belt belongs to us."

Del grinned broadly. "Let's go take it."

ACKNOWLEDGMENTS

Although much of this book was set in a vacuum, it was not written in one. I had a great deal of help along the way. I'd especially like to thank the following:

Chantel Saban, who not only designed my cover, but provided inestimable support and encouragement through the writing process.

My editor, Kereah Keller.

Although I did my best to hide the math, there was a great deal of it involved. Two of the resources I made significant use of were Theodore W. Hall's SpinCalc calculator at https://www.artificial-gravity.com/sw/SpinCalc/ , and Edward Furey's Displacement Calculator at https://www.calculatorsoup.com/calculators/physics/displacement_v_a_t.php

And, of course, all of my beta readers, whose feedback greatly improved the final product: Allison Chambers, Torrin Kearns, Vijay Lakshminarayanan, Tom Luther, Thomas Marsh, Erika McCorkle, Sharon Stern, and Lovender S. White

ABOUT THE AUTHOR

Pat Luther is a Portland native currently living in Eugene, Oregon. He has been a pizza boy, a Kelly girl, a corporate propagandist, and both a purveyor and debunker of conspiracy theories.

In previous jobs, he once helped save the world (you're welcome), learned how to launder money and finance terrorists (didn't actually do either one, officer), and programmed satellites and police databases. He lost one job because the project was shut down by the EFF, and another because Bill Clinton said the wrong thing to an Iranian official.

On his Mars One application he pointed out that he once spent three weeks in a Subaru with five people and was still friends with them all. He was eliminated in the first round

He has volunteered with archaeologists where, in addition to sifting dirt and flying drones, he has evaded poisonous snakes, crossed a pit on a precarious bridge, and once dodged a giant boulder. The boulder wasn't actually moving at the time, but it was still a close call.

Thoughtless is his second published novel.

facebook.com/PatLuthertheWriter

twitter.com/plutheus

goodreads.com/Pat_Luther

CPSIA information can be obtained
at www.ICGtesting.com
Printed in the USA
BVHW081352230522
637776BV00001B/2